STRIKE BACK

DETECTIVE KATE BOWEN MYSTERY THRILLER
BOOK 4

T. R. CROKE

BLUE DOOR PUBLISHING IRELAND

Blue Door Publishing Ireland

Fisherstown, Ballybrittas,

Laois, Ireland.

https://www.trcroke.com

Publisher's Note: This is a work of fiction. Names, characters, places,
and incidents are a product of the author's imagination. Locales and
public names are sometimes used for atmospheric purposes. Any
resemblance to actual people, living or dead, or to businesses,
companies, events, institutions, or locales is completely coincidental.

Book Layout © 2020 Lizzie Harwood

Cover Design by Design for Writers

Strike Back/T. R. CROKE -- 1st ed.

ISBN 978-0-9955976-6-2

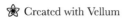 Created with Vellum

For Daniel, Eleanor, Ifelola & Omolara
… and for Eva, always

CONTENTS

DON'T MISS THE FREE STUFF!

I enjoy building a relationship with my readers. It's an important aspect of my life as an author. From time to time I let readers know about special offers, new releases, and other news.

For example, sometimes I offer the series starter, *The Devil's Luck* (**RRP** $4.99), free to everyone joining my mailing list. Simply visit https://www.trcroke.com and leave me your e-mail address. The series prequel, *The Trinity Enigma* is permanently free and downloadable at this link.

1

PARIS - SPRING 2019

The child in the red tee shirt staring at Detective Superintendent Kate Bowen had moments left to live. As Kate's police escort sliced through heavy traffic on the Paris ring road, she gave the little girl a cheery thumbs-up when her armored 4x4 overtook the family's yellow Renault. The impish child stuck her tongue out in response. Kate tipped her ballistic helmet in salute as her convoy motored past on a steady trajectory.

The fleeting interaction reminded Kate that she'd forgotten to buy a present for her niece's upcoming birthday and she called a friend.

'Hi Angie, I need a favor.'

'Hi there, what is it?'

'Would you pick something up for Ellie? Her birthday's on Saturday.'

'Leave it with me. Where are you; what's all the radio chatter?'

Up ahead a cacophony of car horns blared. Traffic was building on the motorway toward Charles de Gaulle airport.

'On a ride-along in Paris—a favor for Mac, I'll fill you in when I see you. Traffic is horrendous.'

'You get all the sweet trips.'

'D'ya' think?' Kate replied, as, without warning, the convoy shuddered to a halt.

'Don't stop – go round, go round!' Special Agent Zach Chapman barked into the radio from the front.

'Someone doesn't sound happy,' Angie said.

'Something's up, I've got to go,' Kate replied.

'The red Peugeot on the right is blocking us,' a reply blared from the radio in French. *'It's stuck halfway out of the lane.'*

'Get it out of the way,' Chapman pounded the dashboard, 'shift it sideways if you have to.'

The *Préfecture de Paris* motorcycle escort swung into action as Chapman bent his long lean frame toward the windscreen.

'Stalling a high-security convoy is a big no-no,' he said. 'And if Secretary Turlington misses his round of golf with the President there'll be hell to pay.'

Kate leaned her elbows on the back of Chapman's seat to get a better view.

'C'mon,' he agitatedly scratched his angular jaw, radio at the ready. They were thirty minutes out from the airport and the clock was ticking.

The cops grabbed either side of the tiny hatchback's rear bumper and hauled it sideways in measured shunts. Suddenly, the officer working the left side stopped and stared into the car.

'Now what?' Chapman said.

Both cops turned toward the convoy and wigwagged Chapman to reverse but that option had gone. Traffic in the lanes to the rear that split obediently moments earlier in response to blue lights and sirens, had locked together again. Kate's stomach knotted; the familiar warning that something was off. Alongside, a car horn tooted. She glanced sideways to catch a bright yellow family car slip by. The little girl in the back seat thumbed her nose as traffic in her lane moved forward while Kate was stuck solid.

As the frantic policemen struggled to unclip their weapons, the Peugeot detonated sending a shockwave of metal in Kate's direction. Chapman roared a warning into the radio that went unheard.

On instinct, Kate grabbed his jacket collar, propelled him into the footwell, and ducked. The blast hoisted their Dodge off the roadway and tossed them violently around the cab. A weapon carry case clattered hard against her ballistic helmet, but a combination of it and the flak jacket Chapman insisted she wore on the ride-along spared her serious injury.

The Dodge withstood the blast, but its engine cut out. Kate's first thought was for the cheeky child as she shook off the debris and used the back of the seat to pull upright.

'Oh God, no!' she exclaimed, covering her mouth in anguish, as she pulled off the helmet's cracked goggles.

The Renault's engine was ablaze, its roof ripped off and everyone inside obliterated. Beyond it, cars that had taken the full brunt of the explosion billowed black smoke. The Dodge had done its job and shielded the black limousine transporting their VIP. Members of the French protection team who stood guarding it when the convoy halted had not been so lucky. Every single one was cut down.

'Get up,' Kate yelled at Chapman as she clambered into the front. Blood trickled down his neck as she grasped his arm and hauled him upright. His eyes were caked with dust and grit and she placed her hands on his shoulders to concentrate his focus.

'It's an ambush, we need to exit, fast.'

Chapman blinked incomprehensibly. Harry the driver was out cold, oozing from multiple lacerations, his head inclined against the door frame.

'Get the door open,' Kate said, 'we don't have time.'

Chapman grasped the handle and pulled but nothing moved.

'Hit it,' Kate shouldered him.

Chapman got the message and rammed his broad shoulder against the passenger door as he pulled its handle. Nothing moved.

'Budge over,' she said, as she lashed kicks at the cracked windscreen.

He followed her lead and kicked it hard until it fell forward. Kate clambered out, slid off the bonnet, and helped Chapman scramble clear. In the open, the full horror struck her like a hammer blow. Acrid black smoke billowed from the red Peugeot while around it, vehicles including a truck blazed out of control. Blood-spattered chunks of metal, large and small, were strewn across the road. Kate's mind was in overdrive and fear gripped her as she surveyed the bomb site. She pulled her gaze from the yellow Renault and pushed Chapman into cover near the Dodge's engine.

'I've gotta check Harry,' he said.

Kate guided him to the driver's door, 'I'll do it.'

Together they wrenched it open and she found a water bottle as she checked the driver's pulse.

'Hold still,' she pushed Chapman against the side of the Dodge, and doused his head and hands, all the time checking for the onslaught she knew was coming. The noise was deafening. Fires burned out of control and piercing screams for help jarred Kate's intense concentration. 'Harry's badly dazed, but still with us. The groaning's a good sign.'

Chapman pushed wisps of wet blond hair from his eyes as Kate wiped the blood from a gash on his forehead. When she was done, he leaned into the 4x4 to settle the heavyset driver into a recovery position. He sprinkled water onto his colleague's face.

'Stay strong, Harry, help is…'

A crack, crack of rounds ricocheted off the Dodge's bonnet. Chapman froze.

'Get down,' Kate grabbed his sleeve and pulled him behind the driver's door.

She peered forward trying to pinpoint an enemy. Where had the shots come from? The thick smoke provided perfect cover for an assault. It swelled into dense plumes as punctured fuel tanks tipped their burning contents onto the motorway.

'I need a weapon,' she said.

'Grab Harry's Sig,' he replied.

Kate unholstered the driver's sidearm with the ease of a veteran. She ducked behind the driver's door with the struggling Secret Service agent as shots peppered the bonnet.

'Can you see where the shots came from?' Chapman asked.

Kate peered through the door's shattered window as smoke billowed everywhere.

'Jesus! Gunmen with assault rifles dead ahead, fifty meters, advancing.'

Chapman blasted toward them from the side of the door. He got lucky, the rapid burst felled one attacker. Kate loosed off a follow-up volley that made the assault group dive for cover. Time seemed to stand still as she checked and double-checked for movement.

'RPG,' she shouted when she saw a shoulder-held weapon aimed in their direction. She sprayed a burst toward the attacker and held her breath.

'They're after the VIP,' Chapman said, as he dumped a spent clip and replaced it. 'Can you hold them off?'

'I can try,' Kate replied.

'Wait for my signal.'

She grabbed the extra clip Chapman offered and directed single shots at the gunmen as he crouched and ran toward the black limousine.

'Stay put,' he ordered the embassy chauffeur who cracked a window open on his approach.

Behind the limo, the French protection team leader knelt in deep distress comforting a dying colleague on the motorway's concrete surface. Most of his team was lost. He was down to two functioning agents.

'Jean-Loup, we need to get the Secretary out of this,' Chapman shouted.

Kate heard Chapman's voice but could not make out his orders. She ditched the helmet and focused on what was coming at her.

'Jean-Loup!' Chapman roared a second time. 'We need to get away.'

'On borrowed time here,' Kate shouted to no response.

Jean-Loup raced to his unmarked car and returned with a briefcase-like device that he kicked toward Chapman. It slid along the motorway until he trapped it with his foot, and shook the ballistic shield open.

Kate glanced back toward the commotion at the limousine. 'Send backup,' she roared. 'I've got to move.'

Chapman jammed the protective shield against the politician's back as he looked in her direction.

'Now,' he signaled.

'Help's on the way, Harry,' she told the driver. 'Stay strong my fr…' An ear-splitting sub-machine gun burst shook her.

'*Allez, Allez,*' a French protection agent urged, 'I'll pin these *connards* down.'

Kate crouched and raced back to the retreating group, as they moved rapidly toward the off-ramp. In the bedlam of gnarled traffic below, Jean-Loup commandeered an

SUV from a terrified mother, frantic as she lifted her wailing child from its safety seat. Chapman pushed Secretary Turlington into the rear and lunged on top of him. Kate leaped into the front as the French cop floored the accelerator and sped away.

2

By the time they reached it, *avenue des Champs d'Elysées* was gridlocked, but not the chaos of noise Kate anticipated. Terror attacks had become a fact of life and Parisians had grown wary. Few car horns honked to complain as drivers sat in the static traffic. Instead, they checked their phones for news updates as exhaust fumes choked central Paris. Jean-Loup summoned a motorcycle cop controlling a junction and ordered him to ride ahead of their commandeered bright red Dacia SUV.

They inched along the *grand boulevard*, dodging on and off sidewalks to get around clogged traffic and maintain momentum. They needed to reach the U.S. embassy on *avenue Gabriel* and the quickest way was via *avenue de Marigny*. Its entrance was blocked, controlled by a snarl of gray metal barricades and a company of CRS riot police. They served as a dramatic backdrop for TV journalists recording reports.

'We need to deliver a VIP under threat to the American embassy, tout de suite,' the motorcycle escort updated the CRS commander.

The commandant peered into the SUV at its blood-stained occupants, 'Do you need your injuries checked out?'

'Just get us to the embassy,' Jean-Loup replied.

'The Elysée next door is locked down but we'll get you through.'

He summoned two of his men and placed one either side of Jean-Loup's vehicle, perched on running boards, and clinging to the roof bars. Television cameras instantly switched their focus to *avenue de Marigny* and narrowed in on the little red SUV driving up its center. The CRS escort communicated continually with rooftop snipers guarding the Elysée Palace.

When the engine spluttered Kate glanced sideways at Jean-Loup's vicelike grip on the steering wheel, his hands streaked red.

'Almost there,' she said.

He wheeled right at the top of the road where his CRS escort descended. They saluted and headed back to their muster station. Jean-Loup spurred the commandeered rescue vehicle to the front of the U.S. embassy and fumbled with the window controls as a Marine Captain approached.

'ID!' an anxious voice demanded.

'Decker, lift the barrier for God's sake. It's Special Agent Chapman with Secretary Turlington.'

'Oh Christ, my apologies, Sir. I didn't recognize you, you're a mess.'

Kate noticed Jean-Loup's grip on the steering wheel relax as the barricade executed a measured lift. Simultaneously, low-tech countermeasures to uninvited vehicles slowly retracted into the ground. He eased the little SUV forward and halted behind the guard room where Kate opened childproof rear doors for Chapman and his VIP.

'You are safe now. I must rejoin my team,' Jean-Loup told him.

The French Protection Service had its headquarters close by. Jean-Loup's trembling voice betrayed the fact that the loss of his colleagues was starting to impact.

'Kate, will you walk with Jean-Loup to his HQ?' Chapman asked. 'It's a street over.'

'Sure.'

'You saved our lives,' he said, as he ushered Secretary Turlington towards an embassy side door. 'We won't forget.'

Kate faced an instant debrief when she arrived at the *Service de la Protection* HQ. The Interior Minister bayed for an immediate report on the catastrophic attack and she helped paint the horrific picture while a nurse cleaned Jean-Loup's wounds and a doctor sutured his lacerations. When she finally got to call her boss, she knew he was close to despair.

'I feared the worst,' Mac said.

He learned of events in Paris from breaking news reports of multiple casualties and had called Kate repeatedly without a reply. By that time, her phone was lost inside the wrecked 4x4, a tiny element of a massive crime scene.

'I got lucky,' she said. 'Chapman put me in a flak jacket and helmet for the ride to the airport. I whined about it until we were ambushed.'

'I'm glad you're safe.'

'Reckon there'll be any blowback?'

The ride-along was unofficial, a courtesy arranged by Mac's FBI buddies and offered by the U.S. Secret Service. Just what the Irish government would make of a Garda officer engaged in a gunfight in Paris was open to debate.

Ireland's neutral stance in international conflicts was sacrosanct to the politicians.

'Don't worry about that.'

'How the hell are we supposed to keep up-to-date with best practice?' Kate asked.

'I'll brief the Justice Sec-Gen all the same.'

'Damn Justice and their politicking; a French Prosecutor requested I make a statement and I obliged. The *Service de la Protection* recognized my assistance.'

'You sure you're okay? Do you need to talk to someone?'

'Are you afraid I'll go rogue and call a journalist?'

'Jesus, Kate! This isn't you. Let me get the Garda Medical Officer to talk through the experience with you.'

'You don't trust me?'

'Kate, stop!'

Both were well versed in the toxic effects of post-traumatic stress disorder. The medical officer regularly updated the PTSD awareness embedded in training programs at Kate's Surveillance and Intelligence Unit. Team members developed an awareness that any life-endangering trauma left a profound mark, which had to be acknowledged and managed.

'I just need rest. A doctor gave me something to help me sleep.'

'All I care about is that you're safe. We'll figure out the rest. Are you sure you're okay?'

'I'm fine.'

'Europe's called an emergency head of services meeting for Berlin tomorrow.'

'Let me go back,' Kate said. 'An early flight from here will get there quicker than one from Dublin.'

'Are you up to it?'

'With some sleep, I'll be fine.'

'There will be plenty to discuss. Today was a barefaced

strike against the West.'

'I'll keep my personal phone on at all times.'

As darkness fell, Kate sat wrapped in a bath towel at the end of a hotel bed, her suitcase open behind her. She stared blankly as tired dark green eyes reflected from the hotel mirror. She once argued with a Garda recruiting sergeant dogmatically bent on recording her eye color as hazel. A common confusion, Kate told him at the time; the green came from a mild amount of pigmentation with a golden tint. It delighted her that only two percent of the world's population had it.

The ancient hairdryer labored on her brunette mop. Kate tossed it to the ground in frustration and brushed absentmindedly until it settled in the style her sister christened 'bedhead' as a teenager. Kate saw no reason to change it any time soon. Both of her eyes had dark circles underneath and she prodded gingerly at red and purple bruising welling up under her left arm. She was bruised and sore from the extraordinary couple of hours she had endured in the French capital. She tried some cool-down stretches. Her ribs ached, it was too soon. She removed light pajamas from her case, tossed the towel, and pulled on her nightwear. Dead on her feet, she lay down, closed her eyes, and tried to tune out the constant ringing in her ears.

She dozed a while and woke to find two missed calls from her mother. She took the phone off silent and called back.

'Hi Mum, sorry to call so late.'

'Katie, nice of you to call back - eventually. Are you home?'

'No Mum, still in Europe. I'm wrecked, can we keep

this short and sweet.'

'Missy, if you don't slow down,' her mother scolded. 'You'll meet yourself coming back.'

'Mum, someone's got to do what I do.'

'It doesn't always have to be you.'

'Is everything okay at home?'

'Fine. You haven't forgotten Ellie's birthday party on Saturday, have you?'

'Of course not. I've got her a present, I'll see you Friday night.'

'What did you get for her?'

'S-sorry?' Kate said.

'What did you pick up for Ellie?'

'It's a surprise.'

Busted!

'Safe travels, my darling daughter,' her mother laughed. 'I'll see you on Friday. Love you.'

Kate closed her eyes and twisted and turned to get comfortable. Doubt nagged. In her thirties now, was it still worth it? The near-death showdowns, the never-ending oversight investigations that followed, replete with bureaucratic critique disguised as recommendations.

No matter what made her weary to the bone, one memory always brought comfort. She recalled it now to suppress the image of the devastated yellow Renault. It was more sensation than imagery. Her childhood fingers locked into her grandfather's rough-hewn hand as they set out on early mornings into dew-laden fields to pick wild mushrooms. He had been a stable male presence in her life after her father absconded back to Wales and left his family to fend for itself. She could never get back their lost years, but a long time ago she vowed to strain every sinew to ensure that the Northern Ireland terror that ruined her grandfather's life would never be visited on others. Not if she could stop it.

3

DUBLIN

Straight from her Berlin red-eye, the squad room's familiar caffeine aroma greeted Kate when she reached home base. The brown-bricked ex-Public Works store was perfect for her Surveillance and Intelligence Unit. Its ivy-straggled outer walls blended with neighboring properties in the wooded valley linking Chapelizod to Castleknock, sprawling Dublin suburbs. Kate had overseen a construction project that converted its underground storage space into car parking to keep transport assets away from prying eyes. It completed a makeover of the building Mac had begun years earlier.

She glanced at the whiteboard with its collection of headshots, SIU's currently engaged targets. Operation names on top, status below. Kate followed the caffeine scent and popped a capsule into their state-of-the-art coffee maker. When it brewed, she draped her coat over her arm, grabbed her travel bag, and shuffled toward her office, coffee cup gingerly balanced.

Ron Sexton popped his head out of the DI's office as she passed. He ducked back to retrieve his journal and followed her. As they walked, he pulled a tweed jacket on over his pristine white shirt and blue striped tie. Short of wearing a uniform, with his sturdy build and dark hair always cut to regulation length, he screamed cop. Sexton brought forensic attention to his surveillance operation planning role.

'I need a word on the Gordon murder,' he said.

'Give me a second,' she replied.

In the sanctuary of her office, she slumped into her chair and closed her eyes. Aside from being sore and stiff from the Paris shootout, she detested flying. Multiple flights in three days had drained her. While the Berlin flight had been uneventful, she needed a moment. By the time Sexton stuck his head around the door minutes later, the coffee was helping.

'There's a case conference at Blanch in forty minutes. I need to be there.'

'Okay, *shoot.*'

He pulled a chair in front of her desk, opened his journal, and read.

'Ben Gordon was murdered at six-thirty yesterday evening as he exited his company's car park in Blanchardstown. The crime scene examination was wrapped up in the past hour. Mainly apartment blocks around there and two people witnessed a blue Yamaha 750cc motorbike pull in front of the victim's car. On hearing the screech of tires, they peered out their windows. Looks like experienced shooters. One witness described a hooded figure executing a kill shot to victim's head while an accomplice scrambled on the ground collecting spent shells from the initial burst.'

He thumbed a page and read on.

'Crime scene techs recovered one shell underneath the car, close to the driver's side front wheel. The bike was found early this morning, burnt out in a forest near Dundalk.'

The link to her hometown, close to the border with

Northern Ireland, grabbed Kate's attention. Media coverage had already suggested a dissident IRA group might have carried out a contract killing. There was no evidence to back up that speculation.

She first learned of Ben Gordon's murder the previous evening as she sat in the Berlin meeting. She had been furiously noting details of violent attacks national Security Services reported, when a flurry of phone texts from Digger, her deputy, distracted her.

'We know from the Khouri case, Gordon had no criminal history,' Kate said to Sexton.

'Am I good to share that with the investigators?' he asked.

'Let me talk to the FBI first. We need to update the profile, check if anything has changed with his squeaky-clean image.'

SIU had profiled the IT entrepreneur when the FBI reached out for help on Rafiq Khouri. The FBI landed Khouri as an ISIS suspect when they identified him as 'the Dark Prince' on a stealth comms wiretap. The communications Khouri exchanged on gaming consul messaging services spooked the FBI enough to send Agent Cody O'Neill to Dublin when Khouri got a job there. The programmer was in his late twenties, a son to a fourth-generation Lebanese family who ran a small restaurant in Brooklyn in New York. The devout Muslim family was unaware that their genius son had veered toward ISIS. His parents simply believed that their boy, who attended CoderDojos from the age of eight, was a star in the IT world.

SIU inquiries at that time found no pre-existing link between Khouri and Gordon. The latter was a model 21st-century successful software entrepreneur. A handsome whiz kid with boundless energy who liked to employ outliers. Key personnel in his company frequently had personality quirks other employers found unattractive. He had taken on Khouri for his genius with algorithms and dismissed his HR manager's concerns about the virtuoso programmer's sullen behavior.

'Update me after the conference,' Kate told Sexton.

'Will do. By the way, call Mac, will you. He's been on twice inquiring when you were getting in.'

'Thanks, Ron.'

Before she put the call through, Kate unfolded a red pamphlet she had ripped from her windscreen in the airport car park. She had disregarded it without a second glance. As she leaned back in Mac's old chair, its added support easing her backache, she read its sparse message. 'It is mine to avenge; I will repay. In due time their foot will slip; their day of disaster is near and their doom rushes upon them.'

More than a little weird, she thought.

A soft tap-tap on her door shook Kate from her reverie.

'Come in,' she said.

Angie pushed the door open and placed a large bag on Kate's desk.

'Best I could do at short notice,' she said.

Kate fidgeted with the bag containing her niece's present.

'Whoa! What's happened to you?' Angie asked.

'I don't look that bad, do I?' Kate asked.

'You've looked better.'

'Grab a seat.'

Kate explained what she had been through in Paris. How a favor for Mac had turned into a life-changing event.

'Why did he ask you? We're a surveillance unit, not a protection unit.'

'Justice won't authorize a replacement for the Chief's spot in Protection and he's trying to cover all the bases. I was just the unlucky one he asked to do the ride-along with the U.S. Secret Service to observe and report on how they do business.'

'You don't say. At least you have Ellie's party tomorrow to take your mind off it.'

'What did you pick her up?' Kate asked as she opened the bag on her desk.

They both laughed as Kate extracted the 'easy-to-assemble' princess's castle.

'Hah, think of the fun Norrie will have to put that together for Ellie,' Kate laughed.

Angie was the first colleague from her surveillance unit that Kate had introduced to her family. Difficult to believe that Angie, pixie-haired and petite was even old enough to be a Garda. Her penchant for changing her hair color was legendary; currently, it was rainbow.

'What do you make of that?' Kate asked, indicating the red pamphlet.

Angie picked up the crumpled paper and smoothed it out. 'Sounds biblical. Where did you get it?'

'Under the wiper of my car at the airport car park when I got in.'

'A bible group seeking converts, maybe?'

'Odd message, if that's the case. Research it and come back to me, will you? I need to call Mac.'

Assistant Commissioner Redmond McEnroe, the boss at Security Branch, was Kate's mentor. A six-foot-plus former oarsman, he had served in SWAT teams and surveillance units for the best part of his service as police. She had flourished under his guidance when he was Chief at SIU.

Skipping formality, he enquired, 'Any update?'

'What I sent before I traveled this morning is the latest.'

The ISIS onslaught had been as devastating in its coor-dination as it had been unforeseen. Just days before the

Paris trip Kate had sat around the same table in Berlin and listened to the same nodding heads agree that the international terrorist threat was two clicks below critical.

'The Middle East conflict has camped on our doorstep, I'm afraid,' Jan Krause, the acting German chair, told everyone in the wake of attacks across the continent.

The death toll around Europe was in the hundreds and rising. The injury toll was still being evaluated. In the UK, London has once again been the target. As reports on the attacks filtered through, a pattern emerged. These were unlike the suicide attacks of recent years. There were no reports of terrorists self-detonating to take as many bystanders as possible with them. No hired cars or hijacked trucks rammed into innocent pedestrians. Instead, well-armed, seemingly well-trained small groups had launched gun and grenade attacks on civilian targets. The *fidayeen*-style attacks mirrored the Mumbai attacks, years earlier. The tactic involved heavily armed small squads of gunmen or bombers launch fluid attacks that responded to local security force reaction in varying the point of the onslaught. Kate told the meeting that it was too soon to link the Dublin murder of Ben Gordon to the mayhem in Europe.

'The attacks are a serious escalation aimed at causing maximum alarm around Europe,' Mac said.

'The common feature is the style of attack, gun, and grenade mostly. France got a real hammering,' Kate replied.

It had been a horrific night. Apart from the attempted assassination of the American Secretary of State, three armed men had entered the exclusive Hôtel de Luxe in central Paris through the kitchens and opened fire in the lobby. Rioting broke out in the outer suburbs and quickly spread to Marseille and Lyon. The far-right *Front Nationale* had mobilized a lynch mob in Lille and tried to storm high-rise apartment blocks, home to North African asylum-seekers. A policewoman died in an exchange of gunfire with FN supporters.

'The continental attacks were coordinated; someone behind the scenes was pulling the strings,' Kate continued.

The attacks demonstrated a high level of planning and honed military skills. The attackers shot by Paris police trying to flee the Hôtel de Luxe had been identified as returned jihadis from the Syrian conflict.

'And an RPG rocket was fired at St. Peter's Basilica in Rome,' Mac noted.

'Well, it was an entrance gate to the Basilica square. All the same, killing two Swiss Guards is highly symbolic.'

'Jan Krause wants us to identify any violent action occurring here in the past twenty-four hours that might fit an ISIS profile. Is that it?'

'In a nutshell. We don't know enough yet about Ben Gordon's murder to say it meets that criteria.'

'I'll need an updated threat assessment by five,' Mac continued.

'I figured as much. We're pulling a draft together.'

'The U.S. president just tweeted that the Dublin murder is a direct attack on American business,' he said. 'Like that helps!'

Kate's workload was stacking up by the time Angie returned brandishing the red pamphlet.

'Old Testament, Book of Deuteronomy 32:35. A biblical denunciation.'

'Bag it for the moment and record when and where I found it.'

'Religious groups do this kind of leafleting all day,

every day. Apocalyptic warnings of eternal damnation. Are you overreacting?'

'Will you just do as instructed,' Kate said.

Minutes later Angie dropped a transparent evidence bag onto Kate's desk and made to leave as Digger arrived.

'You okay?' he asked.

'I'm fine,' Kate said. 'Hang on a minute, Angie, will you?'

She closed the door and asked Angie to pull up a chair.

'I'm sorry I barked at you.'

She didn't want the Paris shootout gaining legs in the unit. Digger and Angie were her closest friends there and she trusted them. She asked them both to keep schtum about it for the moment. Digger sat alongside Angie, distracted by the evidence bag he had seen her deposit on the desk. He barely made the five-foot eight-inch height requirement back when he joined the Garda. The limit had since disappeared. Although the oldest in the room, his wiry frame accentuated a coiled toughness and gave him a youthful look.

'Mind if I take a look?' he asked in his lilting Kerry accent.

He was already reading the pamphlet through the clear plastic when Kate asked why he was interested.

'Mmm…' he mumbled.

'What?' she asked.

He reached into his pocket and pulled out a similar pamphlet and laid it out on Kate's desk. He smoothed it out and read it aloud, '*It is mine to avenge; I will repay. In due time…*' he continued until he had read the full quotation.

'Where did you get yours?'

'Windscreen of my car when I came out of a petrol station this morning.'

'Did anyone else here get one?' she inquired.

In the recent past, SIU had lost a colleague to a

murderous criminal whose gang the unit targeted. It pained Kate that she had gauged that threat inaccurately.

'Nobody's mentioned receiving anything.'

'Make sure everyone on the unit sees it,' Kate said. 'Find out how many are going around. Find out where they're coming from.'

Angie took both sheets to fast-track through forensic examination.

'Well?' Kate asked Digger.

'We're unlikely to get much from forensics but we've no shortage of enemies. Take your pick.'

'Someone is monitoring our movements. Draw up a list of suspects when we find out how many threats have been received.'

By later that evening no other pamphlets had been identified. Angie scooped CCTV footage and was already reviewing it. A tall suspect in black biker leathers and matching helmet with a yellow lightning flash on its rear showed at Digger's morning fuel stop. The suspect casually popped the pamphlet under the wiper of the car before taking off.

The airport CCTV confirmed a motorcycle courier also delivered Kate's pamphlet the previous evening. The rider had a well-worn tan leather jacket and appeared less nimble than Digger's messenger. Angie used traffic camera footage to track the suspect exiting on roads surrounding the airport. She expected the bike to head for the city, but it did the opposite. It turned left onto the slip road for the M1 motorway. It was headed toward Kate's home town of Dundalk and the invisible border with Northern Ireland that lay beyond it.

4

NORTHERN IRELAND - WINTER 1996

The drenched gunman led Harriet Stevenson to a pile of loose hay in the corner of the barn. Without invitation, he wrestled off her wet woolen cardigan. She didn't resist and tugged his soggy black tee-shirt over his shoulders. The first touch of his skin against hers overwhelmed her. His hands raced beneath her skirt and peeled away her pants. He watched her intently as she slipped the straps of her bra off each shoulder before unclipping and dumping it on the pile of discarded wet clothing. Her eyes never left his as, slowly, she lowered her saturated skirt and lay back on the loose hay.

Harriet had discovered the gunman months earlier on one of her regular rambles to get away from the house and A-Level exam preparation. She was sheltering from an April shower in the barn when the mysterious stranger emerged from behind leftover straw bales from winter.

'Don't worry, I'll not harm you,' he told her in a calm voice, his dark brown eyes piercing hers.

She nodded nervously.

'Don't tell a soul I was here,' a finger to his lips.

It was the first time she was spoken to as an adult.

'Our secret,' he smiled.

'What'll I call you?'

'Kevin,' he lied.

Peace talks to end thirty years of sectarian strife in Northern Ireland were stumbling into their second year, beset by mistrust on each side. Whenever the peace initiative stuttered the IRA reminded everyone of its capabilities. The gunman's gang carried out sporadic attacks along the stretch of border skirting the Stevenson home. He convinced the frightened girl not to turn him in and coaxed her into bringing him food until police and army searches eased back. Her wariness dissipated, and in the weeks that followed whenever an attack occurred, Harriet scampered furtively through the fields to check the barn. Their first tryst happened as he cleared supper scraps from the barn floor late one evening. She leaned beside him to help and he stole a kiss.

'You're wild kind,' he whispered. 'I can't thank you enough.'

She blushed and hurried outside; her teenage mind a muddle of mortification as she returned home along the headland of the turnip field that led to her house. Was she falling for an outlaw? All she knew for certain was the touch of his lips sent a sensation through her body she had never before experienced. His accent told her he was from Belfast. Although he never mentioned religion, clearly he was from the other side of the still-bitter protestant-catholic divide. It only added to his allure.

He towered over her now, unbuckling the belt of his blue jeans as she pulled him downwards. They were urgent at first, exhilarated by the danger of discovery. Her youthful body aroused him like nothing he had experienced. She rolled on top as her self-assurance grew, her breasts aroused and slick. An autumnal gust of wind ripped a galvanized sheet from the barn's roof as their rushed passion soared.

Flouting the guerrilla fighter's key diktat of a rapid retreat, the gunman lingered amid mists of sensual pleasure. It proved a disastrous miscalculation. An explosion of noise and light startled their coupling apart. A gaping hole opened where the barn door had been, and four black-clad figures burst through. They moved like lightning, ski masks concealing their faces. The squad leader thrust Harriet aside and crunched his rifle butt into the side of her lover's disbelieving head. Frantically, she scrambled for her clothes while the men in black snapped flex cuffs on her lover's wrists and hauled him, naked, toward a waiting armored car. As the British soldiers departed a local detective entered the barn and arrested her.

The fateful decision upended her life. By the time the child they created that night was born, her lover was in Long Kesh prison. She dodged a charge of aiding and abetting terrorism thanks to her father's connections in the District Lodge. However, despite his strong standing in the community, no local ever employed Harriet. To support her newborn, she trekked across the border six days a week to a mind-numbing mushroom-picking job that paid minimum wage.

Three years later she agreed to marry Bart Wrollesly, a farmer from the other side of Caledon, the market village close to where she lived. Fifteen years her senior, he was the polar opposite of the father of her child. A lay preacher in his local Presbyterian church, Wrollesly promised to accept her illegitimate son as part of the marriage pact.

Before their wedding, she made a secret visit to Long Kesh prison. She wanted to introduce her gunman lover to his son, Kevin, and alert him to her imminent change of circumstances. She knew her lover's name was Sean but chose to name her son with the one used when they were together. The bus trip from Belfast, jam-packed with prisoners' close relatives, was a revelation of chatter and laughter. A stark contrast to the silent world three-year-old little Kevin lived in with his grandparents. At home, the conversation was sparse and confined to talk of work around the farm. He brought along his teddy to show his dad.

At the jail compound, a man in a black uniform smiled at him as he held out his hand to demand the toy. Kevin eyed him suspiciously as the warder poked and prodded the precious companion he snuggled up to every night. He screeched loudly when the prison guard took a box knife, sliced the teddy down the middle, and pulled out its insides.

'Was that necessary?' Harriet demanded, comforting her heartbroken child.

'You should know the routine. No soft toys allowed.'

'Don't you worry I'll mend Ted, he'll be good as new,' Harriet comforted her son as she wrapped him in her arms.

'Don't want him,' Kevin screamed.

Nonetheless, his mother carefully collected all the stuffing and placed it in her bag for repair when they returned home. The unexpected visit was not listed as a close relative; those were reserved for the gunman's legitimate family in Belfast. She took a seat at one of the visitors' tables, her son perched on her knee constantly fidgeting as she waited nervously. Her heart skipped a beat when she caught sight of her one-night lover strolling casually through the yard gate that linked the visiting room to the blocks. He sported a couple of days' stubble, exactly as she remembered. His deep brown eyes were as alluring as ever and once again butterflies hit her tummy. He sat opposite, tossed back a fringe of jet-black hair, and smiled.

'This is a pleasant surprise.'

'This here is Kevin,' she smiled.

'How are you, big man,' the prisoner tickled the child's chin.

They chit-chatted a while. The child constantly butted in with questions and stories, telling his mum's friend what happened to Ted.

'You let your mam fix wee Ted there and pay no heed to these bad men.'

He took the boy's hand to comfort him. Harriet reached across and touched his arm.

'I'll not forget that night,' she said.

The supervisor leaned in, reminding her that personal contact was reserved for family visits, and they were nearly out of time.

'Nor will I,' her lover said. 'But you settle down now with your kin and raise this wee boy right and proper.'

'I promise I will.'

As she walked from the visiting room with her son in her arms, Kevin stared intently over her shoulder. Despite the prison guard's repeated order to move, his father stubbornly remained seated until they reached the exit. At the last moment, he raised a hand and waved a cheery farewell. The boy clung tighter to his mother, a broad grin spreading across his face. This was a day he would never forget.

5

Dublin – Spring 2019

While Angie investigated the threats against Kate and Digger, Detective Pete McNally, the unit guru, pulled intel on Rafiq Khouri together and emailed it to Kate. Pete's time with the unit stretched back to when Mac set it up twenty-five years earlier. He was everyone's go-to guy.

Kate skimmed through boringly repetitive surveillance reports until the final night when the wheels came off. While she and most of her crew navigated the high-octane conclusion of their last big case, exiled SIU Chief, Raphael O'Driscoll, destroyed any chance of concluding the Khouri job successfully.

Kate hovered over the folder marked, 'Khouri interrogation.' It drew her back to an episode she figured closed. There were two sub-folders. She clicked one labeled, 'Digger interrogation' and skimmed the transcripts. He had gotten nowhere with Khouri. The recordings confirmed the interrogation was rushed; the suspect stuck to 'no comment' answers. After scanning the exchanges, she closed the folder.

She hesitated over the second. Reflection on what might have been washed over her when she heard Cody O'Neill introduce himself to the suspect as FBI. She switched to skimming the transcripts. Khouri was less cocky with O'Neill, uncertain of his ground. Their three-hour session terminated when O'Neill concluded Khouri would offer nothing the FBI didn't already know. The suspect fled the country twenty-four hours after release.

Kate called Digger when she closed the folder. He was working in his 'cave' where he crafted the gadgets SIU used against targets.

'Get down to Special Branch and pick up everything they've got on the Khouri arrest,' she told him.

'Will the SB Chief hand everythin' over?'

'Considering the mess his predecessor made, he better. I'll put a call in just in case.'

It worked. Digger carried two large cardboard storage boxes into Kate's office later in the afternoon and dumped them on her desk.

'Hang on to it all. I need a cover-to-cover review. Double-check everything; O'Driscoll's idiots are likely to have overlooked something.'

'More a job for Ron, wouldn't ya say?' Digger retorted. 'I'm tryin' to keep what equipment we have serviceable. When are you goin' to let me order new gear?'

'When I get my budget, you'll get your slice.'

'Where is Ron, anyway?'

'Still at the case conference in Blanchardstown on the Gordon murder. We need to crack on and see if there are any gaps from Khouri's arrest. I'll talk to the FBI and get clearance to brief the investigators.'

Pete McNally reminded Digger that the surveillance on

the Khouri house had been carried out by a skeleton crew of two detectives on the night O'Driscoll raided.

'Whoever they were, call them and tell them I need them here, pronto.'

Joe Forde was the rookie detective who had done most of the running on the final night of the SIU operation at 17A Manifold Avenue. The elder lemon with him had since retired. The crew observed three suspects on site until the Special Branch search party disrupted their operation.

When he received Pete McNally's summons to report to base, Forde called in a replacement and carefully descended the ladder of a Dublin port crane. He was average height, with a solid frame grown from pitching in to put food on the table every day as he grew up on a west of Ireland farm. For the Dublin Port job, his workman's hands won him the crane driver role in the eagle's nest. He pulled light brown hair into a ponytail for the part. The SIU crew was tracking a city organized crime gang whose expected cocaine delivery had still not arrived. It had become a battle of endurance and will.

Back at SIU base, he linked up with his DI. Forde had grown on Digger since his attachment to the unit. He carried out every task thrown at him without fuss. His stints in the port crane for the past week had been 12-hour shifts without toilet breaks but he didn't grumble. Each day he turned up equipped to improvise and got on with the job.

'Dissect this and get back to me. We're huntin' for anomalies,' Digger told him as he handed over Special Branch detective report from the search party that carried out the raid at 17A Manifold Avenue.

Forde headed back to the squad room, poured a mug of stewed coffee, and settled into a quiet corner. When he finished his review, he descended to the Cave again, punched the door code, and pushed inside.

'Timmons and Thompson searched the house,' Forde said. 'They were in and out in under an hour.'

'That pair of *wasters*!' Digger shook his head. 'Did they seize anythin' worthwhile?'

Detectives Timmons and Thompson had been bully boys for Chief Superintendent Raphael O'Driscoll, in his time as Special Branch boss. All three were detested in equal measure.

Forde leafed through the report and pulled out a page. He told Digger apart from a laptop seized from Khouri, three mobile phones had also been confiscated. Some household bills for gas and electricity were taken for further examination along with items of clothing for forensic testing.

'Do they detail what areas of the house they searched?' Digger asked.

'They list the rooms and what was found in each.'

'What about the attic?'

Forde scanned the report.

'No mention.'

When Digger read the search report he was convinced there were gaps. Usually, a specialist team would be called in to take the place apart, but that hadn't happened. Something could have been missed. The name of the real estate company that looked after the lease caught his eye. The boss, Gahan, was a gun nut at Digger's club who had won every fifty-meter pistol competition in recent years. He rang him and after catching up on club gossip, enquired whether he had rented the Manifold Avenue house since the date it was searched. When Digger got back to Kate, it was seven o'clock in the evening.

'You look wrecked. You need to rest.'

'Not you too? I've just hung up from my mother and

she told me I sound tired, should see a doctor and blah, blah… but don't miss my niece's birthday tomorrow. Everyone's a therapist.'

'Cranky as well. It's time to down tools.'

'Did you learn anything about the address where Khouri was arrested?'

'Yes. It's been vacant a while but the rent for 17A Manifold Avenue is still paid each month from a company account in the UK.'

'How do you know that?'

'A friend whose company handles the lease told me,' Digger grinned. 'The two who had been livin' there packed up and left a day after they were released from custody.'

'Houses around there don't stay vacant for long. Why pay the rent but leave it empty?' Kate asked.

'Loose end number one.'

'O'Driscoll's source is number two,' she said.

'Exactly. I found no statement linked to the source of the information that triggered the raid. Was he even interviewed?'

'I'll get a name from Mac and we can check it out with Immigration.'

'What about 17A Manifold Avenue?' Digger asked.

'If the rent money is coming from Britain, I could check the bank account details with MI5.'

Ron Sexton tapped the door and Kate beckoned him in. Digger stayed to hear Sexton's update on the Ben Gordon murder. Witness statements were being scrutinized with re-interviews scheduled where required and forensic reports fast-tracked but there was nothing substantial to report. Investigators agreed the evidence from witness statements indicated a professional hit. No suspects had been nominated.

'We should search that house again,' Digger suggested.

'If the first effort was sloppy,' Sexton agreed. 'It's a no-brainer.'

'Not so sure,' Kate mused.

'Why?' Digger asked.

'Someone's been paying the rent, yet the house lies empty. There's something shady in that. If we send in a specialist search team now it will blow any chance we have of finding out what's going on.'

'We can't sit on our hands and do nothin''

'What about covertly?' Kate asked. 'Think you could take a sniff around? Check the attic out, that sort of gig.'

Digger smiled for the first time since Kate drew him into the investigation.

'You get me the warrant, I'll do the rest.'

Kate's next phone call was to Mac. They ticked off issues that had preoccupied their day. She did not mention the biblical warnings she and Digger had received. She needed more information before assessing if they posed a credible threat. Instead, she outlined her need to identify and locate O'Driscoll's agent. Such identities were a closely guarded secret. Only the Assistant Commissioner at Security Branch and the agent's handler knew it. Mac obliged and wished her a quiet weekend.

'Not likely! My niece's birthday party is tomorrow.'

She rang Daphne Clarke as she drove north along the M1. They had a solid working relationship since Clarke took over MI5's Irish desk. Kate agreed to have Pete McNally pass her the bank account details Digger had secured since she was working an evening shift.

Sexton called and updated Kate regarding O'Driscoll's source, whose intel led to the arrest of Khouri and associates. The Iraqi had failed to keep any recent immigration appointments and was listed for deportation. The next time law enforcement encountered him he would be arrested for repatriation.

As Kate rummaged in the car console for toll booth change, her phone kicked into life. Daphne Clarke.

'There may be a Middle East connection to that bank account,' she said. 'Can it hold until tomorrow to chase it up?'

'Will you be able to make banking inquiries on a Saturday?'

'In Dubai, no problem,' Clarke replied.

'There's a *Dubai* connection?'

'Our first lead takes us there, who knows after that.'

The Boyne Valley Bridge toll booth came into view as Kate thanked Clarke and ended the call. She had left Dublin an hour earlier and only forty kilometers now separated her from her mother's cozy kitchen in her two-up two-down red brick terraced home in Dundalk.

'Enough for today,' she said aloud, as she dumped coins into the toll basket and whirred the window closed. She settled into her comfortable leather seat and clicked her BMW's sound system into life. She hummed along as Coldplay's lyrical intro to *Paradise* kicked in. By the time she parked outside her mother's house, she had enjoyed most of the playlist. Chris Martin was halfway through extolling his mythical love as *A Sky Full of Stars* when she cut the ignition and sighed in relief.

As she leaned over to grab her weekend case from the rear seat she was surprised to see the house in near darkness, only a single light visible. Her mother detested dark autumn and winter evenings and kept her house a beacon of brightness. She abandoned her case, jumped out of the car, and moved swiftly toward the front door.

Usually, Margaret Bowen's smiling face beat her to the punch, pulling open the door before Kate had a chance to get her key in the lock. Her heart beat faster when it didn't happen this time.

6

At Beaumont Hospital hours later, Kate clasped her sobbing sister, Norrie, in a tight embrace. When she found their mother slumped at the kitchen table, Kate had feared the worst. She shook her mother's shoulders and Margaret Bowen tried to smile in response. Kate recognized the warning signs immediately as one side of her mother's mouth drooped and her speech came out garbled. She made a despairing attempt to push upright, her fingernails clawing the table's wooded surface. Distraught, Kate forced herself to remain calm. She summoned an ambulance and dashed behind it to Beaumont Hospital on Dublin's north side, one hour south of Dundalk.

The long journey was a risk, but her mother's close friend, Mary D'Arcy, confirmed Beaumont as the best option. Even though she concealed it well, Margaret's collapse was hitting Doc D'Arcy hard. As a teen, Kate called the pair Laurel and Hardy and got scolded by Norrie for it. Their mother's rake thin stature was the polar opposite of her rotund psychologist best friend and confidante. Doc D'Arcy ferried coffee to the sisters as they waited for news that might change their lives forever.

'Now girls, no tears when they let you in to see your mum, *okay*.'

The shocked pair nodded silently, one on either side of their family friend. Kate was stoic, still focused on what needed doing.

'What should we expect?' she asked.

'Certainly not much by way of conversation,' Doc D'Arcy replied. 'Be guided by what the medical team tells you.'

Norrie burst into tears again and the doctor placed an arm around her shoulders. Two years older than Kate and always more curvaceous, she savored being the most-sought-after Debs night date the year she finished secondary school. She had no interest in college and settled for a library assistant post in Dundalk Library where she indulged her favorite pastime.

'Come on now, Norrie, Margaret will need you and Kate to be strong.'

Kate paced the corridor and an hour slipped by as they waited for news. She bumped into Angie on the landing outside the emergency department and could no longer hold back. Angie held her while she let pent-up emotions go.

'You get back to Norrie,' Angie finally said, 'I'll bring coffee.'

When she joined the little group huddled on low molded plastic seats in the sterile corridor, Angie handed out the paper cups of steaming refreshment. As usual, when seeking information, she got straight to the point.

'So Doc, tell us what happens with a stroke.'

Norrie winced at the bluntness of the question.

'Prepare for the worst, hope for the best,' Kate reassured her sister.

'The brain depends on its arteries to bring fresh blood from the heart and lungs,' Doc D'Arcy began. 'The blood carries oxygen and nutrients and takes away carbon dioxide and cellular waste. It looks like Margaret might have a blocked artery that brought on what's called an Ischemic stroke.'

'What's going to happen to her afterward?' Norrie asked. 'Will she be alright?'

'Norrie, pet, I don't know. We'll have to wait and see.'

Norrie sniffled, blew her nose into a paper tissue, and dumped it in a waste bin. Mary D'Arcy knew it was too soon to tell the distraught daughters that stroke patients frequently displayed psychological distress, mood swings, and other mental difficulties in the wake of an attack.

Three hours after their mother entered the hospital's emergency department Kate and Norrie were told they could see her. She was smiling and mouthing incomprehensibly at nurses who fussed around her. Norrie threw herself onto the bed and held her mother's hand.

'Oops, careful now, your mum's had a big night,' the guy in the white coat chided.

He introduced himself as Aidan Hanrahan, the neuro-endovascular surgeon treating their mother. He replaced Margaret's chart at the end of her bed and removed his black-rimmed glasses. The ED team had carried out a CT scan, he explained. It confirmed the presence of a clot. They had tried clot-busting drugs but when they didn't perform as well as expected, he had been called in. Doctor Hanrahan described inserting a stentriever to grab the offending clot and using an aspiration catheter to remove it. Norrie shuddered at the description of the procedure, while Kate hung on every word.

'What about recovery?' she asked when the group moved out onto the corridor.

'Each person is unique, of course,' Hanrahan told them, 'but your mum appears to be a strong woman. We need to observe her closely over the next few days and monitor how she's doing.'

'What can you tell us at this point?' Kate pressed.

'There's some loss of control over the muscles in the face and mouth, but it's not too severe.'

'I hate the way her mouth droops,' Norrie said.

'We'll have to wait and see whether she has any difficulty swallowing,' Hanrahan continued. 'Even if she does initially, a physio can show her lip and tongue exercises to get things working again.'

'Has Margaret suffered any paralysis?' Doc D'Arcy asked.

Hanrahan explained it was early days, but so far the only loss of function was in face and mouth muscles. The coming hours would be critical and should yield more information on how to map her road to recovery.

As they shuffled back toward the seats on the corridor, Angie reminded Kate her apartment was close by on the north side. She was welcome to crash there; it would save the cross-city trek from her southside apartment. Norrie told her to go and get some sleep, they could switch places in a few hours.

Angie supplied earplugs but it didn't matter much, Kate was restless at the apartment. She tossed and turned, trying to rest until finally surrendering to the inevitable that she would have a sleepless night. As early morning sunlight filtered through a chink in the curtains she slipped out of bed and took a shower. She pulled on a change of clothes from her weekend bag and went out to the kitchen-diner of the cluttered apartment. A lime green cardigan along with multi-colored babygros sat on the countertop, while two white towels occupied the stools underneath the breakfast bar. Eileen, Angie's partner, sat breastfeeding their four-month-old baby.

'Sorry about the noise last night, we're a bit colicky.'

Kate noted Eileen had slipped into the 'new mum plural' when talking about the new arrival. She hadn't noticed Angie doing likewise when discussing their little boy.

'Not to worry, Eileen,' she reassured, 'Being able to rest awhile and freshen up is great.'

Angie returned from a neighborhood bakery with fresh croissants and removed the baby clothes from the countertop to brew coffee.

'I don't get this treatment,' Eileen teased.

'It's Kate's first time here since Flynn arrived.'

'I never got to give you my gift for him, it's in my car. I'd been planning to drop it in on Sunday, then mum happened,' Kate said.

'I'll drop you at the hospital after breakfast,' Angie said. 'I can head to work from there.'

Kate sat in an armchair opposite the happy pair and their cooing baby as she and Angie gulped breakfast. Angie cradled their newborn as she cleared away dishes.

'Want me to take him?' Kate asked.

'Nah, you're good. I need to practice doing things one-handed.'

Kate smiled.

Angie brewed a small pot of green tea for Eileen and left it, together with a croissant and Danish pastry on the low table beside her. She kissed her partner good-bye and nuzzled their son's sleepy head as she handed him over.

'See you later, little man.'

'Be careful out there,' Eileen whispered, as Angie put the key in the door so she could close it quietly.

'I will,' she joked. 'Hospitals are dangerous places.'

Kate was quiet for most of the trip back to Beaumont.

'Eileen worries about you,' she said.

'Anytime she's been close to Garda action, it's been in hospital emergency departments when we're called to subdue violent headbangers,' Angie replied. 'She wouldn't do my job for all the money in the world. I tell her ditto.'

'All the same, it's nice to know someone cares.'

As they approached the hospital Angie mentioned Digger's plan to search the Manifold Avenue house later in the morning. She was going with him.

'You're doing it in *broad daylight*?'

'Yeah, Digger said estate agents check houses regularly. His mate's even providing a company car that Joe Forde will man out front after he lets us in via the rear garden. We'll search while he keeps watch.'

'Make sure Digger calls me when it's done.'

'Roger!'

7

At the hospital, Kate urged Norrie to get home to Dundalk and celebrate Ellie's birthday as planned. Their mother had been sleeping most of the time since she arrived, but was roused when the medical team came on morning rounds. The endovascular consultant led a gaggle of interns to Mrs. Bowen's bedside and challenged them to diagnose the patient. Kate listened on the other side of the drawn curtain as they quizzed her mother. She peered through and tugged Aidan Hanrahan's white coat sleeve. In response he slipped through the curtain, smiling.

'Is this appropriate?' she asked. 'Firing twenty questions at a patient who is only a few hours over a life-threatening stroke?'

Unfazed by Kate's interruption, he replied, 'We're learning a lot by doing it this way. Your mum's reactions in this session will help me guide her recovery. If you don't mind me saying, she's one sassy lady.'

Crestfallen, Kate apologized for jumping in.

'Not at all. The apple didn't fall too far from the tree it seems,' he laughed, as he pulled aside the curtain and returned to his bedside consultation.

Kate walked off the ward and headed for the corridor's coffee machine. It was her second cup of the stuff and she was thoroughly sick of it.

———————————

As Kate paced the hospital corridor, on Manifold Avenue in a nearby housing estate, Fazli Sumbal opened the back door of his rented terraced house and whistled for the tan terrier-cross to come and eat. The animal was hunched in a corner of the tiny garden producing a heap of foul-smelling waste that would have to be scooped up later. Its combo of greyhound legs and short terrier body was every kind of weird. He placed the bowl of cheap dog food on the concrete path and returned indoors.

Keeping a dog was not something he had planned, nor especially enjoyed. When the local social welfare office discovered he was living alone, they recommended a pet and allotted a monthly allowance to pay for dog food. He mentioned the dog in a phone call from the homeland and was told to familiarize himself with the neighborhood by walking it regularly. Soon, he had a mental map of every inch of the long-neglected working-class estate.

His instructions were precise when he was dispatched to number 51 Manifold Avenue; lie low, assimilate into the local Muslim community, and await orders. His mission was to keep watch on a nearby house. His daily routine was boring and repetitive. Since his part-time meat-packing job fell through, he collected a weekly welfare check.

When he returned to the kitchen, he lit a gas burner on the cooker and placed a saucepan of water on it. He measured spoonfuls of ground coffee into a cafetière and cut two slices of bread from a loaf ready for the garbage. He discarded the moldy crusts, lit the grill, and placed the bread on a wire tray dripping with fat from weeks of meat grilling. While he waited for the water to bubble, he strolled into his front room and peered through the Venetian blinds. When he saw the brown car parked near 17A, down the road on the opposite side, he changed his plans. He turned off the gas, grabbed the dog lead, and headed out.

Detective Joe Forde walked slowly around the front garden, checked a drainpipe, and looked upward toward the facia and guttering of 17A. He wore a cheap gray suit with a name tag prominent on his right lapel. Today he was John Cunningham, estate agent. He glanced up and down Manifold Avenue before consulting the list on his clipboard and ticking off another item. Systematically, he opened the green, blue, and brown unused waste bins at the side of the house and scribbled on his list. As he returned to the front garden, he saw the dog walker on the opposite side of the street.

Forde slowed his pace and leafed through pages on the clipboard as he kept the stranger, now staring at him, in his peripheral vision. A nagging thought struck him, some-thing familiar about the dog and man combo. Then it hit him. The night Khouri was arrested he had seen a dog walker on three separate occasions; always close to 17A.

He made much of re-checking the front windows, turned a key in the front door, and walked inside. He made straight for the front room to get a good look at the guy who was more interested in him than looking out for his dog. Possibly Pakistani, Forde thought, young - early twen-ties, medium height, skinny, bushy black beard, and neatly trimmed black hair parted on the left. The same guy he had seen the night Rafiq Khouri was arrested at 17A.

On the landing, Digger was unfolding an attic ladder and about to move their covert search into previously unexplored territory.

'We could have a problem,' Forde said, explaining the unwanted interest.

Angie climbed the ladder to the attic, her head torch cutting through its gloom.

'Go sit in the car and make out like you're doing paperwork. Keep an eye on him and if he continues to show interest, let us know.'

'Roger, boss.'

'Joe, do whatever it takes to keep him out of our hair.'

Forde had barely settled into the front seat and placed his clipboard on the steering wheel when the dog-walker sauntered past. The young detective watched as he crossed the road and entered number 51.

He waited and watched the house in the rearview mirror. The blinds twitched twice and the rookie detective increasingly felt ill at ease. He needed to improvise. Offering his fake business card on each call, he began calling to nearby houses enquiring if they had rooms to rent. Forde stuck meticulously to the side of the street opposite number 51. As he drew level with the dull gray house, its front door opened and the dog and owner walked out.

Forde continued into the next street until he was out of sight. There he called Digger.

'That guy from number 51 has left the house again. It's going to be a hassle keeping him out of your hair.'

'Don't let the bastard out of your sight. We've got hassle too.'

Forde knew the terrain like the back of his hand. He jumped in the estate agent's car and looped to the rear of 17A to get there ahead of his nosy adversary. By the time owner and pet came into view, Forde was already talking to the householder across the street from the rear wall of 17A.

'We're in the area checking the availability of rooms to

rent,' Forde said in a loud voice. 'There's a nice chunk of change to be made if you're interested.'

The dog walker glanced in his direction as the house-holder told him all rooms were taken in his house and he wasn't interested. Forde tried to prolong the encounter with the disgruntled middle-aged man. 'Is there anyone at home next door, would you say?'

'Go check for yourself.'

Forde tried to palm a business card, but the door closed in his face. Across the road his target paused. The mongrel sniffed a lamppost, cocked a leg, and squirted a territorial mark. His owner rattled hard on the handle of the rusted sheet metal gate and raised on tiptoe to peer over the rear garden wall of 17A Manifold Avenue. Nothing had changed in its outward appearance. Forde stabbed the transmit button on the radio in his suit pocket as he stepped over the low garden fence. A small microphone concealed underneath his garish yellow tie was linked to it and he flashed a warning.

Inside, Digger swore as he helped Angie wrench her ankle free from the sheet of plasterboard it had punched through. She had agreed to search the cramped attic and as she squeezed past a water tank, her foot slipped off a rafter and went through the ceiling. Anxious to extract it as gingerly as possible to limit the damage, she called Digger for help.

'We're screwed,' she moaned, as she rubbed her ankle.

Digger retracted the attic ladder when Forde warned of the unwanted attention and waited for news from their wingman.

'Kill the light, will ya,' he said to Angie, 'you're blindin' me.'

Angie her head torch off and sat cross-legged on an eight-by-four chipboard sheet while they waited. As their eyes adjusted to the darkness, a flicker of green light pierced the gloom.

'What was *that*?' Digger whispered.

'LED from the house alarm backup battery, maybe?'

'No, that's in the box bedroom.'

They decided against switching on torches until they knew they were in the clear. Minutes later, the LED blinked again and Digger set a timer on his phone. By the time Forde gave the all-clear, Digger knew whatever was giving off the signal pinged every three minutes.

'Find out what that light is comin' from,' he told Angie. 'I'll assess the damage.'

He exhaled a sigh of relief as he surveyed his hurried repair job. He collected any scraps of broken plasterboard, placed them in his backpack. Then he meticulously swept any chalky crumbs from the bedroom carpet, checking the floor three times from wall to wall.

Luck was on their side, the mishap occurred above a fitted wardrobe and they concealed the damage by relocating duvets stored on its top-shelf. The rough realignment was a stopgap that bought them time, nothing else.

Before wrapping up the search, Digger swiped through the photographs Angie had taken of the electronic unit in the attic. The black metal box was 50 x 30 centimeters and located on a rafter close to the rear eave making it impossible for him to access. Angie's fingertip search traced a socket wired from the bedroom below, which provided an uninterrupted power source. The photos Angie had managed were the best obtainable without disturbing the unit fixed by screws to a rafter.

When Forde confirmed the coast was clear, Angie and Digger slipped out through the rusted rear gate. He re-entered the house and pulled the rear gate's rusted bolt across to secure it. He placed the real estate agent's business card on a kitchen countertop with the inspection date scribbled on the back and exited by the front door.

He walked around the front garden one last time, clipboard in hand, and sat into the car and continued writing. Minutes later the blinds in number 51 twitched a final time as Forde pulled away from the curb.

Kate's mother spent most of the morning sleeping. The signs were mixed; there had been no further deterioration but no appreciable signs of recovery either. Kate had spent five minutes on face-time with Ellie and sampled the racket generated at her niece's birthday celebrations. Part of her was relieved to have missed the full-blown live experience. Digger rang in the late afternoon and updated her on the search outcome.

'Any ideas about what kind of electronics?'

'Maybe a signal detector,' Digger replied. 'Something like a transceiver that would extend segment distances in a network.'

Kate glanced up as the corridor doors pushed open and Norrie walked through alongside Mac.

'Mac's here,' she said, 'I better go. You did good, keep me posted.'

Mac peered through the ward window to check on Kate's mother, but a nurse had pulled the curtain around Margaret Bowen's bed to allow her sleep.

'If you two have business together, you'd better go and sort it out,' Norrie said, 'I'll see to Mum.'

'Let's chat on the landing,' Kate said, ignoring the barb.

Norrie sat by the bedside and, stroking her mother's hand, told her how the birthday party had gone. Margaret Bowen's only response was an occasional smile. She had spoken little apart from responding to the medical team's questions with monosyllabic replies. Her speech was cluttered and thick as if her tongue had swollen and was sabotaging her efforts.

'How is everything?' Mac asked Kate.

She explained her mother was stable for the moment, but recovery would be a long slow process. 'Let's go outside. I could do with some fresh air.'

Their feet rustled leaves on the edge of the footpath as they exited near the Emergency Department. Two yellow ambulances were parked in bays ready for dispatch, another reversed to the ED entrance transferring a patient onto a gurney.

'The Germans are proposing a task force to tackle the ISIS threat,' Mac told her. 'The objective is to identify terrorist networks and destroy them.'

'Politicians always make it sound like it can be done just like that,' Kate snapped her fingers.

'There's a meeting in Berlin on Tuesday. I'll nominate someone else to attend, you have enough to cope with here.'

Kate didn't offer an immediate response. The early spring chill made her shiver involuntarily. 'Is your car close?'

Out of the bracing breeze, Kate went over what Digger and Angie had uncovered at the Manifold Avenue house. Mac had already spoken to the head of the telecommunications section at Garda headquarters and Digger would drop off photos for him to review. Forde's connection of the unidentified suspect to the Khouri arrest meant the morning search had been highly profitable.

'Is your mother up to visitors?' Mac asked.

'If you don't mind, leave it for now. Particularly with Norrie's mood.'

'I'll tell you what, I'll send her flowers,' Mac said. 'I

won't decide on who to send to Berlin until tomorrow morning; see how your mother is then.'

'I'll corner the good-looking doc and see if he can give me a read on what the immediate future holds for mum.'

'Good looking, eh!'

'Just my way of distinguishing one from the other.'

'Stop now,' Mac laughed. 'You've dug a deep enough hole.'

'Honestly!' Kate sighed.

———

She spent a second night at Angie's place, replete with the smells and sounds of a newborn. She slipped out before seven the next morning as baby Flynn settled to his early feed. She found Norrie dozing in an armchair alongside her mother with Doc D'Arcy sitting at the end of the bed.

'How is Mum?'

'Ask her yourself,' the Doc replied.

Kate slid alongside the bed and took her mother's hand. She kissed her cheek and whispered, 'How are you feeling?'

Margaret Bowen slowly opened her eyes and regarded her daughter, her brain crunching the data. Finally, she smiled. It wasn't perfect. The left side of her mouth drooped, but for Kate it was beautiful.

'Like I've been hit by a truck.'

Kate spluttered and leaned in for a hug. Norrie roused on the opposite side and joined in.

'Oh, Mum! You're back!'

'I sound stupid.'

'We can work on how you sound,' Doc D'Arcy chipped in from the bottom of the bed. 'The stupid bit, you'll have to work on yourself.'

All four broke down laughing and crying. The three

visitors spent the next ten minutes coaxing conversation from the determined patient. Kate collared Aidan Hanrahan as he completed his morning rounds and asked for an update on her mother's progress.

'I'm about to take a coffee. Would you like to come to my office,' he invited.

They walked through corridors busy with early morning routines and took a lift to Hanrahan's office in the consultants' suite. Kate accepted a coffee and listened without comment as the specialist outlined how he hoped her mother's recovery would progress. He was optimistic. She had shown great fighting spirit and the fact some motor function was returning, even in a limited way, was a good sign.

'What about relapse,' Kate asked.

'Every recovery is individual, but I think we have grounds to be positive,' Dr. Hanrahan sipped his cup and placed it back on its saucer.

'I might have to travel to Europe to work in the next day or so. Should I cancel?'

'What business are you in?'

Kate dipped into her bag, fished out her Garda ID, and placed it on the table.

'Clearly, this is an important trip.'

Kate nodded.

'Your mum is stable right now. Leave your number and I will call you myself if anything changes while you're away.'

Kate thanked him and walked back toward her mother's ward. Along the way, she let Mac know that she was good to travel. The FBI nor the CIA were not getting directly involved. Instead, Chapman, the Secret Service agent from the ride-along, would represent American interests at the meeting.

'Why don't I travel to Berlin, via Paris?' Kate

58

suggested. 'I need to persuade O'Neill to release FBI data to the Ben Gordon murder investigation team.'

'Good idea. We need to know if Gordon's murder is linked to Khouri.'

Kate returned to her apartment on Dublin's south side in the afternoon. She dumped the contents of her weekend bag in the laundry basket and re-packed it for her overnight stay. She enjoyed a brief, blissfully undisturbed nap, before heading back to spend time with her mother. The airport was close by and Kate delayed catching a taxi for as long as possible. When Norrie arrived, despite her tetchiness about Kate, once again, putting work before family, they hugged affectionately as their mother slept. Kate kissed her mum lightly on the forehead and raced to the airport where she grabbed a seat on the final Dublin-to-Paris flight.

8

NORTHERN IRELAND - KEVIN'S EARLY YEARS

When his mother married Bart Wrollesly, Kevin Steven-son's surname changed but little else. He rebuffed his step-father, loathing the insisted on daily bible study, along with farm chores. Within four years of moving to his new home, a stepsister and brother had arrived. He liked Maud but envied the attention his mother lavished on his stepbrother, Ivan.

At twelve years old, a bust-up with Wrollesly irreparably soured any chance of a decent relationship between them. The stern lay pastor clipped Kevin hard for giving lip at the dinner table. He howled; bolted out of the house and failed to return by nightfall. Neighbors arrived and spread through the fields, searching with Wrollesly for the errant boy. When the search parties returned empty-handed, Harriet berated her husband, threatening to leave if any harm came to her firstborn. Hidden in a nearby hay barn, Kevin smirked as he watched the spectacle unfold.

He strolled in for breakfast the next morning elated that his protest had won the day. Despite Wrollesly's objec-tions his mother wrapped him in her arms and kissed his cheeks. She brushed loose hay from his clothes and set about cooking a fry-up usually reserved for Sunday mornings. Wrollesly was having none of it.

'Put the frying pan away, woman,' he said. 'This boy needs a lesson in discipline. I know the man to do it.'

'Don't worry,' his mother whispered. 'I'll not let him harm you.'

They listened as Wrollesly spoke on the hallway telephone. 'The prodigal son has returned,' they overheard. Next came a bible quote, *'if any man has a stubborn and rebellious son who will not obey his father or his mother, and when they chastise him, he will not even listen to them, then his father and mother shall seize him, and bring him out to the elders of his city... Deuteronomy 21:18-21,'* Wrollesly thundered as if addressing a congregation.

The prodigal son smirked at the memory of his mother doing her own chastising the previous evening. What happened next wiped the smugness away and tainted Kevin's trust in his mother.

When Wrollesly returned, he said, 'You're coming with me, young man.'

'Where are you taking him?' Harriet demanded, pushing her son behind her.

'Lord Humphrey says he has just the place to cool you off.'

'Lord Humphrey!' Harriet repeated. Wrollesly leased his entire farm from the lord of the manor.

When his mother meekly stepped aside, a primal self-preservation instinct surged through the stubborn boy. Wrollesly grabbed him and manhandled him toward the jeep. His mother cried as the jeep reversed in the farmyard. Kevin decided he would take the punishment meted out, he would not concede an inch.

· · ·

The entrance to Lord Humphrey Ashton's Northern Ireland manor was lined with tall oak trees. They blotted out sunshine as Kevin stared out the jeep's side window as they drove up the avenue. The lord of the manor was waiting in a backyard. He strode to Wrollesly's jeep and pulled open the passenger door.

'Why do you think you are here, young man?'

'Fucked if I know,' Kevin replied, refusing to budge.

Lord Ashton looked across the roof of the jeep at Wrollesly. 'You did the right thing.'

Ashton pulled the boy from the jeep by his shirt collar and propelled him toward the manor. Before they reached the stone stairs leading to the main house, he diverted toward a basement, a dungeon in Kevin's youthful eyes. Inside, the musty 'old clothes' odor reminded him of his grandparents' house as Lord Ashton led him down a central corridor. Dim light filtered from the rooms on the right while those on the left were dark as night.

Midway, Ashton's grip on his collar tightened and he dispatched the boy into a disused pantry on the left with a kick in the rear. 'Learn to respect your elders, you cur,' he said.

The tiny room was windowless. Kevin kicked its door hard and demanded immediate release.

'Kick all you like,' Ashton told him. 'You'll get out when you're ready to show respect.'

Kevin kicked until his toes swelled inside his boots. He untied the boots and felt the warm squelch of fresh blood. He stopped and listened. Was Ashton outside the door waiting for an apology? He could see nothing. Something scurried in a corner. He screamed at it to leave him alone. He listened for a reaction in the corridor. Nothing. He was starving, phantom smells of his mother's promised fry-up tantalizing his brain. He fumbled for something to drink. There was nothing but dust-covered bottles on shelves.

Kevin lashed them with a sweep of his hand and slumped to the ground. He was alone and scared.

The next morning Lord Ashton opened the door with a tray in one hand. Kevin lay curled in a fetal position in the center of the cell-like room. The smell of freshly fried sausages wafted in as his eyes blinked furiously in the streaming light.

'Nothing like a night in pokey to rekindle the soul, eh Kevin! What do you think?'

'Go fuck yourself,' Kevin replied, kicking bits of broken glass away from his blood-soaked socks.

'Take another night to think about it,' Ashton replied and slammed the door shut.

The following evening, Kevin's eyes blinked rapidly again as the door was thrown open.

'Get up and get out,' Ashton shouted.

Kevin grabbed his boots in his left hand and hobbled up the steps out of the basement, socks crusted with dried blood.

'There's not much I can do for you,' Ashton bellowed to Wrollesly, arrived to collect the sinner.

'What will I do with him?' he asked.

'You have your hands full, Bart. The lad's got spunk, I'll give him that. Sign him up for Crusaders NI Juniors maybe, rugby might channel his stamina.'

Kevin slapped Ashton's hand away when he opened the jeep's passenger door and offered to help him in.

'This cur was never here, you understand,' Ashton growled to Wrollesly.

His stepfather's ashen face made Kevin forget his pain. He had prevailed, he had conquered.

The teenage years played out as a predictable, stormy saga. When secondary school ended, Kevin headed to Queen's University, Belfast to study a law degree. Tall and robust, with dark hair and deep brown eyes, he reveled in the liberation of college life and everything that went with it. Within weeks he was an exalted, lightning-fast member of the Fresher's rugby team.

As the end of his first year approached with assignments completed and exam prep in full flow, he came across a 'frozen in time' feature in a Law Society newsletter. The piece questioned whether the early release of hundreds of prisoners serving time for terrorist offenses was justified to achieve peace under the terms of the Good Friday agreement. The accompanying photograph of released prisoners outside Long Kesh prison included a face that flooded back memories of a never-forgotten childhood moment.

A primal impulse for a familial connection surged through him, but he hesitated. The itch nagged until a week later he contacted the Belfast Sinn Fein office, explained his request, and left a contact number. It took a month but with one final exam to sit, he received a text message inviting him to meet his biological father in Belfast.

The meet-up was arranged for the west of the city, Andy's café, in Andersonstown. Kevin was already sitting at a table covered with a black-and-white checkered oilcloth when the bell over the entrance door rang to announce the older man's arrival. The roly-poly owner beckoned his old pal behind the counter toward to a tiny room.

'Fair play, Andy,' he said, clapping him on the shoulder. 'Come on,' he signaled Kevin.

Once again they were sitting across a table from each

other; once again Kevin fidgeted. Each observed the other as if trying to figure out what to say.

'Well, will you look at you! All grown up,' Sean O'Hare opened.

'Look at you. Scot-free to roam the world,' Kevin countered.

O'Hare smiled.

'Here, my mother told me I was named after my father. Your name's not Kevin.'

'Best ask your mother.'

Andy arrived and placed two steaming coffee mugs on the table. 'I'll give ye a bit a peace,' he said, closing over the mustard-colored door as he slipped out.

'So, what are you doing with yourself these days?' O'Hare asked.

'University. You?'

'Aye well, if we're to believe our lords and masters, it's a whole new world out there. I'm doing alright.'

'What's alright?'

'Nothing a university man like you'd be interested in. What did you want with me, anyway?'

'To get to know you a bit. Is that so bad?'

O'Hare regarded him suspiciously.

'Don't you have a father?'

'Aye, well me and Wrollesly don't exactly see eye to eye.'

'How's your mother?'

'Doing alright, aye. Two more wee wuns, a sister and brother.'

'Good to hear it. What're their names?'

'Maud and Ivan.'

'What are ya studying in Uni?'

'Law with French.'

'Hoping to be a lawyer, are ye?'

'Haven't made up my mind.'

'To be straight and honest with ye. I don't know how much I can do for ye. I've got a family of my own.'

'I figured as much.'

The student took a sip from his mug but slammed it back on the table. '*Jesus*, that's piss.'

'I'd say you're more a barista man. That pretentious shite is everywhere these days; wee cafés like this one are dying out.'

'Maybe it's not before time.'

That raised a laugh.

'I'm getting out of Belfast,' the older man continued. 'Moving to Portadown to manage a business that myself and a few boys set up.'

'A pity. I thought maybe we could grab a coffee now and again. Proper coffee, not this muck,' Kevin replied. 'Give me a chance to get to know you a wee bit.'

'Did your ma put you up to this?'

'God no. I still remember the way you waved at me the day we came to see you at the jail.'

'I remember an' all. That guard was being a bastard.'

'You remember?'

'Aye. Ye were upset about a wee toy, weren't ye?'

Kevin bowed his head. 'I got over it.'

They chatted a while, ignoring the coffee mugs, now with a slick of grease floating across their surface.

'Thanks for meeting up anyway.'

'Not a problem,' O'Hare told him. 'And, here, maybe we can grab that coffee sometime. We're truckers, it'll bring me this way now and again.'

'You have my number.'

'I do.'

A week on, Kevin had finished his final exam and was cleaning out his student room when he received a text from a number he did not recognize – *want a job for the summer.*

'*What's the job?*' he replied.

'*Helper on a truck.*'

Kevin tapped out '*screw that*' in reply but hesitated over the send button.

Who would offer him such a job? Might it be his real father extending an olive branch?

'*Is it yourself?*' he sent, instead of the dismissive text.

'*Yes or No?*' came an immediate response.

Kevin wavered. Humping loads from trucks around a damp and cold Irish countryside was not how he saw the summer ahead. But …

'*Yes,*' he tapped in reply.

He slapped his forehead. Was he crazy? As he pondered his decision, he received another text with a different number to call for further details. It also instructed him to change his phone number immediately.

9

NORTHERN IRELAND - JUNIOR

Every newcomer to the isolated south Armagh depot picked up a first-day pet name—Kid, Pup, Young Chap, even Squirt. When Kevin arrived, his uncanny resemblance to the boss earned him the nickname, Junior.

By summer's end, he knew that contraband was his biological father's main source of income. The smuggling was on an industrial scale; regular cargo a mere front. On the surface, his father's group kept it simple, dealing contraband cigarettes. Junior suspected illicit drugs were part of the trade, hidden from him.

His new mentor was nothing like the tight-fisted Wrollesly. He paid cash each week, increasing amounts as the summer rolled on. The weeks flew by in a blur of return trips through central Europe into Turkey. He followed O'Hare's advice and pulled his head in at home, gave up arguing with his stepfather. At the end of August Junior broke the news that he had deferred his second year in college.

'You should have talked to me first,' Sean O'Hare said.

'It's my life,' Junior replied.

'Aye, but I might not have work for you in the coming months.'

'Let me drive.'

'You'd need a heavy goods vehicle license for that and it's three grand to train up. Have you got that kinda cash?'

'I've got £1,500 saved, I'll get the rest.'

O'Hare could see much of himself in the young pup.

'Here's what I'll do,' he said.

Junior knew it would take a few months to repay O'Hare the loan but that didn't bother him. He climbed into the cab of a Scania truck weeks later, with his HGV license stuck behind the sun visor, and departed from Rosslare port for Europe. It was a dream come true. His first solo run was through France toward the countries of the former Soviet bloc to the east. Each trip an adventure that fueled a growing relish for risk as the contraband business grew on him and challenged him to learn fast.

As summer rolled into autumn, Junior noticed odd callers drop into his father's yard from time to time. He did not care for them; they were unfriendly and hostile. He learned to avoid them, figuring them for former comrades from the Troubles and surmised their visits as nostalgic. The opportunity to talk to his father every day was almost too good to be true. He was diametrically opposite to Wrollesly, encouraging get-up-and-go, rather than zealously pointing out errors.

As the dusky evenings of late autumn set in, his mentor grew distant and restless. He was out of contact for long periods and seemed distracted. By that stage, the constant tutoring had given Junior a detailed knowledge of company business. As instructed, he had cemented bonds with Turkish suppliers and established new supply lines with Bulgarian gangs. The contraband cigarette runs across the Irish border were in his hands. The college boy knew the territory well from sojourns south with both his Crusaders and university rugby teams.

Junior's natural charisma was sometimes misjudged for softness. When a customer complained to O'Hare about a henchman's broken jaw, the boss knew his protégé could deal with the hard men in the criminal gangs who tried to double-deal them. Junior worked their suppliers hard and forged a trust that built a conveyor belt of product.

As winter snows made the runs east increasingly hazardous, Junior's world imploded. He struggled to cope when word reached him of Sean O'Hare's death in France.

The violent death received blanket media coverage for days. Each revelation shocked and revolted him, each new detail increasing his bewilderment. Was the rumor true that his father had killed one of their drivers in the south weeks before Kevin joined the business? Blinded by a desire for a real father-son relationship he missed the warning signs. Lurking at the heart of the dynamic 'business' was a terror group he would never be part of in a million years. Was the bond with his terrorist father a charade?

As his anger simmered, his problems intensified. The Criminal Assets Bureau from the Republic targeted the 'business' and worked with Northern Ireland counterparts to seize all its identifiable assets. Trucks vanished in a feeding frenzy of police raids that stripped the business empire his father had built of all its possessions. By the end, the only assets remaining were their precious Turkish and Bulgarian contacts.

Junior avoided criminal charges by pleading ignorance to any knowledge of the true nature of the business. He spent twenty-four hours in police custody and played the role of naïve student. Financially broken and emotionally shattered, he returned home to start afresh. His mother supported him, reminding him of the charismatic man his father had been, and the positive qualities he had inherited.

He tried to pick up the threads of his former life; played rugby on the weekends and got in touch with Queen's university to re-boot his college degree. He blanched at the length of the reading list the Law faculty sent him. Being unable to travel was stifling. He missed the addictive battles of will, physical and mental, in the underground life he had briefly sampled. In the back of his mind was the possibility that if caught he might end up in jail. The thought sent a shiver down his spine. As winter evenings in the farmhouse dragged, his agitation grew. Everything changed when remnants of the old gang came calling.

'*Jesus*, that's one wild cold night,' he said, as he returned indoors from a farmyard chat with two of them.

'Don't take the Lord's name in vain in this house,' Wrollesly admonished.

'Who were the boys in the yard, anyway?' his mother asked.

'They might have work,' he replied, pressing a finger to his lips.

Harriet worried about her son. Since Sean O'Hare's death, Kevin's moods swung between anger and rage.

'I'll go watch the news,' Wrollesly grumbled and headed toward the sitting room. 'Maud, turn off that nonsense.'

'Och, do I have to change the channel?' she moaned.

Junior shook his head and closed the kitchen door.

'That man can't act decent, can he?'

'Pull up to the fire and warm yourself,' his mother encouraged. 'What work is going?'

'They're friends of the boss. They want me to see about getting things moving again on the continent.'

'I'll help you,' she replied, to his surprise.

She told him he could take the £5000 he had given her during his working months and use it as a deposit to purchase a truck. She had diligently put aside the bonuses he collected and explained it was all his if he wanted it. He flat out refused to take the money, at first, telling her he intended it as security for her.

'Do you take me for an idiot, is that it?' she demanded.

'What do you mean?'

'I know the money you were giving me wasn't coming from trucking.'

'You still took it.'

'Do you know what they call me around here? *Harlot, IRA whore,* and worse, a lot worse. It's been thrown in my face for nearly twenty years and I'm sick of it.'

'When the Orange men get oiled up around the 12th July they hold back on nobody. None of them dare say anything to *my* face. Anyway, it's nobody's business but your own.'

'Round here everyone knows everyone else's business and they'll *never* forgive me.'

'Fuck them!'

'You take the money and get yourself back on the road. Maybe I might get away from here someday.'

'What about Maud and Ivan?'

'I'll look after them like I looked after you, but I can't take the bitterness much longer.'

In the few months they worked together, O'Hare had demonstrated to Junior what was possible with careful planning and attention to detail. However, his arrest meant details of Kevin Wrollesly's UK passport featured on police watch lists. Using it while smuggling contraband would be downright foolhardy. His mother found his old birth certificate and he applied for an Irish passport using his birth name. The Irish government's desire to welcome members of the northern protestant community into the Irish family ensured Kevin Stevenson received his shiny new passport within fourteen days of applying for it. It opened up unimpeded travel right across Europe.

It took careful planning and ruthless execution but month by month Junior slowly re-built the gang's old operation. He acquired more trucks and flipped ownership regularly as his accountants skimmed the business from one new company name to another to throw the Inland Revenue off the scent. He developed fresh routes in Europe and taught them to new drivers.

For his father's buddies, Junior was a carbon copy of the old man; same drive, same ruthless cut and thrust. Eighteen months after buying his first truck, Junior had seven units permanently on the road and was laundering Dublin drug gangs' profits in the city's flourishing contraband cigarette market.

Although controlling his territory demanded more of his attention, Junior stayed in touch with life on the road. He took on a monthly continental run and used it to pay off his vital contacts, renew acquaintances, or develop new ones. He studied how customs in each country went about their business. When he figured out that people smuggling was what preoccupied French authorities most, he threw the border police titbits of information using his scrappy French skills.

In France, he timed his runs so he could eat a few hours ahead of embarkation. He avoided transit stop dross and went for Breton villages offering decent cuisine. Roscoff had a choice of restaurants Junior loved. He sampled them all. From crêperies in the center offering specialties of buckwheat pancakes and local cider to the finer dining restaurants on the seafront with more expansive menus.

The day the axis of his world shifted, he had parked his truck at the port with hours to spare before sailing. He used the terminal facilities to shower and change and strolled into Roscoff along the coast road toward *Chez Aline*. He ordered a seafood platter and brushed up his rusty language skills discussing with the waiter a white wine to accompany it.

He ate slowly, savoring each delicious flavor and gazing absentmindedly as an instructor put teenagers through basic sailing lessons in the pleasure port. As he was about to down an espresso and head out for a stroll along the seafront, he overheard chatter from the next table that changed his plans.

The middle-aged, mustachioed pair, elegantly attired in royal blue blazers and light gray slacks, were hard to ignore. Their table was a testament to a luxuriously drawn-out lunch. A duo of wine bottles, inverted in their coolers had been supplemented by bowl-like glasses of cognac *digestifs*. As they rambled on about the terrorist threat, inebriation made them louder and less inhibited. France was being torn apart with dissension they said, Islamic radicals and their henchmen.

'*Beressi de Brest, lui, il a vécu un cauchemar,*' one pronounced, somberly.

Junior's curiosity piqued at the mention of the place

where his father died. Who was Beressi and what nightmare had he lived through?

'For once, the cops did well.'

'Irish ones too, I'm told.'

Junior's head tilted. He ordered another coffee and requested the local paper, turning the pages slowly to cover his earwigging.

'Who told you that?' the diner with the silver handlebar mustache asked.

'Beressi himself,' his friend replied. His mustache was more walrus than handlebar.

'He said Irish *flic* were there when he was interviewed.'

'That was kept hush-hush.'

'The *flic* had two Irish cops helping them at the museum ramparts,' he said. 'The terrorist threatened to kill them both, but the woman shot the ringleader.'

Junior closed the paper and left cash with his bill. The waiter retrieved his customer's jacket from the coat stand and opened the door. Junior paused and asked if the gentlemen adjoining his table were police. The waiter beckoned him onto the street. He accepted Junior's generous tip and whispered that the walrus mustache was Roscoff's harbormaster and his guest held the same post in nearby *Saint-Malo*.

In the bright afternoon sunlight, Junior mulled over the enormity of what he had overheard. He Googled 'harbormaster Brest' and confirmed him as Alain Beressi. This made it likely the chatter was accurate. Someone from home, a cop, a woman, had killed his father. As he reached the edge of town and climbed the hill that dropped toward the ferry port on the other side, he had one thing on his mind.

Vengeance.

10

Junior attacked pinpointing his father's killer with religious zeal. Accounts of the trial of Treacy, Sean O'Hare's accomplice, yielded sparse details even in French newspapers. Treacy was serving a prison sentence at Portlaoise prison following repatriation from France. Junior put out feelers to every police contact the gang paid off in Northern Ireland but no one knew anything. Had a British agent ensnared his father? Nothing made sense.

His luck changed when a newly hired receptionist cleaned out the office in his Newry depot. She wanted to bin old copies of the Sunday Chronicle but he held off dumping them. The Dublin weekly specialized in true crime stories and Junior read them all. Months after Sean O'Hare died, they printed an article about elation among Dublin surveillance officers with the return of their former commander. A fuzzy picture of Superintendent Kate Bowen in a UN uniform accompanied an article laden with speculation on her unexplained exile.

As they headed south, weeks later, to collect a debt from a Dublin drug gang, Junior posed a tentative question to two henchmen. Frank Reilly, his right-hand man, was driving the rented Mercedes as Junior stared out the passenger window. He noticed motorway speed limit signs change from miles to kilometers signaling they had crossed the Northern Ireland border into the Republic.

'Did it ever cross ye'r mind who killed the boss?'

After a beat a reply came from the rear seat, 'French cops shot him.'

'Aye, that's what we heard alright,' Reilly said.

He had been close to Sean O'Hare and although Reilly never spoke of it, Junior imagined the pair crossed paths during the Troubles.

'What if there was a different story?'

'How do ye mean?' Reilly asked.

'What if it was someone closer to home?'

He laid out the story he had overheard in France and watched Reilly mull it over.

'Nothing showed here and we dug as deep as we could,' Reilly said.

'Maybe we're looking in the wrong place. What if the answer lies down here?' Junior replied.

When they pulled into M1 motorway services, Junior bought three coffees and brought them to an outside table. He showed his henchmen the newspaper report.

'First, I overhear that an Irish cop, a woman shot my father. Then I come across this report saying,' he jabbed a finger at Kate's fuzzy image, 'that this bitch was shifted offside shortly after it happened. A few months later and she's back home leading a bunch of spies. A bit of a coincidence, wouldn't you say.'

'It would make you wonder, right enough,' Reilly agreed. 'What about it?'

'Dig into it, will you and see if there's anything in it?'

'I'll get the boys in Dundalk to nose around,' he said.

'Leave it to fuck alone,' Reilly's younger associate piped up. 'We've got a good thing going.'

Junior ignored the interruption. 'I need to find out if the story I overheard was bullshit. Frank, would you talk to Treacy in Portlaoise.'

'I'm not sure he'll want to talk to me.'

'Why not?'

'We've had run-ins; he's a mad bastard.'

'Bring him around; promise whatever it takes.'

Weeks later, Reilly pulled his truck off the M7 motorway outside Portlaoise and parked at the nearby services. He ordered a snack from an outlet in the food mall and brooded over how best to approach Treacy. He had been granted a close relative visit on a ruse that he was a cousin of the prisoner.

He took a taxi from the services and lowered himself onto a gray metal bench in the visiting room, as Treacy arrived on the other side of a thick glass panel.

'Cousin Frankie!' Treacy grinned.

His cold, steel-blue eyes still held the luster of crazy.

'Nutser, you're keeping well?' Reilly replied, adjusting the black wand microphone.

They parleyed a while on topics familiar to both, football, events around home, and who was doing what. It was the kind of inane chatter supervising guards were attuned to and the one standing immediately behind Treacy soon got bored. He moved to the end of the visiting room and tinkered with his smartphone.

'Junior was hoping you could help us out.'

'Is this the boy everyone's saying is the boss's whelp?'

'The same.'

'What does he want?'

Reilly lowered his voice as he laid out the information Junior needed verifying.

'He's some prick.'

'Come on Nutser, don't be like that.'

'Fuck him. I've years to do in here. If he needs to know something let him come and ask me himself.'

'He lodged a €100 in your prison account, the maximum.'

'Big fuckin' deal. Tell him to bring another €100 when he's comin' himself.'

Reilly invoked loyalty to their fallen leader but to no avail. A fortnight later, Nutser sat in the same screened visiting area looking at a face he had never seen before.

'Cousin Kevin!'

'Call me Junior. What'll I call you?'

'Nutser; everyone else does.'

'So here I am.'

'They weren't lying when they said you're the spit of the boss.'

'It's him I'm here to talk about.'

Slamming doors as prisoners came and went, unnerved Junior. Old memories rushed back of nights locked in a dank room. He watched the guard pace behind the line of prisoners and draw level with Nutser's seat. This was nothing like he recalled from the visit, as a child, to see his father. This sterile room felt cold and impersonal by comparison.

'Why do you want to know how he died?' Nutser asked.

'Don't be fucking stupid. I can't say anything here,' Junior replied.

'What do you want from me?'

'Were there Irish cops around the night your operation failed?'

Junior knew the implied slur would sting and enjoyed watching Nutser's mouth twist into an impotent snarl.

'Aye, well now someone betrayed us, that's for sure.'

'Don't let that go unpunished,' Junior responded.

'If I ever…'

'Nutser, you've years left in here. Help me.'

'What about my money?'

'Deposited in your account.'

Nutser shifted closer to the screen.

'I heard Irish voices on the quay that mornin', alright. I was on the ground, at this stage, mind you. All the same, I glimpsed a woman and a wiry fucker who looked like one of us. The French were listenin' to what she was advisin'. That's as much as I know.'

'And you couldn't tell Reilly this?'

'Your old man was a God to me. I wanted to see his pup with me own eyes.'

The guard approached on his return patrol and Junior slipped off the metal bench. He needed to unpick any information from the obstinate prisoner's head but had no interest in bonding with him.

'So long, Nutser' he waved. He made to leave but turned as the guard moved away and leaned into the microphone – 'Frank will send you a Sunday Chronicle. Read it and get back.'

The following week Frank Reilly sent the newspaper with Kate's photo to the jail, together with a coded contact number. Nutser replied from a burner he paid a fellow inmate €10 to use.

'*That's the bitch*,' the text read.

11

At her Paris hotel, Kate re-read Cody O'Neill's invitation to breakfast at a small café close to the U.S. embassy. His note, handwritten on high-quality stationery, was old-school and charming. The last time they had spoken by telephone, he had authorized a limited release of information on Rafiq Khouri. Murder squad detectives investigating Ben Gordon's murder were given a carefully constructed brief. It outlined that SIU assisted the FBI in carrying out a surveillance operation on an employee of the victim over several weeks. The Dublin based operation concluded the suspect's arrest and eventual release without charge.

Kate strode along *avenue des Champs Elysées,* the bright blue Paris sky lifting her spirits. Seeing the city's undiminished splendor invigorated her. She located the café and pushed its door open. She was unsurprised that the table O'Neill had chosen commanded a view of the entrance. Old habits. The tall, dark-haired FBI man was movie-star handsome and wore an impeccably pressed dark suit teamed with a white shirt and burgundy tie.

'Great to see you,' he greeted Kate with a peck on each cheek.

'Here we go again,' she said.

O'Neill smiled as she turned her attention to the more thrown-together guy with him.

'Hi Zach, how have you been?'

'All things considered, I'd rather be heading for WA right now.'

The attack on Secretary Turlington scuppered Chapman's planned trip to his hometown in Perth, Western Australia.

'Things will perk up.'

'Chapman will be our guy on the European Task Force,' O'Neill said.

'So I'm told,' Kate replied.

'Let's eat,' Chapman intervened, 'I'm famished.'

The crowded café made open discussion impossible. Kate wondered why O'Neill had chosen here for the rendezvous. They chit-chatted their way through croissants, *pain au chocolat*, coffee, and orange juice.

'Mind if we jump on a train to Berlin?' Chapman asked, as their waiter cleared the table. 'My ears still ring; the doctor advised me to avoid planes if I can.'

'You'd be doing me a favor,' Kate replied.

O'Neill booked their tickets through his office assistant and drove the pair to *Gare de l'Est*. On the way, Chapman sat quietly in the back seat while Kate discussed the Khouri case with O'Neill.

'I can't guarantee any further sharing of intel,' O'Neill told her. 'If your guys develop specific leads, we'll do our best to find a workaround.'

He parked the car and insisted on carrying Kate's overnight bag to the station. As they waited for the Berlin Hauptbahnhof train to shunt onto its track, Chapman sidled away toward ticket-checkers controlling the platform gate to inquire about boarding.

'Any chance we could do dinner and a catch-up?' O'Neill asked.

'Why' she asked.

'Caitlin's spending the summer here with me but I'm sure I could work in a trip to Ireland during the Gordon murder investigation.'

'What about your wife?'

'Staying Stateside,' he continued.

Kate pondered a comeback about his still being stuck in a rut but instead said, 'Paris will be wonderful for your little girl.'

'I hate how we left things back in Dublin.'

As O'Neill's hand touched her sleeve, Kate noticed Chapman beckoning.

'What's done is done,' she said. 'I've got to go.'

She joined Chapman and they sought out their carriage. He stashed her weekend bag in the overhead bin, glanced around, checking their immediate neighbors before pushing in toward the window.

'First long train trip in Europe,' he quipped.

The train moved slowly out the station at its designated departure time, on a journey that would take eight and a half hours. They planned to catch up on lost sleep. Having changed trains at Mannheim, and barely settled, simultaneous text alerts roused the pair. Kate opened her eyes and fumbled with her new phone.

'Meeting's been brought forward,' she said.

'Will we make it on time?' Chapman asked.

'Should do, we're over halfway now.'

The news shook off their lethargy. Kate told Chapman

of her student days inter-railing around Europe; Chapman was all about his home in Perth's western suburbs until his fourteenth birthday. Despite its isolation, Western Australia was heaven to Chapman and his younger sister, Jess. Their house on Parry Street was hidden behind a huge Queensland Box tree that provided relief from the summer heat and nesting for noisy kookaburras.

'How come you moved to America?' Kate asked.

'Dad was a mining engineer. When he went into management, we moved with him to Michigan,' Chapman replied.

'What was it like uprooting to the US?'

'A whole other world.'

Kate glanced out the window; they were leaving behind the rural landscape overloaded with wind turbines and entering city suburbs. A service announcement confirmed they would arrive at Berlin Hauptbahnhof in minutes.

At the station, Carl-Gustav, the agent who had ferried Kate around on her recent Berlin visit, met them and drove to the German Intelligence Service HQ. Once again, Jan Krause chaired the crisis meeting.

'As you are all aware,' he said, 'nothing goes out of date quicker than up-to-date information. Mr. Chapman, please brief us on the attempted assassination of Secretary Turlington.'

Chapman got straight to business. He showed scene photos of the devastation and described how the attack unfolded. The ambush location had been well chosen and although it failed in its objective, the battle-hardened manner of its execution had been impressive. Seventeen people were killed in the blast triggered by the suicide driver of the red Peugeot. Many more suffered life-changing injuries. Seven gunmen died in the gun battle. It was impossible to say conclusively whether any had slipped away from the chaos. Chapman's driver, Harry, was recovering in hospital.

'I would not be here to tell the tale,' Chapman continued, 'were it not for my international colleagues in the *Préfecture de Paris* and *Service de la Protection*.'

Krause called for a moment of silent reflection for the slain police.

Chapman resumed, 'A fellow delegate played a big part in rescuing a desperate situation.'

Kate bristled. Had Chapman not gotten the memo on keeping her out of the picture or was he choosing to ignore it? She shook her head to slow him, but he feigned ignorance.

'Detective Superintendent Kate Bowen was along for the ride that day, casting her professional eye over how the U.S. Secret Service does business. She played a big part in my being here to tell the tale. Damn, can she kick hard!'

He spared no detail in his colorful description of their exit from the Dodge and shootout with an assault group. Kate blushed, unaccustomed to effusive praise. Back home the politicians who demanded the terrorist threat be contained, presumed entitlement to nit-pick how the job was done. A burst of spontaneous applause jarred her as all eyes in the room zeroed in on where she sat.

'A fact our Irish colleague kept to herself,' Krause smiled. 'Would you like to add anything, Kate?'

'I did what any of us would have done. And the media *don't* need to hear about it.'

The gaggle of mostly middle-aged men around the table chuckled in response.

'Any queries for Special Agent Chapman?' Krause asked.

A smattering of tactical evaluations of the attack

followed. When Krause moved on to update reports on attacks in individual countries. Kate chronicled the Ben Gordon murder investigation without reference to the mystery device uncovered during SIU's covert search. Mac was taking the photos to J2 for a military perspective and she did not fancy proffering bullshit excuses for how it might have been missed the first time the house was searched.

'Let's move on,' Krause said as he dimmed the conference room lights. 'The Al-Jazeera news desk in London received this video earlier today.'

A great storm is coming,' the hooded figure on the screen began, his accent British and delivery assured. An ISIS monochrome flag hung behind him.

A storm mightier than the Crusader has ever witnessed. As the Crusader seeks to destroy the lands of the Prophet, so we will lay waste a great city. As you have left us, so we will make you—homeless. Your greatest power will become our greatest weapon against you. When the people rise, it is the messengers of Allah, peace be upon him, who will provide guidance.'

The room lights came up and Krause turned to MI5's head of Berlin station, 'Before we view the remainder of the video, what can MI5 tell us about this suspect, Mr. Symons?'

'My service has identified this suspect as Abdu al-Farouq AKA Frederick Powell,' Peter Symons' whiny voice began. Kate reviled the puffed-up Oxonian. They had worked an old case together, an experience that left a sour taste.

'This ingrate,' Symons continued, 'was born and raised in Washwood Heath, Birmingham our second-largest city. A few months ago, he disappeared from his job as a general operative at Network Rail, New Street station, Birmingham. He had been working on an operations and maintenance crew. He adopted the name, Abdu al-Farouq, twelve months before he dropped out of circulation. The Abdu is short for Abdullah and Network Rail red-flagged the name change to police, who tipped us off. We have nothing to link him to militant Islamic circles.'

'Did he work on passenger trains?' someone asked.

'Not specifically. He was part of a line crew carrying out continual maintenance to keep the network running. Such work is carried out at night. If you can believe it, al-Farouq completed a media studies degree in college under the name Freddy Powell.'

They discussed his radicalization at a suburban mosque in Birmingham, a city where one in five of its 1.1 million population declared Islam as their religion. The majority were peaceful, law-abiding citizens but the elders in al-Farouq's local mosque realized too late they had erred in accepting vast overseas donations. The money came with a radical Imam. During side gatherings after main prayers, he had deluged younger members of the congregation with a hate-filled version of Islam.

Months after they expelled him, six families were struggling to make contact with sons or daughters that they believed were on gap-year travels. By the time the mosque leaders recognized their error of judgment, five young converts along with al-Farouq, were believed to have crossed from Turkey into Syria to fight with ISIS.

Krause resumed the video to a hushed room. Delegates listened as al-Farouq threatened that Europe's transport infrastructure would soon be a shambles. First a threat to destroy a city, Kate thought, now another to hit continental transport networks. She listened, without intervening, as discussion swung back and forth between the heads of national security services trying to pin down a target.

By the meeting's conclusion, all that was agreed was that intelligence would be funneled to a European Task Force in Berlin. If an active terrorist cell was identified, individual countries would be tasked with eliminating the threat. When Krause ended the meeting, everyone filed out for a pre-arranged meal.

'Want to skip this?' Chapman whispered to Kate.

'Gladly!'

'How about lunch at the TV Tower? I hear they've got an elevator that can whisk you to the top in less than a minute.'

The idea of eating in a restaurant 360 meters off the ground made her queasy. Some of the tables even revolved. For Kate that would be like a twist of the knife in an already torturous experience.

'Not for me I'm afraid.'

They settled on a restaurant near the train station that boasted a beer garden. Chapman ordered a stein of local brew to accompany his wiener schnitzel.

'I love to try what the locals eat when I travel,' he smiled.

'But wiener schnitzel's Austrian!'

'Are you Irish always this adventurous?' he laughed, pointing out Kate's Caesar's salad.

'I'm flying in a couple of hours. Wise to give the sauer-kraut a miss, don't you think.'

The beer garden at the rear was jammed so they dined on the terrace alongside a busy pedestrian street. Boats cruised by on the nearby river Spree. Kate looked around as she sipped her sparkling water; with so much going on, the sunny ambiance was lost on her.

'Ever had to deal with a personal threat?' she asked Chapman.

'Nothing I couldn't handle,' he replied, taking a pull from the stein. 'Is someone threatening you?'

'Last weekend my number two and I received warn-ings. Biblical quotations vowing revenge. We've no idea who's behind it.'

'It might be just a crank.'

'It doesn't feel that way. Two of us targeted and the culprit's proven he can get close.'

'Kate, *don't* leave it out there hanging. Go after it.'

'Where to begin is the question.'

When Chapman drained his beer and ordered a refill, Kate asked the waiter to arrange a taxi for the airport.

'Don't wait for someone else to figure it out,' he said. 'You gotta do it yourself.'

12

Back in Dublin, Kate spent the morning at her mother's bedside. There was little change. Margaret Bowen slept a lot and struggled to speak each time she tried. When she arrived, Norrie suggested her sister take a timeout from the hospital. Kate grabbed the opportunity to tune into an operation Digger was running at Manifold Avenue.

Fifteen minutes after leaving the hospital, she twisted in the back of Digger's control van and stretched to shake off weariness from a weekend she was unlikely to forget. Leaving stuffy conference rooms behind and getting back into the surveillance world where she worked best, re-energized her. They were parked streets back from Manifold Avenue and Digger was rotating vehicles to keep numbers 17A and 51 under constant observation. SIU had confirmed Fazli Sumbal as the resident at fifty-one. His visa status was under review. There was a suspicion that his marriage to a teenage Dublin girl had been one of convenience.

'Has J2 got any bright ideas on our attic device?' Digger asked.

'Shaw got back to Mac, alright.' Kate replied.

Colonel Shaw was the cold fish in charge of Army Intelligence. Kate tolerated rather than liked him. The last case they shared earned him a promotion; it only held bittersweet memories for her.

'His best guess is it might be some kind of repeater to boost a radio signal.'

'Nothing much to add then?'

'He's worried it might be an encrypted unit, you know like Tetra, impossible to intercept. He wants us to leave the final analysis for him. He proposes getting a team from the Army CIS Corps, backed up by Rangers, into 17A to remove the device for closer scrutiny.'

'Jesus! That would blow us out of the water,' Digger said.

'Oh, he has a plan! The Army would execute the job in civvies, he said—to assuage any anxieties of the local population. *Very* considerate.'

'Is that man on drugs?'

'The Communications and Information Systems Corps would make sense because these days Ordnance is part of that group.'

'But if they march into the house, we're done.'

'Look, for the moment Mac calmed him down and told Shaw we would keep the Army option in our back pocket.'

'Thank Christ! What a fuckin' drama queen.'

'The Army's got primacy with external threats. Grabbing this case would pull them into the limelight in the fight against ISIS.'

'You've got to buy us time,' Digger replied.

Before she could respond, the radio crackled and Kate adjusted her earpiece.

'A female just walked in the front gate of 17A Manifold Avenue,' Detective Joe Forde reported.

Forde continued his commentary as the woman opened the front door with a key and entered the house. The person of interest was approx. 60 years, short, rotund, gray curly hair cut tight, and a pasty complexion. She carried what looked like an empty blue kitbag with Dublin's three castle crest on either side

'Now Sumbal's on the move,' Forde added, moments later. 'Looks like he's heading for 17A.'

'I bet a pound to a penny they get stuck into each other,' Digger said.

'Standby all units,' Kate ordered. 'Sierra Bravo 5 get ready for a stroll-by. Stay with 'the granny' if she exits.'

To Kate's alarm, Sumbal used a key to try and enter 17A, but the door was deadlocked on the inside. This confirmed his connection to the house; he was likely part of a bigger picture. Detective Becky Kingston, the marathon runner SIU had attracted into surveillance work, ambled on the path near the house. Kate watched the live feed from the camera she carried concealed in her shoulder bag. Sumbal rang the bell and waited. The door cracked open, the security chain engaged, and the granny filling the space.

'Let me in,' Sumbal said, roughly.

Becky's camera caught snatches of the exchange.

'Look, Faz, I'm collectin' Jasmine's stuff, nothin' else,' the older woman said in an indignant Dublin accent. 'I'm not interested in talkin' to you.'

'I will call the police,' Sumbal challenged.

'Do what ya like,' came the reply. 'I'm doin' nothin' wrong, just gettin' her gear together.'

'You must allow me to supervise.'

'In your dreams, pal, now…'

When the door slammed in his face, Sumbal stood outside pondering his next move before eventually sloping back to number 51. Becky Kingston was ambling at a slowed-down pedestrian pace that she maintained until she rejoined Joe Forde, two streets away. A quarter of an hour later 'the granny' exited with a bulging kit bag on one shoulder. She locked up, posted the key through the letter-box, and walked out the front gate.

The return to fieldwork for Kate was brief but rewarding. Sumbal's link to 17A was definitive, plus another lead had been established to the ballsy granny and someone called Jasmine. Kate guessed the incident was likely linked to Sumbal's marriage that Sexton was chasing up with the immigration service. The crew reported 'the granny' was waiting at a bus stop for a city center connection.

'Drop me anywhere,' Kate asked Digger. 'I've got to check back at the hospital and pick up my car. Catch up back at base.'

'Sexton's taking over when we hit the city center. Jane wants me to pick up the kids from school.'

Jane was the farmer's daughter from a neighboring parish back home in Kerry that the fates conspired Digger would bump into on a Dublin street. While a rookie in the uniform branch, he recorded details of her bag snatch in his notebook. They had chatted non-stop in Irish and she gave him her Social Welfare office work number for contact. Digger made her promise that if he located her handbag, she would share her private number. It took him a week of shaking down the thieving fraternity but he achieved his goal. Everything in the bag was thoroughly wet or soiled and her cash was missing along with her bank cards. Even so, the blue-eyed blonde kept her promise and the rest was history.

Digger rarely deviated when hooked on a target. Kate figured whatever truce he had hammered out at home to keep working surveillance had come with compromises. As she exited the van, 'the granny' was confirmed on a number twenty-seven bus heading toward the city center. Detective Becky Kingston had also hopped on board and was sticking with her. Kate zipped her jacket and headed for Beaumont Hospital.

When she arrived in the ward she pushed through the curtain pulled around her mother's bed and hugged her.

'Mr. Hanrahan,' she acknowledged the white coat standing at the opposite side.

'Aidan, please.'

'Aidan wants to hold on to me for another week,' her mother said, slowly.

Kate looked in the consultant's direction.

'Your mum's doing well. We'll monitor her closely over the next few days and try some light physio. All going well, we will consider discharge in the next seven days.'

'That's great news. Thank you, Aidan.'

'I'll look back in on your mum later on this afternoon. I have to pick up my car from the garage.'

'Repairs?' Kate queried.

'Collecting my new Beamer 7-series. To celebrate the end of student debt.'

'Quite the celebration! It's a nice feeling all the same.'

'You studied?'

'Trinity.'

'Me too. I loved it there.'

'Kate left her Masters unfinished to join the Guards,' Margaret Bowen interrupted. 'Imagine?'

'Indeed!' the consultant laughed.

'*Mum*, for God's sake!'

'Your speech was remarkably clear there, Margaret,' Hanrahan joked. 'This is a passionate subject for you!'

Undeterred by Kate's glare she continued, 'they're too hard on her; they expect too much.'

Hanrahan glanced at his watch and said, 'I'd better run.'

'Is it far?' Kate asked.

'The BMW dealership down the road a mile or so.'

'I know the place. I get my modest 3-series serviced there. If you can find someone to drive you, you can take my car.'

'Pat the porter has been badgering me about seeing my new motor. Would it be okay if he drove?'

'So long as he gets it back in one piece.'

'Pat's a BMW nut. He'll be your friend for life,' Hanrahan accepted Kate's key.

He told her they shouldn't be more than an hour and took her parking ticket. As always, it had the aisle letter and parking bay number written on the reverse.

'Thank you for this,' he smiled, as he pushed out the ward door.

Lunch was served and Kate offered to help her mother. Reluctantly, Margaret conceded her daughter could cut the pieces of buttered toast on the plate of scrambled eggs. She insisted on making an effort to feed herself.

Using her left hand for leverage she positioned the fork into her clenched right. She pushed some scrambled egg onto it and commenced the slow trajectory toward her mouth. Unable to lean forward, her trembling arm sent the contents spilling onto the tray. She scooped it up and tried again. After a third unsuccessful attempt, she threw the fork back on the plate. The scrambled egg skidded and landed on the sheets.

'What's the use?' she cried, pushing the food trolley away.

Kate cleaned the mess and wheeled the trolley onto the corridor. She returned and hugged her mother.

'Be patient. Don't expect miracles,' she said, dabbing her mum's eyes.

'I don't want to be a burden on anyone.'

'Don't be silly. Do you want me to nip out and get you something you could hold with both hands, like a sandwich?'

Her mother nodded.

'Look on the bright side is what you always told me.'

'What bright side?'

'Your appetite's back,' Kate smiled.

The hospital was becoming eerily familiar and she found the front door without once glancing for direction signs. A typical Irish spring day, it offered sunshine and showers as she sought out a close-by delicatessen. Kate caught the sunshine part and savored the warmth on her face. She picked up a ham and cheese panini and headed back for the hospital campus.

The dull thud she heard as she approached the entrance did not strike her as anything out of the ordinary. There was a construction site to the rear and she figured most likely the sound had come from there. Then she saw black smoke pour from the front and sides of the underground car park and white-coated personnel race toward its entrance.

'What's up?' she asked the security man at reception.

'There's been an explosion.'

'Do you know what caused it?'

'Not yet.'

'Can I see it on the monitor?'

'Who are you?'

Kate displayed her Garda ID and told him she wanted to check on someone who might be in that area.

'I'm not supposed to give out information.'

'What floor was the explosion on?'

'Level minus 3. That's it. That's all I can tell you.'

Kate froze. That was where she parked her car.

'What aisle?'

'I've already told you too much.'

Kate was conscious she was in a public space. In the reception area, worried people were watching the encounter. She could go either of two ways; get in the security man's face and pull rank or cajole his cooperation.

'I am Detective Superintendent Bowen from Garda Headquarters. See, it says as much on my badge.'

The security man scrutinized the Garda ID a second time.

'If that explosion is anything other than a gas leak, likelihood is I will be investigating it,' she bluffed. 'All I need is basic information to make up my mind.'

'Watch it!' He pointed to a monitor located underneath his desk, away from public eyes.

Kate squeezed behind the counter and waited.

'Camera A3,' he said. 'This captures vehicles descending the ramp to that level.'

'Nothing.'

'B3, this one scans aisle K.'

'Just smoke.'

'C3 covers aisle L.'

Kate racked her memory.

'Smoke again.'

'C4 covers the up ramp toward the exit. Oh shit, that looks bad. I'll try to get a close-up.'

He swiveled on his chair to catch her reaction, but Kate had ducked back into the reception area and was racing toward her mother's ward. She met Norrie returning from a meal break and threw the cooling sandwich at her.

'Give that to mum, I have to go.'

'Kate, what's wrong? What was that noise? Kate...'

It was too late, she had reached the end of the corridor and pushed through the swinging doors, well out of earshot. Her mind ached with flashing images and possibilities; the quick action required, the people she needed to warn and…

'Slow down, slow down please,' a familiar voice said, as her arm was grabbed.

She stared at him, not noticing until the moment his strong arms kept her from toppling over that his eyes had an opal blue tint.

'You're okay!' Kate exclaimed, hugging him, briefly. 'Oh thank God!'

'Of course, I'm alright,' Aidan Hanrahan assured her. 'There was an explosion while I was waiting for Pat to fetch your car and meet him out front. I've been ordered to the ED; my new car will have to wait.'

'You don't know?'

'What?'

'It was *my* car exploded.'

'Oh, sweet Lord!'

His team gathered behind him. Two doctors accompanied by nurses pushed a convoy of loaded gray metal trolleys toward a staff elevator that would deliver them to the ED.

'Oh my God!' Aidan groaned. 'That means Pat is seriously injured.'

Kate stared at the floor.

'Looks that way.'

'Leave it to us,' Hanrahan's registrar urged him, shooing the medical team toward the elevator.

'No,' Hanrahan insisted. 'This is my doing, I'm coming.'

Kate watched them shuttle across the landing. As the lift doors came together Hanrahan stalled them.

'Are you alright?' he asked.

'I'm so sorry.' she replied.

The lift door closed. Kate glanced at the clock over the ward doors—2:55. Digger's school pick-up was… She couldn't be sure, was it 3:00, maybe 3:30. She called his number. It was engaged. Her radio handset was incinerated in the hospital's basement along with her car. Fear spiked. She fought it under control and called Angie.

'Where's Digger?' she shouted.

'Slow down. What's wrong?'

'Get him on the radio, now.'

'Boss, he's picking up his kids from school today. Didn't he tell you?'

'That's why I need to warn him not to use his car.'

'Oh! I spoke to him minutes ago and he was sitting outside the school waiting for them. He switches off the radio when he has them in the car.'

'Get to him and warn him; someone just blew my car up.'

13

With Dr. Hanrahan's team dispatched to the emergency department, the tiny landing at the staff end of the corridor was quiet. Kate paced, frenzied, her phone clutched tightly in her hand, unimaginable possibilities swirling in her mind. *It's not fair,'* she muttered, *'trouble always finds me.'*

Danger came with her chosen profession, she accepted as much but the thought of innocent children suffering was unbearable. A memory, long-repressed, dredged itself from the depths of her subconscious. *Why now?* she protested. She tried to suppress it, leaned both hands on molded plastic seating to steady herself. Each time the vivid memory awoke it ran its course like a movie reel. Events she witnessed in childhood that wrought havoc on the people closest to her and changed the course of her life. She slid onto the seat and buried her face in her hands.

'Why is Grandad sad?' seven-year-old Kate was asking her mother.

'Kate love, you've asked me that question every day for the past week and every day I tell you the same; he misses his friend, Albi. He was Grandad's best friend; now he's in Heaven and he misses him.'

Since she was four years old, Kate had spent weekends at her Grandad's farm helping him with chores. As she grew older and stronger, she helped chop the timber that kept their home cozy each winter.

'But Norrie said he was sad before Albi died because Albi wouldn't talk to him anymore. Why, Mum, why?'

Kate's mother was exasperated, lost for words. Her youngest daughter had been like this from the time she could talk. Questions, questions, always checking and re-checking, wanting to understand everything going on around her. Her daughters nattered incessantly and Margaret confided in her eldest, Nora, more than ever since her husband, Jamie Bowen was no longer around.

They were facing into their second precarious winter as a one-parent family. Margaret was preoccupied with stretching their meager resources to last until the end of each week. For the first few months, her missing spouse had wired small amounts from Wales to the local post office, but it soon dwindled to nothing. By the first missed month, Margaret had already moved on and established a daily routine for the girls. She took a job in a local cigarette factory, quality controlling cartons of smokes that rolled off of a production line. It paid enough to put food on the table and clothe the girls. Life became a blur of breakfast, work, home, dinner, homework, telly, sleep. Repeat.

The times they lived in were far from normal. The IRA's long war strategy was in full flow a few miles from where they lived. Attacks that IRA units mounted against police and British security forces in Northern Ireland levied a terrifying price on the lives of ordinary families like the Bowens.

Kate's childhood nightmare began with waking up to angry voices, an argument in the yard behind her grand-parent's house. Kate kneeling on her bed, shivering in the nighttime chill, listening keenly to the heated encounter. Men confronting Grandad in front of the timber shed beside the garage that housed his dark blue Ford Escort. Those men must have stolen in by the vegetable garden, Kate decided, crept through the orchard and Grandad heard the usual squeak when they opened the gate. She hoped they hadn't robbed the apples or pears, she knew would soon ripen. Her Gran rushed into her room and warned her that whatever happened, she was to remain indoors. Kate stayed at her window squinting into the adult world outside. She did not understand why the men surrounding Grandad had their faces covered with black masks.

Gran pushed into the circle and berated the tallest of the group. Kate screamed when the hooded man pulled a gun and put it to her Gran's head. Her scream changed the dynamic. Her Grandad glanced back in the direction of the house. Kate cried as she watched her Gran push the weapon away and shuffle back indoors. Grandad handed over keys from his pocket.

'Why was that man being nasty to you,' Kate sobbed, her pajamas wet.

'Calm yourself, child,' Gran comforted. 'He's just an aul eejit with a bad temper. He lost the run of himself.'

'Where's Grandad gone?'

'He'll be back in a minute. Don't worry now, girleen.'

'But that man had a gun, he was going to hurt you.'

'Stop your crying now. Let's change your pajamas; your Grandad will be back in a minute. Wait and see, everything will be alright.'

But nothing was right after that night. It took ages for her Grandad to return and when he did, an ugly gash on his forehead oozed blood. Kate rushed to him and hugged him tightly. In her best, big girl's voice, she assured him she was going to phone Mum and get her to call the Guards at Dundalk police station to come help them. For a long time afterward, she did not understand why he told her to leave it until morning.

All through the next day Kate had watched Garda cars drive up and down the laneway beside the farm that straddled the border. She learned that Susanna Patterson, a neighbor's daughter, whom she'd only met once, was missing. The six o'clock news reported that a police constable had been found murdered in Northern Ireland. Kate did not understand how her grandfather's burnt-out Ford Escort could be linked to Susanna's terrible killing but it was, and she overheard his inconsolable anguish from her bedroom that night as her Gran tried to comfort him.

In the weeks that followed she struggled to understand what was going on around her. Grandad lost interest in doing all the things he and Kate loved. There were no more early morning walks through dewy fields to pick wild mushrooms. Even though winter was coming, he allowed his pristine outhouses to descend into chaos. He remained indoors more and more. When his neighbor, Albert Patterson, died he was bereft. Six months after an IRA gang kidnapped and murdered his daughter, Mr. Patterson followed her to the grave. A year on, Kate's Grandad joined them.

As years passed Kate grew to understand what had occurred, a daughter taken and murdered, a neighbor who could not forgive a lifelong friend for something he was forced to do. It lit a fire inside Kate for justice; to take on anyone who would destroy the lives of ordinary people. She would go through hell to fight their cause and mete out retribution.

Digger collected his children in Ron Sexton's job car. He was now running the operation on 'the granny' from 17A Manifold Avenue. When the school traffic warden guided them across the road the excited pair raced to their father's car when he tooted its horn. Digger put a call through to Jane so they could tell her about their school day. He drove back toward his house with his work radio turned off and missed the warnings continually flashed over it. The end of his road was blocked by a uniform squad car.

'What's going on?' he shouted. 'That's my road.'

'A temporary diversion, sir,' the squad driver replied.

His observer was busy diverting traffic. Digger spotted a second car at the top of the road doing a similar job. He stepped out of his car, warned the children to stay put, approached the squad driver, and flashed his Garda ID.

'What's happening?'

'We're waiting on an Army EOD team.'

'Where's the bomb?'

'Not located yet. There's a big panic about a car. Rumor is we're going to have to evacuate the road. What number is your house? '

'Fourteen, the one with the blue car parked in the drive. A mechanic is comin' to collect it in a while and take it away for repair. Who reported a suspect device?'

'Another Guard's car exploded at Beaumont Hospital in the last quarter of an hour...'

'Jesus Christ!'

He ran back to his borrowed work car and told the children to say goodbye to their mum, he needed his mobile phone. It exploded into life before he could punch in Kate's number.

'*Don't touch your car*,' Angie screamed.

'Understood, understood. I'm using Sextons. Is Kate safe?'

'Her car blew up. A hospital porter was driving, long story. She's very shaken up.'

'Get to her. Uniforms have my road sealed off. I'll point out my car and get the kids away from here. Call you in ten.'

Norrie searched for Kate at Beaumont Hospital. She found her sobbing on the landing with her head in hands and recognized her distress. As Kate clutched her mobile phone, vicelike, in her right hand, Norrie grasped the other and pulled her upright.

'Come on little sis.'

At the women's toilets, she held Kate, as she had years earlier when the nightmares came and their mother was too tired to overhear her sobbing. She rubbed her back and repeated the same soothing words—'It's okay, you're safe.' When she released their embrace, Kate splashed cold water on her face and grabbed a paper towel to pat her skin dry.

'That hasn't happened in a while,' she sighed, leaning on the wash hand basin staring at her weary reflection.

Her sister brushed aside wisps of Kate's brunette hair.

'Let's get you cleaned up, otherwise Mum will ask questions.'

Kate told Norrie about her car, the doctor's near-miss, and how fears for Digger and his children had pushed her over the edge.

'Why *do* this?'

'Someone has to!'

'Kate against the world! What about you? Who looks out for you?'

A call from Angie interrupted them. She was five

minutes out from the hospital and Kate agreed to meet her at the entrance.

'Look at yourself, diving headlong in again, not knowing what's around the corner,' Norrie scolded. 'You need to rest,'

'I've got to get back out there. Whoever did this won't stop, I've got to get them first.'

'My sister, the superhero! At least say goodbye to Mum!'

14

Kate blue-lighted it to the end of Digger's road and rendezvoused with an Army EOD officer. He removed the hood from his bomb suit and cradled it under his arm. The harsh conditions of his profession showed on his sweat-peppered face.

'Seventy-five pounds of bomb suit will get you this,' he grinned as he wiped his brow.

'Rather you than me,' Kate replied.

'He's located a device under the driver's side of my car,' Digger said.

'Any ideas?' Kate queried the EOD man.

'Looks like a classic under-car booby trap device. Most likely operating on a mercury tilt switch. I won't know what the explosive component is until I've disarmed it.'

'My car exploded at Beaumont when it drove up a ramp.'

'Do you think both devices are from the same source?'

'Highly likely. Can you defuse it?'

'If it behaves like those in the past, no problem. Recent ones have been shoddy. We'll soon find out.'

Later that evening Kate ordered every SIU detective to

heighten their vigilance. By the time the team assembled for a debrief, they knew Semtex had been used. Four ounces were recovered from underneath Digger's car, twice the required amount for a fatal attack. When the team debrief concluded, she headed to Mac's office with Digger and Sexton.

'Can we connect any of this to what's happening around the continent,' he opened.

'Not so far. Right now, we're stumped.'

'What about recent targets? Is this a gang seeking revenge?'

'Unlikely,' Sexton cut in. 'Bailey's driver, Gerry Buck, for example, he was trying to pull some of his old mob together but got taken out by the opposition three months ago.'

'So who wants revenge against SIU?'

'Lately, we've been doin' routine jobs,' Digger said. 'Nothin' that stretched us.'

'What the hell have we got here?' Mac asked.

'Someone trying to impress his peers, show he's the big dog,' Sexton suggested.

Kate replied. 'The use of Semtex points in one direction only—terrorists.'

'Then don't rule ISIS out,' Mac said. 'They've got tons of the stuff.'

'If ISIS wanted to make a spectacular statement, would they not go after a figurehead like yourself?' Kate asked. 'Your name is out there.'

Digger cocked his head.

'What about you?'

'What do you mean?'

'The Sunday Chronicle printed your name and a photo of you in a UN uniform a few months back.'

'ISIS misses very little when it comes to media,' Mac affirmed. 'Don't rule them out.'

'Could closer to home,' Sexton suggested. 'We know the IRA held back some Semtex from decommissioning after the peace deal.'

'With advance biblical warnings?' Mac replied. 'I don't think so. Anything on the CCTV?

'Both bikes had false plates. The one that put the pamphlet on Kate's car at the airport headed north,' Digger confirmed.

'The car from the Ben Gordon murder was found burnt out outside Dundalk, right on the border,' Sexton chipped in.

'It's a tenuous link,' Kate said. 'We've no idea who ticketed our cars.'

'Why didn't you tell me about them?' Mac asked.

'It was early days. Angie was reviewing the CCTV footage and we wanted to have something to show before we brought you into the loop.'

'Draw up a list of suspects,' he ordered, 'we'll review it tomorrow.'

Kate detailed the security arrangements she had implemented. Everyone checking underneath cars before driving; everyone armed at all times until the threat was extinguished. She and Digger would have armed protection at their homes. At eight o'clock she told Mac she needed to get to the hospital before visiting ended.

'You should rest,' he urged.

When Kate returned to her mother's bedside at Beaumont, she was sleeping. Norrie had returned home and Doc D'Arcy was sitting beside the bed. She signaled Kate to move outside and closed the door quietly. They moved away from the ward entrance and Kate leaned against the wall. The psychologist squared off against the stubborn girl she had known since childhood.

'How are you doing?'

'Norrie's blabbed, hasn't she?'

'She's worried, Kate.'

'I'm fine. Well as fine as anyone can be who's just had their car blown up. Don't worry Doc, I've tons of backup.'

'I don't doubt it. That's *not* what I mean and you know it.'

'I'll be alright. Did you hear how the porter is doing?'

'Kate, the poor man died an hour ago. Dr. Hanrahan asked me to tell you before it got to the media.'

'Oh no!' she leaned her head against the wall and slid onto a plastic seat.

She closed her eyes as the news hit her like a punch in the gut. It should have been her. A twist of fate and she lived; an innocent died.

'Oh, God!'

Doc D'Arcy rubbed her shoulder reassuringly.

'Kate, none of this is your fault, you couldn't have seen it coming. There's nothing you could have done.'

'How is Aidan?'

'His registrar was with him. To be frank, he didn't look good.'

'I should call him.'

'Hold your fire, Kate, give him time.'

They returned to the ward and her mother slept through the next hour. Doc D'Arcy nagged Kate about getting the rest she needed and reluctantly, she trudged to the front of the hospital where Angie collected her and dropped her home. At the apartment block lobby, a protection detective unlocked the entrance door. He rode the elevator with her and checked her apartment was clear before she entered. He took up a post on the landing as she locked her door.

She showered and changed for bed. Disregarding the Doc's advice, she messaged Aidan Hanrahan and was surprised when he called back instantly.

'Pat's death is beating me up,' he said.

'Losing a colleague like that is never easy.'

'We worked on him for two hours straight, but his injuries were catastrophic.'

'I'm so sorry, I don't know what to say.'

Aidan told her he would be back on duty at Beaumont Hospital the next day and they could talk face to face. As Kate hung up she knew he lived alone, and a guilty part of her sensed he wanted to get to know her better.

15

She awoke to a muffled conversation from the landing among her protection detail during the first shift change of the day. She mulled over the events of the previous five days. She had been shot at, almost blown up, *twice,* and had been tasked with uncovering any Irish link to a terrorist plot with the potential to destabilize Europe. More importantly, she had saved her mother from an untimely death. By any stretch, a bad week, and it wasn't over.

The Paris ambush was part of a bigger picture, she didn't dwell on it. Chapman's insistence she don a flak jacket and helmet for the airport run, together with a dollop of good luck, had seen her come out of it unscathed. She thanked her lucky stars. The Ben Gordon murder investigation was still at an early stage with no breakthrough on the horizon. Cody O'Neill had sent an email the previous morning suggesting he make an immediate trip to Dublin to sit in on a case conference. The FBI played its cards close to its chest with intelligence sharing on Rafiq Khouri, a potential suspect in the case so Kate put him off to a later date.

She showered, dressed, and invited Ken James, her

protection detail, to join her for breakfast. He accepted a mug of coffee instead and stayed on post. Angie rang to warn that traffic was choked at the East Link Bridge, so she was running late. Kate relaxed at her breakfast counter taking in the overcast vista of Dublin Bay. A gray mist that matched her mood billowed like a dirty lace curtain across the bay. She was in the dark on who singled out Digger and herself as targets for revenge. Her new phone's shrill ringtone shattered her meditation. *That's got to change*, she thought.

'Hey there!' the friendly voice greeted her.

'Zach, what are you up to?'

'Right now, I'm in the Secret Service office in Paris reading the wires about an explosion in Dublin. Should I be worried?'

'Can you *believe* it, *twice* in a week? An under-car booby-trap device.'

'Jeez Kate, what the hell? Is there anything I can do?'

'We're working every angle to find out where it came from. We still haven't figured out what's going on.'

A knock on Kate's door distracted her. She continued talking as she answered it. Before Angie could step into the apartment, Ken James wagged a finger at her.

'Don't take risks, Super. Always check before opening.'

Kate gave him a wry thumbs-up. 'Get the security peephole changed for a camera, will you?'

Angie stepped inside and closed the door.

'Zach, thanks for the offer. You know I'll ask if there's anything you can assist with.'

'I can tell you're busy. Let me sniff around and get back in touch if I turn up anything useful.'

'Thank you.'

'We better get going,' Angie said.

Kate killed the call, grabbed a kit bag she kept

prepared for last-minute deployments, and headed for the door.

'Why the bag?' Angie asked as they descended the stairs.

'Old habits. Never leave home without it!'

Before her briefing with Mac, she spent an hour at Beaumont Hospital. She insisted her mother not be informed that the explosion the previous day had been an attempt on her daughter's life. She busied herself brushing her mum's hair and helped her apply some perfume. Margaret was smiling and looking cheerier when Aidan Hanrahan arrived wearing his most professional smile.

Kate moved off the bed and drifted outside the curtain Hanrahan had pulled for his team's consultation.

'How is our most popular patient?'

She listened as he tossed question after question, now knowing each one was posed to elicit a long enough response to allow him to assess her mother's speech.

'Are you going to liberate me from here soon?' Kate overheard.

'You're doing well, Margaret,' Hanrahan said. 'When you're ready, we won't detain you a minute longer than we have to.'

Kate smiled at the consultant's skillful reassurances. When Hanrahan emerged, he signaled her toward the corridor and spoke about the kind of home care services that would need to be put in place. He advised that she and her sister begin the process of securing them from the Health Service Executive.

'What time do you finish tonight?' he asked, out of the blue.

'Excuse me?'

'Could we grab a cup of coffee, or a drink if you like?'

'I'm not sure what time I'll be done—it's that kind of job.'

'Okay.'

'No, I'd like to talk. How about I call you later?'

Kate returned to her mother and chatted about overnight hospital routines and her visitors. They were either former clients or volunteers from the local Rape Crisis clinic her mother had managed in Dundalk for years. For Kate, the inane conversation was a relief. She was happy to hear her mother putting an intelligible string of words together. As they chatted, a thought nagged her. How had the bombers known where she would be when they planted their device? Was she tailed? Possible but unlikely. From her earliest days in SIU, Kate developed an acute security awareness and practiced the countermeasures she preached to her rookie detectives. It was more likely they were already in the car park, waiting for her car to arrive.

Her mother asked for a coffee and as Kate walked along the corridor toward the vending machine she diverted to the reception. She recognized the security man as the one who had shown her CCTV footage of her wrecked car the previous day.

'Can I ask another favor?' she inquired.

'You again!'

'Sorry, I took off in such a hurry yesterday.' She leaned closer to the skeptical guard. 'It was my car that exploded.'

'Come back to the office and tell me what you want.'

Kate pushed around the counter and followed the guard to a tiny office at the end of the corridor. He dispatched a replacement to reception and closed the door as Kate pulled up a chair.

'Denis Murphy,' he extended a hand across the desk.

'We got off on the wrong foot yesterday. What can I do for you?'

Kate eventually left his office with days of CCTV footage from the hospital front entrance stored on a USB. She had given Murphy details that Norrie verified concerning their mother's visitors and he matched in the dates and times.

Later as she drove toward Mac's office with a protection car stuck on her tail she rang Detective Jack Quinlan. If anyone could pick out the Dundalk groups from the crowded footage, he was her best chance.

Digger took the early morning hours off work to acclimatize his family to their new situation. Jane was badly shaken by the near-miss. She put on a show for the children, fussed over them ensuring they had all the things they needed for their school day before driving them there. The kids were delighted to be escorted to its front door by two burly ERU detectives.

To preserve her sanity, Jane had joined a local Zumba class weeks earlier. After sessions spent with long blonde hair whipping across her face almost taking an eye out, she decided it had to change and now sported short spiky layers, a dramatic transformation. She finger-combed it into place as she prepared for work at a local café.

'I'll collect the kids this afternoon,' she shouted.

'Okay,' Digger replied, as he launched into their bedroom and picked up his shoulder bag.

'Jesus, don't do that,' Jane startled. 'I thought you were downstairs.'

'Angie's waiting outside to pick me up. I better run.'

'Dan Rooney, if you leave without kissing me goodbye, I swear…'

'*Slán go fóill*[1],' Digger grinned and kissed his wife a passionate farewell.

As the front door banged, Jane worried the life they had built as a family was going up in smoke. Would Sean and Maggie have to move school? What about the house and neighbors—were they safe? One question after another.

When he got to work, Digger checked in with the teams watching Sumbal and 17A Manifold Avenue. He noted that Sumbal had walked the dog twice during the morning and all was quiet at number 51. He told Pete McNally to leave him undisturbed and took a coffee with him as he retreated to the Cave.

An engine warning light on his car had saved him. It triggered on his drive home, the evening before the car was booby-trapped. He had told Jane not to use the car until he got the fault checked out. She had arranged for a neighbor to bring the kids to school and had pushed past the car to cycle to work.

He wiped his whiteboard clean and began making a list of suspects they had worked on in the previous two years. By the time his coffee mug was empty, the board full. Nothing sprang out at him from the list. There had been operations against a militant Republican group that successfully prevented armed robberies. Those groups might have access to Semtex but he reckoned it unlikely given their general ineptitude. The assassination attempts on himself and Kate had been well planned and executed.

SIU would nail the perpetrators, he assured Jane the previous evening. In reality, he knew it was a lottery. He had no idea who had tried to kill him and was scratching his head for a motive. One person was dead. He and Kate had been reprieved through good fortune and little else. It was a situation that could not endure.

16

Late afternoon on the day Kate's car exploded, Junior veered off a two-lane highway when he read a sign indicating a truck stop ahead. It was his first time using the Black Sea route and he didn't like it. Bulgarian roads were poorly maintained and satellite coverage dropped in and out making navigation problematic. Today was the big one. The day when a plan he had taken months to put together would finally bear fruit. He meticulously planned to be nowhere near the scene of the crime.

His final stop before crossing the Romanian border was a lakeside café near the city of Burgas. A wave of humidity greeted him when he pulled open the fly screen and pushed through its faded red door. The spices and unfamiliar odors took him by surprise. He glanced at the menu but got nowhere. It was only offered in the local lingo. As the line at the counter shuffled forward, he glanced at what other diners were eating and listened to their orders. Most shouted the same thing.

'Bouh-tich-kee, coffee.'

Donuts with coffee. That would do, everything else, particularly the plates of foul-smelling tripe looked repulsive and made him want to retch. Phone in hand, he waited in line at the counter scanning news sites hoping one would connect. He repeated the overheard order when he came face to face with the middle-aged woman behind the counter.

'Sure, only the best for our English friends,' came the heavily-accented reply.

'Irish actually,' Junior corrected her. His attention diverted as his phone screen lit up when the local signal connected at last, 'For fuck sake!' he exclaimed.

The server scowled at her rude customer.

'Apologies, I …' he pointed to his phone.

It took him a second to realize that explaining his apology was wasted. The server's vocabulary was limited and she had already lost interest. She brewed his coffee and grabbed three brown buns from the warming cabinet. She placed them on a chipped plate, showered them with icing sugar, and returned to the counter with a practiced pirouette.

'Very good Buhtichki, you will like. Fifteen Lev,' she said, sliding the order.

Junior pulled two tens from his wallet and told her to keep the change. He found a seat by the window offering the best chance of holding a signal with news that shocked him.

'A fucking porter…' he muttered, as he scrolled through the report.

He wolfed down the snack as he checked other sites for mention of the hospital explosion. It was obvious reporters were aware of the identity of the intended victim but were respecting an embargo not to link Kate's name with the attempted assassination. Before leaving the café, he went to the men's room and splashed ice cold water on his face. He twisted the spluttering tap killing the flow of brackish water and stared at his reflection as he dragged wet fingers through his jet-black hair. Before his precious WiFi signal dropped, he scanned airlines serving the nearest airport and made a booking.

Outside, he picked his way across the pot-holed car park until he reached his truck. He swore at the easterly wind that whipped ripples across the nearby lake and chilled him to the bone. Snow was coming. He slammed the door and started the truck's heater.

Engine-warmed air blasted his face as he searched the cab, tossing papers and a jacket onto the floor. He located the unused phone under the front seat. Junior clicked it into life and stared out across the lake. His temper flared and he punched the steering wheel repeatedly as he listened to the clicks and burrs of his phone seeking to connect. His right hand throbbed as he finally got through.

'What the fuck, Frank? You promised we were solid on this.'

'Aye, well the targets were right, sure enough, but here we'll not talk about it like this,' Reilly warned. 'Your blood's up; so wait 'til you're home to talk business.'

'Get another driver out to Varna airport with keys to take over this yoke,' Junior snapped. 'I'm catching a flight to Manchester tonight. I'll be in Dublin in the morning and I'll see you in the usual spot at dinnertime.'

By noon the next day, Junior was sullen and hungry. The re-heated pork pie the owner of the Dew Drop Inn in Dundalk offered as a snack did not improve his mood.

'What the fuck, Frank? Solid, you said, One hundred percent wasn't it.'

'We targeted the right people. It didn't work out. We'd no way of knowing a fuckin' hospital porter would end up driving her car, did we?'

They settled into a discussion on the failed operation. Reilly's grasp of detail was the reason Junior entrusted him with the gang's innermost secrets.

'We worked a long time to identify her, you know that,' Reilly explained.

The gang had quickly tagged the sister, Nora, as married to an Army officer, stationed at Aiken Barracks in Dundalk. They confirmed Kate's home place was still the two-up, two-down red brick house in the center of town. Tailing either Nora or her husband got them nowhere. Kate was seldom seen around the town anymore. Their breakthrough came from Gary McEvoy, a local drug dealer, in the border town. He had known her as a teenager; they had knocked around in the same group. He told Reilly, Kate Bowen had been a fearless kid, up for anything.

McEvoy knew the mother lived alone and was well-liked in the area. When word got out she had been taken ill, his partner traveled with several local women to visit. When his partner confirmed Margaret Bowen's two girls were with her in the Dublin hospital, McEvoy tipped off the gang.

'In any case, we didn't want to do anything in the locality that might hurt the mother,' Reilly explained. 'She's popular, like.'

'Fair enough,' Junior replied.

'Let this go. You've got a good thing going here. Don't rock the boat.'

'You're fucking having me on! I doubt that bitch will lie down. It's either her or me now and I'll not repeat my old man's mistakes.'

17

As all hell broke loose in the wake of the explosion, the surveillance operation Kate had briefly overseen at Manifold Avenue continued unabated. An SIU crew followed 'the granny' to a Dublin inner-city flat complex and spent the night rotating vehicles and ground personnel while they watched it. By shift's end, they had identified her as Greta Connolly.

Kate read the night shift sergeant's report when she returned from the hospital the next day. Enough watching and waiting, she decided and pulled her crews from the location. She gave Sexton and Angie the go-ahead to interview the older woman.

The complex housed long-term tenants and Sexton was the perfect fit to make the approach. He grew up in a similar block on the other side of the river Liffey. Greta Connolly warily opened her front door and invited them in when Angie flashed her Garda ID. She introduced herself as a detective with an immigration query.

Greta Connolly's family had been street traders for over seventy years. Each generation overcame different challenges at their fruit and vegetable stall. They were cagey with cops. Greta didn't mind the local ones who cleared illegal traders off the streets. A visit from detectives, on the other hand, spelled trouble.

When Ron Sexton quizzed her on her daughter's marriage a year previous, Greta feigned shock. She told him that her daughter, Jasmine had left the family home months earlier and gone to England.

'Mrs. Connolly, you're not seriously trying to tell me you didn't know Jasmine was married,' Sexton said.

From the corner of his eye, he caught Angie steering the younger sister, Chantal, toward the kitchen.

'You can call me Greta. What'll I call you?'

'Detective Inspector Sexton: Answer my question; you knew your daughter had married Fazli Sumbal, didn't you?'

'Jesus Mary and Joseph, you've done your homework!'

'You've met Sumbal, I presume?'

'When Jaz brought him home, I asked her was there no Dublin lad she could have picked.'

'What sort was he?'

'To be honest, a proper little bollix. Jaz was keen on him but I never liked him. He'd say feck all when he was around the place. And when he did, it was slaggin' off the way we live in Dublin. I told him to go back to where he came from if he hated it so much.'

'Where's Jasmine now?'

'I told you Jaz is in England, Birmingham.'

'Is she separated from your man?'

'Faz she used to call him. Jaz and Faz, we teased her that the combination would get them on the stage,' she laughed.

Greta was clever, using distraction to avoid the main issue. Maybe her daughter was in trouble for aiding Sumbal to get residence in Ireland. Sexton didn't take the bait.

'Did she go to Birmingham to get away from him?' he asked.

'D'ya know what I'm not sure. She told me she wanted a fresh start but I'd swear they're still in contact.'

While Sexton grilled Greta, Angie sat in the kitchen and chatted with Chantal.

'Do you miss Jasmine?'

'Suppose so.'

'How many brothers and sisters do you have?'

'Three brothers, Jasmine's me only sister.'

'So, you've got a room all to yourself now?'

'Yeah, Jasmine took down her posters and all. Said she was done with that.'

'What was her best poster?'

'One Direction,' Chantal said. 'Niall was her favorite. He's Irish, isn't he?'

'Yeah. He's gorgeous!'

'D'ya want to see my room?'

'I'd love to.'

Chantal had re-postered the walls with Justin Bieber images and Angie admired each one. She sat on the bed and chatted with the young girl who seemed delighted to have anyone engage with her world.

'Jasmine even left me her jewelry,' she explained.

'Give us a look.'

Chantal went to a rickety brown wardrobe and opened the door, but slammed it shut immediately. Not before Angie saw it was stuffed top to bottom with cartons of cigarettes. The place did not smell of smoke and Angie concluded that Mrs. Connolly sold more than fruit and vegetables from her Moore Street stall. Chantal switched to a chest of drawers and pulled out a tangle of cheap accessories. There were bangles, bracelets, and necklaces. She slipped a gaudy sample on Angie, who cat-walked across the floor, before returning it around the child's neck.

'Chantal, get the door will ya?' her mother shouted when the doorbell rang.

'Did Faz have any mates?' Sexton asked.

'There were two brown lads he knocked around with; before you ask, I don't know their names.'

'Do you have any pictures?'

'Ma, it's the milkman looking for his money.'

'Tell him to come back next week. And bring me the little red photo album from my room.'

The chubby pre-teen dropped the album to her mother and hurried back to Angie.

'There he is, that's Faz and his pals. Jaz is in the middle.'

'Good looking girl,' Sexton observed. 'Like her Mammy!'

'Go away, ya chancer!'

'Has she been in touch since she went to Birmingham?'

They had spoken a few times but Jasmine did not have a regular contact number. As far as her mother was aware, she still worked as a shop assistant at Birmingham's New Street train station. It was a newsagent that sold coffee and snacks to commuters. Greta claimed she had no address for her daughter.

'Jaz moves around a bit, sleeps on pals' couches.'

While Chantal was busy with the doorbell, Angie had used her time alone to rummage through the chest of drawers. She hit pay dirt as she delicately opened the envelope of what appeared to be a bank statement. Jasmine's account deposits had spiked in recent months from low hundreds to thousands. She used her phone to snap rapid photos of the statement and Jasmine's passport. By the time the excited child returned, she had everything back in place.

Sexton wrapped up his interview by re-checking notes and taking a copy of the photograph of Sumbal with

125

Jasmine and his mates. He thanked Greta Connolly for her cooperation.

'That fecker still lives on Manifold Avenue but I wouldn't be one bit sorry if the Guards sent him packin',' Greta told them as they left.

'Get anything?' Angie asked as the pair descended the concrete stairs.

'Bits and pieces,' Sexton replied.

'I hit the jackpot.'

'How are Jane and the kids?' Kate asked Digger.

'She's on edge and they're delighted with the attention they got leaving for school this morning,' he replied. 'We've just told them the lads will be around for a little bit. They don't need to know the gory details.'

'Good idea. Where are you at the moment?'

'In the Cave, why?'

'Quick question. Did you double-check everything on the search of 17A?'

'Of course! Why ask?'

'What about the Timmons and Thompson search?'

'I read their report.'

'Double-check it, will you?'

'Why?'

'Sexton interviewed Greta Connolly this morning. She told him that she called to 17A because one of her friends who lives on the road told her that there was activity at the house recently. Mrs. Connolly believed the house was being re-let and went to collect Jasmine's belongings.'

'Maybe she saw Joe Forde in the front garden and figured him for an estate agent as I intended.'

'No. Sexton checked the dates. She noticed two men in

overalls at the house days before you and Angie searched it. Said they looked like tradesmen.'

'Maybe they were. I'll check with the estate agent.'

'Do that anyway but talk to Timmons and Thompson about the search. If the attic was checked and found empty, it means the electronics may have been recently installed and might be linked to the Ben Gordon murder.'

'Or maybe it was in the attic all along and *they* missed it.'

Reluctantly, Digger did as ordered. He had neither the time nor stomach for a face-to-face meeting with the pair. Andrew Timmons called back an hour later and gruffly demanded what he wanted. They discussed the 17A search, going through each room and checking what Timmons said against the report. The defensive detective repeated that he had nothing to add to what was already in the report.

'So you checked downstairs, while Thompson dealt with the prisoners?'

'No, I checked downstairs after the prisoners were secured. We dumped them on the kitchen floor and kept them there until we gave the place a good going over.'

'Thompson did upstairs?'

'Him and two of our crew.'

As with downstairs, Digger took him through each room.

'Thompson told me they had to rummage into the back of a wardrobe to find the opening rod for the attic door.'

'You don't mention that in the report.'

'A minor fucking detail.'

'No, numbnuts! You didn't mention you searched the attic.'

'I didn't, Thompson did it.'

'Jesus Christ! You wrote the bloody report and didn't mention it.'

'Anyway, why are you worried about it now?'

'None of your business! Get in touch with Thompson and ask what was in the attic when he searched it. Ring me back, pronto.'

His wife and family had almost been wiped out and he had no idea who was behind it. Digger hurled his coffee mug at the wall in frustration. He kicked the pieces out his way and walked dejectedly to the squad room. 'Fuck it,' he muttered, 'now I need a new mug.'

18

Jack Quinlan arrived unannounced at SIU in the afternoon. On his way, he had called in to see Margaret Bowen at the hospital and was dismayed to see her in a dependent state. Kate assured him that her mother was making progress and things were looking up.

'Down to business,' Quinlan said, 'that CCTV you sent me this morning…'

'I know, it'll take a while to review,' Kate replied, 'it always does.'

'I viewed some of it before coming down. I've picked out some of the Dundalk women from the bits I've watched, and the lads are checking the rest.'

'Anything I should worry about?'

'Maybe.'

'Spit it out.'

'Remember Gary McEvoy?'

Kate nodded nervously.

'Well, it was his latest squeeze who gave three of the women a lift. She stayed in the hospital reception area while they called to see your mother.'

Kate looked away from Quinlan toward the trees,

greening up with spring growth outside her window. Her past just sucker-punched her and she needed time. Her mother's daily advice to the teenage sisters came flooding back. Every morning as she got them ready for school, she had counseled her daughters to look out for each other until she got home at six-fifteen. Every day of Kate's early teenage years was a trial of one confrontation after another with her mother. Everything, from the length of her school uniform skirt to the food in her lunch box, was fodder for argument.

When the sisters got in from school each day, they scoffed the prepared snacks their mother had left in the fridge. Being the eldest, Norrie, in theory, saw her role as taking care of her younger sibling during the two after-noon hours they had to themselves. In practice, she rolled over each day when Kate shouted she was going out and returned to devouring her latest Judy Blume library book.

While Norrie juggled leisurely reading with swotting for her Junior Certificate, Kate's independent streak warped into rebellion. Always attracted to the rough and tumble, a nearby derelict factory had proven a magnet too strong to resist. Kate spent most afternoons there, hanging with boys from the school opposite hers. They swung from old pipes, broke windows, and kicked dirt or threw crap at each other. Kate who loved the rowdiness; was as strong as any and could run faster than most.

When her group switched their attention to the local shopping center the fun changed. They hung around mostly, trying to avoid the elderly security man who regu-larly herded them from the mall. On sunny days they retreated to nearby fields and it was there Kate first heard of Scooby snacks. The bright-colored pills looked like sweets to her. Gary, the oldest boy in the group said he could get £5 a pop for them at the Friday night disco. He told their gang they could all make easy money if they did some runs for him.

Kate was nabbed en route to her first drop.

Two cops from the local Garda station, one in plain clothes, arrived at the Bowen household with Kate in tow as her mother got in from work. Margaret Bowen's back ached from leaning over a cigarette factory conveyor belt all day. She was shocked to hear of her young daughter's descent into delinquent behavior. She knew she hung out with boys rather than girls and figured it was a teenage phase she would grow out of in time. As she sat at her kitchen table, fighting back tears she listened to the young detective talk about the wild behavior this type of drug was generating around town. Kate had been banished to her room to await her punishment. Upstairs, she had listened intently, her ear pressed to the floor.

'Search Kate's room,' the young detective advised. 'Do it on your lunch break while she's at school.'

'Oh, I couldn't do that. We trust each other. I mean I respect the girls' privacy.'

'Would you prefer we arrive with a warrant and do it,' Detective Jack Quinlan came back. 'Because that's where this young lady is headed.'

Margaret Bowen was silent as she processed the advice.

'Leave it with me,' she finally said.

'If you find anything suspicious, at all,' he advised, 'call me and I'll investigate it myself.'

'Will you charge her over the pills she had this time?'

'I have to wait and see what they turn out to be; most likely ecstasy, or MDMA.'

'What's that?'

'The kids call ecstasy everything under the sun, E, Scooby snacks, Shamrocks, the list goes on.'

Upstairs Kate had almost sniggered. When Gary was around it was all they talked about.

131

'The stuff dealers sell on the street these days contains anything from LSD, cocaine, heroin, amphetamine, and methamphetamine. Rat poison and dog de-wormer are some of the mixing agents they cut it with. That's what we're dealing with.'

'Oh my God, is Kate using?' Margaret Bowen had asked.

Kate remembered recoiling at the thought.

'Not today anyway,' Quinlan replied. 'But it's best to be diligent and get her on the right path.'

In the weeks that followed Kate's life changed dramatically. Margaret Bowen followed Quinlan's advice and tossed over Kate's room a couple of times a week. The young detective told her tests on the pills came back as prescription paracetamol with a color coating. Kate was grounded for a month which drove everyone crazy. Weeks on from her brush with the law, Quinlan called again. He informed Margaret that a Ju-Jitsu club had started in the town and suggested it might be a way of channeling Kate's energy. Six months later, Margaret Bowen was tired of searching her daughter's room. By that stage, *'Hi Mum'* notes were appearing in pillowcases and on wardrobe shelves.

Kate took to the new sport with gusto. She excelled, zipped through the grades, and achieved her black belt faster than anyone in her age group. It took over her spare time and she drove Norrie crazy as she practiced for hours in their shared bedroom. She relished competition and became a national junior champion at seventeen.

Having attainable goals transformed Kate's life. Her school grades improved from average until she made the top five in her class. At sixteen, she took a weekend job as a chambermaid in a local motel. She handed her wage packet to her mother, who returned a small amount of pocket money and squirreled the rest away for her daughter's education.

For Kate, Gary McEvoy evoked only bitter memories. He had manipulated her as a teenager and she felt remorse for the worry her behavior had caused her mum.

She finally asked Quinlan, 'What's the runt doing these days?'

'What he always did, selling all kinds of shit around town.'

'Who's he running with?'

Quinlan laid out the scraps of intelligence they had compiled on McEvoy and his local operation over the years. A born survivor with loyalty sold to the highest bidder, he ran with whoever kept him supplied with product. His ability to dodge the losing side in frequent drug wars kept him alive.

'His partner coming to the hospital could be significant,' Kate said.

'It was unusual,' Quinlan agreed. 'McEvoy's bird never worked with your mother at the Rape Crisis center. I'll call you in the morning, I'm meeting one of the other women tonight.'

'Thanks, Jack—for everything.'

19

Digger arrived at Kate's office and talked through the events of the previous twenty-four hours. She could not recall ever seeing him so despondent.

'Thompson says they climbed into the attic of 17A and found nothin' suspicious. He claims they emptied the black plastic bags, examined the contents, and put them back.'

'So no radio unit.'

Digger nodded.

'Do you believe him?'

'I wouldn't believe the gospel from that little rat but the way Timmons talked about scrabblin' around in the wardrobe for the rod to open the attic door makes me think he's tellin' the truth. I found it in the same place.'

'Is any of this connected?' Kate asked.

'Do you mean to the bombs under our cars?' Digger asked.

'Yes.'

'I don't know. If ISIS is planning a spectacular over here, they might want to eliminate the risk of someone like us foulin' up their plans.'

'Given the attacks in Europe over the last few days, we can't rule it out, but it seems more personal to me.'

'How do you mean? Bailey's mob, maybe?'

SIU had taken out a major Dublin crime gang months earlier.

'What's left of the Bailey gang is scattered,' Kate said.

'I'm goin' up the walls with someone shadowin' me all the time.'

'It's only been a couple of hours, for God's sake.'

'I can't work like this. I can't think straight.'

'You're going to have to get used to it for a while.'

'Give me somethin' useful to do.'

'Angie found something interesting in Jasmine Connolly's bank accounts. Help her chase that up. Sexton's following up Fazli Sumbal.'

Politicians were piling on the pressure to determine who or what was behind the assassination attempts. Kate was relieved that Mac was shouldering the burden of holding them at bay so their investigation could proceed unhindered. As she ended one call, Chapman kicked off another. She had barely said 'hello' when he asked, 'Do you know what our main job is?'

'Zach, I haven't time for this. I was targeted for assassination yesterday; we're kinda busy trying to figure out what sonofabitch planted the bomb.'

'Humor me!'

'The Secret Service does more than protect the President, I know that much.'

'We were established to protect the U.S. financial system from the counterfeiting of the national currency. That remit means we've had to get savvy about cyber financial crime. Long story short, Kate, the cyber threat means we have people placed with a lot of different agencies.'

'Okay.'

'I reached out to our guy at the CIA and had him do some trawling. A few things popped up that didn't mean much to us but might mean something to you.'

'Can you send it to me?'

'I've just sent a file to your secure email. It's a bit a dog's breakfast but if you can sort through it you might pick up something.'

'We'll take a look at it. Thanks, Zach.'

Kate had not properly checked her burgeoning inbox in an age. It groaned with neglect as she clicked it open and read a second message from Cody O'Neill enquiring how the Ben Gordon murder investigation was progressing. He wanted to know if he could assist further. Still angling for a trip to Dublin, she smiled as she clicked it closed. Chapman's email headlined, *Don't Ask, Don't Tell*. It had an attachment which she ignored until she read through his message.

Kate,

I kicked around ideas on adding something useful to your investigation. Perps often return to the scene of their crime and in your case, I figured there was a chance they might want to brag about their success in its immediate aftermath.

A colleague suggested using keywords like target, bomb, explosion, and other derivatives coupled with a narrow timeframe encompassing the time your car exploded, to see if we could pick up any chatter.

Nothing popped from boards, chatrooms, and other social media, so we looked at cells. We targeted short duration calls; a smart terrorist won't dilly-dally on the phone.

Hundreds of thousands of possibilities popped up. We applied a few analytical filters to reduce them to a couple of dozen, attached. I'll leave you to sift through and see if anything shakes out.

Zach

Kate clicked open the attachment and saw pages of printouts listing Irish numbers. Keywords were highlighted in yellow in the conversation transcripts that followed on succeeding pages. *Don't ask, don't tell, indeed,* she thought as she hit print.

Pete McNally raised an eyebrow when he deposited the pile on her desk minutes later. 'That took a full ream,' he said.

Kate grabbed a handful and leafed through page by page. She was uneasy reading one after another private conversation. She had no idea the Americans' reach extended so far and took care to shred each completed sheet. Angie called half an hour into the mammoth task that Kate could not risk delegating.

'Want to grab lunch?'

'Love to.'

'Toasted sandwich in the Boatman's okay?'

'Sounds great.'

'Pick you up in five.'

Kate took a final bundle and quickly scanned the blizzard of printed words and numbers. Her shredder hummed as page after page died an early death. She was ready to ditch the exercise and take a break when a testy exchange caught her eye.

What the fuck, Frank? You promised we were solid on this.

Anger screamed off the page.

Aye, well the targets were right, sure enough, but here we'll not talk about it like this. Your blood is up; so wait until you are home to talk business.

The digital transcription eliminated nuance and accent, but Kate figured the speakers as Irish. The caller rang from a +353 country code, Kate's jurisdiction, the number dialed was +44, The UK; both cell phones. Who was Frank and why was he urging caution?

Get another driver out to Varna airport with keys to take over this yoke. I'm catching a flight to Manchester tonight. I'll be in Dublin in the morning and I'll see you in our usual spot at dinnertime.

Had a van or truck broken down? Was it that simple? The caller/driver sounded irked by someone's sloppiness. The instruction to meet at a regular unnamed rendezvous hinted at darker motives. Or maybe not. Either way, she had to follow the lead. She locked what remained of the printout in her office safe and contacted Angie to call off their lunch date.

By the time Angie returned with a deli sandwich, Kate had spoken with Zach Chapman again. There was no voice recording available for the call that interested her. Chapman used contacts to confirm an Irish passport holder, Kevin Stevenson, had traveled from Varna to Manchester on the date of the call. Kate asked Daphne Clarke at MI5's Irish desk to check the UK end and she duly confirmed a passenger with the same details traveling on the Manchester to Dublin flight the following morning. Stevenson had no criminal record. Kate traced the number to a pre-paid unit purchased in Dublin months earlier. Although having no subscriber listed was unsurprising, the call data was. It had zero traffic until the call to Frank.

The Police Service of Northern Ireland confirmed the UK mobile as pre-paid and purchased in Newry, across the border from Kate's hometown. They had never encountered it and offered nothing on Frank's identity.

The Passport Office retrieved Stevenson's application and immediately forwarded Kate an e-copy, complete with the scanned passport-size photograph.

'Who *are* you?' she asked aloud.

20

A radio call from Joe Forde irked Digger. He was stuck indoors when he should be with his crew on the ground. Sumbal had returned home to 51 Manifold Avenue from another dog walk around the estate. The second report brought better news. Immediately after dropping the dog home, Sumbal exited the house again. This time he walked straight to 17A and used a key to open the front door. Deep in his Cave, Digger smiled and clicked into action.

'Stand-by,' he radioed Forde. 'Stay out of sight.'

He thumped the keyboard on his laptop and ensured the live feed he activated was recording. As Angie cleaned away her attic mishap, he had secreted two miniature cameras there. One was trained on the attic door, the other where the electronic unit was secured. He activated them both, he was back in the game.

The attic door creaked open and Sumbal's head appeared turtle-like in the loft space. Digger noted beads of sweat on the suspect's forehead as he flicked on a head torch. He pulled an iPad from underneath his sweatshirt and shifted across the rafters to get closer to the Radio Shack unit Angie had photographed. Once close enough, he connected both devices via a cable and paused. He hummed as he began typing on the iPad screen. The suspect tapped in strings of data Digger could not see and double-checked it, running his finger along each line several times. Sumbal edged cautiously backward toward the attic door and as he did, his foot snagged on the plastic bag of old clothes used to cover the hole caused by Angie's misstep while they searched the place.

'Ah, nuts!' Digger exclaimed.

He watched helplessly as Sumbal lifted the black bag and examined the hole punched through to the bedroom wardrobe below. Sumbal shook his head and mouthed something Digger could not figure out, before clicking off his light and descending the ladder.

In the hours that followed Digger's emotions swung between dejection to amusement and finally, relief. Sumbal returned to his house, pulled on a jacket, and took the number twenty-seven bus to the city center. Digger's crew stuck with him as he drew close to Greta Connolly's flat. An animated shouting match at her front door ensued, with Sumbal accusing her of damaging the house while she collected Jasmine's clothes. He demanded she give him money to repair it. When the argument got heated, neighbors from nearby flats emerged. One warned Sumbal to watch his language and asked Greta if she needed the Guards. She assured him she could sort this guy out herself. Sumbal argued he was getting by on welfare and could not afford to lose the deposit he had paid for his friends. His appeals fell on deaf ears, and he shuffled off the landing and returned home.

Kate printed the name, *Operation Ares*, onto one of the squad room whiteboards. Angie worked with her drawing together everything they knew on the audacious assassination attempts.

As Kate dictated them, Angie transcribed leads. The board filled up with disparate snippets of intel, names of suspects, and sightings but little to connect any of it.

'Where do you want to put this photo of Stevenson?' Angie asked. 'Wow, he has really dark brown eyes, they're something about them.'

'Leave him off for now. We need to find out more about him.'

'Khouri's a real lump of lard, isn't he?' Angie said.

'Last time we saw him he was,' Kate replied. 'That was months ago.'

'Do you want him on the Manifold Avenue board?'

'For the moment, yes. He has a definite connection to 17A.'

She left Angie continuing the task when Jack Quinlan arrived. The veteran detective told her that local drug pusher, McEvoy, was making furtive inquiries about her. When she returned to look over Angie's work she added his name to the Op. Ares board, with a photo of his pudgy, pasty face.

'Now there's a looker,' Angie joked when she saw the addition.

A call from Sexton interrupted their analysis.

'Guess what?'

Kate put the call on speaker.

'Tell us.'

'Remember O'Driscoll's tout?'

'The guy Immigration want to get their hands on?'

'I've located him.'

'Great work. Did you arrest him?'

'What's left of him is in the city morgue.'

'Crap! How did you make the ID?'

'Greta Connolly's photograph of Sumbal and his

mates with Jasmine Connolly was the clue. His friend had a tattoo on his neck which I took as an Islamic symbol. Turns out it was a Zodiac sign. He hadn't been seen for months, so I started digging by reading pathology reports on six John Does at the morgue. It stuck in my head that one had a Zodiac tattoo. It turns out what I took for Arabic script is a Gemini tattoo and our guy was born third June 1996. I'll give you his details when I get back.'

'Sounds great but a tattoo, is that enough to be sure?'

'This guy was on a rape charge that O'Driscoll spiked to turn him as an informer. I knew there was a good chance a DNA profile might exist. Sure enough, the Store Street Garda who processed him retained the case paperwork. I had the two sets of DNA compared and bingo; we got lucky.'

'Great piece of work. See you when you get back.'

Kate stepped back to review their work. She added John Doe to the Manifold Avenue board and connected a line to Rafiq Khouri's photo at its center. She studied the round face and bushy black beard of the overweight programmer and wondered. It annoyed her that she knew nothing of where he was, what he looked like these days, or what he was up to. The John Doe had been at the meeting the night Khouri and the other two suspects were arrested. Strands, like a spider's web, connected from Khouri to 17A Manifold Avenue and from it to Sumbal and Jasmine Connolly. Greta, her mother, featured on the whiteboard as a connection to the same address and also to Sumbal.

The pieces of the puzzle were building up. But, what was the big picture? When Digger briefed her on Sumbal's recent testy exchange with Greta Connolly at her flat, Kate grasped the opportunity. She needed to get a legal copy of the bank statements Angie had photographed earlier and diverted Sexton toward the city-center flat with a mission to cajole copies from the cagey Dubliner.

Digger gave him a covering crew in case things turned sour. As he climbed the concrete steps of the gray block, teenagers scurried in different directions. Sexton figured he had disrupted a drug deal. The door to the Connolly flat was open. He tapped lightly and asked if anyone was home but got no reply. He pushed it open and followed the sound of the conversation toward the back of the flat.

'Come on hurry up; I need to get out,' he heard Greta say.

Plastic bags rustled and drawers slammed shut.

'God bless the work,' Sexton grinned as he entered Chantal's bedroom.

'Oh Jesus, Mary, and Joseph! You're after putting the heart crossways in me,' Greta spluttered.

Chantal climbed down from the chair she had been standing on stacking cartons on top of her wardrobe. Her bed was strewn with cartons of cigarettes and she pushed them off as she sidled alongside her mother.

'That smoking will kill you, Greta,' Sexton broke the tension.

'G'wan out to the kitchen and put the kettle on, Chantal, we'll be out in a minute,' Greta shooed her daughter. 'What are ye like walkin' into a person's house like that, Mr. Sexton?' she scowled.

'The front door was open. I shouted was there anyone home.'

'Ya did in yer arse. What do you want?'

'Greta, I need to look through Jasmine's stuff and I'd like your permission to do it.'

Mrs. Connolly made to protest but Sexton raised a finger to his lips.

'Without your permission, I'm going to have to go to court and get a search warrant. Now having to seize anything here connected to lawbreaking would be a proper pain in the arse!'

'What're you after?'

'I just want to have a look around. You make a cup of tea, I won't be long.'

By the time Sexton emerged, he had moved around the mountain of cigarette cartons and searched all the areas Angie mentioned. When he returned to the kitchen, Greta dispatched Chantal to watch television.

'Let's have a chat,' he said, placing a bundle of printed bank statements on the table. 'I need to take these,' he explained as he wrote out a receipt.

Connolly signed without quibble.

'Is Jasmine in trouble?' she asked.

'Well now Greta, you tell me. Are you getting her to pay for stuff in England?'

'What do you mean?'

'The cigarettes, does she get them for you?'

'Jesus, Mary, and Joseph, not at all! Junior's the man for the fags.'

'Who's Junior?'

Connolly was crestfallen; she had said too much.

'He's from the North. That's all I know.'

'How does he get in touch?'

'I haven't seen him in months. Someone else does the runs for him these days.'

'So, he's given it up?'

'No, he's the boss now.'

'Young or old?'

'A good lookin' young fella.'

'Alright. Listen, remind me again where Jasmine works.'

For the third time that day, Greta Connolly explained that she was employed in a snack shop at the main railway station in Birmingham. Her daughter's banking anomalies were a red flag and Sexton hoped Greta Connolly would not tip her off. He queried whether she had any other source of income, but there was no second job. He left the flat complex alert to the possibility that something or someone had skewed Jasmine Connolly onto a dark, dangerous road.

21

As Kate turned her screen off after a day working mostly indoors, her old college roommate, Betty Fitzpatrick called.

'Got time for a coffee?'

'Fitz, you pick your moments!'

'Kate, people are saying that it was your car that blew up at Beaumont yesterday.'

'What people?'

'You know, gossip.'

'I can't talk out of school, you know that.'

'How's your mum?'

'Doing better, call out and visit if you like. She'll be in Beaumont for another few days and you know she'd love to see you. She knows nothing about the explosion.'

'So it was your car.'

'*Betty*! I'm too tired for this.'

'Meet me at Blackboard. We need to talk.'

'Honestly, it's not a great time.'

'There's something I'd like to share.'

'I've got minders everywhere I go at the moment.'

'Bring them along!'

The ERU decided to put Kate in one of their armor-plated vehicles until the threat against her abated. As she sat in the Audi's back seat the city's docklands district flashed by in a blur. Her old stomping ground from her rookie days had utterly changed. The abandoned factories and warehouses had vanished, replaced by a business district of office blocks with apartments thrown in to house the new kids of the high-tech industries. The bright lights ahead marked a vibrant square with a Daniel Libeskind-designed theater as its centerpiece. Traffic stalled as show-time approached and people rushed for curtain up.

Kate would cut back through the same area when she was done with Betty. Their mother was in good form Norrie had assured her, but Kate needed the reassurance that only a bedside visit could bring.

The car dropped her to the front door of the restaurant. Last time Kate met her friend here they drank one Mojito too many. When she pushed through the swinging doors Betty was her usual chic, sat at the tiny bar sipping a drink. Her flowing auburn hair, offset a pale smiling face combined with high cheekbones to ensure heads turned whenever she walked into a room.

'Sparkling water?' Kate mocked, as they hugged.

'It's midweek.'

'Same again, please,' she signaled the barman, slipping her coat off and slinging it over the back of her barstool. She settled an elbow on the counter and weighed up her beaming friend.

'Chin-chin, Betty Boo!' she said.

They clinked glasses and Kate stopped midway toward replacing her glass on the counter.

'What?' Betty smiled.

'You're pregnant!'

'Ah, you've gone and spoiled the surprise.'

'You're practically glowing,' Kate laughed, as they embraced again.

When the two met in Trinity College in their late teens, they had struck up an unlikely friendship. Kate was a bridesmaid when Betty married her artist boyfriend. They chatted about the details, due date, and whether or not Betty wanted to know if it was a boy or girl in advance.

'I know you're swamped at work, but I didn't want to just text you.'

'Of course, but I do have to get across town and see mum before visiting ends. Can I share your news?'

'My second mother! Of course, you can. Tell her I'll see her soon.'

'She'll be thrilled.'

Forty minutes after getting together for the first time in ages, the pair went their separate ways. Kate headed to the north side of the city and pushed through the crowded corridor where night shift staff coming on duty mingled with visitors.

Her mother was alone. She seemed so fragile as she napped and her expression worried Kate. Was depression setting in? She roused immediately Kate touched her shoulder, happy to see her younger daughter, and was delighted with Betty's news. Kate was surprised when Aidan Hanrahan entered the ward fifteen minutes after visiting time ended.

'Are you here to throw me out?' she asked.

'Not at all. I just need to check something with your mum,' he replied.

Kate waited in the corridor while the consultant went through his routine. It was odd that he was still working. Then it hit her; she'd forgotten to call him.

'Working late tonight?' she asked, as he left the ward.

'I thought you might call in for a visit. You promised to let me know if we could grab a coffee this evening.'

'It went out of my head. Can we do it another time?'

'Maybe I should detain your mother until you say yes,' he joked.

'Try telling her that.'

Once her mother was settled for the night, Kate left the hospital. Buoyed by Betty's great news, the sharp, the chilly breeze that swept through the entrance doors jolted a reminder that someone out there wanted her dead.

Jack Quinlan called as she was driven home. As usual, he was true to his word and had interviewed one of Margaret Bowen's visitors. She told him that Gary McEvoy's girl-friend, Cheryl, actually offered to drive Margaret's friends to the hospital. On the way, she had chatted about Margaret although admitted she didn't know her. She mentioned that Gary and Kate had knocked around a bit while at school. Cheryl was full of questions about her. Why did they not see her around Dundalk anymore? Some of the women believed Kate was teaching but one let slip she had joined the Garda Síochána a few years earlier.

The questions never let up on the return journey. Had they seen the Bowen girls? Had they chatted? How were they bearing up? Cheryl went silent when one of the women inquired why she seemed more interested in the daughters than their sick mother.

'One final thing,' Quinlan added. 'I'm retiring at the end of the month.'

Bemused at first, Kate offered her congratulations and told him she would be in touch.

22

Mac canceled his usual management meeting the next morning in favor of a one-to-one with Kate. Nothing seemed different as he returned to his private office from a conversation with his staff officer. Just a week earlier, he had confided that when things calmed down, he would be taking time off for medical reasons. A routine prostate examination had yielded results that concerned his GP. The doctor had been in touch twice to remind him of the urgency of being properly checked out. If he was worried, he concealed it well.

They rapidly concluded their brief on the threat against herself and Digger. Apart from Quinlan's nugget of information from Dundalk regarding Gary McEvoy's apparent interest in finding out about her, Kate was no further on in identifying where the threat was coming from. She explained McEvoy's background as a local drug dealer but omitted their historic connection. Mac pledged to spare nothing, manpower, overtime, whatever it took to find out who was coming at them.

'Do we have any intel to offer the European Task Force?' he asked.

'I'm considering whether or not to tell them about Sumbal and 17A. We don't have a full picture yet and you know how they like clarity in Europe.'

From the Berlin meeting, they knew ISIS had close-knit groups operating around Europe with international support. The Spanish delegate described how the local group that carried out the Barcelona attack also had plans to attack France. They were part of a tight trans-national terrorist cell; all Moroccan in origin and extensive travelers throughout Europe.

'How about we give J2 a shot at figuring out what that attic device in 17A could be used for?' Mac asked.

Kate said nothing.

'Look, the Army is more experienced with international terrorism. They've dealt with Hezbollah and the like in the Middle East.'

'We've had experience with them here too,' Kate replied.

'Granted but the Army's technical capability far exceeds ours. It's time to use it and get that clarity we're seeking.'

'So what do you want me to do?'

'Get the Army specialists into 17A and let them figure out what the hell that signaling unit in the attic is being used for.'

'Digger will hate this but I'll get him to set it up. Sumbal worries me,' she added.

'What about Jasmine Connolly?'

'Since we passed her Birmingham address to MI5, they're watching her. They've linked a phone to her and traced where it has pinged around Birmingham in the last eight months.'

'And?'

'It's mainly in the Washwood Heath, Sparkbrook areas. Both have a large Muslim population. They're carrying out more background checks, she's moved around a lot.'

'Keep me posted on any developments. What does Sexton make of the Connolly family?'

'He's only met the mother, a street trader in Moore Street, fruit and veg. Angie noticed contraband cigarettes in a young daughter's bedroom but they don't strike me as likely part of any international plot. The mother detests Sumbal.'

'What about the rest of the family?'

'Jasmine has three brothers all working in Dublin, one in the army. None of them have ever been in trouble. They appear like a decent working-class family.'

Mac slid a photograph of a Middle Eastern male across his desk toward Kate. 'I'm going to have to talk to O'Driscoll about his dead informant.'

'I'll take the photo but keep me out of *that* conversation if you can.'

'What did Sexton find out about the informant's killing?'

'A few weeks back, a trawler fishing in the Irish Sea spotted the body in the water and called the coastguard who recovered it.'

'What did the post mortem tell us?'

'The pathologist reported an earthy odor from the corpse.'

'So he drowned in freshwater and was in it a few days,' Mac said.

'Exactly,' Kate replied. 'Maybe dumped into the Liffey at the quays before being washed out to sea.'

Sexton was chasing up the pathologist on how the victim had lost three toes from his right foot. The skin on the feet had degloved during recovery and the report was silent as to whether the damage occurred pre- or post-mortem. A murder squad team had been assigned and the lead investigator had requested a fresh autopsy be carried out.

'He's Iraqi, is that right?' Mac asked.

'Correct. Interpol is notifying next of kin.'

Mac switched attention to Rafiq Khouri. Had the FBI any idea where he went after release from custody in Dublin? Had O'Neill said anything about where the suspect is at the moment?

'He traveled to Brussels from Dublin,' Kate told him. 'After that, we've no idea.'

'What's O'Neill's take on him?'

'When we discussed it in Paris he mentioned that the American military in Syria was impressed with the ISIS internet communications. FBI nerds suggested the system bore similarities to Khouri's set up in his cyber world.'

'Do they think Khouri's in Syria then?'

'Speculation only; they've got no evidence to back it up.'

Kate slipped the John Doe photo into her folio and stood to leave.

'By the bye,' Mac added. 'Quinlan's retiring at the end of the month.'

'He told me so last night. I'll miss him.'

23

Junior's new company headquarters was in an industrial unit on the outskirts of Newry. The unit consisted of admin offices and a drive-in workshop for basic truck repairs. It blended neatly with other start-up businesses in the estate; a new company with big ambitions.

It was still dark when he unlocked the office at six-thirty. The receptionist wouldn't arrive until nine o'clock. Still brooding two days on from his failed attack, he was agitated when at eight-thirty Trevor Crowe, the portly president of Crusaders NI, walked in. What did he want?

I'll not be staying long, Kevin,' Crowe said, as he pushed through the door.

The corpulent solicitor was immaculately dressed in a bespoke navy pinstripe suit. They had known each other since Junior joined Crusaders NI and grew into one of the best inside centers ever to play for the club. Being a key part of a team driving for promotion in a league where the club struggled for so long gave Junior a disconnect from the life of crime he had slipped into.

Instinctively, he shuffled paperwork on the club president's approach.

'What can I do for you, Trevor?'

'Kevin, life is about choices, you know that. We all live by their consequences. What I have to do right now is about the hardest thing I've ever had to do for Crusaders NI. So, I'll go ahead and read the prepared statement agreed at last night's board meeting.'

Junior settled in his chair, eyes riveted on the club president. He shifted as the corpulent lawyer unfolded a single sheet of paper. Crowe coughed softly into a clenched fist and began reading.

'Per club rule 12.4, and effective immediately Crusaders NI Rugby Club expels Kevin Wrollesly and terminates any association with him or companies associated with, or connected to him. We acknowledge the commitment Kevin brought during his time with the club and thank him for his contribution to our development. The club's decision is unanimous and *final*.'

When he finished reading, Crowe placed the statement on the desk and stared at the floor. Junior felt ambushed. He should have seen it coming but planning the attacks south of the border had blindsided him.

'So that's it, is it? Good luck and *fuck* you.'

'Kevin, please let's not quarrel. We'll not go into the whys and wherefores.'

Junior leaned back in his executive leather chair and stared at his former friend. An important part of his persona just went up in smoke in front of his eyes. He leaned on the chair's chrome armrests and drew himself upright.

'Don't let the door hit your arse on the way out.'

When Crowe's black Mercedes departed Junior reflected on the callous choices life had forced on him. He should have played the game he loved for years to come with the club that held him in legendary status. Perhaps he could have even finished his law degree. His class would graduate next year. A law degree might have given him a shot at transforming the business into a legitimate enterprise. Instead, all that promise had been pilfered by the rogue cop who killed his father. However foolish the old man's intentions had been in trying to re-ignite an armed struggle, he had deserved a chance to surrender and take his punishment.

Apart from stripping away his sporting heritage, the club president's visit was a warning. Word was out on him. Nobody was fooled anymore that his business was legit; police would come sniffing soon. Frank Reilly had re-organized the contraband offload into different yards around south Armagh when it arrived in from the continent. His network of contacts probed deep into former IRA controlled territory, tracts of the countryside that received scant attention from police patrols, even in these more peaceful times. Junior paid handsomely for using the hideouts.

Two days on from the explosion in Dublin he still had not figured out how it had gone wrong. When he calmed down and listened to Reilly's explanation of how they had planned the operation, he accepted his number two had done his homework. He had used Semtex supplies his group still controlled and persuaded a bomb-maker Sean O'Hare had trained to build the two devices. Reilly opposed giving the targets advance warning by leafleting their cars, but Junior had insisted on it. He wanted the bitch to squirm.

The beautiful irony was that remnants of O'Hare's Saor Nua group agreed to claim the attack as revenge for killing their leader, putting Junior in the clear. He strongarmed every drug gang he supplied to play their part. A Dundalk biker from Gary McEvoy's gang agreed to deliver the pamphlet warning to Kate's car when a budding south

Dublin gang tailed her to Dublin airport. They followed Digger later and made a leaflet drop.

When the operation failed, Reilly was grabbed and beaten up by erstwhile comrades. They warned him if anyone in Saor Nua was linked to the attack he would be shot.

―――――――

Harriet Stevenson grew impatient when the cash her son had promised did not materialize. Kevin had promised to make enough money that would enable her to move away from the loveless marriage she had endured for too long. While he repaid all the money she loaned him, there had been little else. He told her he had to re-invest in the business for it to grow.

He was rarely home these days and when he was, he avoided the heart-to-heart chats that kept their relationship close. Initially, she thought a girlfriend might be turning his head. He denied having a regular partner, insisting he had a lot going on. When she saw a television report on the Dublin car bomb days earlier, she was sad the attack was directed against a policewoman. Women were a soft target. She figured it for just another violent incident in the gang wars that seemed to go on down there all the time.

'I'm done with Crusaders,' Junior said when he called her a few hours after the club president broke the news of his expulsion.

'Why's that?'

'Crowe came to Newry earlier to tell me the club had decided to expel me.'

'That's shocking. Come over for your tea and we'll chat about it.'

'Is the boss around?'

'He'll be gone to an evening cattle mart. I'll make sure

he takes Maud and Ivan with him; we'll have the place to ourselves.'

Later that evening Junior drove the twenty-six miles to Caledon. It took him forty minutes but as he pulled into the neat farmyard he relished the prospect of the fry-up he hoped his mother would have prepared. She did not disappoint. After consuming the rashers, sausage, and black pudding, accompanied by lashings of freshly baked white soda bread, Junior felt revived. He stretched out and used a final slice to wipe yellow streaks of egg yolk from his plate. His mother refilled his mug with piping hot tea and he moved from the table to an antique smoker's chair close to the warm solid-fuel cooker to finish it.

'You'll miss the club,' his mother ventured.

'Of course, I will.'

'You've enough to be doing anyway.'

'I didn't expect it to last forever but I never thought they'd do what they did, expel me, like.'

'That was rough.'

'Ungrateful bastards!'

'How are we doing otherwise?'

Aware his mother wanted away from the oppressive house she had lived in all her married life, Junior wanted to make it happen. He looked around the kitchen and through the lace curtains into the yard beyond.

'Maud and Ivan are with the old man, aye?'

'They are.'

'We're doing alright. Here, I'm going to tell you something now that you'll have to keep to yourself,' he said, quietly.

His mother looked at him. Was this the big news she had waited for? A deposit on the place she'd need to care for her two younger children.

'I found out who killed Sean.'

'What… what?'

'You heard me.'

'What does that matter now?'

'What does that matter? Jesus Christ, Mother, I'd expected better from you.'

'Son, Sean is dead and gone.'

'I know, but I'd only started getting to know him when the chance was whipped away from me.'

Harriet took her son's hand in hers, just like when he was a kid and it soothed him. She worried the fiery, unpredictable quality that, as a teenager, so attracted her to his father was coming to the surface in his progeny.

'That's a real shame but there's nothing we can do about that now.'

'*Isn't there?*' he snarled, snapping his hand from her clasp.

'Son, don't get upset!'

'When you let Wrollesly lock us up and me only a nipper, I didn't get upset. I'm not upset now.'

'Son, come on don't be like that now. That's the past.'

'Maybe you don't want anything done but I'll not let it lie.'

'What do you mean?'

'Never you mind! You're better off not knowing.'

'God almighty, child, don't waste any chance we've got to get away from here.'

'I'll get you what you need, wait and see.'

'Don't you get yourself hurt doing something stupid.'

'Forget about it. That's the boss back now,' Junior said, leaving the chair to confirm the headlight flash through the kitchen window was his stepfather's jeep. 'I'll go out and help him. Looks like they didn't sell and he'll be like a bull.'

24

Kate gave Digger the search warrant she had sworn in front of a judge. She told him to coordinate with DI Bill Twomey from ERU on smuggling the Army comms and ordnance specialists into 17A.

'Do you not trust what I sent you in my report?' Digger asked.

Usually, operational momentum built over time on jobs, and instinct guided Kate on the optimum time to strike. This intervention would not be a full-on strike to arrest targets. The chances of a four-man team getting in and out without being noticed were slim.

'You've identified the device as a transponder but said there were likely 'RadioShack' alterations with circuit boards you could not account for without taking the thing apart. I had no choice but to ask the Army if they could explain it.'

Digger sighed, 'I'll do my best to get them in and out unnoticed.'

He traveled with Twomey to a south city army barracks to plan the logistics of their insertion. Twomey's six-foot-five rock-solid frame filled the car.

'Stick close to me this evening.' Twomey's tight haircut and tank-like body screamed 'cop' and Digger bristled at the notion of trying to pass him off as anything else.

'Fuck sake, enough of this protection shit. I can look after myself.' he replied.

'You didn't see the bomb coming, did you? You stick with me, brother, I'll be glued to you.'

Digger's scrawny shoulders rose and fell in defeat. It was pointless arguing with his all-action colleague.

Two hours after arriving at the army base, Digger and Twomey departed having briefed both teams on their roles. Digger explained the layout of their target area, down to the noisy bolt that kept the rusty rear gate shut. The agreed plan was to enter the house in relays after dark, with as much delay between the two teams as circumstances dictated. An SIU team would keep Sumbal's house under constant surveillance to ensure he posed no threat. Twomey's number one squad would be nearby as backup and Army Rangers in civvies would deploy as a reserve to protect their specialists.

At SIU Kate was chasing shadows, uncertain where to go with Zach Chapman's suspicious phone call lead. She had to chase it down and mulled over sharing it with Daphne Clarke at MI5. Given that Chapman's initiative was off books, she decided to tread softly. She had talked to Clarke earlier about progress on Jasmine Connolly. Everything was quiet. Connolly was working at New Street railway station in Birmingham selling newspapers and coffee as usual.

Kate settled on an informal approach with an old friend. It had been a while since they touched base. She rang his Enniskillen office and was surprised when his phone answered on the first ring.

'Good morning Superintendent Tyrell.'

'What about ya, Kate? Long time, no hear.'

'I'm good, Alan. You?'

'The finest now. Getting used to more noise about the house.'

Their paths had crossed at Trinity College and diverged into different strands of policing with two different forces. She occasionally used his Northern Ireland uniform resources to stop and check targets that had slipped SIU and crossed the border.

'You're not hanging about. I've just about recovered from your wedding last year,' Kate laughed.

'A wild night.'

'A wild weekend, more like.'

'How is the new addition?'

'Ava, she's wonderful.'

'Lovely name.'

'And what can I do for you?' Tyrell laughed.

Kate outlined recent events in Dublin and he was horrified to learn she had been one of the targets.

'There's one lead out there hanging. I need a steer on how to go with it.'

She described learning of the disgruntled truck driver who had dropped everything in Bulgaria and flown to Dublin within hours of her car exploding.

'His name is Kevin Stevenson with an address near Caledon village. Don't ask and I won't tell how I learned about this guy.'

'Right. We should be able to do something for you. Caledon's not a million miles from us here.'

'Keep it word of mouth, Alan, no written record. My source is super-sensitive.'

'Aye, alright. We'll give it our best shot. I'll get one of

my seasoned detectives to do some nosing around; I can count on her to be discreet.'

'We're in the dark about the attacks. I know our ballistics people have been examining the recovered device and comparing the bomber's signatures with your guys. Nothing has shown up yet.'

'Leave it with me.'

Dublin Corporation built The Elms estate, the suburb containing Manifold Avenue, during the eighties in response to a burgeoning social housing need. The gray three-bedroom units were cheek by jowl with red-brick new builds crammed into any leftover plots of land. Streets had one or two well-maintained dwellings, but the majority of tenants simply paid their rent, leaving maintenance to Dublin Corporation. The rundown condition of the estate reflected the local authority's empty coffers. Cul-de-sacs, where local gangs congregated, were strewn with litter, broken glass, and a burnt-out car or two. The hundred-plus acres of urban sprawl was solidly working class.

To Digger's frustration, the spring evening extended long and bright. It beckoned a crisp, cold night. Two streetlights behind 17A were broken, darkening the road. The working lamps in the street spread fuzzy orange fluorescence toward the rear gate. Getting in and out unseen would only work if they got their timings spot on. Not too early or so late into the night that any activity around the house might spook a neighbor and trigger a 999 call. Getting the team through the rear gate fast would be a priority.

Detectives Joe Forde and Becky Kingston manned a mobile unit and knew the terrain better than most. An hour into the op, Digger prompted Kingston to push flyers for a local pizza shop through letterboxes on Manifold Avenue. At 17A, if the coast was clear, she was to scale the side alley gate, get to the back garden, draw back the bolt securing the rusty gate and get out fast after securing a miniature camera onto the wall.

Ten minutes after she completed the task Sumbal went walking again. Digger was convinced their operation was blown. He watched helplessly from the command van as their suspect loomed into view at the rear of the house. On previous occasions when observed in this area, he'd pushed against the rear gate to ensure it was secure. The dog stalled a couple of feet shy of the gate and cocked a hind leg at a broken lamp post.

'When the gate swings open, swoop in and grab him,' Twomey ordered into his radio.

'Wait!' Digger said, pointing toward the fuzzy orange feed on the monitor.

A group of teenagers roaming the estate came into shot. The teenage pack leader was struggling to control his Doberman Pincer. It lunged straight for Sumbal's mongrel.

'Get a proper dog, ya Paki bastard,' the pack leader jeered and pulled hard on the long leather leash restraining his purebred killer. To avoid confrontation, Sumbal scooped his pet under his arm, dashed across the street, and headed home.

'Back in business,' Digger grinned.

When Joe Forde reported Sumbal slipping the lead off the mutt in the front garden, Digger decided it was time to move.

He insisted Twomey wear black workman's trousers, a navy donkey jacket, and a blue woolen Dublin supporter's cap. They left Pete McNally manning the command van and exited toward their target. Digger had Twomey carry a workman's tool bag in the hope it might divert attention from the club-like hand toting it. It was the best he could come up with to keep the ERU commander from sticking out like a gorilla in a troupe of chimpanzees.

'Take it easy, will ya!' he whispered, as Twomey shouldered the rusty rear gate. 'It creaks like a fucker.'

Digger closed it carefully and used the key his estate agent buddy loaned him to unlock the rear door. They shifted cautiously through the kitchen into the narrow hallway and climbed the stairs. As he opened the attic door Digger told his colleague to go sit on a bedroom floor and keep out of sight. Reluctantly, Twomey settled on the dusty carpet and slid a paperback from the bedside locker to check out the cover.

'Touch nothing!' Digger hissed.

Digger was edgy, back in the house where his last visit ended sourly when Angie punched a hole through the ceiling. The army team was already in his earpiece seeking clearance to approach. He told them to stall.

Kingston monitored the feed from the rear gate camera and when she gave him the all-clear, Digger beckoned two CIS Corps specialists to advance. He slunk through the tiny garden, unbolted the gate, and brought them through.

'Remember this is a semi-detached house and the neighbors haven't heard a noise in a while,' Digger whispered. 'When you're movin' about, go slowly and quietly.'

'Easy and slow does it for me every time,' Commandant Sweeney, the EOD specialist, replied.

Digger guided the pair upstairs to the landing. Twomey would keep watch on the front while he funneled the pair, one at a time, into the attic. Sweeney who, days earlier had defused the device found under Digger's car, was first. He edged across the attic space, leaned forward, and commenced an assessment of the mysterious unit.

'Nothing suspicious on first observation.'

He moved on to a fingertip examination of the unit and delivered the same verdict.

'Philips screwdriver, please.'

Digger obliged and held his breath as the bomb specialist unscrewed the cover and slid it off.

'Oh!' he said.

'What's up?'

'I need to unscrew it from the rafter to take a closer look.'

Digger edged close enough to the attic entrance to enable him to drop quickly. He watched Sweeney use a pencil from his tool belt to mark a tiny 'x' over each screw hole. It would enable him to return it to its original position if that operational decision was made. Digger's plan to keep the attic uncrowded changed instantly when the EOD man whispered, 'Jennings, get up here.'

He edged cautiously backward to allow the communications expert to operate. Almost an Angie replica, Captain Myra Jennings' lithe frame moved cat-like as she climbed the ladder and peered into the attic space. She used the light from Sweeney's torch to shift cautiously from rafter to rafter.

'Sir?'

'What's your read on the LED counter?' Sweeney whispered.

Jennings ran her fingers quickly over the integrated circuit boards that made up in the unit, identifying and accounting for each one. The LED readout clocked her examination at twenty seconds.

'I don't see its purpose. DI Rooney was right when he described it as a RadioShack job. Somebody has added circuits. The LED has nothing to do with its core function as a transponder.'

Digger poked his head into the attic as Sweeney scratched his chin.

'Eighteen minutes on the timer,' he said. 'It's counting down to something. Did you interrupt the power source?'

'Yes, regardless, we're out of time.'

'What do you mean?' Digger whispered.

'Countdown timers mean one thing to me; something is going to blow. We need to search the house fast.'

'I knew this was a terrible idea,' Digger replied.

Sweeney spoke quickly, 'If there's a device that might explode we need to get surplus personnel out of here and evacuate people from nearby houses.'

He disconnected the power cable as he spoke and handed the unit to Jennings, telling her it was safe for analysis.

'We'll need it for evidence,' Digger reminded her.

'No time to talk, less than eighteen minutes,' Sweeney snapped.

As they swiftly maneuvered from the attic Twomey said, 'I know someone who can tell us if there's something here. Sumbal.'

Sweeney ordered Jennings to evacuate fast and bring two from the Ranger team to help him search. Digger's head was swimming. His options for keeping the operation covert had sunk like stepping in quicksand. Twomey waited impatiently for a decision.

'Evacuate with Jennings, grab that Sumbal bastard, and get him over here.'

When the pair departed, Digger and Sweeney searched methodically. Digger went to the garden and checked two gas cylinders connected to a kitchen cooker. He disconnected the gas leads and checked each cylinder thoroughly for concealed devices. Blue flashing lights distracted him. The lights halted outside the rear gate. He heard voices directing someone to the front. A uniform Garda edged the creaking rear gate open and shone a torch in his direction.

'Stay where you are, don't move!'

'Switch that feckin' thing off and get over here.'

'Don't get lippy with me,' the uniform replied, pulling his ASP baton from its holder and extending it with a reassuring snap. 'Last chance, move away from the cylinders and lie on the grass.'

'I'm DI Rooney from HQ, my ID is in my left inside pocket,' Digger told him as he stood and righted the second cylinder. 'We need your assistance.'

The uniform kept the ASP poised over his shoulder ready to strike as he shone his torch on Digger's ID card.

'What do you need from us?' he said, retracting the baton.

'Standby for orders.'

He ducked back inside where the EOD man was working systematically at the heating cylinder in the airing cupboard. Despite the panic, he was respecting Digger's now redundant order about creating as little light and noise as possible.

'Uniform cars are here. How many houses should we evacuate?'

'Get all the houses on Manifold Avenue emptied immediately.'

Digger delivered the order to the uniform Garda. 'Say it's a gas leak to keep people from blind panic,' he added.

When he returned to the landing, Sweeney was lying on his back with his head in the airing cupboard, straining to reach the rear of the copper hot water cylinder.

'A favorite hiding place in the Middle East,' he grunted, 'the results aren't pretty.'

Digger switched on the landing light.

'No point pretending anymore. Sumbal will be here any minute if I know Twomey.'

'I need my gear, urgent, urgent,' Sweeney shouted into his radio.

Outside, the commotion was building. People, pulling on jackets and coats, traded cozy front rooms for the chilly night air as numbers swelled on the street. More uniform guards spilled into the area to shepherd the throng toward safety.

Digger ordered Joe Forde and Becky Kingston to assist the army team in getting through the inner cordon around the house. Shortly after Sweeney's barked order, they ran through the back garden with a ranger humping the EOD man's precious kit bag. The house was a blaze of light now and Digger immediately caught the expression on Fazli Sumbal's terrified face as Twomey pushed him through the rear door. Blood spurted from his nose and the scrape on Twomey's knuckles told Digger the big man's patience was shot.

'Keep him down here,' he told Twomey.

He ran back upstairs and found the EOD man on his back with his legs still sticking out of the airing cupboard.

'Found something?'

'This one's a doozy.'

'Can you work on it?'

'Get everyone except Sergeant Daly out.'

'We have the suspect downstairs.'

'Is he cooperating?'

'He's not said much.'

'Less than ten minutes left on the clock. I'll question him in the kitchen.'

Downstairs, Sweeney shot questions at the trembling prisoner. Twomey cuffed Sumbal on either side of his head when his initial replies were blatant lies. The best the EOD man hoped for was confirmation of no secondary devices. His brief interaction with Sumbal convinced him it was a useless exercise. The guy was a fanatic, not to be trusted.

'Leave,' he told the kitchen interrogators. 'Daly come with me.'

Twomey grabbed the handcuffed prisoner and slammed his head against either side of the door frame when he screamed *Alu Akbar*. Sweeney welcomed the return to the silence that usually accompanied his job.

'Onwards and upwards,' he told his sergeant when they reached the landing.

'Seven minutes, forty-three seconds. Do we trust the clock?'

'Five minutes, then we leave. No time for suiting up, helmets only.'

'Roger.'

Over the next four minutes, Sweeney described what he was seeing. An assembly of circuit boards and traps he had never previously encountered. Despite the evening chill, beads of sweat rolled down Sweeney's neck from the confines of the stuffy helmet.

'Twenty seconds to extraction,' Sergeant Daly cautioned.

'Fucking pig!' Sweeney swore. 'People on the street should lie down, pass it to DI Rooney.'

Daly had never heard his senior officer swear and recognized defeat for the first time. He shouted a warning into his radio as he rapidly repacked tools on the carpet before clicking the tool kit closed. Outside, people grumbled as uniformed Gardaí shouted warnings to take cover on the cold concrete.

'Three seconds!'

'Damn!' Sweeney exclaimed, as his sergeant grabbed his hand and hauled him to his feet.

They descended the stairs steadily; a trip would stall their retreat and delay was lethal. Sergeant Daly allowed his boss to run ahead of him and saw him duck to avoid hitting the top bar on the rear gate's steel frame. The kit bag snagged on the gate's bolt receiver and as Daly tugged it free the night sky filled with an eruption of light and noise. He was blown backward as shattered pieces of concrete roof tiles and rubble showered onto the street.

The copper heating cylinder the device had been strapped beneath shattered and the top half soared through the roof and landed in the rear garden. Commandant Sweeney sheltered behind the neighboring wall, hoping it would not topple and trap him.

When Digger and the back-up team reached him he was frantically tearing rubble away from Sergeant Daly's body. The Ranger unit took over clearing it as a doctor from the standby ambulance gingerly removed the sergeant's helmet.

The shockwave from the blast shattered the top half of 17A's rear wall and the snagged kitbag proved disastrous. One half of a concrete capping stone caught Daly square in the face as he was blown back into the street.

The Garda chief at Dublin's Command and Control center triggered the major emergency plan on Digger's warning. A fleet of ambulances rushed to The Elms and ferried civilians to a triage station at the edge of the estate. Kate stepped from the Audi her protection team used to get her there and joined Digger alongside Forde and Kingston. They bowed their heads in silence as paramedics loaded the stricken soldier into an ambulance.

A fire crew hosed neighboring houses to contain the blaze the explosion had ignited. They diligently heeded Commandant Sweeney's warning to the Chief Fire Officer not to allow his men to approach the suspect house. What remained of 17A and the garden would be searched for secondary devices when the fire was extinguished. All power to the block was cut and away from the glow of the fire, the night took on an eerie murkiness.

Sweeney was in the rear of a Dublin Fire Brigade ambulance when Kate reached him. He was in shock. A paramedic wrapped an extra blanket around his shoulders as tremors set in. It had been less than a quarter of an hour since the catastrophic consequences of his inability to neutralize the complex device showered down on them. He had little time before his body's natural morphine wasted and his body shut down.

Kate climbed into the ambulance, squeezed past the nurse, and sat opposite. She recognized Sweeney's struggle, trying to stay focused, knowing everything had changed.

'Give us a minute.'

'Make it quick,' the paramedic urged.

She exited the ambulance and closed one door.

'You did good!' Kate said.

Sweeney looked at her and frowned.

'You saved lives tonight. No civilians were badly injured. Cuts and scrapes are what I'm hearing.'

Sweeney hung his head and shook it.

'But not Sean Daly.'

Kate reached over and squeezed his arm.

'Wait and see how he does.'

Sweeney raised his head and slumped back against the side of the ambulance.

'I should have gotten out sooner.'

'Get your injuries treated and don't second guess your-self. Can you tell us anything about the device?'

'Whoever put it together was no novice.'

'We're still trying to identify everyone connected to the house. There's one dead and three are missing.'

'Give the names to Colonel Shaw, he'll know to look for any stand-out bomb-makers we have on record.'

'Were there any remarkable features?'

'I'll get notes to colleagues; they'll guide Shaw.'

Kate figured she was running out of time when Sweeney's eyes closed and opened in slow motion.

'We searched that house twice and found nothing. So, the bomb must have been planted recently?'

'I don't know. The house is thirty years old and the copper cylinder is original. Whoever planted it was smart. They stuck it in the hollow base of the cylinder and slid a plywood sheet beneath to conceal it.'

'Have you seen that before?'

'Last tour in Lebanon while I was clearing a vacant house of IEDs, I saw a twist on it, but this was highly skilled work.'

'What about the bomb from Digger's car? The same source, do you think?'

Sweeney sat upright and scratched his head. He shook it and brushed the dust from his hair. Gray concrete specks settled either side of him on the black ambulance bench.

'Definitely not. The bomb under DI Rooney's car was a pressure plate device, a variation on what we encountered along the border in the nineties.'

'And the one in the house?'

'Straight out of Afghanistan. Up-to-the-minute technology and assembly,' Sweeney replied as he slumped forward. Kate caught him and helped him lie out on the stretcher. She thanked him and exchanged places with the returning paramedic who pulled the door shut and signaled the driver to depart. The houses to the rear had been evacuated in the wake of the explosion and the road at either end was controlled by uniform Gardaí.

Kate walked with Digger to the shattered rear wall and stared at the smoldering house.

'Get everyone back to base,' she said. 'The media will feast on this. We need to be ready.'

25

She called Norrie en route and told her she would not make it into the hospital that night. Margaret Bowen could communicate, chatting slowly and cautiously with the nurses looking after her. Norrie told Kate their mum was badgering every doctor about when they would release her back into the community. Each one said the final decision lay with Mr. Hanrahan. It reminded Kate to text him that a bad week had just gotten much worse and their coffee date would have to wait.

When she reached base, Mac was on the phone in his old office, talking with Colonel Shaw. He signaled Kate to listen in. Their conversation was somber. If the operation's disastrous outcome was to trigger finger-jabbing, it had not started yet. Sergeant Daly died shortly after arrival at Connolly Hospital. Mac suggested a joint press release offering no comment pending a full forensic examination of the site. Shaw turned the offer down, pointing out that Defense Minister was en route to the hospital to make the grave press announcement on the soldier's death.

'Superintendent Bowen has joined me from the scene,' Mac said. 'Have you anything to add, Kate?'

'Sumbal is in custody and both number 51 and what remains of 17A are locked down crime scenes. I've withdrawn all SIU personnel from the area. Commandant Sweeney is in good shape, all things considered. He's cut and bruised, of course, but I spoke with him in the ambulance. Here's what he told me.'

Kate outlined the details Sweeney had shared concerning the bomb and the highly skilled hands that put it together. Shaw said he would have his people work through the night to identify suspects. Mac signed off, agreeing to share everything they had on 17A since it entered SIU's orbit as a suspect house.

Mac called Commissioner Fox and agreed to update media security and defense correspondents. He would tell them that the explosion occurred during an ongoing security operation and request they continue to report the suspected cause of the blast as a gas leak.

Kate awoke the next morning to her new phone's unchanged, shrill ringtone and groaned when the screen told her it was only five thirty-five.

'The *Daily Express* broke ranks,' Mac said. 'Its front page is reporting a security blunder that cost a soldier's life. The commissioner is livid.'

'Assholes!'

'Get in as quick as you can, we're scheduled for a working breakfast with the Justice Minister at eight.'

She showered and allowed cool water to run longer than usual to spark herself into life. She chose a perfectly tailored navy suit with a crisp white blouse for the morning meeting. She checked her look in the hall's full-length mirror and headed to the kitchen. The express coffee maker grunted into life and she downed an espresso. As she stepped onto the landing, her protection officer called the lift.

Instead of heading directly to the Phoenix Park HQ, they swung by her SIU office where Sexton was briefing the early morning crew. She needed to plug into the energy of her unit before facing the music in the Commissioners' office. Keeping her office door ajar, she reviewed emails. One from Daphne Clarke leaped out from the list.

The first paragraph outlined how their target, Jasmine Connolly, had dropped her MI5 tail late the previous evening. Clarke's prose was sparse, but Kate sensed the pandemonium the development had caused. The second paragraph brought better news. They had picked up a trace. The suspect had purchased a ferry ticket on the 02:40 a.m. sailing from Holyhead in Wales to Dublin.

'Hold the phone!' Kate called to Sexton. 'Check the early morning ferry arrival time into Dublin port, will you?'

Why the hell didn't Clarke call, Kate wondered?

The roll-on, roll-off ship docked at 05:55, an hour earlier. They were too late. All passengers had disembarked and the last of the heavy goods traffic was being cleared through customs as they spoke. Sexton advised her to leave it to him.

Kate tapped a one-line reply to Clarke advising that SIU would undertake to house the suspect. Surveillance around Connolly's home would likely throw up a sighting of Jasmine. SIU would also cover the streets around Sumbal's house in case she turned up there. Before she logged out, she read a short email from Alan Tyrell in Enniskillen asking her to call him as soon as possible.

Commissioner Fox sat at the head of the large oak table that dominated his conference room. Mac to his right and a private secretary and press officer to the other side. Kate grabbed the seat next to Mac as Fox checked his watch. He was an ally, but the kind of political pressure he functioned under meant nobody around him got an easy ride.

'Nice of you to join us, D-Superintendent.'

She slid her folio case onto the table's shining surface and extracted her report. It outlined the investigation that led them to 17A Manifold Avenue and detailed the joint Army/Garda operation that culminated with the previous night's explosion.

They spent forty minutes hashing out details of how the Commissioner and Mac would tackle the breakfast meeting with the Justice Minister. Fox wanted Kate along, but Mac argued it might be viewed as counter-productive to have operational personnel mired in political meetings. Fox conference-called the Army Chief of Staff via his press officer and agreed to host a joint media briefing later in the day. Both press officers would repeatedly tell the media they could give no further details on ongoing security operations. They would neither confirm nor deny the Dublin explosion was linked to recent European attacks.

'Let's get out of here before they change their mind,' Kate shot at Ken James waiting in the corridor.

Her day was already clogging up with demands she was struggling to sync. She called Alan Tyrell as she diverted her protection detail to Beaumont Hospital so she could nip in to see her mother. Tyrell told Kate he was driving with a colleague and they would have to speak later. Margaret Bowen, on the other hand, was feisty and eager to talk when she arrived.

'When will they let me out of this place?' she asked.

'What does Aidan say?' Kate asked.

'He talks more about you than me.'

'Don't be silly, Mum.'

'You're even dressing up for him.'

'Mum!'

A nurse's aide arrived and spared Kate further interrogation. She assisted her mother from the bed into a wheelchair and explained she was going to help her to shower. Seeing her resilient mother so dependent made Kate well up. She had been a fit and active sixty-five year old until she suffered her stroke. Norrie was doing all the heavy lifting on making arrangements for the fulltime care she would need in the foreseeable future.

'Mum, I've got to get going or I'll be sacked,' Kate said, as she kissed her good-bye.

'Talk to Aidan.'

'I promise. If you see him this morning, tell him I'll call in the afternoon.'

'I certainly will.'

As her protection detail whisked her back to SIU, she called Alan Tyrell and adjusted her folio to support the notepad she scribbled on furiously.

'Have I got a story for you!' he told her.

'I'm all ears, Alan.'

'This Kevin Stevenson, AKA Kevin Wrollesly sounds like one interesting boyo.'

'Tell me more.'

Kate recorded every detail. The local detective had an aunt living in Caledon and she filled in the background on Harriet Stevenson's teenage tryst with an IRA man that had scandalized her father and the town years earlier. The fact she had married and had a family with a solid member of the local Presbyterian community took some of the heat off her. However, the tempestuous teenager's firstborn was a living reminder of local bitterness during the Troubles.

'Wow! That's interesting.'

'That's only the half of it! I've had my detective unit open a file on him as a result of your inquiry.'

'Why?'

'I'd read about a shit hot center for Crusaders NI called Wrollesly and rang Trevor Crowe, an old rival from my rugby days. Wait till you hear what he told me.'

Kate's curiosity grew as each snippet of Wrollelsy-Stevenson's story unfolded. His early promise as a player, the sudden drop out of a Queens' law degree for a job as a truck driver, and finally his expulsion from Crusaders NI rugby club the previous day.

'What was that about?' Kate asked.

Tyrell explained that the club president had sworn him to secrecy on the reasons for the expulsion. He agreed to share it with Kate on that basis. She wrote bullet points on a fresh page as Tyrell outlined the belief club officers formed based on the strong rumor in the community that Stevenson was involved in large-scale smuggling. He was a club sponsor and Crowe told Tyrell if word got out that the club was accepting dirty money to fund its talent academy, parents would withdraw their children in droves and senior players would follow. Kate flipped back through her notes as Tyrell spoke about the deep roots the sport had in the community and the political importance of the all-island team that represented Ireland at international level. One detail was missing.

'I don't suppose you know who Stevenson's real father was?'

'He was a seasoned operator called Sean O'Hare; sentenced to fifteen years for the attack on security forces that preceded his arrest but, of course, he got an early release as a result of the Good Friday Agreement. He's dead since I believe.'

Kate's head spun as she tried to process the information.

'Are you there, Kate?'

'You're certain about Stevenson's father?'

'I don't have DNA confirmation if that's what you mean. What I do have is the fact that Harriet Stevenson was arrested with him in the nineties. My detective talked to the arresting officer; retired now, of course, and he said it was obvious from her semi-dressed state what the pair had been up to.'

'Is it possible she had more than one lover?' Kate asked, clutching at straws.

'Can't rule it out but it's unlikely.'

'Okay,' Kate sighed. 'Alan, there'll be a follow-up on this.'

'How come?'

'I was there when Sean O'Hare died. From what you've told me, his kid, Kevin Stevenson or Wrollesly, is likely the one who tried to kill me.'

26

Sexton rotated his teams around different surveillance points on Jasmine Connolly's home. The inner-city dwellers had a nose for sniffing out police and Sexton knew as much. He was raised on the other side of the Liffey with the same constant hide and seek game. It would be difficult to keep the operation going long term.

There was no sighting of Jasmine during the early morning. Her sister, Chantal ran to the corner shop and picked up a liter of milk, bread, and half a dozen eggs, an indicator of an extra mouth to feed. In the early morning, Greta Connolly had a short conversation with a neighbor before heading to Moore Street.

During the morning Kate switched her navy suit for the jeans and blue blouse combination she had stashed in a squad locker. At midday, she spoke to Daphne Clarke to find out how the young Dubliner had given her MI5 tail the slip. Clarke admitted an embarrassing lapse and hinted that a team leader faced suspension as a result. They discussed the Dublin explosion and combed through the possibility of a connection between the two events. Kate had nothing to link them. When Digger poked his head in the door it was her signal to sign off.

'Daphne, we'll keep you posted.'

'Cheers, mate, appreciated.'

Digger looked as if he had not slept much; dark circles evident under his eyes.

'Target's on the move.'

They headed to the squad room to tune into the pursuit. Neither could risk joining the operation on the ground with ERU protection detectives on their shoulders. Jasmine Connolly moved swiftly and confidently through her old neighborhood onto O'Connell Street, the capital's main thoroughfare. It was busy with bus, tram, and taxi traffic but the wide boulevard made it relatively easy to keep her in sight. Sexton speculated she was going to meet her mother, at her nearby Moore Street stall. However, Jasmine walked past the turnoff and crossed O'Connell Bridge. She headed through the grounds of Trinity College, exited at Nassau Street, and veered into the tourist throng of Grafton Street.

'She's trying to drop you,' Kate warned Sexton. 'Stick tight.'

Despite the warning, twenty minutes later Connolly managed to ditch her pursuers after browsing in Stephen's Green shopping center. SIU detectives scoured side streets in the busy city center for a sighting of their target.

'Feck sake,' Digger swore, frustrated at being cooped up. He paced in front of the squad room whiteboard viewing the threads of the Rafiq Khouri/Sumbal case.

'What do you make of Sean O'Hare's son turning out as the likely nut who tried to kill us?' Kate asked, changing his train of thought.

'*Briseann an dúchas trí shúile an chait,*[1]' Digger replied instinctively in Irish. 'It's the only way it makes sense to me.'

'How do you mean?'

'From what we know, Stevenson grew up in a rural Protestant community with no history of violence or criminality. The opposite they were staunch Christians. If it's not his nature, what was it that skewed him into criminality?'

'Opportunity, maybe. It's something we need to find out.'

Digger returned to the whiteboard. 'Does this Connolly connection come back to Khouri? Does anyone even know where Khouri is? What's the big picture?'

'His only known link to 17A was the night he was arrested there,' Kate told him. 'I shared that detail and an account of last night's explosion with the European task force.'

'What about your FBI man? What's he sayin'?'

'*My FBI man* is playing his cards close to his chest.'

'I didn't mean anything by that,' Digger replied.

'I'd hope not,' Kate replied. 'It's time I rang him, anyway,' she added as she headed back to her office.

The investigation into the murder of Ben Gordon, Khouri's old boss, was progressing but no one had been arrested or even identified as a suspect. Despite the Dublin explosion and the known link to Khouri, O'Neill was guarded about divulging any intelligence. Kate was in no mood for his half-answers and lost her temper.

'Cody, where the hell is this guy? What is the FBI doing about him?'

A long pause. Did she hear a whispered aside? She couldn't be sure.

'Kate, the truth is we're not certain.'

'But you have ideas?'

'He hasn't returned to the States, so Syria's an obvious possibility.'

'Obvious? Do you think that lump of lard is capable of fighting?'

'He might be running ISIS communications.'

Exasperated, Kate knew there was little to be gained from pursuing a line of inquiry focused solely on Khouri. Nobody had figured out if he fitted in the bigger picture.

'Will I shoot over to you guys? Maybe there's something tangible I can add to the Gordon case,' Cody continued.

'I'll speak to the investigating officer and get back to you.'

'I'd love for us to have dinner. How's your mum doing?'

'Mum's doing good, thank you. Right now, dinner is impossible, Cody but I'll get back to you on the Gordon murder.'

'Great, thanks. Lovely to hear your voice, Kate.'

Sexton's crew searched city center shops, streets, and alleyways trying to re-establish contact with Jasmine Connolly. They came up dry. Angie suggested Sexton allow her call to the Connolly household on the off-chance that Chantal, the target's pre-teen sister was home alone. The pair had hit it off during their initial visit and Sexton needed something to get back in the game.

After a mad dash across town, they sauntered along the landing to the Connolly flat and rang the bell. Angie used the ruse of losing her phone and wanting to check if it had fallen from her pocket in Chantal's bedroom. It got them inside the front door. MI5 had been tracking Jasmine Connolly's phone for weeks and it stopped pinging the previous evening. There was only one conclusion, the phone had been dumped.

'You're chirpy this morning,' Angie remarked to Chantal.

'Jaz is home.'

'Your sister from England?'

'Yeah.'

'That's great. She must be delighted to be at home.'

'No, she's grumpy. Ma says it's all the travelin' and she'll be grand when she has a rest.'

'Oh sorry, I didn't know there was someone asleep in the house.'

'No, ye're alright. No-one's asleep. Jaz went out; she told me not to tell Ma.'

'Mmmm!' Angie looked in the young girl's eyes. 'And I'd say you don't like keeping secrets from your mam?'

'No, but Jaz begged me.'

'Did she say when she'd be back?'

'No, she left her phone here, said it was dead. She told me to plug it in and charge it but warned me not to switch it on. She borrowed mine.'

Angie made much of looking around the flat for her ghost phone and asked Chantal if it was okay to look under her bed. Once again, the child seemed comfortable with Angie in her room.

'It's not here,' Angie said. 'I'm sure I will find it in the silliest place.'

Chantal laughed.

'Text me when you find it.'

'Sure, write your number on my hand,' Angie invited stretching out her arm.

'Ya sure?'

'Of course! Ohh that tickles!'

She caught Sexton's grin from the sitting room as the child scrawled the number. When they left the flat he pinged the phone immediately and located it heading toward the Elms estate. Why was Jasmine Connolly

185

heading there? Was there another safe house? A check on its activity identified one call to a Birmingham number.

'Angie's gotten us something,' Sexton explained when he called Kate, indicating the direction his crew was headed.

'The Elms?' Digger repeated, scratching his head.

He made a quick phone call from the Cave and returned to the squad room. Kate was pacing, lost in her call with Sexton. They had not pinpointed their target yet, but it was only a matter of time, as his crews flooded the area. Digger nudged her elbow.

'Jasmine Connolly's at Manifold Lane station askin' about her husband.'

'*What?*'

'She's called to the hatch at Manifold Lane inquirin' about her husband. She's sittin' in the public office right now.'

'*Holy crap!*'

'Vince Hyland's there to collect Sumbal for an interview. He's refusing to speak English and they couldn't get an interpreter until this morning. What do you want to do?'

'Tell Ken James to get the car, we need to go there now. Get Vince on the phone and don't let Jasmine Connolly leave. He needs to interview her before Sumbal.'

Detective Vince Hyland was Kate's go-to guy when it came to interviewing high-profile suspects. The veteran interrogator had an avuncular quality that made him seem like everyone's best friend. His gift for getting the most tight-lipped tough guys gabbing was unique. Some put it down to his round, ever-smiling face. He made it seem like he had just dropped in for a chat, the timbre to his smooth

Dublin accent resembled a reassuring flight captain telling his passengers to sit back, relax and enjoy the ride. He was attached fulltime to the Criminal Assets Bureau that targeted the ill-gotten gains of organized crime gangs, but they released him whenever Kate required his silky skills. Years earlier she had shadowed him for weeks to improve her interviewing technique. In the end, she conceded she was unlikely to ever match his ability to find a track into the most stubborn of minds.

The tabloids were having a field day. When word spread that a broadsheet had leaked the security operation, other papers raced to catch up. Their online editions freely speculated on possible mayhem in the capital as a terrorist cell operated with impunity in Dublin.

Sumbal was housed at Manifold Lane station to separate him from regular prisoners. Kate and Digger listened in an upstairs office as Hyland began an interview with Jasmine Connolly. The station's antiquated facilities meant no recorded interviewing was possible and prisoners requiring interrogation were shipped to the nearby Elms district headquarters. They had reached the station and kept Jasmine Connolly waiting until Digger rapidly rigged the interview room so he and Kate could listen in.

They caught a glimpse of Connolly in the corridor as she walked from the public office to the windowless interview room. Kate recognized her immediately as a younger version of 'the granny' she had seen at 17A days earlier. A pale round face still held a youthful look and she didn't make much over five feet in height. The beige parka she wore had seen better days and swung loosely around her full figure. Underneath she wore faded black jeans with slashes on either leg and an oversized dark blue sweatshirt. Wisps of her dark-as-night hair protruded from the front of a gray headscarf. Despite tatty clothing, she moved almost regally ahead of the Garda directing her, unfazed by the police surroundings.

'Good morning, Jasmine,' they heard Vince begin, his tone calm and sociable. 'Do you understand why we want to have this chat with you?'

'Is it about Faz?' Connolly asked, her Dublin accent unchanged by her time away from home.

'Mr. Sumbal, yes, we'll talk about him later but let's get started. You are here at Manifold Lane Garda station of your own free will, is this correct?'

'Why are ya sayin' that?'

'Jasmine, I'm treating you as a cooperating witness, so this interview will not be voice-recorded. Even so, there are a few formalities we must observe.'

'Fair enough.'

Hyland read over the usual caution advising his interviewee she did not have to say anything that might incriminate her and opened by asking where she had met her husband. He listened as she recited a well-rehearsed story about how they met by chance on a Dublin street, how they had married quickly, and when she could not find work locally, she had gone to Birmingham and picked up a job at a railway station newspaper kiosk. When questioned about the coincidence between her return and the events close to Sumbal's home the previous night, she denied any connection. She was only returning home to see her mother. Hyland coaxed background information from her about the noisy, loving family she had been raised in and steered the interview back to her relationship with her husband. She faltered. Kate perked up as she and Digger sensed a mood change. Connolly became emotional for the first time, changed tack, and confessed that marrying him was a mistake. She did not like him anymore and admitted the reason she had gone to Birmingham was to get away from him.

'She certainly has her mother's gift of the gab,' Digger remarked to Kate.

Kate smiled.

'Why did you come here this morning?' Hyland asked in the stuffy interview room.

'To let him know I'm divorcing him and get him to sign the papers. I don't think it'll come as any surprise.'

'Is now a good time?'

'I've to be back for work in Birmingham three days from now.'

'Who told you he was in custody?'

'Put two 'n' two together, like. After the house explodin,' I figured you'd be roundin' up all the Pakis.'

Upstairs Kate adjusted her headphones and shook her head. She knew that line was stretching the truth. Connolly was likely on a train from London to Holyhead ferry terminal before the explosion occurred. There had to be a specific purpose for her trip. Was it just a family visit or something more sinister? Her anti-surveillance tactics en route to the station pointed to the latter.

'That's not how we operate.'

'Isn't it?'

'No.'

'Can I see my husband?'

'We'll come back to that. Talk to me some more about growing up in Dublin.'

Kate listened impatiently as Jasmine Connolly talked about a happy childhood despite her father dying shortly after Chantal was born. It was clear she had been close to her mother. Hyland was subtle. Kate could see where he was going, forming a bond that might prize the truth from the canny young woman. Finding out whether her marriage was genuine or one of convenience was vital.

The way she told it, the second time around, was that she did not hesitate when the young, attractive Pakistani man asked her to marry him. The problems began within days of leaving the Dublin Registry office. He changed, became domineering and she quickly recognized she had made a huge mistake. All she was looking for was a chance to get her life back.

'When can I see him?'

'We'll get to that. You told me you were raised a Catholic, your mother took you to mass in the Pro-cathedral every Sunday. Did you convert to Islam when Sumbal came on the scene?'

'None of your business.'

'It's a factor relevant to our investigation. Answer the question.'

Connolly pushed back the chair and stood away from the table.

'I'm not puttin' up with this intimidation.'

'You're free to leave any time you wish, Jasmine, but if you walk you won't get to see Faz,' Hyland told her. 'Is that what you want?'

Kate held her breath while the standoff played out.

'Islam's a beautiful religion if you must know.'

The sound of the chair legs scraping the tiled floor told Kate that Connolly was resuming her seat.

'But one that treats women badly.'

'That's a Western view. In the Qur'an, the Prophet, peace be upon him, tells us men and women are equal.'

'Faz is a Muslim and he treated you badly.'

'And are all Catholic men saints?'

'So you have converted to Islam.'

'I'm at peace with the world for the first time in my life.'

'Let's take a break,' Hyland offered. 'I'll get you a drink of water.'

He filled a plastic cup from a corridor dispenser, dropped it on the table in front of her, and exited.

'What do you think,' he asked Kate in the upstairs room.

Kate pointed out how Connolly had lied about her reasons for starting her journey to Ireland. Hyland said he would probe that angle further when he returned. They were in a tiny unused office in a side corridor of the first floor of Manifold Lane station. A sharp knock on the door startled all three.

'What is it?' Hyland shouted.

'Your interpreter's arrived,' came the reply.

'Bring him through and put him in the Inspector's office. Tell him I'll call when I'm ready.'

'It's a her and the Super's office said to remind you that she's on an hourly rate.'

'I know that!' Hyland replied, without bothering to open the door. 'Now where were we?'

They brought him up to speed on everything SIU knew about Rafiq Khouri, his links to 17A Manifold Avenue, and Islamic terrorism. Digger briefed him on their surveillance of Sumbal in recent weeks. Kate told him about the classified intelligence MI5 had shared about their investigation into Connolly in Birmingham and how she seemed embedded with an Islamic group there. MI5 speculated but could not definitively prove the people she stayed with during her time in the city were radicalized. It encapsulated the shifting threat posed by radical Islamic terrorism that had ballooned internationally since the Syrian conflict. Choosing the right suspects to focus attention on was a constant challenge.

An alarm sounded on Hyland's phone.

'Her break is over. Let's see if I can rattle her cage.'

27

Hyland introduced himself to the interpreter en route downstairs. He told her the interview she came to work on was delayed but requested she stay.

Kate put on her headphones and adjusted the volume. As Hyland repeated the interview formalities, Connolly declined to hear the caution again. He reassured her she was free to leave at any time. This was partially true. Kate told him if she walked to let her go. Digger would arrest her immediately she stepped outside the station.

Hyland skillfully walked Jasmine Connolly back over her reasons for coming home. She claimed not to know where her husband resided anymore. They had lived together at 17A Manifold Avenue for a couple of months, but she believed Sumbal moved out shortly after she left. Kate's briefing armed Hyland, he was ready for her lies now. When he constantly tripped her up and pointed out inconsistencies in her answers, she snapped.

'Are ya goin' to let me see me husband, or what?'

'We'll get to that. I've one or two more things I would like to talk about.'

'I'm done talkin.' Let me see him or I'm out of here.'

'One moment,' Hyland said, as he gathered his notes and left.

Upstairs he had a hurried conversation with Kate and Digger.

'Should we go ahead and let her see him?' he asked.

'What's to be gained?' Kate asked.

'Might loosen her tongue.'

'What's the downside?'

'She could pass him a message,' Digger suggested.

'Or vice versa,' Kate added.

'I accept, there's a risk here,' Hyland said. 'If you prefer, I'll just use what she's told me when I'm interrogating Sumbal. Some of it might be useful.'

'No, she's the key player here; he's a foot soldier.'

'Does she speak their lingo?' Digger asked.

'I doubt it, although she has admitted she converted to Islam.'

'If we put the two of them together we should get the interpreter to tune in,' Digger suggested.

'Will she question the ethics?' Kate asked.

'She's here to work on Garda interaction with Sumbal.' Hyland said. 'I'll explain that monitoring the meeting is essential.'

'What custody Sergeant is on duty?' Kate asked.

'Dooley,' Digger replied. 'He's a pure mule! You'll have to talk nice to him.'

Kate rang Sergeant Dooley and requested he come to the Inspector's office. When the barrel-chested, stumpy Sergeant arrived, the interpreter exited and continued her conversation with Vince Hyland in the corridor. Kate outlined what she needed from the Sergeant.

'Jesus Christ! I've two families going at each other in the public office over their dogs fighting. If I give you Sumbal I'll lose one of my guards to escort him.'

'I know you'll do your best,' Kate cajoled.

The blocky sergeant left the office grumbling that he alone would have to keep the peace. Vince Hyland guided the interpreter to the cupboard-like room Digger and Kate occupied and offered her a chair.

'Five minutes,' he told her, as Digger handed her a set of headphones. 'Record everything spoken in your language and alert Superintendent Bowen if anything of concern crops up.'

Digger told his ERU escort seated outside to go for coffee and grab one for Ken James who had stayed with the car in the station yard. As Hyland waited in a downstairs corridor, arguments raged unabated in the public office between the warring families. A Garda threw his eyes skywards as he opened a cell door and beckoned the prisoner forward. Sumbal's face was bruised and his nose sported two white strips of sticking plaster.

'We talk now?' he asked Hyland.

'Turn around, hands behind your back,' the custody Garda ordered.

'So you speak English,' Hyland replied, as handcuffs clicked onto the prisoner's wrists.

'Very little.'

'I've someone who wants to see you first.'

The Garda led the way and as the interview room door opened, Hyland noticed Sumbal bristle when he caught sight of who was waiting for him.

He turned, 'Why is she here?' he whispered.

'Ask her yourself,' Hyland replied. 'Just a few minutes,' he warned the accompanying Garda as he closed the door behind him.

After pushing Sumbal to a sitting position on a chair opposite his wife, the Garda unlocked one cuff and re-attached it to a metal bar on the side of the chair. Sumbal stared at him with contempt.

'In case you go getting any ideas,' the Garda winked and stepped back into a corner of the room.

Connolly asked if he was being well cared for and he replied he had seen a doctor. She mentioned three people from Birmingham who enquired about his wellbeing. Upstairs in the cluttered office, Vince Hyland leaned over the interpreter's shoulder to see the scribbled names. Sumbal was responding with monosyllabic answers to his estranged wife's questions.

Vince shared Kate's headphones as they listened intently.

'Not much love lost there.'

'Hard to believe they were ever married,' Kate replied.

'Let's face Kaaba and pray together,' they heard Jasmine Connolly suggest.

'I cannot kneel,' Sumbal replied.

'Shuffle your chair and bow your head. It's alright, isn't it, Guard?'

'Knock yourselves out!'

'Kabba's the direction of prayer, isn't it?' Kate queried the interpreter.

'Yes. Not always east, as everyone thinks,' the interpreter replied.

The four listened to the chanting, slow at first. Kate found Connolly's fervor alarming and was surprised she seemed to know the prayers better than her husband.

The interpreter jerked suddenly.

'No, no, this is not right; these are prayers for the dying.'

'Oh, Jesus Christ!' Kate shouted, 'she's not fat, she's wearing something. Stay put,' she screamed at Hyland and the alarmed interpreter as she bolted out the door, with Digger in close pursuit.

She raced downstairs and pushed open the interview room door. In an instant, she lashed a kick at Jasmine

Connolly separating her from her husband. It sent her sprawling against a wall and Kate was on her in a flash, trapping her arms behind her back.

'Help me get her out,' she shouted to Digger.

He grabbed her legs as she struggled with the strength of a trapped animal. In the corridor, she unleashed a kick to the side of his head that threw him off balance. Kate's grip slipped under the extra weight and Connolly faced off, hunched over feral-like ready to attack. She gobbed spit in Kate's direction before Digger took her ankles from under her with a well-aimed kick and swept her to the ground. Kate reached out to grab her parka and spin her onto her back.

'Ye's are too late!' Connolly screamed, scrambling underneath the dark blue sweatshirt.

Digger grabbed his Sig.

'Take cover,' Kate screamed as she dived away from Connolly and careered into the stairwell.

Digger dived in the opposite direction, sliding along the floor until he hit a pillar. He was scrambling to get behind it when an ear-splitting explosion ripped through the confined space. The narrow corridor transformed into a lethal alleyway of suicide vest ballbearings laced with shards of breaking glass and filled with dust and smoke. The station's fire alarm clanged into life as a confetti of burning sheets of paper swirled through the air. The ceiling's white tiles shattered and hung suspended, some on live electric wires. An acrid smell pervaded the corridor as screams rose from the public office. The walls, floor, and ceiling were smeared with blood, guts, and brain matter.

In the moments between the explosion and its aftermath, Kate sensed an utter calm, her eyes locked tight; her brain in overdrive protecting her from the grim reality around her. When she blinked her eyelids open and brushed debris from her face, her head ached from colliding with the stairwell in the dive that spared her life. Although fate channeled most of the blast away from her, proximity to the explosion left her hearing severely dulled.

'Digger!' she shrieked.

She scrambled past Jasmine Connolly's grotesque remains, her body torn in half. Kate moved swiftly past the interview room door where the custody Garda was struggling to get Sumbal upright. The solid block wall that separated them from the corridor spared them serious injury, but both were cut and bleeding.

'I'm here,' Digger moaned.

The concrete slab surrounding the high-tensile steel column he took cover behind had shattered in the blast. Kate picked her way through the rubble and cleared concrete chunks off Digger's legs. His eyes were closed and his face pockmarked with lacerations oozing blood.

'Jesus,' he groaned, 'we sure know how to pick them.'

Kate grabbed him in a bear hug.

'Stop, stop,' he yelped, 'My arm's busted.'

'Oh, Christ! Sorry Digger, I'll get help.'

'What a mad cow!'

'Forget about her.'

Kate helped Digger into a sitting position. She undid the belt of her jeans and looped it around his neck to support his damaged arm.

'I'm alright until the medics arrive,' he said. 'Check Sumbal.'

Despite his loud protests, Kate assisted the injured custody Garda in getting Sumbal back to his cell. They knew they could not leave him there for long. The station Inspector raced from his upstairs office along with Vince Hyland. Ken James heard the explosion and bolted inside. Kate ordered him, along with Digger's escort to help extinguish small fires burning along the corridor.

'Take over,' the Inspector requested, handing Kate a bright red extinguisher. 'I need to check on Dooley.'

As he moved toward the public office, the sound of approaching sirens filled the air.

'Get the medics in here first,' she pointed to Digger, 'DI Rooney needs immediate care.'

By early afternoon, blue and white crime scene tape cordoned off the front of the station. A gaggle of media congregated behind an outer cordon and camera crews struggled to get worthwhile shots through the wrought iron railings. Ambulances had departed before they got there and just two fire units remained.

Already a blurred image of the smoke-filled corridor had circulated on social media and been re-broadcast by the mainstream press. The photograph had Kate with her back to the camera, alongside Vince Hyland and Ken James dousing flames with fire extinguishers. She had no idea who snapped it but reckoned the culprit was from either one of the warring families in the public office or emergency services personnel first on the scene.

Sexton and Angie had arrived soon after her call for assistance. Digger was whisked away by paramedics along with the others injured. Angie dashed to a nearby deli and brought back energy drinks and sandwiches. When Kate had tried to eat, overwhelming nausea gripped her as images from the corridor flashed before her eyes. She left the food untouched but downed cans of Red Bull in swift succession.

When told the Commissioner was en route to Manifold Lane, she cleaned the blood and dirt from her hands and face in an upstairs washroom. She welcomed the freezing water on her skin and grimaced as she pulled back on her smoke-suffused clothing. The ringing in her ears ebbed and flowed and her head hurt.

An incident room was set up in the Inspector's office and for the second time, that day Commissioner Fox coordinated a meeting from the head of the table. Two explosions in the capital within twenty-four hours suggested a terrorist organization operating with a free hand. This was not how the government wanted Ireland perceived, a haven for terrorists. Fox needed answers; the independent policing oversight body, GSOC, was already looking over his shoulder, its investigators on site.

Mac sat next to Kate, her clothes smeared in blood, and filthy from dust and smoke. He knew the adrenaline that sustained her in the explosion's immediate aftermath was long gone.

'Kate, I appreciate you staying on duty,' Commissioner Fox opened. 'Walk me through what happened.'

She regurgitated the case history she had delivered at the morning conference and outlined the dynamic situation she was managing throughout the morning.

'All my command decisions were made with the primary goal of protecting lives,' she said.

Commissioner Fox nodded agreement.

'Sumbal has to be part of a bigger plot. Something big enough to trigger Jasmine Connolly's suicidal journey from Birmingham.'

Fox listened, scribbling the occasional note as Kate outlined her contact with MI5. She did not labor the fact of MI5's loss of their target in Birmingham. This was the everyday challenge surveillance teams faced. Emphasizing another agency's failure served no purpose.

Jasmine Connolly had arrived at Manifold Lane Station as a wife seeking to speak with her husband. There was no reason to arrest her and limited powers existed to search her in advance of her brief interaction with her spouse. There was no female Garda available to pat her down. The custody Garda had demanded the laces from her Doc Martins and left them with Sergeant Dooley in the public office. Similarly, she had surrendered the belt from her jeans and emptied her pockets before being allowed into the holding area.

Commissioner Fox accepted confronting a prisoner with his or her partner was common practice, used to persuade a suspect to talk. He had no doubt GSOC would offer a different viewpoint on its efficacy and appropriateness. He enquired about Digger's condition and was told he was undergoing surgery for two broken bones in his arm. His ERU armed guard was with him at the hospital.

'Thank you, Kate,' he concluded. 'Your swift thinking today kept a horrific situation from being a whole lot worse.'

Kate nodded her appreciation.

Mac suggested that while he and Commissioner Fox worked out a narrative with the press officer to satisfy media demands, Kate could take her team back to SIU, re-assess current intel and try to paint a clearer picture of the ongoing threat. At the rear of the station, Kate edged gingerly into the ERU car, Angie tagged along. They exited the rear of the station to avoid the posse of cameras at the front. A lone cameraman clicked furiously as their car sped away.

———

'Jump in the shower,' Angie suggested back at base. 'I'm sure someone will have something to loan you that fits.'

'I've got my suit from this morning. It'll do.'

Kate lingered under the jets of warm water, it soothed her aching body. She had been in this territory often enough to know the pain was both physical and psychological. Although she had been spared injury requiring medical treatment apart from minor cuts and bruises, she had not contemplated the psychological scar. That would show itself when she tried to sleep.

Angie chatted with her while she showered and changed. It helped her clarify the sequence of events that had become a jumble in her head, one scarier than the next.

'Sit, that cut to your head needs a fresh plaster.'

'No need to fuss.'

'The hot water has made it bleed again. You need to get that cut stitched.'

'There's no time.'

Angie stripped off the old plaster and applied a fresh one from a first aid kit.

'I'd get it checked if I were you.'

'What time is it?'

'Seven fifteen.'

'Oh crap, that time already,' Kate replied. 'I need to get to the hospital to see Mum or she'll be asking where I am.'

'What about Mac's orders to work on the case.'

'Jeez, give it rest, will you! I'll ask Ron to keep it ticking over.'

'Sorry, just thinking out loud. Sexton's gone to break the news to Greta Connolly.'

'That will have to do until I get back from the hospital. Meantime I need to eat. Where's that tuna wrap?'

'Ron took it.'

'I'll grab a sandwich on the way to the hospital. Do you want to come along?'

'Wouldn't miss a chance to see your mum giving you a hard time!'

Kate touched her right temple. The thought was already giving her a headache.

When they arrived at the hospital, they ducked into a ladies' loo so Angie could fix Kate's hair. She did her best to conceal the plaster with a wisp of hair near her hairline. When they reached the ward, her mum was sitting on a chair beside the bed wearing a lime green dressing gown and pink slippers. Right off the bat, she quizzed Kate on when she would be getting out of the hospital. Had she spoken to Aidan yet?

Nurses came and went. They doted exceptional care and attention on her mother and Kate was on first name terms with most of them. As if on cue, minutes after they arrived, Aidan Hanrahan popped in to see his 'favorite' patient.

'Angie, can you keep Mum happy while I chat with Aidan?'

'Of course!'

'Walk with me,' he said when they stepped into the corridor.

'Mum wants to know when she's getting home.'

'We'll chat about your mother in a bit. What about you?'

'What *about* me?'

'Kate, I've spent the afternoon in the emergency department helping patch people up as a result of an explosion in Manifold Lane Garda station. Now you show up looking like this.'

'Jeez, you sure know how to make a girl feel great. This is my best suit.'

'Kate, I recognize trauma when I see it.' They had reached the end of the corridor and he was face to face with her now.

'You're cut,' he said, reaching out and raising the lock of brunette hair Angie had clipped into place.

Kate swatted his hand away.

'It's only a scratch.'

'Come with me, I'm going to examine it.'

Before she could object, he led her along a connecting corridor, unlocked his office with a swipe card, and sat Kate on a chair as he switched on a blindingly bright light.

'Now let's see,' he said, as he stripped away the plaster Angie had applied earlier.

'Ouch, twice in an hour.'

'That cut needs a stitch, otherwise, you'll have a permanent scar.'

He requested an ED nurse come to his office and she cleaned the wound as he prepped a suture kit to insert three stitches. He outlined his plans to transfer her mum to a Dundalk nursing home. They hoped to have a bed available in the next few days.

'I've recommended four weeks of recuperation, knowing your mum, she'll be kicking to get out in two,' he smiled. 'The health service will cover the bill.'

'That's incredible. How did you swing that?'

'I might have twisted an arm or two.'

'Can I tell her tonight?'

'Of course!'

As Harahan finished, the nurse collected the waste and departed. He covered his handiwork with a plaster.

'Take that off before you go to bed tonight it will heal quicker.'

Kate squeezed his arm.

'Thank you for everything.'

'Want to talk about what happened today?'

'I can't.'

'I take it this isn't the first time you've encountered a dark situation. You know you need to talk to someone.'

'I'll talk to Doc D'Arcy, she's mum's best friend. She's helped me in the past.'

'Good. When are we going to get that coffee?'

'Do you ever give up?'

'I'd like to get to know you better. Is that so bad?'

Caught off guard, Kate stuttered an elongated nooo as she checked herself in a tiny mirror from her bag.

'Nice work,' she pecked him on the cheek. 'Thank you for putting me back together. I'd better rescue Angie before mum drives her crazy. And I need to eat.'

Back at her mother's bedside, Kate played second fiddle as her mum cooed over dozens of baby photos Angie displayed on her phone.

'I've just talked your mum through how same-sex couples have babies,' Angie laughed.

'Mum!' Kate exclaimed.

'I was curious,' Margaret said. 'And anyway Angie, you'll make a great, ahm, parent.'

When the trio stopped giggling, Kate shared the nursing home news and studied her mother's reaction.

'You're putting me in an old folks' home!'

'Don't be like that, Mum, you should be pleased. It's to give you time to recover. They have 24-hour nursing care there. Exactly what you need until you're strong enough to come home.'

'Are you going to tell me what happened your head?'

Kate sidestepped the question and sat back on the bed. Finally, she dismissed it as just a scratch that Aidan had checked out and everything was fine.

'So your fancy suit is working,' her mum remarked.

Where was the attitude coming from? This was not like her mother. Was it an effect of the stroke or her hospital confinement, Kate wondered? Taken aback, she scolded her for teasing and kissed her goodnight. As she and Angie exited the main entrance, Ken James pointed toward a shiny new seven series BMW parked in the staff parking bay.

'The doc wants a word.'

Kate looked around cautiously and walked to the

gleaming motor. Despite her weariness and need to be else-where, Hanrahan deserved a hearing. The driver's window whirred open and the new car smell hit as she got closer.

'Wow! Good luck with your new wheels.'

'Thank you!'

'You said you needed to eat. I know a place,' Hanrahan beamed. 'Hop in.'

'Can't you see I've got company,' she said, pointing out Angie and her ERU shadow.

'You've got an armed guard! Are you some kind of Garda royalty?'

'Hah!' Kate laughed.

'Bring them along.'

Kate told him tonight was out of the question and waved good-bye with a promise to call the next day. Ken James drove to her favorite Chinese takeaway and she chose a meal-for-four combo. As they drove toward the SIU base savory aromas suffused the armor-plated car and she updated Norrie on their mother's planned recuperation closer to home. She would eat dinner and try to refocus on two cases that combined to threaten her very existence.

28

Earlier the same evening, Sexton had picked his way through empty cardboard boxes as trading for the day wound down on Moore Street. Trade was slack at Greta Connolly's fruit and vegetable stall.

'I need an urgent word, Greta,' Sexton said. 'Get closed up and we'll go.'

'This better be important,' she shook her head.

News of an explosion at a Dublin Garda station spread among the traders hours earlier. Greta was numbed when Sexton broke the news that Jasmine was dead, the central player in causing the blast.

'It has to be mistaken identity, Mr. Sexton,' she said, as he drove her home. 'When I left her this morning, Jaz was sleepin' off the effects traveling all night.'

When they arrived at her city-center home, her sons, Adam and Barry were looking after their little sister. Chantal ran to her mother crying, 'It's not true what they're saying about Jaz, is it Ma?'

'Mr. Sexton says it is. There now, love, calm down and tell me what Jaz did this mornin'?'

The brothers sat either side of an aging Formica-topped table, one beside Greta, and the other with his arm around his little sister. Sexton stood with his back to a kitchen counter. Chantal related the same story she had told Angie earlier in the day.

'Jasmine woke up in a grumpy mood. She just got up and went out,' Chantal sobbed. 'Her phone was dead, so I loaned her mine. I told Angie all this earlier when she called here looking for her phone.'

Heads turned in Sexton's direction and the atmosphere in the kitchen shifted from distress to suspicion.

'It's nothing, Greta,' he said. 'Remember Angie, who was with me when I called here a few days ago.'

Greta nodded.

'She couldn't find her mobile and we were retracing our steps to try and locate it.'

'Phone my arse,' Barry, the eldest son, piped up. 'Youse were lookin' for Jaz; it's that Sumbal bastard's the problem, isn't it.'

Sexton was caught in a bind. The Army corporal was no fool and he needed to tread carefully to keep cooperation working with the family.

'I'll be honest, Mr. Sumbal was arrested last night. We wanted to get a number for Jasmine to talk to her about him. We were as surprised as anyone to find out she had come home.'

'So the other Guard hadn't lost her mobile,' Greta cut in.

Sexton held his hands up.

Circumspect about how much SIU already knew of Jasmine Connolly's affairs, he replied, 'We hoped you might give us Jasmine's number so we could talk to her about Sumbal.'

'Take Chantal into the sitting room, will ye lads,' Greta instructed.

Sexton went over every minute Greta Connolly had

spent with her daughter. Midway through the conversation, her Army corporal son, Barry returned and sat beside his mother. Jasmine had walked in unexpectedly from the early morning ferry, Greta explained. She was already in her kitchen, preparing to head out and pick up the fruit and veg she would sell from her stall during the day. After hugs and kisses, she poured her daughter a cup of tea and quizzed her about how Birmingham was working out for her. Jasmine's answers were vague and snappish. Her mother put the surly attitude down to tiredness and told her daughter to get some rest.

'I love ya, Ma, was the last thing she said to me,' Greta said, tearfully, staring at her hands. 'I don't understand. Why did she go to the Garda station, anyway?'

'Jasmine called to Manifold Lane and asked to speak to her husband. She said she wanted to get him to sign divorce papers or something to that effect,' Sexton explained.

'She told me this morning she was divorcing him, alright. So what happened?'

'You know what a suicide vest is, don't you, Greta?'

'They're the bombs in them Arab countries.'

Sexton nodded. 'It seems Jasmine was wearing one when she died.'

'Oh, Jesus, Mary, and Joseph!' Greta wailed.

Barry threw his arms around his mother to comfort her.

'Oh my God! What possessed her?' Greta sobbed, her son now clasping her shoulder. 'What will the neighbors make of it?'

'Listen, I grew up in Oliver Bond,' Sexton told her. 'Whenever anyone suffered a death in the family, everyone got together to help out. You'll see, it'll be the same for you.'

'Jesus Christ Almighty,' Greta sobbed. 'The wheels are

comin' off. Junior was around town this morning squeezing everyone for money; his knuckles skinned from beatin' people to get cash off them.'

'Shud up, Ma,' Barry advised. 'This lad's a copper.'

Sexton said he would leave the family in peace and call back tomorrow. Barry ushered him into the narrow hallway toward the front door.

'Jaz's phone is charged,' he overheard Chantal tell her mother in the kitchen.

Sexton hesitated, turned, and brushed past Barry before he had a chance to protest.

'I'll need to examine that,' he told Greta as she stared at the blank screen. 'It would be great if I didn't have to get a warrant to seize it.'

'Leave me Ma in peace, will ya,' Barry shot at him.

'I need it,' Sexton insisted.

Greta handed it over and as he prepared to leave, Sexton looked toward Chantal.

'Do you know Jasmine's code?'

'No.'

'Okay, now feck off, will ya?' Barry was growing more irritated by the minute.

Sexton ignored him and focused on Chantal. 'What's your password?'

'One Direction forever.'

'Did Jasmine know that?'

'*Yeah, of course!*'

'I'll be in touch, Greta. Look after your Ma, lads.'

Later, as Kate pushed through SIU's squad room door, Sexton was in the DI's office putting the finishing touches to his report.

'Let's eat,' she said. 'I'm famished.'

In the Cave, Pete McNally turned Jasmine Connolly's phone over in his hands. He knew three unsuccessful attempts to unlock would block it and might even wipe its contents. He came up to the squad room and picked from a generous bag of prawn crackers as he updated everyone on Digger's condition. He was out of surgery; the broken bones in his left arm had been pinned and screwed. He was conscious and had spoken to Jane, who was still at his bedside.

Angie texted him immediately, teasing that he would do anything to get off work, Digger replied with a shot of Sean and Maggie's names on his plaster. Jane had written their names in large careful letters with a Superman logo to reassure her children that their hero dad was strong and would be fine.

When Pete told them he was trying to unlock Connolly's phone Angie asked Sexton, 'What did Chantal say her password was?'

'One Direction forever.'

'And there's a chance Jasmine might use the same?'

'The two sisters were close, shared the same bedroom for years. You know yourself, there's a good chance they might use the same code.'

'*One Direction Forever.* There has to be shorthand for that,' Angie mused. 'Who'd know?'

'Try Digger's Maggie,' Kate suggested.

Seconds after texting Jane, Digger's daughter had given him an instant response—1D43VR, One Direction fans used it all the time. When Pete tapped it into the phone the screen lit up and unveiled a glimpse into the final days of Jasmine Connolly's young life.

There was a slew of texts. A theme ran through them. Their tone made Kate think the texter was male. The messenger exhorted Connolly to carry out a holy task. With her husband alive everything they planned was threatened. Sumbal was reporting increased activity around the Dublin house. Some of it had to be security services or police. They could not risk letting him fall into police hands.

'We know this guy,' Pete held the phone up as he accessed the picture gallery.

The selfie featured Jasmine Connolly's smiling face alongside a black-bearded twenty-something with a red-and-white checkered keffiyeh. Although he posed with a neutral expression, like a pop star bored by his adoring fans, dark dispassionate eyes stared directly into the camera. He seemed at ease with this kind of devotion.

'Abdu al-Farouq aka Freddy Powell from Birmingham,' Kate said when Pete passed the handset. 'He worked with Network Rail there. The Brits believe he's the one delivering the threats in the latest ISIS video.'

'There are lots of pictures of him. Looking at the metadata, they were taken a few months back.'

'Grooming her.'

'Tons of messages last week.'

Pete zapped through the messages that flew between the pair in recent days. It was clear the young woman was in the thrall of al-Farouq and prepared to do his bidding.

'Print them all,' Kate ordered. 'Mac needs to see everything.'

She didn't need to voice the obvious with her team, they were well aware. MI5 already had most of this information, they had held back from sharing it. Even when she dropped her pursuers and came home, Daphne Clarke did not share the knowledge that the young Dublin woman had likely converted to a radical strain of Islam. The only notification of the suspect's travels had been an email in the middle of the night. A standard memo that provided no background intelligence.

Kate was disillusioned, but unsurprised, that MI5

looked on the Irish with disdainful regard. She had naïvely allowed herself to believe Clarke was different. She needed to get the intel to Mac and plot their way forward. The information pointed to a deeper conspiracy in the UK. Was this why MI5 had played it tight? Their target, their prize.

Kate flicked through Sexton's report on his visit to the Connolly household when she went back to her office to call Mac. The call went directly to voicemail suggesting he and Fox were either talking to the Justice Minister or the media. It gave her time for a thorough reading of the report and as usual, Sexton had spared no detail.

'Ron,' she shouted, after reading a paragraph toward the end of the meticulous report.

Sexton pushed her door open.

'What's this about Junior pressing everyone for cash?'

'I've no idea, her son Barry told her to shut up at that moment.'

'Do we know who Junior is?'

'Likely her contraband cigarette supplier. When I called unexpectedly to her place a few days back, I caught Greta and the young one red-handed, packing away a resupply. I ignored it, we have bigger fish to fry. She told me Junior's from the North, but she hadn't seen him in ages. Someone else was doing the runs for him.'

'I wonder is he ex-IRA or plain criminal?'

'Criminal, I'd say, and desperate for money from the sound of it. Greta said his knuckles were skinned from fighting.'

'Old or young?'

'A young lad, according to Greta.'

'Unlikely to be ex-IRA in that case. Is there any chance it's Kevin Stevenson,' Kate thought out loud. 'I'll check it with Alan Tyrell in Enniskillen tomorrow.'

'Let us follow it up. You're shattered; go home and rest.'

'I will when I've talked to Mac but if you have any paracetamol, I'll take a couple. My head's splitting.'

An hour later Kate left Mac's office. He said he would mull over the Connolly messages before contacting the Brits in the morning. They had not fed the Connolly information to the European intelligence center and this gave Mac leverage. Kate touched base with Vince Hyland who told her doctors had ordered overnight rest for Sumbal. They would reassess in the morning whether to allow any interrogation to go ahead.

Back at her apartment Kate brushed the dust off her navy suit before hanging it up. The prospect of Sumbal's interrogation being stalled preyed on her mind. Why did someone want to get rid of him? What did he know that was so important? Any delay in questioning him could be disastrous.

The clock ticked relentlessly toward midnight and beyond to a new day of God knows what. She needed to shower and get some sleep. She dumped her underwear in the laundry basket and was about to turn on the shower when an idea hit her. She pulled on a robe and dialed a number.

'Is it too late for coffee?' she asked Aidan Hanrahan.

'Give me in twenty minutes. Does the rooftop bar at the Tara suit you?'

'Perfect.'

The change of plan meant Kate settled for a splash of cold water. She grabbed fresh underwear, sprayed deodorant, and spritzed Dolce & Gabbana Light Blue on the nape of her neck, its fresh, zesty fragrance instantly revitalizing.

Aidan Hanrahan slid off his seat when Kate walked into the Tara hotel's buffet bar. Midnight was fast approaching and small groups, mainly couples, dotted the room. Most enjoying a nightcap. A tinkling piano background soundtrack in the modern bar seemed combined with subdued lighting to encourage customers toward bed.

Hanrahan asked Kate where she wanted to sit. She chose the counter as it offered reasonable privacy. Kate called for two decafs and thanked him again for tending her forehead earlier. The painkillers he had supplied had lost their edge and the paracetamol Sexton gave her made her nauseous. Tightness around the wound was adding to the throbbing in her temple. The explosion had caused tinnitus that dulled her hearing throughout the afternoon. It seemed to recede in the back and forth of conversation during the earlier debrief but in the tranquility of the late-night bar, a relentless din reverberated in Kate's head.

'You'll feel better after some sleep.'

'Is it that obvious?'

'Trust me I'm a doctor.'

Kate laughed and immediately regretted it.

'Oh, don't make me laugh,' she winced. 'A few hours' rest is my plan. Before that, I need to ask a favor.'

Side by side, the large mirror behind the bar reflected their tired faces. Conspiratorially, Aidan leaned an elbow on the black marble bar and looked directly at her. He listened as she outlined the urgency of removing medical obstacles to questioning Sumbal.

He pulled back, lifted his decaf, and sipped. 'Boy, do I feel stupid? I was looking forward to the prospect of a normal conversation.'

'Sorry, it has to be like this but isn't saving lives a doctor's core motivation?'

'It is, but ethically, I can't poke my nose into another doctor's affairs.'

'What I'm asking could save many lives.'

'Leave it with me, I'll see what I can do,' he sighed. 'Now, can we talk about something else?'

They steered clear of familiar topics like her mother's care, or their work, and zeroed in on what they did for leisure. He was a college champion tennis player and tried to play each weekend. Kate trumped him as a former all-Ireland Ju-Jitsu champion, explaining whenever she got time these days she loved coaching juniors. An hour on, as they parted Kate joked her protection officer was duty-bound to keep her in sight at all times. Smiling, Aidan leaned in and kissed her cheek, with a promise of an early call.

29

The botched bomb attempts in Dublin cost Junior dearly. When the operation failed to kill its intended target the Saor Nua IRA gang meted out a severe punishment beating to Frank Reilly, his trusted sidekick. It took hard graft and more than a few thumps to come up with the money they demanded to let the matter lie. Most of it came from Dublin drug gangs and Junior beat the rest from contraband cigarette sellers.

His hands ached as he drove the rented Mercedes north along the M1 motorway. The previous night, he had ordered a bucket of ice in a Dublin hotel to ease his swollen knuckles.

'Give up this madness,' Reilly implored. 'See what it's costing us.'

Was he beginning to doubt him as a leader, Junior wondered? 'No turning back now, Frank,' he replied. 'The die is cast.'

His trawl of Dublin's underworld had gathered most of the money needed to keep Saor Nua off his back. He would make up the rest. Reilly sat in the passenger seat, sullen and silent for most of the journey. The welts on his bruised face made him look like he had come off worst in a heavyweight fight. He told anyone nosy enough to ask, that he had crashed his car a few days earlier.

The beating had scared off three drivers; they quit instantly on seeing Reilly's swollen face. Junior knew they would struggle to fill the slots immediately. He would take on some extra runs and they could delay others until everything settled.

'We'll offer them fifteen,' he said, as they picked up speed after crossing the Boyne Valley Bridge.

'Jesus, are you mad? They'll do me in.'

'They'll do nothing of the sort. They know what side their bread is buttered on.'

'Junior, I'm serious. Don't mess with these people. I'm lucky to be still above ground.'

'We'll see.'

By the time they crossed the border into Northern Ireland, Junior had relented and said he would make a first and final offer of twenty grand. He told Reilly about the visit from the rugby club president and the increased risk that came with it. He ordered him to tell Saor Nua he needed new drop-off points and to take any added costs from their payoff. His accomplice shifted uncomfortably in his seat.

'That's not the way these boys do business, Junior. When the Dublin bombs missed their targets the heat increased on them. The twenty-five grand is to cover the cost of volunteers having to go on the run.'

'None of them have the contacts we have. Or know the routes like us. So they can feck right off.'

'I'll show you where I want to be buried.'

'Feck sake,' Junior retorted, 'don't be so melodramatic.'

They spent the rest of the journey in brooding silence. Junior knew his mother would not be happy receiving just five thousand. She needed four times that amount to restore the family home her father bequeathed her the previous year. After Grandad Stevenson moved into a full-time care facility for his final two years the place had fallen into disrepair. Neighbors leased the land and to cover the nursing home cost Harriet had to supplement the lease income from the paltry monthly sum Wrollesly allowed her to spend.

A sense of injustice gnawed at Junior. His father's death had gone unpunished; his *real* father, not the one who had tried to force compliance onto a sparky teenager. It was unfinished business from which he could not walk away. When he pushed the Dublin drug gang for more information, they reported both detectives had an armed guard everywhere they went. The woman was the target now; he told them to keep watching.

Kate awoke to the sound of loud knocking on her apartment door the next morning.

'Hang on a moment,' she shouted.

She fumbled for her phone on her bedside locker and stared at its blank screen.

'Oh crap,' she groaned.

She grabbed her dressing gown and pulled it together as she shuffled to the front door.

'I was about to call the caretaker,' Ken James smiled. 'Assistant Commissioner McEnroe wants a word.'

'Come in, Ken,' she gestured, accepting his phone as she closed the door and headed back toward her bedroom. 'You know where the coffeemaker is.'

'How are you this morning?' Mac asked.

'More tired than I thought. I forgot to recharge my phone last night,' Kate replied.

'Do you need to take a day or so to get back on your feet?'

'No, I'll be fine.'

'Good news. Vince commenced Sumbal's interrogation this morning.'

'Brilliant! The medical people cleared it, so.'

'Yeah, Vince told me the registrar had a road to Damascus-like conversion overnight. He was all smiles this morning and talked about not impeding the Garda's important work.'

'Good. I'll be in within the hour. What time is it anyway?'

'Ten o'clock.'

'Ten! Oh my God, why didn't you call Ken earlier?'

'Kate, after what you and Digger endured yesterday, the least you needed was rest.'

She showered and dressed quickly and Ken James handed over a travel mug of fresh coffee at the kitchen door.

'Let's crack on,' she said.

Daphne Clarke was chirpy when, at Mac's request, Kate put through a midday call on a secure conference line. She smiled as her image projected onto the large conference room screen. He and Kate sat side by side, silent while anti-intrusion countermeasures completed their cycle.

'You alright, mate?' Clarke began when the line cleared.

'Kate is fine,' Mac interjected. 'No thanks to you.'

The blunt interruption caught both women off guard.

'Is this the new British attitude to European cohesion against terrorism?' he continued. 'Tear up the agreement before the ink is dry?'

'I'm uncertain how to respond to that outrageous statement, Mr. McEnroe,' Clarke replied.

'*Your* unwillingness to share intelligence, almost cost the lives of an entire station party yesterday,' Mac said

'That's a bit of a stretch.'

'Is it? This morning I shared the intel we gathered from Jasmine Connolly's phone with the European group.'

'I've glanced through it. It looks promising.'

'You've known most of it for weeks and kept it to yourselves.'

'I beg to differ,' Clarke said.

'Is there anything else you're not telling us?' Mac pressed.

'Mr. McEnroe, I think it's best we conclude this call and I get my boss to ring you back.'

'Do that.'

The screen went blank and Kate stared at Mac as he settled into the executive chair behind his desk.

'Was that wise?' she asked.

He waved her protest away.

'At this stage, I don't give a damn.'

Kate was well aware of Mac's fractious relationship with Clarke's predecessor, Peter Symons.

'You had me sit here and watch while you tore strips off Clarke. Will that help?'

'I wanted her to see the result of their irresponsibility.'

'What, I was just a prop that looked like shit?'

'Don't you get it? The only way these people react is when a gun's put to their head. I needed impact and you're living, breathing proof of a highly dangerous situation. Clarke needs to go back to her boss and leave him in no doubt, we're holding MI5's feet to the fire on this one.'

Kate stood and stretched gingerly, deciding to leave Mac grapple with the politics of international policing. She needed to get back to the investigation.

She met Sexton at 51 Manifold Avenue in the afternoon. It was still cordoned off. The pair donned crime scene overalls and pulled on nitrile sterile gloves before approaching. An Army EOD team had cleared the house and a specialist search team was systematically deconstructing the place room by room. Sumbal's kitchen cupboards were searched and emptied, then removed from the wall to check for possible cavity concealment behind. Other team members lifted floorboards and checked underneath.

'Have you examined the attic yet?' Kate asked the sergeant in charge.

'The Army CIS corps was here earlier and the EOD man examined the device we located there. He took a few hours working on it and declared it was a transponder of some sort.'

'Where is it now?'

'Still up there. CIS is sending a communications tech to remove it.'

'So they're satisfied it's not booby-trapped like the other house?'

'They told us it's safe; there's no known device within a range that poses a threat. I wouldn't have my team here otherwise.'

'In case they get ideas about holding onto to whatever that attic device is,' Sexton told the sergeant, 'remind them that it's evidence in a criminal investigation and we've got primacy.'

'Will do, Inspector.'

Angie had parked up in a nearby pub car park while the pair carried out their site visit. As Sexton concluded his briefing with the search team sergeant, she rang Kate to warn that a television news crew was en route to film Garda activity around the house. Neither wanted to feature on the nine o'clock news so they slipped off their overalls in the back garden and gave their names to the Garda at the rear gate.

'Want a dog?' he asked Sexton.

'*What?*'

'The suspect's mutt is tied up over there in the corner. The DSPCA kennels can't take it, they're full. We'll keep it fed while we're here but after that, we'll have to get a vet to put it down.'

'I know someone who might look after it,' Kate interjected.

'Seriously!' Sexton remarked.

'Get the dog. We'll go there next.'

When they drew up in front of Digger's house, his children, Sean and Maggie raced out the front door to greet them. Kate was glad to get the unnamed mutt out of her life. The newspapers she spread on the back seat contained some of the leakage but not the smell from numerous times the dog squirted on their way over.

'She's gorgeous,' the kids yelled.

'Easy now,' Sexton said.'

'Am I supposed to feel safer with that thing around?' Digger laughed, as he sidled along the driveway past his parked car, his right arm suspended in a navy-blue hospital sling.

'You're home!' Kate exclaimed, hugging him. 'Jane kept that quiet.'

When Kate called her to inquire if they would care for the homeless pooch, Jane didn't hesitate. It would be an ideal distraction for the children to help them past their worries about their injured Dad. Maggie took the lead from Sexton and steered the mutt toward the back garden.

'More a licker than a killer, I'm afraid,' Sexton laughed. 'I got it in the mush, twice on the way over,' he added, wiping his cheek.

'Come inside,' Digger invited.

From a distance, he appeared okay, but his face was pockmarked from his close encounter with death twenty-four hours earlier.

'I'll dump the newspapers and follow you in,' Sexton replied.

'First door on the left,' Jane said. 'I'll drop in coffees. How do you take yours?'

'Black, no sugar, thanks.'

Kate was already sitting in a well-worn red leather wingback chair when he pushed the door open. It was obvious photography was Digger's passion. One side of the room had a white Ikea unit packed with camera bags, lenses, and tripods of varying sizes. Shelves were crammed with snap-on attachments and filters. Sexton pulled up a borrowed kitchen chair and looked around the room.

'You're a proper culchie!'

The walls were dotted with photographs, testifying to Digger's rural predilection. While he thrived on the pressure of pursuing human targets in any terrain, he was most at ease waiting out wildlife. Elusive red squirrels, kingfishers darting along riverbanks, and stags at rut in Killarney's national park all featured in stunning images.

'Cozy, all the same,' he added.

'Jane insists on callin' it my den. It's one of the reasons I bought the house. I needed somewhere to store my gear and somewhere I could get a bit of peace.'

'Better keep that dog out.'

'He'll get a root up the backside if he pokes his nose in here.'

The aroma of coffee filled the room as Jane appeared carrying a tray.

'Love the new look!' Kate said.

'Thanks, Kate, he hates my hair short. See, I told you,' she jibbed Digger.

He cast his eyes skyward as he handed out the mugs. 'Don't mention the war.'

'I'll leave you to it,' she said, as she set the tray on the antique desk.

All four corners of the desktop's tan leatherette inlay had come unstuck and curled with age. Kate searched for a spot to put her coffee on it after the first sip.

'Stick it anywhere,' he told her. 'What's the latest?'

'Vince is back in with Sumbal.'

Digger sipped and nodded.

'Good! Anything new on Connolly?'

Sexton updated him on the phone data they had accessed. A vital unknown was where Jasmine Connolly acquired the suicide vest she used. Did she bring it with her from the UK or pick it up when she shook off her tail in Dublin city center.

He grinned when Kate told him that Mac was using the phone intel to bash the Brits for their stingy intelligence sharing. For Digger, assessing the new developments was a break from contemplating his injuries and he soaked up every morsel. He agreed MI5 must have known that al-Farouq was grooming Jasmine Connolly.

'Anythin' further on that Stevenson suspect for the bombs?' he asked.

'There might be but I'm not sure yet,' she replied.

Digger winced as he shifted in his secondhand office chair, listening intently as she repeated what her PSNI mate had passed on concerning Kevin Stevenson AKA Wrollesly. His probable biological link to Sean O'Hare, one of the deadliest foes the unit had ever taken on.

'Ron turned up a nickname with Greta Connolly— Junior,' Kate continued, 'we think might be Stevenson.

224

He's a contraband cigarette supplier who's been throwing his weight around Dublin these past few days.

'Do we know where he was when the bombs were planted?'

'Early days with that lead, we think he was out of the country. Alan Tyrell promised to get me more information. All the same, we need to stay focused on Sumbal.'

Kate was conscious of Digger's discomfort and nodded at Sexton who took the cue. He stood up, collected the cups, and opened the door.

'Remember he needs rest,' Jane called, protectively from the kitchen.

'Take it easy,' Kate said, her hand on his elbow. 'I'll call.'

Sean and Maggie appeared with the dog still on its lead. Its light brown color matched the jaded leatherette on Digger's desk. It sidled forward and licked Sexton's hand as if expecting a return car trip.

'Any name yet?' he asked.

'Lazarus,' Maggie suggested. 'Teacher's telling us about him in school and how he was saved.'

Everyone laughed.

'*Maith an cailín!*[1]' Digger said to Maggie. 'Lazarus sounds great,' he patted the mutt on the head.

30

Digger trudged upstairs after Kate and Sexton left. The anesthetic from the operation to reset his broken arm had floored him. The thump of a heavy motorcycle engine on the street didn't help the hangover-like headache he had struggled to ignore while talking to Kate and Sexton.

As he paused on the landing and used the banister to steady himself, a subliminal wariness aroused. The bike had slowed momentarily, then accelerated away, something might be amiss. He glanced out the window to check if his ERU minders had been quick enough to catch a glimpse. Both were seated in a car, yards from his house, absorbed in their phones.

The night after the attempt to blow up his car, he had installed a relay of cameras around his house. He shuffled into his bedroom and opened the laptop that connected the loop. He replayed the recording and caught one letter and two numbers on the bike's registration plate. The black leathers looked familiar but the yellow lightning flash on the helmet sealed it. He rang Pete McNally immediately.

'Show Angie the footage I'm sendin' you pronto, and have her call me.'

'Howya feelin' me aul' flower?' McNally enquired.

'No time to talk. Show Angie the grab and we'll chat later.'

Angie rang back minutes later and confirmed two things. The bike was identical to the one that ticketed his car with the biblical warning a week earlier. It was linked to a south-side drug gang. The helmet also matched and the rider looked of similar height.

'Warn Kate she likely has a tail. I need to talk to Twomey.'

The two ERU detectives more interested in web surfing than guarding their colleague were instantly replaced. When Twomey learned of their negligence, he hot-footed it to Digger's house and ordered the distracted pair back to their Dublin base. They would surrender weapons and stand down. Their only hope of retention in the unit would be a re-take of the next basic training module to determine if they were worthy of a second chance. Six weeks of hell lay in store.

Kate and Sexton executed counter-surveillance moves on receiving the message. Since the murder of one of SIU detectives by another drug gang, she vowed never to back off such a target again.

Sexton commented after a beat. 'If we keep going around in circles, the guy will just piss off. It'll be rush hour soon.'

'Find us somewhere quiet.'

He looked at her quizzically as she had a hurried conversation with Ken James, outlining how she proposed to deal with the threat. She needed his active participation if they were to take out their pursuer.

'The boss said to keep you safe, nothing else.'

'Ken, help me, or don't help me, you decide.'

'I'm in,' Ken, sighed, double-checking the mag in his Sig Sauer.

Sexton eased away from traffic lights near the Pepper Canister Church, not far from Dublin city center.

'Turning left,' he announced.

'We'll be making a sharp exit, get ready,' Kate said.

Sexton turned slowly and entered a warren of side streets leading toward Merrion Street. He maintained a steady speed enabling him to check the rearview mirror. The bait was taken. As he turned into Stephen's Lane he saw the bike stall at the top of the road, then ease forward after them.

Out of sight, Sexton slowed to a crawl to allow Kate and Ken James to get in position. When they exited the car, he drove around the corner of the narrow lane, out of sight. Their suspect tail duly followed and as he did Ken James advanced from cover to the center of the road.

'Halt and dismount,' he shouted, one hand aloft displaying his Garda identification badge, his Sig Sauer in the other behind his back.

The suspect braked hard and sat upright. He was bigger than Kate had figured, six foot four at a minimum. The suspect glanced behind and to his left, assessing his options. In an instant, he revved the bike and lunged forward. Ken James dodged aside but Sexton reversed hard around the corner, blocking his escape route.

The rider changed tack immediately. He stepped the bike backward to gain space to turn and flee. Kate emerged from a doorway and kicked out hard at the leg the suspect was using to keep the bike upright. She connected below the kneecap. As bike and suspect collapsed in a heap in the center of the road Ken James pounced and knelt on the prisoner's back. The rider struggled and roared as his arms were secured with flexicuffs behind his back.

'Stand him up,' Kate ordered.

Ken James grabbed the suspect's wrists and ordered him to kneel.

'Youse bastards!' he roared, refusing to budge. 'Get me a fuckin' doctor.'

Sexton joined the party.

'You'll need one if you don't move,' he replied, dragging him upright.

'Fuckin' torture, this is.'

'Let's get a proper look at you,' Sexton chuckled.

After flicking the visor and seeing hate-filled eyes staring back at him he made to loosen the strap under his chin. The prisoner lunged a head butt that might have injured Sexton, but Kate saw it coming. She kicked him hard, this time behind the kneecap of his other leg.

'Fuckin Garda brutality, this is! I'll have yer fuckin jobs. Fuckin bastards,' the suspect roared.

'Talkative chappie, aren't you?' Sexton pushed the helmet's visor as he pulled him upright for a second time. 'Let's see how chatty you are at the station.'

'You've fuckin nuttin on me, I'm just going about me business.'

'And what business is that?' Sexton demanded. He had the helmet strap loose now and yanked it off the suspect's head, followed by the black ski mask.

'Mind me fuckin hair, ya bastard,' he blinked.

The suspect's limp shoulder-length straight hair was dyed jet black and tied in a lank greasy ponytail hanging over his biker jacket.

'Obstreperous today! You need to cool it, Dickie. We've got a lot to talk about.'

If taken aback by Sexton's immediate identification, the suspect gave nothing away. As Sexton talked, Ken James unzipped the leathers and commenced searching the prisoner for concealed weapons. There was no weaponry but he extracted the suspect's wallet.

'What's a Dublin man like you doin' in a job like this?' the prisoner snorted indignantly at Sexton.

The DI edged forward, almost on tippy-toes, so he could get in the suspect's face.

'I'm your worst nightmare, Dickie,' he told him. 'I live to put shit like you in jail.'

He handed Kenny back the driving license that confirmed what he already knew; the suspect was Dickie Wallace, an enforcer for a south-side drug gang. When ERU reinforcements arrived, he pushed Wallace's head forward as he dumped him into the rear of the van.

'Youse haven't told me what youse are arresting me for?'

'Assaulting a Garda for starters,' Sexton told him.

'I thought I was being ambushed.'

'Now who would want to do that?'

'Ah fuck off.'

'Enough guff,' Sexton retorted and slammed the door.

'Mind my hair,' came the muffled cry.

He walked back to where Kate was engrossed in a phone call. She broke off the conversation to tell him Vince Hyland had an update on Sumbal's interrogation. She asked him to stick with Wallace; confident he could get something useful if given time alone with him in an interview room.

'It would be better to turn it over to Kelly, the Drug Squad know more about Wallace's gang.'

'Do you mean the same D-Super who bled my budget dry with whims he claimed as solid leads?'

'Wallace is one of their targets and we have bigger fish to fry.'

'He was targeting myself and Digger, so that makes him ours for the next while. See what you can get from him. Have Pete download everything off his phone and call me.'

She switched seats with Sexton and wound through city center rush hour traffic to drop him at the nearby station where Wallace was being processed by the custody sergeant. He hoped to rile the suspect enough in the interview room to get him to spill something worthwhile. Fueled by adrenalin from the action of the arrest, for the first time in days, Kate felt invigorated. She had sent a message to the criminal underworld. Nobody got a free shot at her unit.

She called Digger and thanked him for the heads-up as they drove across town to the main station close to the Elms estate. He sounded re-energized. One of the gang targeting them was identified and under arrest.

'Get some rest. You know we'll keep you in the loop.'

'What about this Junior guy up North? Any chance of getting a tail on him?'

'Andy Tyrell is looking into it for me.'

When she drove into the yard at the rear of the Elms station Vince Hyland was outside smoking a cigarette. The gray, featureless two-story building had been acquired back in the eighties from a bankrupt builder provider when the Elms estate was completed. It was designated a district headquarters with a superintendent and detectives commanding the top floor. Its best feature was the large yard that afforded generous parking. Over the years, sheds had been added for storage, forensic examination of vehicles, and other essential police requirements. The gloomy evening triggered sensors on perimeter lights and in one corner Kate saw the charred remains of her precious BMW.

'Walk with me, Vince.'

'Am I good to grab a cup of coffee?' Ken James asked.

'Sure, Kenny.'

'He should have been a hairdresser with a name like that,' Vince joked as they walked away.

'He's one of the toughest dudes I know.'

'This is yours?' he queried as they reached the blackened wreck.

Kate nodded in reply.

'Do you think Sumbal's mob planted the bomb?'

'I don't know. The EOD man said there was a night-and-day difference between the device that destroyed the house and the one that wrecked my car.'

'What does he mean?'

Pointing to the wreck Kate replied, 'The one that did this was old school. The one in 17A was up-to-the-minute tech.'

'That confirms what Sumbal's said all day. He knows nothing about targeting Irish police.'

'Did you get anything useful from him?'

'Let's go inside and I'll go over what I got. His final break is coming to an end in a few minutes. I'll have you updated by then.'

Vince said the morning with Sumbal had strained every sinew of his patience. He had been reticent about answering anything. He moaned continually and complained that being in a police station the previous day almost got him killed. There was little doubt he was traumatized by events at Manifold Lane station. It was only when Vince talked him around to acknowledging the fact his former comrades wanted him dead that cracks appeared.

Sumbal admitted there had been thirty or more young men, but also women, aroused by the radical Imam's preaching in Birmingham. His world imploded the day he was ordered to move to Dublin.

'Why did he come here?' Kate asked.

'He said Abdu sent him with money and instructions to rent a house.'

'So it's al-Farouq who's calling the shots. That makes sense. Where does Jasmine Connolly fit into the picture?'

'We were getting into that next. It's like pulling teeth, I have to drag every scrap of information out of him.'

'Did he come to Dublin alone?'

'He rented the house and he likely chose Connolly as cover to make him legit. He said two others came later and stayed a few months in the house.'

'That's 17A Manifold Avenue he's talking about?'

'Yes.'

'And what about the other house, number 51, where he was arrested?'

'He was ordered to move out of 17A after Special Branch raided it last year. He says he does not know what it was being used for but he was ordered to keep watch over it. Number 51 was available so he rented it.'

'He's lying saying he doesn't know what it's being used for; my crews clocked his comings and goings there.'

'I'll question him about that next. I agreed with the Registrar to take him to the hospital to be checked out at seven o'clock.'

'Make sure wherever he goes, his ERU escort goes with him,' Kate ordered.

'Sure.'

'Vince, I *mean* it. If Sumbal has to have a rectal examination, I want an ERU man chained to him at the other end.'

'I'll leave nothing to chance,' he grimaced.

'When will you break for the day? You must be tired.'

'I'm okay for a while. I'll keep going and see what gives. Call you later.'

As Kate emerged from the district detective unit office Vince had sequestered, Ken James was waiting. She stalled when her phone buzzed and checked its screen.

'It's Chapman,' she said. 'I better take it.'

Kenny resumed his seat. She spoke briefly, ended the call, and threw the car keys to him as she strode toward him.

'Find me a payphone asap.'

'That'll be a challenge.'

'Shopping centers still have them.'

Why? Kate thought as they sought out the nearest payphone, why the off books call? '*Call me at the place we ate breakfast,*' Chapman had asked. This wasn't the guy she thought she knew. He wasn't into the intrigue of international security cooperation like Cody O'Neill. She had to look up the Paris café online to find its number. When she got through to him, the Secret Service man's cryptic message mystified her—the *non-essential staff at the Paris U.S. embassy were being teed up for emergency evacuation.* What lay behind such a decision?

'Why tell me like this?' she asked.

'No questions, Kate.'

'Why tell me then? Is it connected to my case?'

'No questions.'

Kate hung up with an uneasy feeling, unsure what to make of all the cloak and dagger.

31

She drove directly to Beaumont Hospital to check on her mother when the call ended. Aidan Hanrahan met her as she used a hand sanitizer station in the foyer. He was heading home at the end of a day that started hours before hers.

'Hi, you're looking refreshed,' he smiled.

'Refreshed! That's all you've got?'

The remark threw him, but he recovered quickly.

'As good as I've got after 12 hours non-stop between wards.'

'How's Mum doing?'

'Haven't you talked to Nora?'

'You can call her Norrie, we all do. We haven't spoken yet. Busy day.'

'We're sending Margaret to Brackenhill Nursing Home, outside Dundalk tomorrow morning. Everything's arranged.'

'Brackenhill's a nice place. Is she happy?'

'To be honest, I think she's apprehensive, you'll need to reassure her.'

'Thanks so much for all you've done for her.'

'My pleasure. Have a good night!'

The automatic doors slid open as Hanrahan hit the doormat but he paused and turned back.

'Pointless asking if you'd like to eat later, I suppose.'

'I'd love to, but it'll be a while before I can call it quits.'

'I don't mind eating late. Do you know the Blackboard?'

'My friend Betty and I go there all the time.'

'Say ten o'clock; I'll get the owner to squeeze us in.'

Us, Kate thought. Maybe.

Her visit with her mother was fraught; Margaret Bowen was sulky. She scolded Kate for not visiting earlier and was furious that she had to read about Digger in the newspaper. For the umpteenth time, she ripped into Kate for not confiding in her about work.

Kate steered the conversation to her mother's imminent move closer to home. Aidan was right, she was nervous about it. Were her daughters planning to pawn her off into a care home? Did they expect that at only sixty-five she would spend the rest of her life there?

Kate told her she had spoken to Mr. Hanrahan about her condition. He was impressed with her progress and saw no reason why she would not make a full recovery to independence. After twenty minutes of verbal jousting, Kate kissed her mum goodbye and said she had to run.

'Oh for God's sake, you're always rushing,' was her mother's parting shot.

Junior stashed the money wrested from their southern clientele in a safe at the company office in Newry and called off the meeting with the gang. He ignored the gang's demand for sterling; he would pay euros instead.

The next day he counted the stash into bundles, five

thousand euros in each. He placed three in a brown paper bag and stuffed another bundle inside his zipped leather jacket. He threw the remaining five thousand back into the safe, locked it, and jumped into the Mercedes with Reilly.

As it hummed along twisting country roads Junior repeated that he would not dance to someone else's tune. Frank Reilly worried that the face-to-face with Saor Nua might turn nasty. As they switched off the main road he told Junior to slow down and guided him through Armagh city's hinterland toward their rendezvous. They wound their way along tight byroads where spring ditches spilled a fresh growth of thorny brambles toward the roadway.

'This car better not get scratched,' Junior joked, trying to lighten the mood. 'I wouldn't want to lose my deposit.'

Reilly said nothing.

'Remember, our opening gambit is fifteen.'

'Don't rile these boys,' Reilly warned. 'They're sore enough as it is with killing the wrong target.'

'How did that even happen? Huh! How the fuck could we have known a hospital porter would end up driving the bitch's car?'

'I've no idea.'

'These guys have nothing going that gives them near the income I put their way. Whatever else they are, they're not stupid enough to shoot themselves in the foot. They'll want to keep a good thing going. Maybe I need to knock some sense into them.'

'They're not stupid, hey. They know more pressure is comin' from the cops and they don't want to do jail.'

'If they weren't sloppy in the first place, they'd have nothing to worry about.'

'Jesus, don't say that when we meet them. Slow down for God's sake, there's a turn comin' up.'

They wheeled left and a text message from Reilly's

phone drew an instant response. 'The place is half a mile further on,' he told Junior.

As they rounded a corner they saw a sliding gate slowly retract. Junior sped onto the concrete slab between a dwelling house and outhouses and spun the car around for the exit. The red gate had galvanized sheeting screwed to its frame blocking any view from the road. As it cranked shut Reilly received a text ordering him to the last shed in a run of outhouses that looked like they had never been used for agriculture. This place was a farmyard in name only.

Junior grabbed the bag from underneath his seat and unlocked his door.

'They want me on my own,' Reilly warned.

'Fuck that, the money goes nowhere without me.'

'We'll just get in and out fast. Don't you go losing your rag.'

'You know me,' Junior winked. 'Mr. Cool!'

When the shed door pushed open it revealed a four-man group. Junior was unfazed by their military fatigues and black balaclavas. They were a rag-bag collection of shapes and sizes. From giveaway short, about five foot one or two, to distinctly portly. Only their spokesman conveyed anything close to a menacing presence.

'You never learn, do you, Frankie?' he said as he beckoned Reilly forward. 'We told you to come on your own.'

The portly one aimed a kick at Reilly's legs, but Junior deflected it with one of his own. It sent the overweight assailant sprawling. Seconds later, he heard a click as the midget jabbed a pistol into his right temple, hammer cocked.

'I insisted I come along,' Junior said. 'Can we stop messing around and get down to business.'

'You're gettin' to be more trouble than you're worth,' the leader told him.

'What do you say, Frank stays here while we do the talking?'

'In the house,' he beckoned.

'Be nice to him now, boys, won't you?' Junior grinned.

Fifteen minutes later, the pair walked from the farmhouse, the leader carrying the bag with the cash.

'No more fuck-ups,' he warned, as the yard gate cranked open.

Junior beckoned Reilly toward the Mercedes. They walked calmly to the car and Junior inched it through the gate. As he watched it slide shut in the rearview mirror he whooped triumphantly.

'He took fifteen grand, no argument. You've been reading these boys all wrong.'

'I don't believe you.'

'I'm telling you.'

'That fucker's not soft. What did you tell him?'

'I told him he'd have to earn the other five grand.'

'Jesus Christ, you're crazy. You've made him look bad in front of his men.'

'Will you whisht, man. He'll get the rest of his money when he gets me what I need.'

'What is it this time?'

'A weapon. I'll do what needs doin' myself.'

———

When Kate met Mac for a late evening debrief, they had plenty to catch up on. Sexton had succeeded in convincing a judge that Dickie Wallace's behavior bore strong indicators the suspect was part of an organized crime group, worthy of further investigation. The judge rubber-stamped an extra twenty-four-hour detention. Word was out of Wallace's arrest. Kate dodged calls from an irate drug squad superintendent wanting to take over the case.

She told Mac about Zach Chapman's call concerning the brewing evacuation of all non-essential U.S. embassy staff in Paris. Those concerned were on standby for a swift departure. Kate had no idea what had prompted this move and Chapman had not been prepared to discuss it further.

Mac relayed the frenzy of activity his barbed exchange with Daphne Clarke had provoked. An afternoon conference call had been hastily arranged with the head of MI5. Their reticence to share intelligence promptly was left unexplained. The organization head outlined MI5 evaluations of possible targets based on the data harvested from Jasmine Connolly's phone weeks earlier.

Al-Farouq had worked extensively with Network Rail before dropping out of sight. The crew he worked with maintained lines that ran from Birmingham toward Manchester and further north to Preston and Carlisle. Possible targets along that route were being evaluated. Sellafield nuclear reprocessing plant was located on a spur off the main northern route along the Cumbrian coastline. However, National Rail crews maintained this line and al-Farouq worked for Network Rail. Nonetheless, security re-evaluations continued at all vital installations.

There was no indication of what the major strike threatened in the earlier video would be or where it would take place. They worried about Sumbal's admission to Vince Hyland that he had relocated to Dublin on Abdu al-Farouq's orders. It meant Ireland was woven into whatever plot was being hatched.

MI5 finally shared insights into the radicalized Birmingham group. At 19, Connolly was the youngest, the remainder were in their mid-twenties or older. Seven had died in the Syrian conflict. Three female radicals had volunteered to enter de-radicalization programs and provided a full account of their ISIS activities in return for repatriation. A further five were being detained while consideration was given to withdrawing their British citizenship. That left upward of 10 male converts unaccounted for; MI5 worried that all were potential terrorists. Their families had been interviewed. All insisted they had not heard from their sons for months.

'We'll need a full report from Vince today,' Mac said. 'Sumbal must be able to account for some of them.'

'Have you any thoughts on why the Americans would pull their embassy people out of France?' Kate segued.

'Not really, my feeling is the Brits are not telling us everything.'

'We've got to find out what they don't want us to know.'

'If you manage that, the gin and tonics are on me.'

She left his office at nine-thirty, leaving her no time to shower before meeting Aidan. After a mad dash across the city, she changed into a white blouse and black jeans. When Kate suggested the night shift detective wait at the apartment, he countered that there was no way in hell he would even consider it. Later, as she and Aidan Hanrahan shared a chef's plate of antipasti, he sipped coffee at a corner table.

'Will this be forever?' he nodded toward the armed guard, as he sampled a white wine.

'He's with me until we find out who planted the bomb under my car.'

They changed the subject and chatted about theater.

'Ruth Negga was amazing as Hamlet last year,' Aidan said.

'Missed it,' Kate replied. 'It was on in The Gate, wasn't it?'

'Yep! What did you see last?' he asked, steepling his fingers.

'I haven't been to the theater in ages. The last thing was a revival of Dancing at Lughnasa in the Abbey,' Kate replied, tugging her right ear. It reminded her that she had forgotten to pop in her diamond studs.

'Let's make that our first proper date, then,' he leaned forward and took her hand. 'Let's go to the theater.'

Kate blushed, caught off guard initially but smiled at his wide and easy grin.

'Let's do that.'

They sipped decaf espressos rather than desert and the chef came to their table to ensure everything had been okay. They chatted a while but it was obvious he was anxious to close up. Moments later Kate and Aidan bumped heads as both moved toward the restroom area at the same time. Aidan turned and smiled.

'Can your shadow see around corners?'

Kate smiled. Like a teenager at her first disco, butterflies hit her tummy. She hadn't felt this way in a long time. They kissed passionately; a sweet, lingering moment of tenderness.

'I'll check out theater listings tomorrow,' Aidan laughed.

32

As dawn filtered through her bedroom curtains the next morning, she lay in bed savoring the semi-conscious moments of bliss before logic took over and commanded reality took center stage. She cherished the secret kiss. It rekindled a longing for the elusive feeling of happiness ever-present in her early childhood. She smiled, her eyes closed, recalling her grandfather's stories as they tramped in the dew-laden pastures of late August picking fresh mushrooms in the early morning. This was the light the fairies liked Grandad told her, as the wee folk scampered home after a night's mischief. Her eager young eyes always scoured the ditches to see them but never caught a glimpse. At 6:05 her alarm broke the spell and she tumbled from the warm bed toward her wet room for a wake-up shower.

Kate arrived at SIU at 7:15. Late the previous night Pete McNally had extracted a message thread from Dickie Wallace's Encrochat phone. The fresh intel changed the picture on the value of detaining Wallace further. Sexton questioned him until eleven o'clock and charged him with obstructing a peace officer in the course of his duty. The custody sergeant released him on station bail and Wallace flipped the bird at the station as he roared out of the yard, his motorcycle and ego dented.

The message thread linked him to a suspicious furniture consignment that had left the port of Belem in Brazil four weeks earlier. When Sexton tracked down the twenty-foot container, it was still in transit. By the time Kate arrived at SIU, he had reinstated the stalled Dublin port operation to cover its expected arrival later that day.

Kate needed neither the distraction of taking on a drug investigation or a turf war. She touched base with Detective Superintendent Richard Kelly, the attention-seeking drug squad boss whose case Sexton had re-ignited. He had inveigled SIU support for his operation weeks earlier with intel that a Southside gang was putting a major drug deal together. Digger's detection of Wallace's motorbike tracking Kate was the first major break.

His vanity irritated Kate and she brushed off complaints that valuable time had been lost by her reluctance to pass the case to him the previous evening. Drug squad detectives had identified the consignee company at a rented warehouse on Dublin's south side. Established four months earlier, the firm's warehouse lay unused in the same period.

'This is it,' Kelly excitedly told Kate.

'The cocaine consignment you said was due weeks ago?'

'My intel is spot-on.'

'My overtime budget is shot playing your waiting game.'

The cargo had reached the UK's busiest container port in Felixstowe two days' prior and had been transferred by road to a smaller one on Britain's north-west coast. It was being shipped to Dublin on another freight vessel that left Heysham at midnight. The nine-hour crossing afforded the time to get surveillance crews re-positioned.

'My crew will stay in the background while SIU tails the container to wherever it's dropped,' Kelly said. 'We'll take over from there. We'll do the bust.'

'You're welcome,' Kate replied.

She went to the squad room where Angie was updating crew allocations on whiteboards. She wrote #8 alongside the Dublin port operation.

'You're chirpy this morning,' she said.

'Not a sin, is it?' Kate replied.

'Just saying. Don't get your knickers in a twist!'

'I'm happy Mum's going to be closer to home from today.'

'Will you miss the dreamy doc?'

'Who?'

'Oh come on! I saw the way you looked at him.'

'Look, I've to get to Mac's morning meeting. Where's Kenny?'

'I heard you snogged!'

Kate groaned.

'Dish,' Angie whispered. 'What's he like?'

'He's nice. Now I've got to go.'

Mac was brewing espresso from the coffee machine in the corridor as Kate entered the Assistant Commissioner's suite. 'None for me, thanks,' she replied to his offer. Instead, she pulled a paper cup from the water cooler and filled it before following him to his office.

'Bring me up to speed on Sumbal,' he said.

She went through his interrogation. Vince Hyland had exhausted forty-eight hours of the seven-day custody period granted by a judge. Sumbal was still a mystery. Was he a soft touch on the periphery or central to the plot? Why had there been an attempt to eliminate him? The interrogation was a battle of wills. Sumbal gave minimal responses, and Vince believed a primal fear was locking in critical intelligence.

Mac had passed a report from Army communications expert, Captain Myra Jennings, to the European intelligence network. She had taken the transponders located in both houses on Manifold Avenue apart. One had been adapted to trigger a bomb if disturbed. Their core function was to pinpoint the location of aircraft in flight or vessels at sea. Programmed to transmit a coded signal when pinged, transponder units operated over thousands of miles.

'Any speculation on why ISIS might use transponders?' Kate asked.

'The Europeans haven't commented and the Brits have stated the obvious that there's a strong possibility ISIS have an attack either by air or sea at an advanced stage of planning.'

'Cody O'Neill and the FBI speculated that Rafiq Khouri might be running comms for ISIS in Syria.'

'Do you think this might be Khouri's work?'

'I don't know. After O'Neill mentioned it, I double-checked our surveillance reports for his time in Dublin last year. I found no gaps in our coverage that would have allowed him to do much outside of work and PlayStation.'

'Do we have anyone on the books we could target?'

'All known suspects from Khouri's network are in custody. Vince is going to show Sumbal the morgue photo of O'Driscoll's tout today. It might get him gabbing.'

'Is there anything else?'

'Sexton is getting a name for the friend who tipped Greta Connolly off about the callers to 17A Manifold Avenue days before she went there. We need to interview that witness.'

'Okay. Brief me in the afternoon; the Justice Minister is going to pressure us until this is over.'

Kate met Sexton at a control point he had established in a disused warehouse parking lot on the port perimeter. It was familiar territory for her, she had spent her early Garda years chasing tearaways off such premises as they picked at the decaying bones of the near-derelict buildings. The area was undergoing a 21st-century transformation as high-tech firms flooded in to occupy the glass tower blocks that replaced defunct warehouses. High-rise, high-price apartment blocks had been built to meet urgent housing demand.

The live feed on a monitor in the control van focused on a dockside crane offloading the freighter. Kate watched it as Sexton briefed her.

'Any idea when they'll get to Wallace's container?'

'Joe Forde says they're quick. He observed them operate for a couple of weeks last time the drug squad believed the container was due.'

'What happens when the container is offloaded?'

'It's placed on a waiting truck and heads for customs control. They check the paperwork and may select the load to pass through the mobile cargo scanner.'

'Kelly hasn't alerted Customs, has he?'

'I put him off the idea. If Wallace has an inside track, it might be there. We'll have to take our chances.'

Kate nodded in agreement and pointed to the screen as the crane operator smoothly swung a container from the ferry onto a waiting transporter.

'Where is that going?'

'It's entrepot trade—containers stored at Dublin port for transshipment onwards, USA, most likely. Customs don't touch them. There's a big Panamax due tomorrow. It'll probably go on that.'

'And what is a Panamax?'

'A ship that can sail through the Panama Canal. I only know that because the harbormaster gave me a tour when we started the op. He likes to yap and I'm a good listener.'

Kate smiled as Sexton focused on the repetitive forward and backward movement of the crane. As usual, he was leaving little to chance.

'I need Greta Connolly's pal interviewed.'

'Straight away?'

'I know the last thing you want to do is trade control of a live operation for an interview room with a bewildered witness but it's urgent.'

'I could ring Greta and get her mate to call into the Elms station to give a statement,' Sexton said. 'Angie could talk to her.'

Kate needed the witness interviewed without delay but her instinct was to allow him to continue directing the live operation.

'We'll get it sorted.'

'I'll call Greta now.'

Kate manned the monitor while Sexton made the call. She watched, fascinated, as the crane operator skillfully picked up cargo containers like pieces of Lego. The crane's spreader lowered slowly and locked onto each container's corner castings. On one lift Kate watched the operator deftly raise three containers in one movement.

'Okay Greta, thanks,' she overheard Sexton in the background. 'By the way when is Jasmine's funeral?'

Kate was conflicted. Days earlier, Greta Connolly's daughter had injured Digger in an attempt to kill them both. Yet she felt only sympathy for a mother who had lost her daughter. Sexton scribbled the date and time for the funeral mass before ending his call.

'Greta tells me the witness's name is Nancy Marnell and she's given me her contact number.'

'Perfect.'

'In fact, Nancy was over with her last night.'

'And?'

'She thinks the two who called to 17A weeks ago were the same two in the photo Greta has of Jasmine with Sumbal and his mates.'

Sexton scrolled through the picture gallery on his phone and showed Kate the photograph he had snapped on one of his visits to the Connolly flat.

'Special Branch arrested this one with Khouri. I can't recall his name offhand; I've no idea who the other guy is.'

'Okay, so we know one of them but don't know where he is. Send me another copy, will you?'

'Done. Are you sure it's okay for Angie to interview this witness?'

'You stick with this, I'll make arrangements.'

'Thanks, boss.'

Kate watched a roll-on, roll-off ferry execute an inch-perfect docking further along the quay.

'Any idea if the ships here use transponders for tracking at sea?'

'The harbormaster will tell you.'

'Okay. You know the drill. If anything changes here, let me know immediately.'

As they drove toward the Elms station Kate was silent. She usually chatted with Ken James between destinations. Today was different. The information linking the visit by Khouri's associates to 17A Manifold Avenue weeks before the house was destroyed, triggered a tsunami of new possibilities.

Had Sumbal armed the device? Digger's cameras caught him transferring data to it days after two suspects called to the house. The place had been searched on two separate occasions by different Garda teams and no bomb had been discovered. It seemed logical that Sumbal's associates had planted it. The EOD report confirmed that disconnecting the device from its power source had armed the deadly IED and started the countdown clock. If a Garda search party had come across it in a routine search, it would have wiped them out.

Vince Hyland's interrogation of Sumbal had developed a clearer picture of his family background and upbringing. The gruesome image of the remains of his associate only elicited the comment that many were martyred in the Holy Jihad. When Vince pointed out that his associate had been drowned like an animal, probably by people he thought were friends, the only visible reaction was a shoulder shrug. The prisoner was due back at the hospital for a check-up at two o'clock. Vince intended ratcheting the pressure in the afternoon. Forty years imprisonment was facing Sumbal for the murder of Army Sergeant Daly.

When Nancy Marnell called to the station hatch at one-thirty, Vince rang Kate.

'Sumbal is gone to the hospital under escort for his medical check-up,' he explained. 'I'm free, do you want me to have a word with her?'

Kate jumped at the opportunity, it spared her having to drag Angie away from base. Nancy Marnell was an unknown quantity but if anyone could get something useful from her if was Vince.

As Kate drove back to SIU, Angie called her. Dublin port's harbormaster had clarified how shipping traffic was tracked. In recent years, VMS, or vessel monitoring system had replaced the old automatic identification system that a ship's captain could switch off and on if he perceived a threat, such as pirates. The AIS system had also proven vulnerable to hacking. The new VMS was contained in the cone-shaped antenna visible on the wheelhouse of many boats and wired to a locked transceiver and the ship's control panel. The harbormaster explained that synthetic aperture radar mounted in satellites could detect a vessel's position regardless of the weather. It seemed to Kate that if ISIS was planning a seaborne attack, keeping it under wraps would be nigh-on impossible.

33

In her office, Kate pressed play on her copy of the Jan Krause video viewed at the Berlin conference. It seemed a lifetime since she first heard al-Farouq threaten to reduce Europe's transport infrastructure to shambles. Was that a real threat or was the ISIS target a city? She viewed him with renewed horror. This monster brainwashed a naïve Irish teenager to sacrifice herself for his cause.

He might be the brains behind the group operating in Ireland and if so, he was capable of killing anyone who stood in his way. Rafiq Khouri could be part of the plot. Kate could not rule it out. No European security service had identified a cohesive group or plan and the obese coding genius was in the wind.

Kate re-evaluated everything she knew in the case. She read the intelligence snippets contributed from around the EU. It was a collection of disparate sightings and meetings of ISIS suspects or persons of interest. Frustrated, she called the senior officer investigating the Ben Gordon murder hoping for something that might fill in the blanks.

To most people, D-Superintendent Fergus Baker was the classic murder investigator; every action measured, nothing left to chance. Kate knew another side of his makeup. Baker was an alcoholic who had not touched a drop of the hard stuff in twelve years. They had served together at Pearse Street station. When she arrived, she had looked up to the senior Garda on her unit. He had ten years' experience under his belt and a gift for solving crime when he applied his mind to it.

However, when he turned in to work after a week-long bender and belligerently insisted on pulling on a uniform, Baker's sergeant put his star man into a patrol car and drove him to a rehab clinic. His counseling sessions began after weeks of drying out and the station sergeant recruited Kate to join him in confronting Baker regarding the impact his drinking had on colleagues. It took a push from her mother to go through with it but she was glad she had played a part in getting her senior colleague on the road to sobriety.

Baker's determination that his recovery would stick grew with each promotion through the ranks. Although the Hugo Boss suits he favored hinted at a 21st-century image, his short-back-and-sides haircut was old school. His investigations mirrored his style: no excess, everything carefully calibrated. Detectives on his team learned quickly not to arrive at his case conferences with any loose ends.

'Any breaks with the Gordon case, Fergie?' Kate asked.

'Slow as hell,' he replied, 'but we have a pair of Estonian guns-for-hire in the frame. We're working on locating them.'

Ben Gordon had been shot as he exited his office car park. The Estonian pair were suspects in three other European murder investigations stretching back five years. In two cases investigators believed the surviving spouse paid to have their loved one murdered.

'That information shifted our focus toward the victim's personal life,' Baker explained.

Staff at Gordon's company told interviewing detectives that they suspected he was having an affair with the personal assistant he had brought from the U.S. head office. When confronted with the information, the P.A. acknowledged it, insisting that Gordon loved her and had vowed to leave his wife. The new lead put Gordon's wife, Lilith, firmly in the spotlight and the trail led to California.

'I'm just back from three days with the San Francisco police,' Baker said.

Kate remembered seeing press photos of an elegant woman, dressed in black, arriving at the company's Dublin offices the day after the killing. The media reported a remarkably stoic woman whose references to her deceased husband were curt and confined to his professional life. She reassured staff that their jobs were secure and a new CEO would be appointed without delay.

'I have to swear you to secrecy on the next piece of the puzzle,' he continued.

Lilith Gordon's family trust fund had bankrolled her husband's tech start-up. Shortly after coming to Dublin and with Lilith's consent, Ben repaid the loan. The contract exchanged with her trust fund lawyers included an unusual clause that she would assume control should her husband leave the business.

'I get the feeling there's more,' Kate said.

'A lot more.'

Baker explained that an insurance pay-out provided additional motivation for Mrs. Gordon to want rid of her straying spouse. Like most U.S. businesses sending key staff to Europe, Gordon's company had taken out a substantial life insurance policy to protect their investment. Along with another policy on the mortgage for their San Francisco mansion, she stood to gain a $10 million windfall from his death. This circumstantial evidence did nothing to connect the grieving widow to the unidentified gunmen. Baker figured his only hope of breaking the case was to track them down.

'Thanks for the update, Fergie.'

'Good to catch up, Kate.'

What she heard convinced her there was unlikely to be any link between Khouri and Gordon's murder. The timing was likely coincidental with the worst night of terrorist violence Europe had experienced in decades. The tangled leads led nowhere. There was no escaping the fact Khouri had been arrested at 17A Manifold Avenue, an address since wiped off the map. While she ruled Khouri out of the Gordon murder case, she retained his name on the whiteboard tying together intelligence strands linked to 17A Manifold Avenue.

Sexton's number flashed up.

'The container's on the move,' he told her.

'Is anyone shepherding it?'

'Would you believe it? That arrogant prick Wallace couldn't stay away. He's tailing it, two cars back.'

'Don't let him get under your skin. We can't be certain there are drugs on board. It might be a dry run.'

'Wallace's presence makes me think it's the real deal. When the driver drops the trailer, we'll let him go and wait out Wallace's next move.'

'When they go to ground, hold Kelly back. Don't let him jump too soon. Give Wallace and Co. time to open the container and start offloading.'

'I'll do my best; will keep you posted.'

Kate analyzed Jasmine Connolly's links to the lethal threat that almost sucker-punched her. MI5 had been tracking her, yet dragged their feet on offering a complete profile of her involvement. Zach Chapman's furtive call suggested that between them, the Brits and Americans were holding back something else.

Before she could change her mind, she dialed the U.S. embassy in Paris. She waited to be connected to Chapman's office, not proud of what she was about to do. When pushed into a corner, her instinct was to come out fighting. She hoped the bond forged in their near-death skirmish on the Paris ring road would take the strain.

'Kate, you caught me,' Chapman answered. 'I was about to shoot through. What are you up to?'

'Zach, If I'm honest, I'm running blind. Hard to see the wood for the trees on the subject we discussed in Berlin. Have you seen the intel from the European group?'

'Berlin sends me a daily email. It's bollocks.'

'I'm glad someone else thinks so. Are you picking up anything under the radar?'

He hesitated.

'Nothing to get excited about.'

'I'm hearing you've activated an evacuation protocol for non-essential staff. You must have a hell of a good reason for that, huh?'

'No comment.'

Kate winced. She could not back down now, she had to force it. Had she chosen the right approach? Embassy calls were recorded and she had likely put huge pressure on Chapman. She hoped he would take the hint and respond.

When Chapman offered no response, Kate changed tack and briefed him on her investigation into the Dublin explosions. The ISIS timeline for planned attacks was likely disrupted by Jasmine Connolly's mission failure and Sumbal's arrest but they could not be certain of that or take it for granted.

'Is there going to be another group meeting?' Chapman enquired.

'None I've heard of. Have you seen Cody today?'

'We had coffee together half an hour ago.'

'Is he free?'

'I'll check. By the way, did you get to the bottom of those threats?' Chapman asked.

'Some progress; I'll fill you in next time we meet.'

'Glad to hear it, Kate. I'll put you through to Cody.'

Kate's conversation with O'Neill was brief and professional. She updated him on the direction the murder investigation was going without revealing the sensitive information Baker had ring-fenced.

'Coming over to talk to the murder squad at this stage would be pointless,' she continued.

'So you figure Khouri is out the picture?'

'Are you telling me he's not?'

'I didn't say that. Chapman's our point man on the European group but the FBI holds intelligence relating to plots.'

'Is there something you're not saying?'

'I'm saying there's something to be gained from Assistant Commissioner McEnroe, you and I having a face-to-face.'

'I'll mention it to Mac.'

'How is your mother?'

'Doing well, thanks. She moved to a nursing home yesterday to recuperate.'

'I'm glad to hear she's doing well; I know caring for an ailing parent is hard work.'

'We'll be fine.'

Kate had lifted the phone to call Mac when she received a text telling her to call a familiar Paris number before five o'clock, French time. She raced to the lift and pressed the button for the basement car park. Ken James took off in pursuit, pushed the doors open, and squeezed in.

'Jeez, Super, you freaked me out.'

'Sorry Kenny, I just need a payphone, fast.'

'I'll find you one.'

They ditched the car in a sprawling shopping center car park and swiftly hunted down a payphone. Mothers strolling with children paid little heed to the couple running up the escalator toward the top floor. Kate had rifled all of Kenny's loose change en route and keyed in the number.

'Are you trying to get me fired, Kate?' Chapman demanded. 'I thought we trusted each other.'

'You big boys must think we're stupid in Ireland or you just don't care. Either way, we're the ones in the firing line.'

'I went out on a limb for you and you've thrown it back in my face. You don't know what happened in Dublin has any connection to what's happening elsewhere.'

'Why the hell are you prepping your people to leave?'

There was static on the line.

'I'm almost out of change here can you call me back?'

No response.

'Please, Zach.'

'All I'll say is, it's about exposure. Think rays and particles.'

'*What?*'

Kate pressed her forehead against the wall as the line went dead. Had she managed to burn the only person offering her insight? She liked Zach and respected his loyalty to his service. She had no clue what he was talking about but knew something was brewing. Something Western powers wanted to keep quiet.

Back at base, she was surprised to see a familiar face sitting with Angie in the squad room.

'Digger, what the…? You're not certified to return to work yet. How did you even get here?'

'Guilty!' Angie admitted.

'I needed a camera to plug a gap in the coverage around my house and Angie swung by.'

'So how are you, anyway? And why are you scrutinizing the case boards?'

'I'm fine, I'll be back on my feet in no time.'

'Jane better not blame me for you being in work,' Kate said.

'No chance. She's glad to have me out of the house for a while,' he joked.

'Has she taken time off work to look after you?'

'Until the day after tomorrow.'

'Come into my office, we better get you back home asap.'

Angie closed the door when all three were inside. Digger's mood was brighter and he was moving more freely than the previous day. His face was still pockmarked raw from the explosion.

'I hear Sexton is getting to finish the juicy port op.'

'What's the latest with it, anyway?' Kate asked Angie.

'The truck just dropped the trailer to a warehouse the gang rented a few months ago,' Angie replied. 'Sexton allowed the driver to leave, unchallenged.'

'What about Wallace?'

'He tailed off before the trailer reached the warehouse. He has done a drive-by since. It's a waiting game.'

Kate leaned back in Mac's old chair and looked out the window as leaves on nearby trees agitated in a stiffening breeze.

'We're supposed to be grappling with a gigantic ISIS plot but we're running around after drug dealers.'

She outlined the confrontational approach she had taken with Chapman.

259

'Ouch!' Digger winced. 'Could be terminal for any relationship you were tryin' to cultivate there.'

'Any idea what the hell he's trying to say—*it's all about exposure, rays, and particles.*'

'Sounds like some kind of nuclear threat to me,' Digger said.

'Nuclear?'

'Remember Chernobyl? Do you think if a western government suspects a radiation exposure risk, they'll allow it to go out on Sky News? No way! They'll keep it tighter than a duck's arse.'

'Radiation?' Kate said. 'Surely someone would tell us.'

'Maybe someone just has.'

Angie butted in. 'If the non-essential staff at the American embassy in Paris are on standby to get out fast, that means the threat is either in France or within range of it.'

'The Brits' stinginess about intelligence sharin' points the finger in their direction,' Digger said.

'Is there any way we can find out if American embassy staff in London are on standby too?' Kate asked.

'I know our London liaison guy,' Angie said. 'He might know something or at least he could dig around.'

'Do it,' Kate said.

Angie's fingers fluttered out a rapid text message, asking the London Garda Liaison Officer if he had heard whispers.

'Where do we fit in?' Kate pondered. 'We have neither nuclear energy plants nor nuclear weapons on the island of Ireland.'

'Sumbal is the key to the whole thing.'

'Digger, please go home and get some rest before Jane starts ringing me.'

'Give me something to keep me busy.'

'I'll sleep on it and call you tomorrow.'

Angie and Digger left Kate to consider her next

move. Guilt gnawed, and she called Norrie to enquire how their mother had settled in at Brackenhill. Kate had not been able to visit the nursing home yet. Norrie was on a visit and assured Kate the place was lovely and everyone was treating their mother better than the Queen. Before handing the phone to their mother, she switched to a face-to-face call. An unrelenting interrogation followed before Kate finally ended the call with a promise to get in to see her as soon as possible. By that stage, her mother had berated her for not letting her know how Digger was progressing. Her final barb was to tell her that she needed to use a better moisturizer as she looked washed out.

Vince Hyland was next on Kate's list, but he beat her to the punch, calling as she tossed her personal phone into her shoulder bag.

'Sumbal's interrogation's suspended.'

'Why?'

'He had to be admitted to the hospital.'

'Did he take a turn for the worst?'

'You could say that.'

'*What* happened?'

'Sumbal informed his ERU minder he needed to use the toilet and the detective set out to accompany him as instructed.'

'My precise orders.'

'Then, a nurse intervened. This *Florence Nightingale* insisted the prisoner deserved the same dignity as any other patient.'

'We're well aware of that,' Kate said. 'Other patients are entitled to expect protection from the likes of Sumbal too. For God's sake! What happened?'

'Let's just say, it didn't go well. I don't know where Sumbal reckoned he would escape to, but he came out from the toilet brandishing a pair of syringes he had retrieved from a Sharps bin, one in each hand, threatening to stab anyone who intervened.'

'No!'

'Yes, but he didn't get far, the ERU man dropped him with a straight left. Sumbal hit his head on a trolley on the way down and lights out. The doctor treating him said there's no chance I'll get near him until tomorrow at the earliest. I'm going home to rest.'

Kate groaned.

'What about Nancy Marnell? Did you get anything useful from her?'

'I'll email her statement. Chat tomorrow.'

Kate closed her eyes and tried to process the myriad of clues and angles this case had developed. She felt utterly drained.

34

Kate held an end-of-day meeting in Mac's office to discuss known intelligence. He told her to get Cody O'Neill over to Dublin the next day, the short notice might encourage him to be more forthright. The unsanctioned clues from Chapman could not be factored into any threat assessment for the Justice Minister who hounded the Commissioner's office for hourly situation reports.

When she was done, she traveled with Angie to the control van Sexton was using for the operation against Wallace's gang.

'We're in good shape here. Wallace is being smart, biding his time.'

'Angie's staying with you overnight?'

'Yep. I'll kip on the floor for a few hours.'

'Keep me up to speed.'

Kate sat in the front passenger seat as Kenny drove to her apartment. He handed over to the night shift. She considered inviting Aidan Hanrahan around for supper, but exhaustion hit the moment she closed her front door and deadbolted it. As she caught her reflection in the hall mirror, her mother's earlier acerbic comment on her jaded look sealed her decision. She poured ice-cold sparkling water and savored its effervescence. If she ran a bath she would surely fall asleep and settled for a quick shower. Wrapped in an oversized robe, a gift too good to toss from an old boyfriend, she settled into her brown leather couch and switched on Sky News.

It was too late for dinner so she settled for crackers and cheese. As she sipped her drink she noticed Hanrahan had sent a text message inquiring about her day. They tapped a flurry of texts back and forth as she wound down. Unsure of her feelings for him, she signed off her final text with an 'x' and killed the television news.

Early the next morning in his Enniskillen office, Superintendent Alan Tyrell read the support request from the UK National Crime Agency. The agency had been operating in Northern Ireland for three years and muscled in as the lead against economic and organized crime that crossed international borders. Local detectives were adjusting to the takeover.

He had spent a brief blissful spell the previous evening boating on Lough Erne with his wife, Marissa, and their six-month-old daughter. Marissa needed to get out of the house, but the humid evening brought the midges out early. They were on the water for just an hour when he had to turn the cruiser toward shore. The midnight and 4 a.m. feed left Tyrell yawning as he turned the pages of a briefing document.

The crime agency intended to carry out raids in the next forty-eight hours. Their target was Kevin Wrollesly aka Stevenson. It explained why he had received a muted reaction to his request for a surveillance operation on the suspect. The agency needed ten of his men on standby as back-up for the raids. The briefing document on the suspect gave little away and Tyrell read into its sparse detail that the agency was protecting an informant.

He was alarmed at how the greenhorn criminal had built a multi-million-pound operation in such a short time. Sources spread throughout Europe into Bulgaria and onwards to Turkey supplied him with a reliable stream of drugs and contraband cigarettes. It appeared Stevenson had rapidly constructed a dependable supply chain from a handful of contacts Sean O'Hare had given him. Tyrell scheduled an eleven o'clock meeting with two of his inspectors to allocate the resources that would temporarily drain his district. He placed the agency request in a tray reserved for open projects, yawned and stretched.

A gnawing need for his first cigarette of the day hit and he slipped on his grey overcoat before heading downstairs to the station yard. He had promised Marissa he would give them up now they had a wee one, just not today. He fished his phone from his pocket and dialed Kate's number. She stifled a yawn as she answered the call.

'So we've both had late nights?'

'Hi Alan, it's been non-stop here the last few days.'

'You've more exciting reasons for being whacked, I reckon.'

Kate laughed. 'How's Junior?'

Her overworked brain blanked out the child's name that she knew Tyrell had shared.

'Now it's funny you should say that. Marissa and Ava are fine, but Junior's a name you'll be interested in.'

'It's not Kevin Stevenson, is it?"

'The very man Kevin Wrollesly aka Stevenson. How did you know?"

'The name came up just recently. I meant to call to see if you had any joy getting surveillance going on him.'

'No joy there but here, something you should know is that we're raiding him in the next forty-eight hours.'

'You must have something good to go on.'

'Not me I'm afraid, the national crime agency is leading the charge.'

'Any chance you could let me know when he's in custody?'

'It'll be my pleasure. Keep it to yourself for now.'

'Thanks for the heads-up.'

Something nagged Kate but she could not put her finger on it. Surveillance instinct, an itch seasoned officers get as cases progress, had been richly nurtured by her vast experience. She double-checked her resources, worried they were stretched too thin. Eight of her crew were still immersed in a drug bust that smelled like it was going stale. Sexton reported nothing had moved overnight. Scraps of intel that usually coalesced into a coherent picture remained disparate.

She missed being able to bounce theories off Digger and fidgeted with paperwork as she waited for Vince Hyland to resume the Sumbal interrogation. She had shared the story of his attempted escape with Hanrahan who promised to do his best to ensure the prisoner could not hide behind a medical excuse to avoid further questioning. An extra detective was added to his escort detail and Sumbal was en route to the Elms station by midday. Armed with Nancy Marnell's testimony, Vince Hyland was waiting, hoping to prime Sumbal into talking.

Kate read the statement one more time. Nancy Marnell had needed little coaxing and surprised them with the level of detail she provided. She explained to Hyland how she had seen men at the Manifold Avenue address a few days before her friend called to 17A to collect her daughter's belongings. She was keeping an eye on the place for Greta who had asked her to warn her if she thought the house was being re-let so she could go and retrieve Jasmine's things.

Nancy's afternoons were spent watching television from a comfortable armchair of her front room. Game shows started when the lunchtime news ended and mid-afternoon nature programs filled in the time until the soaps came on after the six o'clock news. She hated having her routine disturbed.

However, when she noticed the white van arrive outside 17A, she immediately took an interest. She watched the driver go to the van's back door where he was joined by his passenger. Nancy wasn't surprised both looked Middle Eastern, she knew Jasmine Connolly had made the mistake of marrying a fella like that.

The driver reached in and pulled out a black toolbox from the body of the van. Then he stood back while his passenger lifted out a wooden box before closing the rear doors and locking them. He had a key to open the front door and by the time they emerged, Nancy had used her stairlift to get to her bedroom for a better view. It enabled her to write down the van's registration before the rental drove off. She said the whole thing had taken about half an hour because she had missed that day's entire episode of *Countdown*.

Pete McNally tracked the rental company and roused a branch manager to recover CCTV. He retrieved clear images of the driver as he filled out paperwork in the company's reception. He picked up the second suspect when he checked a car park camera. Even though the outdoor images were not as crisp, as he climbed into the passenger seat during the handover, Kate confirmed his identity as Sadiq Zardari. When Special Branch arrested him months back,

Cody O'Neill provided solid background information on him. American forces had detained Zardari in Afghanistan around 2009. He was one of the hundreds that U.S. marines held as they pushed the Taliban back into Helmand province. After two weeks of detention and basic interrogation, he was classified as not worth further investigation and released. Nothing had cropped up concerning him with any friendly intelligence service until his Special Branch arrest.

It was likely the pair in the footage planted the device underneath the copper heating cylinder that destroyed the property. It pointed to a well-funded militant group active in the capital working to a carefully crafted plan.

She copied the CCTV footage to Zach Chapman, requesting assistance in identifying the driver. Since the Americans had identified Zardari, Kate hoped they might be able to identify this guy too. She walked to the case board and added Nancy Marnell's invaluable information. She placed a headshot of Zardari and his unknown accomplice on the board. She linked both to 17A, along with the date and time they had called there.

She updated Mac and left him to pass the news to Commissioner Fox and the edgy Justice Minister. Zardari was an experienced fighter and since American intelligence had identified him, she invited Chapman to share the reported sightings in Ireland with the 27-country European group and MI5. Kate's mind was in turmoil. She was hemmed in by unknowns and sucking up to Chapman to get their working relationship back on track. Her stake in the game had risen.

Junior drove his mother to her father's old house on the other side of Caledon village. Her pleading tone forced him into making the trip. He felt guilty that, as months went by, and his cash flow increased by multiples, he had not gifted her sufficient money to make the house she grew up in, habitable again. Having to pay thousands to the Saor Nua group had put his plans back by months.

'You know the boss is at me to sell this place,' his mother told him.

'He's rotten when it comes to money, you know that.'

'He is, aye.'

'But he might be right about selling.'

'What do ye mean?'

'Sell it off to hell and use the money to buy yourself somewhere nice and cozy. Get away from him like you want.'

His mother shot him a look that killed conversation for the rest of the trip. When they opened the back door into the kitchen the smell of must was overpowering. Junior slid open the top panel of the narrow sash window that faced onto the farmyard.

'Do the same in the parlor, will ye?' his mother asked.

'You haven't answered me. Why not sell the place and buy something nicer?'

His mother said nothing as she walked ahead of him in the short hallway. The two front rooms at the end were locked. She used a key to open the one on the right and as the door swung open, she sighed.

'God, I loved playing here as a child. Get the windows open there, good lad.'

Junior never shared his mother's sentimentality for the place. Dust covered everything. An oak fire-surround framed the open grate and a dark-brown mantel completed the nineteenth-century tableau.

'Mother, stop avoiding.'

'Son, you don't understand, part of me died when I left

here. Having you, loving you, and minding you was what kept me going.'

Junior saw tears slip down his mother's cheek and walked over to comfort her.

'It'll be alright, Mother. Let's walk down the field and check the shed down there. The fresh air will do us good.'

They walked along the headland of the fields now rented to a neighbor, along with the barn. Junior pulled its sliding door open effortlessly.

'They're maintaining it well.'

Deep in thought, his mother didn't reply. She walked around the empty bay, loose straw scattered from bales drawn to the bay next door for bedding cattle. Junior put his arm around his mother's shoulder and drew her close.

'We'll get you away from him, don't worry.'

Back at the disused farmyard, he helped his mother climb into the passenger seat of the truck and guided it gingerly out the narrow gates. He had other places he needed to be; to make the trip worthwhile he had scheduled a pick-up from one of his legitimate customers.

'Let's go to the pub and grab a sandwich,' he suggested.

'Righto.'

His phone beeped an incoming message before they turned onto the main road and he checked its screen. The office number flashed and he almost ignored it until he read the first words the software captured as a headline— *police with a warrant...* As he dropped the phone on the seat beside him his mother glanced at its screen. He covered it with a jacket.

'Mother, lunch is off, I'm afraid,' he said, as he revved onto the main highway.

'Is there trouble?' she asked as the truck picked up speed along the narrow country road. 'Can you at least drop me home?'

'I'm rushing, maybe a neighbor might do it.'

'No neighbor around here would offer me a lift.'

Junior took a long look in his rearview mirror as he approached a crossroads. He carefully scanned the other three roads for police cars as he slid a fifty-pound note across the dashboard to his mother.

'Take a taxi from the post office in the village,' he said, 'It's the best I can do, I have to run.'

'You're leaving me in the lurch,' she sighed.

'It's not like that,' Junior said.

'Men are never done tormenting me.'

'Come now, Mother, don't be morose. Jimmy the taxi will welcome the fare.'

'Go on about your business, son. You know I love you.'

The village was approaching and Junior feared a police checkpoint might be waiting for him. He was preoccupied, scanning the byroads from his elevated viewpoint in the truck as he swerved into a public car park.

'I love you too, Mother,' he said. 'Take care now.'

35

Kate checked updates from the European intel group. Were al-Farouq's video threats hollow words or had recent events in Dublin disrupted his plans? Daphne Clarke had finally received clearance to share an MI5 intelligence package on Jasmine Connolly. The information share ended with a curt sentence outlining Connolly's death in Dublin. A separate intel snippet outlined how the UK Marine Accident Investigation Branch was scrutinizing a cargo ship that had dropped anchor at Douglas in the Isle of Man following an outbreak of sickness on board. When Kate noticed Heysham as the ferry's final destination, she called Sexton.

'All quiet with the container?'

'Dead as a dormouse.'

'What was the name of the ferry that container came off?'

'The *MV Liverpool.*'

'The Brits are reporting that the same ship is moored at the Isle of Man right now and the crew is sick.'

'What's that about?'

'I've no idea but I'm sure as hell going to find out.'

'I'll advise Kelly.'

'Tell him not to go near the container until we get further information.'

Daphne Clarke explained that she had included the report of a sickness outbreak on the ship in case it drew media attention. MI5 did not want other intelligence services speculating unnecessarily on the nature of the problem. There was no additional information, but given the unique connection Kate's crew had to cargo from that vessel, she promised to contact the Marine Accident Investigation Branch and seek further data.

Kate passed the clarification to Sexton and added that she was meeting FBI liaison, O'Neill for lunch but would be contactable at all times. Mac ducked out of lunch at the last minute so it would just be the two of them. She went to the women's locker room and changed into her navy suit. She adjusted the shoulder pads and leaned toward the mirror to finish off her token make-up. Using a tissue to blot her lips, she put the finishing touches to the *Nude* lipstick she had carefully applied. Their brief, intense relationship was in the past but she was edgy about once more sharing a lunch table with Cody O'Neill.

He chose a restaurant close to Dublin's American embassy. For Kate, it meant negotiating snarled city center traffic. She spoke to the maitre d' and glanced casually around until her lunch companion's enthusiastic wave caught her attention. O'Neill had the best table in the house; the restaurant valued the embassy as their prime customer.

Kate dodged busy waiters in the crowded bistro as O'Neill watched, smiling, from the secluded corner. He greeted her with a peck on each cheek. The amber musk of his aftershave, rich and honey-like, impulsively made her close her eyes and smile. As always, he dressed to impress. A navy-blue suit, white shirt, and gray tie combined perfectly with black shoes polished to a high sheen. She accepted a prosecco aperitif and apologized for Mac's absence as they perused the menu.

'How is your Mom today?'

'She's good, the nursing home staff are fantastic.'

Kate did not tell him her only contact had been a hurried text with Norrie before work. It was almost two days since they had spoken face-to-face, and guilt bugged her.

'So, what are you holding back from us?' Kate asked immediately after they ordered lunch.

'How about we keep business for Mr. McEnroe's office. Kate?' he replied. How are you holding up?'

'Overworked as usual. You?'

'Looking forward to Caitlin coming over. It will be great to have her in Paris the whole summer. I hope she likes it,' he said, stroking his dimpled chin.

'I'm sure it will be nice.'

'To better times,' he lifted his glass.

She clinked and listened without interruption while he regaled her with tales of the legendary status her name gained with each re-telling of the Paris attack. That day had receded in her memory, overtaken by more recent deadly events.

Although lunch passed quickly, conversation flagged as dessert plates were cleared and coffee served.

'Have you heard about that UK cargo ship's crew coming down sick?' Kate asked.

'I haven't had a chance to check my mail in a couple of hours.'

Kate filled him in, outlining how she had a crew watching a container that had come off the *MV Liverpool* the previous day.

'Do we know what type of bug the crew caught?' he asked.

'I've heard nothing further. Daphne Clarke is checking it out.'

'Daphne's good people.'

Kate fiddled with her coffee spoon and glanced around. An uneasy feeling gripped her. Was she being watched? She checked each waiter out as they exited the kitchen into the bistro. Nothing suspicious. She excused herself and walked slowly to the restroom. Nothing showed in either direction.

'There's *something* you're not telling us?' she said, as she resumed her seat.

He remained deadpan, taking time to formulate an answer. Probably the lawyer in him, Kate imagined.

'I'm sorry Kate, you've lost me,' he finally said.

'Don't bullshit me. Holding back intel almost got myself and Digger killed.'

'Don't put that on us.'

'What are you big boys not sharing?'

O'Neill leaned his elbows on the immaculately white linen cloth draped over their small circular table and places his hand over hers.

'From the get-go, I loved that you never held back.'

Kate snapped her hand away.

'I d-didn't mean…' he stuttered. 'You know I mean our professional communication has always been open and friendly.'

'You're deliberately muddying the waters.'

O'Neill changed tack. 'About channels of communication, you should have sent that footage of Zardari and the unknown to me rather than Chapman.'

'He's your point man on the European group. I knew you would see it eventually.'

'The FBI is the lead intelligence agency, I told you as much yesterday.'

Kate looked away.

'Hey, let's not sweat the small stuff,' he continued, 'when we get to Mac's office I'll tell you what I know.'

'Fine, I'll get the bill.'

'Lunch is on me.'

'You're our guest!'

'I insist,' O'Neill said, placing four fifty euro notes on the side plate. He didn't wait for change.

Junior drove cautiously outside Caledon village. If the police were raiding his office, he reckoned it would not be long before they showed up at Wrollesly's place. He called Frank Reilly's number as he drove and punched the roof of the cab in frustration when the call did not connect.

Their backup plan, should the police come knocking, was to scoot across the border and link up there. He needed to keep moving and the safest place was outside the jurisdiction. The border was five miles away; ten minutes' driving on the main road would have him safely across but if he stayed on the A28 the police might have a checkpoint in place to trap him.

Close to panic, he drove hard, away from the border. The route brought him back toward Caledon. He slowed to the thirty-mile an hour limit as he entered, relieved not to meet either of the two taxis that served the village. He ignored a friendly wave from a neighbor used to his comings and goings as he swerved onto the Derrycourtney road. He drove from memory, veering left for Glasslough after a few meters onto the narrower by-road. The rig straddled its entire surface and Junior checked his rearview mirror for anything in pursuit. He drove cautiously, knowing that he needed to get out of the rig with his company name emblazoned across the front.

The bridge over the Blackwater river marked a crossing point into the rolling hills of Monaghan. Rays of sunshine filtered through banks of black clouds to the west throwing a sparkle onto its fast-flowing surface. Junior whooped as he maneuvered the truck over the narrow bridge and across the line.

He welcomed the dense cover that forests either side of the road afforded his flight from the law. The farmers who owned the land had long since given up trying to scratch a living from its stony, gray soil. The wet, infertile, and exposed sites provided perfect growing conditions for Sitka Spruce and other non-native conifers. When the government offered incentives to plant trees, many jumped at the opportunity.

The truck's tires squelched as he veered off the paved road onto the track that led to a clearing. Showers of gravel sprayed the surviving trees as he spun around and switched off. A huge swathe of trees had been harvested from the forest edge skirting the road ahead and the clearing that had previously been hidden from view was now opened up.

The big engine's growl died with a shudder and peace returned to the forest. Junior tried Reilly again but got no reply. He mulled over the details of their backup plan in his head. Grab as much cash as possible and meet at Moll's Roadhouse in Dundalk. The £5,000 he had stashed in the office safe was now a hostage to fortune. Paranoia nipped at his psyche. He hesitated over the handset deciding which contact to call to swop his truck for another set of wheels and a wedge of cash.

He rested his head on the steering wheel. If the police were raiding his offices, they were tracking his phone. He switched it off, pulled out the SIM, and dumped it out the window. With any luck, the phone had stayed connected to network towers in the North before he killed it. The pungent aroma from the remaining conifers hit him as he jumped from the cab. The earthy fragrance did nothing to calm him as he paced the muddy clearing trying to think straight.

A knot of nervous energy, as he climbed back into the cab his boot clipped something that skidded across the floor. Junior swore and leaned to retrieve it. He came up gripping a rugged smartphone, the burner he had used to check in with Reilly from Bulgaria. It might prove a life-saver. The phone's blank screen worried him until he scrambled underneath the driver's seat and found its charger. He drummed his fingers on the dash and chewed on an energy bar until it powered up and he made his first call. He called his mother next to check that she had gotten home safe. There was no reply. He dialed Wrollesly's land-line and his sister answered.

'Maud, is Mother home?'

'She's with you, isn't she?'

'No, I dropped her in the village and gave her money for a taxi.'

'Why did you do that?'

'Something came up and I had to run.'

'Kevin, Daddy's out in the yard talking to police. What's that about?'

'How would I know? Look get me the number for Jimmy the taxi, will ya. I'll check that she's on her way.'

'Kevin, I'm scared.'

'Don't be. Everything's going to work out.'

Jimmy the taxi's wife told Junior that his mother had indeed booked a taxi with them. The destination concerned him.

'Where did he pick her up?' he asked.

'Outside the hardware.'

'And you're certain it was her father's place she went to, not home to Wrollesleys.'

'No doubt at all, son, wanted a while in her home place, was what she said.'

Junior hung up mystified. He would have to change his wheels before he could venture back across the border to check out what was going on with his mother.

36

While Kate shared an awkward lunch with Cody O'Neill, Ron Sexton's crew punched in another tedious hour staking out the warehouse on the stop-start drugs case that was draining SIU's budget.

Her phone rang as Mac greeted Cody O'Neill and invited him into his office.

'It's Ron! I better take it,' she said, hanging back in the corridor.

Sexton asked, 'Have the Brits given us any further intel on that ship?'

'Give them a chance, I only sought further information an hour ago.'

'Someone better get their finger out. One of Wallace's gang has just driven by the container warehouse. We need a decision; go or no-go for hitting it if he goes in.'

'I'll call you back immediately.'

The lack of information regarding what caused the ship crew's illness presented a dilemma. Detectives opening a container offloaded from the vessel would be exposed to an unquantified risk. Also, courts would take a dim view if criminals were knowingly allowed to approach it, without intervention.

'Can I have a private word?' Kate asked when she returned to Mac's office. His reaction surprised her.

'We're all friends here. Grab a seat.' Hesitantly, Kate sat into a leather armchair.

'Can we hit that container if the gang approach it or should we back off until we hear from Daphne Clarke?' she asked.

'Stay away from it,' O'Neill intervened.

Kate and Mac looked at him in surprise. His normally inscrutable face could not mask an obvious concern.

'I mean, I would stall if I were you.'

'For God's sake, give us something,' Kate said.

'I can't tell you what I don't know for sure.'

'Is it a nerve agent attack similar to Salisbury? Is that what's going on; the superpowers playing spy games?'

'Not that I'm aware.'

'What is it then? Non-essential staff has been drifting away from your London embassy. Why?'

'Who told you that?'

The UK Garda liaison officer had told Angie it would be inadvisable to make a direct approach to determine whether non-essential staff were getting out of London. Instead, on a late afternoon, he went to the Horse and Groom, a regular haunt for embassy staff and a good place to meet and greet or simply observe. He chit-chatted with contacts and looked out for the usual faces. By the time he left he knew seven regulars were prepping to go on 'home leave.' He told Angie that in his experience, allowing seven consular staff to take holidays at the same time was unheard of.

'Are you going to query everything I say? I need to tell Ron to back off or not.'

'Could I get a glass of water?' O'Neill coughed.

'I'll order Ron to keep everyone back from that bloody container, just in case,' Kate said.

As Mac walked to his drinks cabinet, she made the call to Sexton ordering him to keep his distance from the target. Mac broke the seal on a bottle of sparkling water and passed it across the coffee table to the FBI man, along with a Waterford crystal tumbler. O'Neill twisted the cap and poured the entire bottle. Kate and Mac waited patiently as he sipped and pushed back on the couch. Was he playing for time—hoping events would spare him an awkward discussion?

'ISIS longs for the capability to set off a dirty bomb in a major western city,' he began. 'The FBI worried when I picked up ripples that the Brits were sitting on information that their nuclear security had been compromised.'

Mac shook his head.

'None of this has been shared with Europe,' he said. 'The Brits are playing with fire.'

'When I mentioned the rumor to them, they flat out denied it.'

Kate and Mac exchanged glances.

'We trust our allies and understand their need to avoid public panic at all costs,' O'Neill continued.

'So?' Kate asked.

'We reached out again and offered our help. The information that came back surprised us—a potential radiation hazard. A batch of re-processed nuclear fuel that's unaccounted for.'

'That's *unbelievable*,' Kate said.

'A breach of this nature won't weaponize ISIS with nuclear capability, but a chaotic dispersal of radioactive material via a conventional explosive device would be hugely destructive to a major city.'

'How destructive?' Mac asked.

'We're talking about huge evacuations and potentially large parts of a city being made uninhabitable for years.'

'Like Chernobyl?' Kate asked.

'Not on that scale, but who's going to buy real estate in a city that's suffered major radiation exposure.'

'So it would create chaos, many thousands made homeless,' Kate said. 'Just like ISIS threatened.'

O'Neill laid out the facts as he knew them. Used nuclear fuel only exhausts part of its potential energy by the time it is removed from reactors. The British and French nuclear industry reprocesses it, a practice due to end since uranium became widely available. The U.S. decided it would never reprocess or recycle spent nuclear fuel.

'Britain makes billions by accepting spent nuclear fuel from around the world, reprocessing it and storing it,' Kate said. 'They've been doing it for over twenty years.'

'And doing it safely,' O'Neill replied. 'There have been no reported radiation leaks in over 7,000 shipments world-wide since 1970.'

Kate and Mac said nothing, unsure where the conversation was headed.

'You're aware of the thermal process at Sellafield that reduces the spent fuel to granules?'

'THORP,' Mac answered. 'I read somewhere it's due to be shut down.'

'A group from the embassy was shown how it's done. It's highly impressive. They bury the re-processed granules in sealed containers on-site under multiple feet of concrete. The nuclear fuel is incredible. Even though its job is done, it retains energy and emits heat strong enough to radiate through several feet of concrete.'

'Okay. So, what went wrong?' Kate asked.

'An audit of the expected outcome from a processing run was considerably underweight,' O'Neill outlined. 'A supervisor caught it the day after it occurred. The temperature on the incident increased when a staff member from the shift could not be contacted.'

'And the Brits sat on this at a time when ISIS launched its most deadly strikes in Europe and threatened a city or the continent's transport infrastructure? Incredible!'

'You must understand, Kate, this would constitute a big loss of face internationally for Britain. Hard to blame them for trying to keep a lid on it.'

'What about the threat to citizens wherever this damn stuff ends up?'

O'Neill did not reply. Kate's phone interrupted the heated discussion.

'I better take this, it's Ron,' she said, as she slipped into the corridor.

'The lid's come off,' she said when she returned moments later. 'The harbormaster just told Sexton that Isle of Man authorities have declared a class-7 hazmat incident on the *MV Liverpool*.'

'Class 7!' Mac said.

'Class 7—radioactive materials. Anyone in the Warm Zone must be decontaminated.'

'What about the container?'

'It will have to be checked and decontaminated.'

'Looks like the Brits' plan to keep their nuclear waste theft watertight just sprung a big leak,' Mac said to O'Neill.

'Best assign a crime task force superintendent to manage it, have him lock down the warehouse,' Kate said. 'The crime task force is the first responder to hazmat incidents, they're trained to deal with it.'

'They'll cordon off the area and keep everyone back from the container?' Mac asked.

'It's the only option.'

'Do you have a drone to send in to get a radiation reading?' O'Neill asked.

'Dublin Fire Brigade will handle that part of the operation, they've got drones,' Kate replied. 'The standard protocol to reduce radiation exposure includes time, distance, and shielding.'

'You remembered something from your stint with the crime taskforce,' Mac said. 'Do you think the radiation risk is within tolerable limits, then?'

'I'm not a scientist but it's reasonable to assume the cause of the scare is something from the Heysham ferry. We don't know if it's our container but in the time we've been on it, it's all been in the open air, so that's good. Nobody has reported any adverse health reactions.'

'Early days,' Mac said.

'In my view, it's reasonable to assume that the likelihood of severe contamination from our container is low,' Kate said. 'Given the time and distance between the *MV Liverpool* and crime taskforce personnel, the hazmat suits should keep them safe.'

'The Wallace operation will be blown.'

'Lockdown is our only option. We can't let him swoop in and take it while we're distracted.'

The trio split up to handle their slice of the crisis. O'Neill said he needed to update the FBI's Critical Incident Response Group and Mac shuttled him toward the conference room. The FBI man breathed a sigh of relief having advised Quantico of the unfolding drama before it broke on CNN. It was a short respite. When Kate learned a Panamax vessel had sailed out of Dublin earlier with several containers from the Heysham ferry, his perspective altered. The *Viking Prince* was headed for New York. Over eight million souls lived in his homeland's most populous city. In barbed calls with his MI5 counterpart, O'Neill demanded immediate evaluations on the scale of the radioactive threat heading in his direction.

37

A radioactive hazard was off the charts compared with anything SIU had faced in the past. Kate double-checked her crew's safety. The crime task force superintendent established a one-kilometer perimeter around the warehouse, on arrival. A public service radio and television broadcast advised residents within three kilometers to remain indoors and keep doors and windows closed while a possible contamination incident was investigated.

D-Super Kelly ranted that she was overreacting and sought to replace her crew with his drug squad detectives. The crime task force on-scene commander shut down his request. Garda crews in white hazmat suits and helmets set up a checkpoint directly in front of the warehouse, controlling entry and exit. There was nothing further Kate could do, the decontamination procedure would have to run its course. Sexton pulled his crew back to an area agreed with Dublin Fire Brigade. When Pete McNally told her Vince Hyland was waiting in her office, she cut Cody O'Neill loose and returned to base.

On arrival at the squad room, Pete was working from the Inspector's office with the phone on speaker as he two-finger typed on a laptop. Vince stayed in Kate's office while she shouted him a coffee invitation.

'No milk, no sugar,' he replied.

As the coffee brewed, she tuned in to Pete's conversation with a snappy Dublin Port official.

'We need the harbormaster to confirm the number and a description of containers loaded onto the Panamax that left for New York,' he said.

'You know the harbormaster has a major operation ongoing here decontaminating the port,' the irate secretary replied.

'I'm aware of that but I need the information nonetheless.'

'He's meeting Dublin Fire Brigade at the moment, you'll have to wait until he gets back.'

'Can you confirm the name of the vessel at least?'

'The *Viking Prince.*'

'Thank you. Tell your boss it's urgent.'

'Every time the phone rings today it's urgent. Good luck with the container descriptions, by the way!'

'What do you mean?'

'There's four thousand six hundred and thirty-one on board. Apart from a number and a different color here and there, they're all pretty much the same.'

Kate deftly balanced the coffees on her slim folio, headed for her office, and shut the door with her heel. Vince looked exhausted. He was sitting on a gray chair in front of her desk, his usual smiling features replaced with a weariness that attested hours of intensive effort. She placed the coffees beside his pile of handwritten notes.

'It never stops,' he said.

'You and me both,' Kate nodded toward the pile of paper. 'Tell all.'

'The statement is handwritten for now, I didn't want to delay getting it typed. We'll go back over everything later when Sumbal's had a few hours kip. To be honest, I don't know whether to believe the devious bastard or not. What he's telling me could be total BS.'

'Where is he now?'

'In a cell at the Elms.'

'Does he need to get back to the hospital?'

'No. The custody sergeant offered him medical attention, but he refused. He said he was happy to stay in the cell provided we didn't allow visitors.'

'Can't blame him on that.'

'He seems calm. Relieved, to be honest, and that's a reaction I look for in suspects when they get a big secret off their chest.'

'What's he saying?'

Vince sipped his coffee and retrieved reading glasses from his jacket pocket. They magnified the bags under his eyes.

'Statement of Fazli Sumbal, born 10 October 1995, Lahore, Pakistan taken at the Elms Garda station, Dublin on ...'

Kate sat forward and hung on every syllable as Vince laid bare a conspiracy that had challenged, exasperated, and almost killed her. When he finished, she asked him to read through it again.

Sumbal knew no names; Vince sorted through the maze of identities using photos of the main players Kate had supplied. It enabled him to construct a narrative that fitted almost seamlessly with unfolding events.

Sumbal admitted his role as a lookout on the two safe houses at 17A and 51 Manifold Avenue. He swore the transponders in both attics were the only ones he knew about. Vince was inclined to believe him. 17A had been compromised weeks before Greta Connolly called to it. A decision was taken to rig it with an IED to deny the enemy any evidence that might risk uncovering their grand plan.

Sumbal followed instructions supplied via a WhatsApp video to set its timer.

Zardari and his sidekick stayed with Sumbal weeks earlier, predating Kate's crew's surveillance on the house. While he cooked them a meal in the tiny kitchen, he overheard snatches of conversations between the pair. They had been chosen for a sacred mission. The American, Khouri, had been spirited out of the Caliphate and was on his way. Sumbal swore he had no idea where he was at present.

Kate scribbled notes as Vince continued reading through the question-and-answer fencing match.

D/Garda Hyland: Is an attack planned in Ireland?

Sumbal: No.

D/Garda Hyland: Is an attack planned for another location?

Sumbal: Yes.

D/Garda Hyland: Where will the other attack take place?

Sumbal: America, I think.

D/Garda Hyland: Precisely where in America?

Sumbal: I do not know. Zardari say the name red hook will be spoken of like the Towers.

D/Garda Hyland: Red hook? What does that mean?

Sumbal: I do not know.

'Any ideas?' Kate asked.

'Not a notion and I didn't want to interrupt him too much once he started to spill.'

Kate called O'Neill. He was still at Mac's office.

'Does the name red hook mean anything to you?'

'*Red Hook* is a container terminal in Brooklyn, across the harbor from the Statue of Liberty. Why do you ask?'

'I'll send Pete to pick you up. You need to hear this.'

Sumbal's statement confirmed what Kate had begun to believe; al-Farouq's warning about reducing Europe's transport network to a shambles was a smokescreen. The statement continued in a similar vein. Snippets of conversations Sumbal overheard in his kitchen as he cooked a meal for his overnight guests. Both were high on the rush of being selected for a mission that would grab world headlines and light up believers around the globe with renewed zeal for the holy jihad.

When O'Neill got to Kate's office, he listened as Vince read Sumbal's statement for the third time. He pored over a copy as Vince read. When he was done a silent dread hung in the room as O'Neill re-read every word with a lawyer's eye for detail.

'Great job.'

'It's what I do,' Vince replied.

'Does it mean what I think it means?' Kate asked.

'There's no other way to read it.' O'Neill said. 'A major attack on my homeland is imminent.'

Pete put the call through to Kate when the harbormaster called back and she listened to his woes of getting the port decontaminated and back in business.

'What about the *Viking Prince*?' she asked.

'I've spoken with the captain and he's keen to continue his journey.'

'That seems odd. Is he not morally obliged to put his crew's health before any other consideration?'

'To be honest, I'm glad he's not turning back.'

'What about his crew and possible contamination?'

'The captain has double-checked the stow positions. You have to remember the *Viking Prince* is far larger than the *MV Liverpool*, picture an elephant and a mouse. The offending containers are near the bow and the ship is on the open sea. He's happy they're far enough away from crew quarters not to pose an immediate contamination threat. As a precaution, the crew will suit up when out on the deck. He's advised the New York Port Authority and decontamination crews are on standby there.'

'Okay. Look, thank you for your co-operation over the past few weeks. We appreciate it.'

'You're welcome!'

'Before I go,' Kate said. 'Was there anything out of the ordinary about the ship's stay in Dublin?'

'Hold on, I'll look up the report.'

She waited as a flurry of keyboard clicks fed down the line.

'I see it left port a half an hour ahead of time, that's a bit unusual, I suppose. Five hundred and twenty-one containers disembarked, ten taken on board, along with four passengers for a cruise to the United States.'

'Four passengers? I thought it was strictly cargo.'

'Cargo vessels take on passengers from time to time, always at the Captain's discretion.'

'I didn't know that was possible.'

'It's up to the Captain. If he has room on board and the passengers are not looking for luxury, the law of the sea says he can do it.'

'Do you have the passenger names?'

'Three British passport holders and one American. What's your email address and I'll send you the names. It'll spare me embarrassing myself trying to pronounce them.'

'Did you copy their travel documents?'

'That's the immigration officer's job. Shane Dobson processed them.'

'I'll check with him. What was the early departure about?'

'It's nothing special, I think. Ship captains request it from time to time, especially since the forecast says he's going to meet heavy weather in the North Atlantic.'

'Okay,' Kate said. 'Thank you once again for your help.'

Immigration Officer, Shane Dobson was the last Mohican, the final Garda left with the Garda National Immigration Bureau before it transitioned to civilian control. Kate knew him; he ran the social club at Pearse Street, the city center station where her career began. Every Garda there had his contact number and she searched her private mobile's contact list to dig it out.

'Shane, long time no see, Kate Bowen here.'

'Kate who?

'Bowen, ex-Pearse Street.'

'Oh, I remember you now, Kung Fu Kate. What's up?'

'I need a favor.'

'You're with that hush-hush squad now, aren't ya?'

'Yes. You were working at the port earlier?'

'I was.'

'Did you deal with the big container ship going to America? The *Viking Prince*.'

'You're enquiring about the four that got on it, aren't ya?'

'Yes.'

'I effin knew they were dodgy.'

'What can you tell me about them?'

'There was an American, who only spoke once to say thank you, two Pakistanis with British passports who didn't speak at all. 'Lenny Henry' did all the talking.'

'Huh?' Kate laughed.

'He sounded just that English comedian when he launched into his thickest Birmingham accent. He said they had met up in Europe and decided to give Freightliner cruising a go because it was dirt cheap.

'Did you believe him?

'Sounded like bollocks but their travel documents passed all the tests.

'If I showed you photos would you be able to pick them out?'

'Sure. Or I could just send you the photos of the passports I snapped with my phone.'

'Shane, you've never lost it! Send them straight away, will you.'

'No problem but here listen; I sent these photos to Fordey before the ship left. He was suspicious of the group too. Now to be honest he didn't acknowledge receiving them so I figured he'd let the whole thing slide.'

'Wait a minute. You sent the pictures to who?'

'Joe Forde. He's ex-Pearse Street and I got chatting to him the past few weeks in the port. He's been working down here in a crane.'

'When did you talk to him?'

'Just after the four passengers went on board. He asked me about the best way to slip on board to talk to the Captain about them.'

'And what did you tell him?'

'Blend with crew members was the only way to get on without drawing attention.'

'A no-brainer!'

'To be fair to the lad that's what he did, he tagged along with four that arrived in a taxi and ran up the gangway.'

'Did you see him get off?'

'I didn't.'

Kate thanked Dobson for his help and immediately called Ron Sexton.

'What's happening there?' she asked.

'Waiting behind a factory unit one kilometer back from the warehouse while Dublin Fire Brigade sets up a tent to start decontamination.'

'Angie is on her way with search party overalls and new undies for you all. Is Joe Forde with you?'

'No, he gave us top cover until we cleared the port. When his job in the eagle's nest was done, I told him to return to base.'

'Have you heard from him since?'

'No, but I had no reason to hear from him. Why?'

'It's a long story. Call him on the radio, will you?'

When Sexton received no reply, Kate checked with Pete McNally whether Forde had shown up at base during the evening. He hadn't. She double-checked with the harbormaster's office to see if he had been detained for decontamination at the port. His name was not on their lists. The photos Dobson send Kate confirmed what she feared. Rafiq Khouri, al-Farouq, Zardari, and his unknown sidekick had used false passports to board the *Viking Prince*. And her rookie detective, Forde, was some-where amongst them.

Joe Forde badged Captain Matt Tucker immediately he got on board the *Viking Prince*. Within minutes he knew he had made a big mistake. The captain was cooperative but preoccupied with readying the ship for departure, annoyed that four of his crew had left it to the last minute to return from a city trip.

Earlier, as he descended the port crane, Forde could not believe his eyes when he caught sight of Rafiq Khouri waiting alongside the *Viking Prince*. Struck by how much weight the ISIS suspect had dropped since he last saw him at 17A Manifold Avenue, he needed a closer look to be certain. When he saw Shane Dobson working at the immigration portacabin, he decided to use it to get a better view of the suspect. Up close, he recognized Khouri's face instantly and picked out his companion alongside as al-Farouq from the photo displayed on the SIU whiteboard.

The pair walked up the gangway of the *Viking Prince*, with two others trailing behind. The rookie detective made an instant decision to follow them and warn the ship's captain before calling in his incredible detections. If he could get the crew off safely, an ERU squad could sweep on board and take on the terrorists.

He had barely finished introductions with the captain when the sound of raised voices approaching signaled trouble. Forde darted into the chart room behind the bridge.

'It's just the crew in high spirits, for heaven's sake,' Captain Tucker shouted after him, startled by his reaction.

Forde climbed into a floor-to-ceiling cupboard, lined on one side with sliding drawers of sea charts. He patted his pockets for either his radio or cell phone, but he had left both beside Captain Tucker in the bridge. He listened intently. The shouting was quickly replaced by one person speaking calmly in a British accent. Forde suspected it was al-Farouq. His orders were distinct and precise.

'Confirm your name.'

'Captain Matthew Tucker.'

'No stupid actions Matthew, or your crew will die. Get the vessel moving immediately.'

'We're thirty minutes shy of our departure slot. I can't go anywhere until the controller gives permission.'

'Well, tell him you need to leave now.'

'It'll do no good.'

Forde heard a click. 'Do it,' al-Farouq warned. 'Or die yourself.'

'Who'll skipper the boat then, eh?' Tucker replied.

Forde warmed to him in that instant.

'Sadiq, remind the captain here who's in charge,' al-Farouq replied, coldly.

Forde winced when he heard Tucker cry out. In the next few minutes, he listened as the captain forced a good-humored exchange with the vessel traffic controller to cajole an earlier than planned removal of his ship from the port. The controller conceded and wished him fair weather. Pilot boats guided the monster carrier into a channel with sufficient under keel clearance to navigate safely and Forde's heart sank as he felt the ship begin to roll and pitch gently on its slow trajectory out of the port. He could see nothing, but what he overheard told him he was in deep trouble.

38

While Kate pieced the jigsaw together, Sexton's crew assembled as specially trained firefighters diligently worked through their decontamination protocol. They cleared personnel and vehicles within two hours and the crew returned to the SIU base.

Most took a second shower and ditched the overalls for personal clothes in the SIU locker rooms. Sexton was happy to take his mate's word that the fire brigade protocol had eradicated any risk. He changed into the spare set of threads he kept in his locker. The only thing missing when he joined Kate in the squad room for debriefing was his ever-present tie.

'You look positively shabby without it,' she joked half-heartedly as he took a seat beside her in front of the returned crew.

Kate rapidly changed plans for the debrief. Her crew's health was the top priority and the Garda chief medical officer spoke first. He offered concise advice on what to look out for in the days ahead. Any flu-like symptoms should be reported immediately, however, based on the information to hand, he reassured everyone that they had experienced minimal exposure to radioactivity. Kate thanked him and invited any queries. When none materialized, Pete McNally escorted him from the room.

She briefed the crew on events since the Hazmat-7 incident was declared by the UK. She outlined how Dublin port was closed down and the containers taken from the *M.V. Liverpool* were being tracked. Decontamination protocols were well in hand. Detective Superintendent Kelly, the disgruntled drugs squad boss, said his crew would deal with searching the container and offloading its cargo when cleared to do so. He left the room without a single word of gratitude for the weeks of SIU input to his case.

'So here's where we're at,' Kate continued. 'You know from Ron that Joe Forde is unaccounted for, but likely onboard the vessel.'

'I've tried ringing him,' Angie said. 'His phone is either switched off or out of coverage.'

'Could a coast guard helicopter get him off?' someone asked.

'That's out of the question, I'm afraid,' Kate said.

'So what's happening?'

'This is massive,' Kate explained. 'It's a lethal international threat and dealing with it has been taken out of our hands. The Irish Naval Service is providing logistical assistance to NATO allies who are assembling a task force along with the Americans to confront the menace.'

'There must be something we can do.'

'Twomey is en route to Cork with an ERU crew. We'll man our comms 24-7 and pray Joe finds a way to make contact.'

'There's other work needs doin',' a familiar voice came from the back of the room.

'Jeez Digger, what on earth? Have you been hiding?'

Digger grimaced a noncommittal reply as he stood. His

broken arm was still supported by a blue hospital sling, the red rawness of his pockmarked face beginning to fade.

'You're not cleared to return to work,' she said. 'Are you trying to get me fired?'

'Pete rang, this can't wait.'

Kate sighed and beckoned him toward the front.

Digger stood behind the top table and used his good hand to scrawl a mobile phone number on the whiteboard. He then perched awkwardly on the chair Kate pulled clear of the table.

'The same day the boss's car exploded in Beaumont this number was used to contact Frank Reilly, a known smuggler from South Armagh.'

'We found that out in recent days,' Kate said.

'There hasn't been a peep from it since until it went active today at 2.15 p.m., pingin' off masts in north Monaghan.'

Kate took up the impromptu briefing.

'Kevin Wrollesly aka Kevin Stevenson is the suspect who rang Reilly. Pete will distribute photos, later. I learned earlier today that the PSNI is looking to lift him. They suspect he's smuggling contraband cigarettes like his father, Sean O'Hare, who dragged him into the business. Given that his gang had grown very big, very quickly, drugs have to be part of that mix.'

'Looks like the PSNI missed him.' Digger said. 'if he's pingin' around different parts of north Monaghan for the afternoon.'

'What do we know about him?' Sexton asked.

'Very little,' Kate said. 'He was raised outside Caledon in County Tyrone, as Kevin Wrollesly, with a Presbyterian, lay preacher for a stepfather. He was Kevin Stevenson until his mother married. She's from the other side of Caledon, nearer the border.'

'And he came at you two presumably because he found

299

out about your links with his real father's demise,' Sexton added.

'The Prison Service at Portlaoise confirmed that he called to see Nutser Treacy months back,' Digger replied. 'We need to arrest this buck, fast.'

He outlined that 'Junior' was believed to be his nickname among associates. The suspect had called some garages along the border indicating a transport problem. The longest call was to a chop shop run by a Monaghan gang. This lot morphed into a serious threat when they hooked up with an Eastern European mob that stole high-end cars to order, stripped them down, containerized the parts, and shipped them East under false invoices.

Sexton thumbed pages of his journal to his interviews with Greta Connolly.

'If it's the same 'Junior' Greta Connolly spoke about, he's been in Dublin the last few days squeezing money from his customers.'

'Maybe he knew somethin' was brewin',' Digger said.

'This is the running order for the next 24-hours,' Kate said. A two-man crew will monitor our radio traffic and deal with any queries from Twomey's ERU squad. Who knows? Joe might manage to contact some of us so everyone keeps their phone switched on and charged. It's too soon to send a crew to Monaghan to locate Junior but we'll continue to monitor the phone. I'm going to Dundalk now and will likely head to Cork with Twomey later. Anyone not rostered on, go home and rest up.'

The clatter of shifting chairs mixed with the murmur of muted conversation filled the squad room as Kate headed for her office. Sexton and Digger joined her as she called Alan Tyrell. She put him on speaker, introduced Digger, and allowed him to update the PSNI commander on where the electronic trail was leading.

'Something spooked the national crime agency,' Tyrell said, 'they triggered the raids early.'

'Do you have anyone in custody?' Kate asked.

'Not a single soul. I was scrambling to find enough bodies to cover all locations. The agency wanted to hit everything simultaneously and missed Junior at his Newry office.'

'Had they a team on him?'

'He left the office before the arrest team got there. He's been staying in a flat in Newry for a couple of weeks and was only in the office half an hour before he drove home, picked up his mother, and headed to the other side of the village for a while.'

'I'm guessing Caledon is not the biggest place in the world.'

'You got that right! The surveillance crews were wary of venturing into the heartland and lost him on side roads near the mother's home place. His phone went dead soon after.'

'Send us a fresh photo, I've only got his passport one. We'll try to locate him on our side.'

'The most recent one we have is an arrest photo from the time Sean O'Hare died. I'll mail it to you.'

'He's probably changed transport. What was he last seen in?'

'One of his company trucks.'

Digger rolled his eyes: how was it possible to lose a target that size?

'Do you want us to arrest him or alert you if he crosses to your side?' Kate asked.

'It'd be better if you could tip us the wink that he's crossed the border and we'll lift him.'

'Roger that. The night crew will monitor the target phone. Bye for now, Alan.'

Kate told both her DIs there was nothing to do but rest.

'What about you?' Digger asked.

'Not sure yet. I'll bring Mac up to date and go on to Dundalk; I haven't seen my mother in days.'

'Will you stay with Norrie?'

'No, at Mum's.'

It would be her first time sleeping in the two-up, two-down house in the center of town without her mother.

'What about Kenny?'

Her ERU escort was still part of the package. Mac insisted she and Digger remain under protection until the threat against them was neutralized.

'Joe Forde has thrown a spanner in the works. How do we extract him? I should probably fly down to Cork.'

'With all you've been through these past few days?' Digger said. 'Leave Twomey to extract Forde. Joe's a good lad, he'll keep out of harm's way until they get to him.'

Kate nodded, unconvinced.

Mac had taken care of briefing Colonel Shaw as the case leaped forward.

'J2 pulled out all the stops,' he told Kate.

'What have they got?' she asked.

'They figured out who built the device that killed Sergeant Daly.'

The Irish Army photographed and analyzed IEDs deactivated and recovered during patrols with United Nations forces. Any unique feature, a signature that pointed to a skilled hand was noted and carefully recorded for investigation. They identified the IED from 17A Manifold Avenue as the work of Abdul Waleed, an ISIS bomb maker they had encountered in the Golan Heights. Local traders reckoned he was an Afghan. Kate compared the photo Shaw sent Mac to the passport photos on the four expert forgeries used to get on board the *Viking Prince*. She now knew, along with an IT tech genius, a master manipulator and experienced warrior, the deadly ISIS cell headed for the USA included an expert bomb maker.

'I'll manage the container vessel,' Mac told her. 'Go to Dundalk. You can direct any operation that's required to arrest Junior from there and visit your mother when time permits.'

The *Viking Prince* was plowing toward New York carrying a container of irradiated material that might make swathes of the city uninhabitable for decades if exploded in a conventional bomb. NATO decided it had to be stopped mid-ocean. The Irish government's cabinet security committee met in early evening session and rubberstamped consent to the Irish Naval Service assisting NATO and Allied forces to deal with the threat. The Naval Service's Haulbowline Island headquarters in Cork harbor would be the logistical base for the mission.

As a military task force mustered off Ireland's south coast, Kate remained in Dublin to double-check Sumbal's confession. The essential elements of his original declarations chimed with events, but she needed certainty that nothing changed when his final interview concluded. It was after ten o'clock when Vince finished rechecking every detail. By then little had been added to the original.

She passed O'Neill a copy of Sumbal's definitive statement when she and Mac met him at the American embassy close to eleven o'clock. Darrell Jackson, a U.S. military liaison officer they knew from a previous operation, joined them. Cody O'Neill and Jackson were hitching a ride on the chopper that would ferry Mac, Twomey, and an ERU crew there.

As Kate concluded her briefing, she glanced through an embassy window. An Air Corps helicopter turned a wide arc over Dublin Bay and headed back for a landing pad at nearby Saint Vincent's Hospital.

'Is that for you?' she asked Twomey.

'Affirmative,' he replied.

'Rather you than me. I hate flying.'

When Kate told Norrie she was staying in Dundalk overnight, her sister dropped by their mother's house and turned the heating on. By the time she reached it, with her bodyguards in tow, the house had cooled. She left an extra blanket on the sofa bed made up for Kenny in the front room. The night shift detective ventured into the small backyard when they arrived and checked the lane behind the house. She warned him not to disturb the neighbors. He stayed street-side overnight in the car.

Mentally drained, the moment Kate slipped under the covers of her old bed she drifted into a restful slumber.

39

Early the next morning Junior grabbed his phone from the bedside locker to silence its piercing alarm. He swung his legs off the bed's lumpy mattress at Moll's Roadhouse and eased upright onto its edge. Leaning forward, he squinted through faded beige curtains covering the room's single window to scan the cars parked below.

The hotel's car park on the northern edge of Dundalk overlooked Carlingford Lough. The dull cloud cover in the eastern sky reflected gunmetal gray on the lough's shimmering surface. He tried to refocus his attention on the car park. In the last few hours, the world he knew had been blown to smithereens.

He swapped his truck in the late afternoon the previous day with the chop shop gang for a rust bucket car, a weapon, and a wad of cash. He used his new transport to nip into Northern Ireland again and check out what was going on with his mother. It made no sense for her to return to where she had just visited. He parked a mile from his grandfather's old house and cut through fields he knew like the back of his hand to check out whether the place was under surveillance. It took him sixty cautious minutes.

He noted two unmarked cars parked up with no good reason to be there. He ducked down, concealed behind a hedge to consider his next move. Approaching the house was out of the question. He tried her phone again, once more with no reply.

He avoided calling Wrollesly's landline to check whether she had returned home. Something deep inside him worried that she had made her mind up never to return there. He scanned the farmyard a final time and decided his last throw of the dice in locating her would be to check out the shed at the outfarm a few fields away. He double-checked the watchers' vantage point and figured they had no sightline on the shed. At its rear wall, he hesitated, holding his breath and listening for tell-tale sounds that a police squad was waiting to pounce. Satisfied there was nobody, as evening gloom turned to the dark of night, he skirted around the side and pushed through the shed's open door.

His heart skipped a beat at the memory of three straw bales stacked one of top of the other, sufficient height to secure to a rope to a roof truss and tie a sturdy knot. His mother's limp body suspended at the other end of it. He had scrambled to reach her, tears streaming down his cheeks.

'In the name of God, Mother, why?' he had whispered, as he cut her down and kissed her cheek. 'Why?' he repeated as he laid her on loose straw beneath and freed the noose from around her neck. He had lain it next to her body, then covered her face with her coat before slinking back through the door and back across the fields.

Frank Reilly never showed at Moll's Roadhouse but it was too late for regrets. Junior had to push on and punish the bitch whose brutal killing of his father had triggered the disastrous turn his life had taken. He stepped into the en suite's turquoise bath, lifted the shower from its cradle, and turned it to full. A brown zig-zag water stain ran along its base. He gasped as a shock of ice-cold water cascaded over him and blasted the cobwebs from his lack of sleep. As he toweled off, he roughed two days of black stubble on his chin before discarding the dank bath towel on the floor and dragging on his sweaty check shirt and black jeans.

Although food was the last thing on his mind, Junior knew he needed to eat. He ordered coffee and toast to his room and tuned his phone's FM app to a local radio station. The car park again; he pulled the curtain aside for the umpteenth time and checked it. The blue van with the rear doors open had not been there last time. He spied through the crack in the curtains until he saw a bread delivery man stroll from the service entrance door with two empty wooden pallets. He continued watching as the delivery man placed them in the rear, shut the van doors, and accelerated toward the exit.

He startled at a knock on the door.

'Breakfast,' came a cheery announcement.

'Leave it outside.'

He eavesdropped warily before opening his door and collecting the breakfast tray. As he crunched through cold toast dripping with runny marmalade he listened to a local news bulletin. There were no reports of police raids or arrests, nor any mention of his mother's death. He ditched the food and went scouting the corridor to check the section of the car park obscured from his room's view. It was all clear.

He descended the winding stairs and dropped his key on the reception counter where he had paid cash the previous night. The ancient night porter, his feet propped beside a CCTV monitor, rustled his newspaper in acknowledgment as Junior advanced toward the front door. When he caught movement in the white Transit van parked opposite, he pulled back instantly, returned to the desk, and grabbed his key.

'Left my damn phone in the room!'

Taking the stairs two at a time, he was already on the first floor as the porter nodded assent. Junior slowed, whipped out the Walther pistol, and breeched a round; ready. A bead of sweat rolled down his back as he brought his breathing under control. He eased the hammer down carefully, before returning the weapon to his trouser belt. Racing to the third-floor landing, he cast an eye beyond the car park toward the street out front and backed out of view. Minutes ticked by as the white van consumed his attention.

'Wonderful isn't it,' a voice interrupted.

Junior's heart pounded as he swung round to face a middle-aged man.

'Oh God, sorry if I startled you. I figured you were here for the wildlife, like myself.'

Junior eyeballed the guy. He was kitted out in army fatigues; a DSLR camera with a telescopic lens hung around his neck. They were similar height but unlike Junior's rugby hardened body, age had added a paunch around the photographer's middle.

'Where are you headed?' was the quickest comeback he could conjure up.

'The mudflats. Are you shooting today?' the guy persisted.

For a moment, Junior startled and adjusted his gilet to ensure the pistol was concealed. Finally, figuring the guy was talking about cameras rather than guns, he replied, with a shrug, 'No gear.'

He had neither interest in wildlife, nor experience of photography. For a second or two neither said anything. Would it be worth the risk, Junior wondered, as he considered whether the amateur snapper might help him exit the hotel. He glanced out the window trying to catch any movement from the van that would confirm his suspicions.

'Mind if I take a quick peek?' Junior pointed at the camera slung around his neck.

'Be my guest!'

Junior accepted the Canon and aimed it out the window. He dallied a moment on the lough shore before swinging the lens toward the street and narrowing in on the white van's rear window. He fidgeted with the focus until the blurred image cleared. He exhaled a soft whistle as Frank Reilly's worried face came into sharp relief. A camera on a tripod beside him near the van's rear window was fitted with a telephoto lens and focused on the hotel entrance. A shadow told Junior that Reilly wasn't alone. The bastard had turned traitor.

'Would you mind keeping an eye on my gear for a minute while I grab my tripod from my room?' the photographer asked, unaware that Junior had already decided his destiny.

He figured the curious nature lover had seen too much of him and would eagerly help police. He allowed him to move ahead, but followed him to his room and knocked him cold with a single blow. He grunted as he lifted his victim onto the bed and stripped off his camouflage jacket and mottled green trousers. He checked the birdwatcher's gear bags and found cables. It took all his strength to prop him upright on the single chair in the room and secure his arms and legs. As the victim mumbled into consciousness, Junior grabbed a fistful of toilet paper and stuffed it in his mouth. He ripped a pillowcase and tied a strip of it around his head to keep the gag in place. His mesmerized victim stared at his assailant in dazed confusion.

'Now, will you remember me when the Guards ask who did this to you?'

An indignant snort of blood and snot from the victim's nose answered the question.

'I know where you live, Gareth Devlin,' Junior goaded, as he ripped the neatly printed tag from the camera case. 'Tell them nothing.'

He glanced at Devlin a final time as he picked up the shoulder bag. The victim was becoming bug-eyed, his head rocking from side to side in frantic, silent pleading. Junior paid no heed to his victim's labored breathing as he pushed past him. The ill-fated birdwatcher's head rocked faster in desperation as the door clicked closed.

Kate roused as her phone vibrated; she could just about make out that it was Digger.

'Morning,' she yawned.

'Junior's phone pinged in Dundalk just now. Where are you?'

'I'm at home like I said I was going to be. Any news of Joe Forde overnight?'

'Mac is on that, you know he'll keep us in the loop. Is Kenny with you?'

She sat up on the edge of the bed.

'He was downstairs last night when I turned in, I presume he's still there.'

'Good!'

'What time is it?'

'Seven-thirty. What time did you get to Dundalk last night?'

'Two in the morning,' Kate yawned a second time.

As she thought about what action to direct, she leaned and looked out the window onto the familiar pavement below. Her armor-plated protection car looked out of place in the narrow street.

'Update the morning shift on Junior and send them here. I'll call Quinlan in a while and see if he's heard anything.' she said.

She called Mac first. There were no overnight developments with the *Viking Prince*. Nothing had been heard from Joe Forde. Satellites tracked its progress as it held a course for New York.

'Is Ken James with you?' he asked.

'Doesn't leave my side. He's sorting out a backup at the moment in case things get rowdy with Junior.'

'Okay, keep me briefed.'

She was barely dressed when the night shift detective rat-a-tat-tatted the front door.

'Breakfast!' he said, offering three coffees and a bag of croissants from the nearby 'shop local' supermarket. As a teenager, Kate had cleaned its aisle spills, when she worked there on evenings and weekends. As they wolfed down the croissants, he jumped at the offer of the sofa bed for a couple of hours.

'We're sticking around Dundalk, right?'

'For a while, anyway.'

'I'll get the head down for a few hours, so. Don't forget me when you're heading back to the Big Smoke.'

'As if!'

Kate called Jack Quinlan as Ken James drove her to Brackenhill Nursing Home. She updated him on PSNI's efforts to locate Junior.

'A phone we know he uses is pinging around the town this morning.'

'Feck, I'm on my own today.'

'Digger is sending you a photo.'

'Is he back working already?'

'Wild horses couldn't keep him away from the hunt for this guy.'

'Call if you need me.'

Brackenhill Nursing Home was a purpose-built single-story T-shaped building, located three miles from the town on a hill overlooking the Dublin-Belfast railway line. The top of the T held the kitchen, admin offices, and a doctor's surgery. The remainder comprised single or double en-suite bedrooms and a large inviting common room.

The swathes of daffodils alongside the pathways from early spring were on the wane. Clematis adorned the outside walls of the accommodation wing, its blossoming flowers replacing the fading yellow with a vibrant blue. Clumps of dogwood, with summer green leaves emerging, split the parking area in two. Kate introduced herself to the owner-manager, a solid, middle-aged woman with teased bouffant hair dyed jet-black, and a permanent smile.

'Margaret's settling in well with us,' she beamed.

Kate doubted that was entirely true.

'She's not inclined to leave her room. We've been trying to get her involved in some social activities. Is she a little reserved, perhaps shy about mixing with people?'

'That's the opposite of who Mum is; I'll see what I can do to encourage her. Room 21, is it?'

'That's it, second from the end, on the right.'

'Thank you.'

Margaret Bowen sat in a chair staring out the window when Kate entered her room. She walked around the single bed and kissed her mother on the cheek.

'Is he your latest?'

Her mother's speech had improved significantly since leaving Dublin, but Kate sensed she was still self-conscious about it.

'Is who my latest?'

'The fella you drove in with in the fancy car.'

'No, Mum, that's Ken, a colleague I'm with today.'

'Are you working in Dundalk?'

'You know even if I was, I'm not supposed to tell you.'

'Nothing changes!'

Kate sat into a visitor's armchair and chatted with her mother. She explained how she had found it impossible to get out of Dublin the previous two days but had chatted with Norrie about her. She received non-committal answers to most of her questions about the nursing home. The staff was nice, the food was fine, she slept well but she stopped short of saying she liked the place. Kate was steering the conversation toward encouraging her to be more sociable when her phone buzzed.

'It's Jack Quinlan, Mum, I have to take the call.'

'Tell him I said hello.'

'Jack,' Kate answered, 'I'm with my mother at the moment.'

'How is Mrs. B.?'

Without giving her the chance to object, Kate handed the phone to her mother.

'She can tell you herself.'

She pushed the phone into her mother's hands, with a broad smile.

'Hello, Jack,' her mother began, each word carefully articulated. 'Thank you for asking after me; I'm doing good, thanks. Now I'm going to hand the phone back to this little imp.'

Kate laughed as she took back the phone. It was great to see her mother rise to the challenge, and it was a long time since anyone had called her an 'imp.' She walked down the corridor and took a seat in the empty common room.

'Thanks, Jack. You put a smile on her face.'

'Mrs. B. is one of the old stock, there's not many like her left.'

'What's up?' Kate asked.

'In case you're looking for me later, I'll be out of circulation for a bit. There's a suspicious death at Moll's Road-house. I'll be at the scene for the next few hours.'

'Molls? I worked there for one summer. Who found the body?'

'A chambermaid. The victim was tied to a chair, but reports indicate he fell over. I'll know more when I see it.'

'Did you get Junior's photo?'

'I did. A hardy looking dude.'

'Rumor across the border is that he's Sean O'Hare love child.'

'You're kidding me!'

'True apparently; he could be behind the bombs under our cars.'

'God Almighty! I'll keep my eyes peeled.'

'Thanks again, Jack.'

Kate returned and chatted with her mother. When Digger sent a text that Pete McNally was driving a control van to Dundalk she kissed her good-bye, promising to call back later in the day.

'Don't leave the house in a mess,' Margaret Bowen called, as her daughter departed.

Kate smiled, her mother was on the mend.

She rang Pete and set a rendezvous for the motorway services on the edge of town. Ken James drove back via her mother's house, woke the night shift, and took him on board before heading out. He could drive the conspicuous ERU car back to Dublin, Ken would stick with Kate on the operation to nab Junior or shepherd him over the border.

Jack Quinlan surveyed the cramped bedroom at Moll's Roadhouse, irked that paramedics had untied the victim from a chair. The overweight middle-aged man lay on his back beside the single bed in a tee-shirt and underwear.

Seeing the bindings in place might have indicated a hasty action or demonstrated a skilled killer. He had interviewed the night porter who said Devlin was a regular at the hotel and he took him to be a birdwatcher. The manager compiled CCTV that Quinlan planned to view when he was done with the paramedic. No one suspicious featured on the guest list.

He leaned over the body and noted fresh bruising on both sides of his face. The victim's wallet was empty apart from a driving license that identified him as Gareth Devlin, a retired civil servant from Dublin. Was the death a sexual adventure gone sideways? The head injuries indicated violence, but Quinlan would have to wait for the State pathologist to give a definitive cause of death. The victim's car keys were on the bed and his vehicle was still in the car park.

He instructed two uniform Gardaí to seal the entire third floor as a crime scene and do likewise around the victim's car. For now, he would make a call on the death as suspicious, but investigate it as murder. He dialed the emergency department coordinator who had dispatched the ambulance from Our Lady of Lourdes hospital in Drogheda.

The young paramedic admitted to Quinlan that when he saw the victim manacled, his instinct was to free him and examine him properly. Quinlan pressed him to recall the precise position the victim was in when the crew arrived.

'He was face down, his wrists and ankles tied to the chair. It was like he had tipped forward.'

'Were you wearing gloves when you untied him?'

'Listen, when we arrived at the hotel I grabbed a trauma bag and ran the room. I untied him immediately.'

'Gloves on at that stage?'

'On reflection, no. He was gagged as well, you know.'

'Come again?' Quinlan asked.

'The poor man had been gagged. If you ask me, I wouldn't be surprised if he suffocated.'

The detective knelt beside the victim and peered under the bed. There was a torn pillowcase, stained red with blood and green with dried snot. A wad of toilet paper lay beside it. He told the paramedic they would need his fingerprints for elimination purposes and agreed to meet at Dundalk station in the afternoon to record a statement. He then called his Superintendent and advised that an incident room be established immediately. Quinlan slowly scanned the room, taking in its every detail. He knew it would be videoed and photographed by the crime scene techs but nothing beat taking time to focus on each element. The smell was something that could not be recorded, but nothing stood out apart from the room's poor ventilation.

This would be his final murder case; his days as a cop were almost done. The time was right to part ways with the job he loved. He snapped off the latex gloves and issued final instructions to the Garda preserving the scene. No rubbernecking by hotel staff, nothing to be disturbed until the scene of crime techs got there. He descended the twisting staircase deep in thought and whispered a silent prayer that he could bring closure to the victim's family before his time ran out.

40

The unbearable tension and hours cocooned in the tight chart room cupboard behind the compass bridge drained Detective Joe Forde. The vessel's pitching and rolling made his legs and shoulders ache. Moving a muscle invited discovery. How many hours had he been marooned there? Time became a blur of pain and deep concern. The chart room was windowless, the sliver of artificial light that came through the cupboard doors gave no sense of day or night. Had his squad even missed him yet?

As his knees succumbed to the constant ache, he began to wobble. He had to move. He thanked his lucky stars for his Sig Sauer personal issue pistol, securely holstered underneath his right arm. A left-handed shooter, his range scores weren't going to win any competitions but he was confident of hitting something in a close quarter encounter.

In the hours since they first assaulted Captain Tucker, Forde had listened intently to the hijackers' demands. They sounded remarkably calm and highly organized. When the numbers on board were demanded, Tucker confirmed he had a twenty-man crew. He cried out in agony when forced to re-confirm the number repeatedly. The violence was relentless and cruelly meted out.

Al-Farouq called the shots. Forde overheard snatches of conversations he had with Khouri about controlling the ship's navigation. He feared the discussion might spark a chart room visit that would uncover him. He vowed to greet anyone opening the cupboard with a lethal response. Khouri assured al-Farouq that charts would not be needed. His software would take care of everything.

When Forde heard al-Farouq say that he and Waleed were suiting up to go on deck he was unsure what to make of it. Al-Farouq ordered Khouri to watch the captain and kill him if he tried anything suspicious. The chilling order made up Forde's mind.

He waited until the bridge went quiet, opened the cupboard door, and stepped out. He took a few cautious steps to release the lethargy and prepare for diving into danger. An idea struck him when he saw two sea charts spread on a table. In large black marker, he scrawled *Forde on board* across one. If help ever came, he wanted them to know he was somewhere on the ship. He gripped his Sig tightly in his left hand and tiptoed toward the door leading to the bridge. Taking a furtive peek was out of the question, it opened inward. He prayed the element of surprise played long enough in the milliseconds he would have, to take out anyone confronting him. Breathing in deeply, he grabbed the door handle.

'Drop your fucking weapons,' he shouted, as he dived out and slid across the floor into the bridge until he hit a sidewall. He pointed his weapon frantically toward the other end of the bridge.

Rafiq Khouri's response was immediate and chilling. He jabbed the submachine gun he carried at Captain Tucker's head.

'Drop *your* weapon, or he dies,' he snarled in a New York drawl that smacked of privilege.

Forde realized in the instant he should have come out shooting. Captain Tucker looked toward him, his hands raised aloft, eyes pleading. Seconds played like hours as Forde held Khouri's crazed stare.

'Captain, you should have told us we had company,' the American said, and without warning fired a burst that killed Tucker instantly.

Forde responded with three shots, and Khouri dropped to the ground. He didn't hang about to see if he had killed the madman. He raced down narrow corridors, ducking in and out of empty cabins seeking somewhere to hide. If cornered in the tight corridor his chances of survival would be minimal. With his options rapidly running out, he made up his mind. He followed signage that led toward the engine room. There, at least, he imagined he would find some cover.

Midday approached as Junior parked and slammed his car door three times before the lock held. To get to Gary McEvoy's council house unnoticed, he parked up in a neighboring housing estate and cut through fields that backed onto it.

He didn't trust the local drug pusher enough to talk on the phone; didn't trust him, *period*. As Junior approached the house wind-whipped sheets of old newspaper twirled in a swirling dervish of filth overflowing from a bin out front. The ragged appearance of the place confirmed his impression of McEvoy as just another low-life. Movement at the back of the house caught his eye. He vaulted the low front wall, eased the side gate open, and slipped through.

There was no mistaking the portly pusher as Junior

approached silently from behind. Near the rear of the garden, McEvoy shuffled alongside pigeon coops, the legs of his gray sweatpants spilling over a pair of cheap blue Crocs. He wore a matching gray top with the hood pulled up as he doled out handfuls of birdfeed on both sides of the coop.

'We need to talk,' Junior said.

'Fuckin' Jaysus, you frightened the shite out of me,' McEvoy jumped. 'I'll kill Beryl for leavin' that side gate unlocked.'

'We can't talk out here.'

'Come into the shed.'

Inside Junior leaned against bags of bird feed stacked along one wall while McEvoy perched on a kitchen stool, consigned for outdoor use.

'Where's Frank?' McEvoy asked.

'Forget about Frank.'

The mention of Reilly's name stabbed a shard of bitterness through Junior. His betrayal stung.

'I need you to point me toward the cop. You know her family.'

McEvoy was already nervous. The chef from Moll's Roadhouse had canceled a pick-up this morning because the place was crawling with cops. He had no inkling the activity was linked to the edgy operator standing in front of him.

'I'll put out feelers and get back to you.'

'Today, I need it today.'

'It doesn't work like that. She's in Dublin.'

'She has a sister, hasn't she?'

'Yeah, Nora; she's married to an Army man. What do you want with her?'

'The other bitch would get up here pretty fast if her sister needed her.'

McEvoy squirmed on the stool. Was Junior unhinged?

Was he seriously considering grabbing the older sister to use her as bait? He didn't want any part of that plan. He slipped off the stool and reached, elbow deep, into a sack of pigeon feed to retrieve his supply phone, sealed in a plastic food bag. His hourly checks on it kept business turning over nicely.

'What number can I get you on?' he asked.

'I need to dump this' Junior replied. 'I'll call you from a payphone.'

The crafty hood never missed a trick.

'Need a burner?'

'Can you sort me out?'

'€100 will get you what you need.'

Junior peeled off two fifties from a tight roll of notes and handed one of them to McEvoy.

'The other fifty on delivery.'

McEvoy's impulse was to bargain but thought better of it. 'Ring me in the afternoon and I'll get a young lad to deliver.'

As he slipped out the unlocked side gate, Junior turned to McEvoy, 'Today, I need that info, today.'

Digger typed one-handed as he triangulated the town map of Dundalk on his screen. He inserted pin drops on mobile masts around the town and isolated the area Junior had moved through. It had been erratic since six-fifteen when the phone first pinged off a mast on the northern side of the town. The signal died fifty minutes later and nothing had shown up anywhere until after midday when a mast on the southern side pinpointed him. He was being ultra-cautious as he yo-yoed around town.

'Looks like he stayed on the northern side of town last night,' Digger relayed to Kate. 'There's one hotel and six

B&Bs in that end. I'll give Quinlan a bell and ask him to check them out.'

'Forget Jack, he's investigating a suspicious death.'

'In Dundalk?'

'At Moll's Roadhouse, it's more like a big B&B really.'

'Junior's phone pinged off the mast down the street from it this morning.'

'I'll tell Quinlan. Our crew can check the B&Bs.'

When Kate spoke to Quinlan he told her it looked like a murder at Molls. He intended to review CCTV while he waited for the State pathologist.

'You're up to your eyes, Jack. Will you let your Chief know we're working on his patch?'

'Will do. Have to talk to him anyway about loosening the purse strings; this investigation is going to take over-time. Any leads on Junior?'

'He's around town but being smart with the phone. Switching it off and on. Digger mentioned his phone pinged close to Moll's early this morning.'

'Where was the last trace?'

'Near Slievemish housing estate.'

'McEvoy's out that side.'

'I know.'

'I'll get the uniforms at the station to check CCTV for sightings of him.'

'Great. Chat later.'

Kate steered clear of town. Too many people knew her, so she couldn't venture onto the streets, and the van wouldn't blend in for long. Pete McNally drove it to a forest car park north of Dundalk. She double-checked the radio signal with the crews, walking, cycling, and driving around her hometown and maintained 15-minute checks throughout the stormy afternoon. When darkness fell she could venture closer. She sent a '*Hi*' text to Aidan

Hanrahan but figured he was working an afternoon shift at the hospital when she received no reply.

Street lights illuminated the drenched streets as darkness descended and Pete shifted in the front seat when Kate's phone pinged an incoming text.

'It's nothing,' she assured him.

Kate stared at the screen trying to make sense of Hanrahan's delayed reply—*'Did you enjoy yesterday's lunch with your hunky companion?'*

Kate scrunched up her nose. Was it possible she had missed him the previous day at the south side restaurant?

'That was work. If you saw me, you should have come over.'

'Was treating Mum to lunch and you seemed deep in convo.'

'So?'

'Is everything okay with your mother?' Pete asked from the front of the van.

'It's nothing to do with Mum,' Kate replied.

'In Belfast tonight for a conference in the morning,' Hanrahan messaged. *'I was thinking of calling in to see your Mum on my way up.'*

'She'd be delighted. What time?'

'After 8.'

'Might even make it there myself.'

'C U then.'

Squalls had slanted in off the Irish Sea all day while Kate's rain-soaked early crew scoured the town in a fruitless search for Junior. After an eight o'clock shift change, fresh faces took up the task. Sexton ran base control as Kate paced the edge of town in a recce with Ken James. She knew the town's side streets and alleys better than her crew. The early hope that Gary McEvoy would lead them to Junior had proven overly optimistic.

It seemed the weather was keeping him indoors as he was a no-show on CCTV. Kate cut through rough ground to skirt the Slievemish estate, trying to get a bead on his house. She contemplated a walk-by but dismissed it; too many people knew her in this estate. Angie offered to do it instead. As rain seeped through the seams of their wet gear, Kate decided it was too risky and doubled back to the control van parked behind an abandoned school.

With the lull in the action, she pondered whether Junior had slipped across the border again and double-checked with Andy Tyrell in Enniskillen. He confided that an informant had nominated sites and the PSNI were checking places where the suspect might hide out. A police search party had found the body of a woman at an outfarm linked to where Junior spent his early childhood. An investigation had been launched to identify her and ascertain the circumstances of her death. There had been zero sightings of the suspect so far.

As she savored coffee Angie poured from a thermos, her phone vibrated.

'*Have just parked at Brackenhill, will you make it?*'

Kate groaned as she read the message. The fruitless search for Junior had shunted a visit to her mother to the back of her mind.

'The dishy doc again?' Angie asked.

'He's called in to see Mum. He's there right now.'

'We're all good here. If anything breaks, we'll let you know.'

'I look like something the cat dragged in.'

'Do you have a hairbrush?'

'In the boot of the ERU car back in Dublin.'

'Take my travel brush. You'll be all prim and proper for your mum. And the dishy doc!'

Kate pulled a face and tapped a reply to Aidan Hanrahan telling him she would be at the nursing home in twenty minutes.

Jack Quinlan called as Kate walked along the nursing home corridor. Conscious of the elderly clientele, she kept her voice low and dodged into the deserted common room.

'This is becoming a habit, Jack, I've just popped in to see my mother again,' she said.

'We need to talk,' Quinlan said.

'You're driving; what's up?'

'I'm heading out to Brackenhill. Meet me in the car park. I think *your man* is *my man*.'

'Come again?'

'The CCTV from Moll's Roadhouse shows Junior stayed there last night. The footage I've got makes him my number one suspect for murdering Gareth Devlin.'

'*Holy crap*! Has the pathologist confirmed the cause of death?'

'Suffocation and I've got footage of Junior coming out of Devlin's room. He signed the victim's death warrant when he gagged him; Devlin was a severe asthmatic.'

'Junior's a PSNI target.'

'If I get him for murder, they'll have to wait in line.'

Kate finished the call and walked into room 21 to find Aidan Hanrahan scanning her mother's charts. He stood as Kate entered, his deep blue eyes smiling behind black-rimmed spectacles.

'Everything looks good, Margaret,' he said.

'Hi, Missy!' Her mum greeted Kate as she kissed her cheek. 'Does that mean I can go home?' she asked Hanrahan.

'You're not quite there yet,' he smiled, folding his spectacles into a bright red case. 'Use your stay here to work on getting mobile, they've got great people to help you. Talk as much as you can, you're doing well.'

'That shouldn't be a problem,' Kate laughed.

'Thank you, Aidan,' her mother smiled.

The trio chatted as Kate kept watch for Quinlan's car outside the window.

'You're not even listening to me,' her mother scolded.

'Jack is dropping in for a chat before he heads home,' Kate replied. 'I'm just watching out for him.'

'I'm sure he wants to see you, more than me.'

'Mum, come on! Did you hear he's retiring soon?'

'Lucky him with his big pension.'

'Don't be like that. He's always been good to us if anyone's earned a pension, he has.'

'I'm only kidding,' Margaret replied. 'You know I'd say the same if Jack was here.'

'Please don't.'

Her mother laughed.

'Sorry you're hearing all this,' Margaret said to Hanrahan.

'I better hit the road for Belfast, anyway,' he smiled, in reply.

Kate stared out the window as headlights swept into the car park and extinguished abruptly.

'That's Jack. Can you stay with Mum for five minutes?' she asked Hanrahan.

'I don't need a babysitter,' her mother protested.

'I'd be delighted,' Hanrahan replied.

Outside, Kate waved to Ken James to indicate she was joining Jack Quinlan in his car.

'That's one miserable night,' she said, as she jumped in.

'Kate, get back-up here straight away,' he said. 'I think Junior might be heading this way.'

'Jesus, Jack! You could have told me this on the phone.'

'I don't trust them.'

'Bullshit! You wanted to make sure you got out here to nab him before me.'

'I admit I want him—badly. It's my final murder case, I need to get him.'

'Are you certain he's headed here?'

'As sure as God made little green apples! I got an anonymous call telling me as much.'

'Jack, for feck sake! You know better than to trust an anonymous call.'

'I recognized the caller.'

'Who?'

'Gary McEvoy.'

'Oh!'

'Get back-up and we'll wait the bastard out.'

Kate rang Angie and told her to direct everyone to Brackenhill. She dashed to the SIU car Ken James had driven her to Brackenhill in but found it empty. She was dialing his number when she saw him beckon from between two cars close to the entrance. She crouched and ran to join him.

'Something's off,' he said, handing her an ultra-thin bulletproof vest. 'Put this on.'

It was the concealable type of body armor SIU favored for its snug fit rather than the higher-spec Ken James used at the Emergency Response Unit. Kate removed her rain jacket and pulled it on

'Jack Quinlan's just told me Junior might be headed this way,' she said, replacing the rain jacket and zipping it. 'What spooked you?'

'I saw something, a shadow,' he replied. 'That car's headlights killed my night vision.'

He pointed to the elderly visitors as one removed a wheelchair from the back seat and unfolded it. She helped her incapacitated passenger maneuver into it and locked the car. Then she began to plow the wheelchair slowly through the gravel toward the ramped entrance. Ever the Good Samaritan, Dr. Aidan Hanrahan saw the struggle from inside and emerged to assist.

'Someone's scouting the grounds,' Kenny said to Kate.

'Stay here,' Kate said. 'We'll check the grounds when backup arrives. I need to warn the hospital that their night is about to be disturbed.'

She ran up the ramp past an alarmed Aidan Hanrahan. 'Get everyone inside as quickly as you can,' she said.

At the reception, she spoke rapidly to the bouffant coiffed matron whose permanent smile transformed into a frown.

'What do you want us to do?' she asked.

'Close all doors. Keep the corridors clear. Everyone must stay in their rooms. We will commence a search shortly.'

Kate walked quickly to her mother's room.

'Love you, Mum,' she said, as kissed her goodnight. 'Reception asked us to close the room door,' she said. 'I'll see you tomorrow.'

Hanrahan walked out of the deserted common room where Sky News was playing on a muted television as Kate returned toward reception.

'Best get moving,' she told him. 'I'll call you later tonight.'

'What's going on?' he asked.

'Garda stuff you don't need to know about.'

Instinctively, her right hand reached toward her belt but she had left her weapon in Angie's care back at the control van. Hanrahan wrapped his arms around her waist and kissed her passionately before she could protest. She pushed him away.

'Seriously, you need to get out of here,' Kate smiled, briefly.

'This is about the guy who tried to kill you before, isn't it?'

'Go!' Kate said, pushing him ahead of her.

Hanrahan's hasty kiss did not go unnoticed. Unseen inside a clean utility room, venom swelled in Junior's heart as he watched the stolen kiss. This bitch had robbed him of so much in his life. It was time to strike back.

41

Ken James spied movement to his left as Kate walked smartly with the doctor to the seven series BMW. He watched her wave as it reversed out before turning to head back toward reception.

'Ken,' she said, quietly, 'I need you inside for security. I'm unarmed.'

Before he could reply, she sensed a rushed frontal assault before Junior flashed into her line of vision. He had slipped through a side door into the car park and was closing fast. Kate's instinct was that anyone charging so fast had to be intent on tackling her to the ground. Ju-Jitsu taught her to position and deflect, use an opponent's strength and speed to repel the attack. Rapid blinding flashes and the thud-thud of shots altered her strategy.

'*For my father, you murdering bitch,*' Junior raged.

Ken James realized he couldn't make the takedown tackle. He had barreled toward the charging assailant but the raised weapon forced a change of tactic. He launched himself between the weapon and Kate. In the blurred aftermath, he lay motionless at her feet.

At the exit gate, Aidan Hanrahan caught the surreal

scene in his rearview mirror. Flashes, someone hitting the ground, then a looming figure pointing a weapon at Kate's silhouette. He slammed his car into reverse and floored it in the direction of the assailant. The revving motor and lights threw Junior, and he aimed shots at the fast-approaching BMW that shattered its rear window and forced it to a halt. Kate used the distraction to counterattack.

She grabbed Junior's wrist and wrenched his elbow in one swift move. The pistol fell from his grip, but he seized her arm and dragged her to the ground. Gravel dug into her back as he rolled on top and seized her throat with frenzied strength. He scrambled for the gun, but Kate locked her free hand on his shirt collar and forced her left leg across his chest using her right heel to slam down hard on his knee. The scissors sweep move spun her momentarily on top and she pushed away from him.

The sound of sirens filled the night air, the cavalry was coming. Junior lurched, snatched the weapon, and pushed himself upright.

'Die, bitch!'

'Drop the weapon,' Kate heard from behind.

In a fog of lethal action, Junior snatched the trigger and loosed off wild shots in the direction of the shouted order. Behind her, a scream of pain rang out. She knew Quinlan was hit. Junior re-directed the weapon at her but the hammer fell on an empty chamber. As he fidgeted furiously to replace the empty magazine she crouched and delivered a roundhouse kick that connected hard with the side of his head. The impact spun him backward and she heard the stomach-churning sound of his head strike the concrete curb of a shrubbery bed. She raced forward and wrenched the weapon from his hand as a troubled life extinguished right before her eyes.

Backup cars swarmed into the nursing home grounds.

The avenue quickly choked and SIU crews tore across manicured lawns to reach the victims. Kate hollered for first responders to check Quinlan and Kenny. As her team pulled Junior's body from the shrubbery and double-checked for signs of life, she flung the BMW's door open. Aidan Hanrahan lay slumped over the steering wheel.

The engine room of the *Viking Prince* was an alien world to Detective Joe Forde. Control panels, massive steam ducts, compressors, switches, and thousands of other components were arrayed on different levels. This was the beating heart of the beast. The sign on the engine room door urged anyone entering to use ear protectors due to noise. The last thing Forde needed was to block out sounds. The machine noise around him was massive and constant.

He cautiously checked the huge space but failed to locate a single crew member. He moved through each level gripping a yellow handrail for support as he moved downwards. In the workshop, there were lathes, grinders, and other tools on workbenches when he checked it out. He verified access points into the engine room but found no vantage point that would cover them all. Hours of anxious watching and waiting left his nerves shredded.

Al-Farouq used the ship's public address to taunt him.

'Come out, come out wherever you are, Mr. Forde,' his opening mocking salvo. 'We found your message and we *will* find you.'

Half an hour later, he upped the stakes.

'No more distraction, Mr. Forde,' al-Farouq said. 'Give yourself up or two of your crew members die. You decide.'

At least they had figured him as crew, not a cop. Forde took solace from that. Twenty minutes later, he squirmed as two voices shouted their names over the tannoy and pleaded with him to save them. Almost instantaneously, shots and screams rang out. They never stood a chance.

'Two more very soon, Mr. Forde,' al-Farouq said. 'Stay tuned,' he added, coldly.

Forde had no way of knowing whether or not the threat had been carried out. Given Khouri's execution of the captain, he believed it was real and determined that if he was to survive, he would have to fight.

Off the Irish west coast, a NATO carrier group steamed north-west in pursuit. Commandant Christophe Marais pushed the nuclear-powered aircraft carrier, *Charles de Gaulle*, out to twenty-five knots when satellites abruptly lost all trace of the *Viking Prince*'s position.

'Khouri's likely hacked the VMS,' Mac told the commander. 'ISIS is probably tracking it via what remains of their transponder network.'

'My guys will work on picking up the locator signal from Joe Forde's radio,' Twomey said.

'That would give us a bearing,' Commandant Marais said. 'I will deploy fighters to get us visual contact.'

An Irish Coast Guard Sikorsky S92 had dropped Twomey's ERU crew along with Mac, Cody O'Neill, Darrell Jackson, and Colonel Shaw onto the carrier's deck the previous evening. Three Blackhawk helicopters swiftly followed, each packing teams of SAS and US Navy SEALS, shipped out of the UK.

As the weather worsened, Twomey's team picked up Forde's radio signal. The special ops teams itched for action. Commandant Marais maneuvered the carrier head-on into a stiff polar wind to enable two Rafale fighter jets to take off to provide top cover. SEAL commander Frank Bullock worked out a plan of attack and reluctantly tweaked it to embed Twomey and two of his crew. When a Rafale pilot reported visual contact two re-fueled Blackhawks departed in pursuit, the third chopper held in reserve.

At ninety minutes flying, they descended in the darkness toward their objective and the strike group abseiled rapidly on to the *Viking Prince*'s deck. With the teams delivered, the helicopters banked sharply to track a safe distance behind. As the vessel rose and fell in the Atlantic swell, the group moved stealthily toward the bridge in a closed triangle formation. On a frigid night, they anticipated little opposition until they made the ship's interior. Still, they moved furtively over the containers constantly checking for tripwires. When they reached the bridge, its interior was empty.

'Fuck!' Bullock exclaimed as he stepped inside. 'Blood spilled. Lots of it.'

Bill Twomey exchanged glances with his colleagues. 'That's Forde's radio,' he pointed to a counter.

'Check the chartroom,' Bullock ordered one of his men as he pored over the ship's controls. He confirmed all equipment was working normally.

'Look at this,' the SEAL returned, pointing out the scrawl across a sea chart.

Bullock turned to Twomey. 'Looks like your guy has his head screwed on.'

Twomey looked around the bridge. 'I count two strike marks at the end of the bridge with most blood. Exchange of fire, do you think?' he asked Bullock.

'Likely.'

Wary that entry had been too easy, Bullock studied the ship's schematics a final time. During operational planning, the strike group had identified each cabin, cupboard, and potential hiding place. Satisfied that no unforeseen factor had entered the equation, he unleashed his team to their mission—search, capture, or destroy. Twomey's crew would sweep in the rear and carry out a secondary search for their colleague.

A white-hot flash erupted behind the bridge. The enemy in action. Bullock killed the ship's lights and watched in horror as a missile streaked from the deck below, slicing through the darkness straight at their air support. The black sky ruptured into a blaze of chaff and flares from the Blackhawks.

'Ours,' Twomey said, as he and his two-man crew clicked their night sights in place and crawled out of the bridge.

The superheated countermeasures duped the missile's guidance system, but it detonated beneath the lead chopper. Shrapnel flayed its undercarriage and the chopper yawed and plunged toward the ocean. From the bridge, Bullock watched anxiously through night vision binoculars as the pilot struggled to level the craft off. Meters from the turbulent waters, he managed it and hauled the Blackhawk 180 degrees. He overheard the mayday message the pilot radioed as he set out for the safety of the carrier.

An icy gale howled as the ERU men crawled on to the deck. Two sets of stairs separated them from their objective. At the base of the first Twomey scuttled along the deck and peered cautiously over the edge. His glance caught Abdul Waleed reloading a missile launcher on Sadiq Zardari's shoulder. The Afghan handled the weapon with veteran proficiency and dropped to one knee, ready to launch a second strike.

'Fire at will,' Twomey ordered.

The trio raked the deck with sustained bursts before Twomey grabbed a rail and vaulted to the lower deck. He scrambled sternward and kicked the missile launcher aside as his sergeant confirmed both hostiles bleeding out.

The loss of the lead Blackhawk wiped out the strike

group's radio communication with the *Charles de Gaulle*. Frank Bullock linked up with his SEAL squad in a cold room off the ship's kitchen. They heard shouts for help from what remained of the twenty-man crew. Along with Captain Tucker, four had been summarily executed with a single shot to the head.

Shouts to halt interrupted them checking out the survivors.

'Get down, stay down,' Bullock ordered the ship's crew, as he raced toward the danger.

The SAS had sprung a hijacker from hiding. Bullock lay flat on the floor and aimed his MP7 submachine gun at the oncoming noise. Two of his squad took up positions either side. The chase brought al-Farouq into his sights.

'Give it up, son,' Bullock ordered when he loomed into view.

'Death to the West,' he screamed in a broad British accent before a sharp burst from Bullock's weapon put him down, blood oozing from both legs.

'Toss the gun,' Bullock told him. 'It's over.'

'Nothing's over,' al-Farouq taunted. 'Alu Akbar,' he screamed and pointed his pistol towards the SAS squad that had chased him down. A single shot dispatched him.

The ship's medical officer told Bullock that he had treated one of the hijackers for gunshot wounds. The SEAL squad located Rafiq Khouri in the hospital treatment room on the upper deck, barely breathing, unable to speak. He had taken one of Forde's hasty shots in the neck.

Bullock ordered his men to lash the prisoner to a stretcher and meet him on the bridge.

'Talk to your boy,' he told Twomey handing him the public address mic.

'Good idea,' the big man agreed and used the tannoy to assure Forde that the ship was secure. Ten minutes later an SAS man led the disheveled detective to the bridge.

'Kate's going to have questions for you,' Twomey said.

'I'm glad I am here to answer,' Forde replied.

Frank Bullock used a Sat phone to report to carrier command that they had accomplished their objective. He held the phone aloft so the strike group could share the whoops and hollers that greeted his news.

'We've got a big problem,' he gazed in frustration at the control panel.

'What's that?' he heard Mac ask.

'We can't stop the ship.'

Bullock sent two of his team onto the cargo deck to check the Dublin containers. The Geiger counter readings from one confirmed worrying radiation levels. Pentagon experts had estimated that any uncontrolled dispersal of radiation would cost New York City billions of dollars and disrupt life there for years. The ship had to be halted.

As a last resort, Bullock emptied a mag from his MP7 into the control panel. The *Viking Prince* plowed on. Commanders conceded that Khouri had managed to jump ahead of known navigation system research to develop AI software that hijacked the Panamax. Bullock kicked the prisoner's stretcher.

'What did you do, you son of a bitch?'

Commandant Marais decided to consign the *Viking Prince* to the bottom of the ocean. He sent the reserve Blackhawk to extract the strike group along with the crew and prisoner.

'Sorry, boss,' Forde said, sheepishly, as he stepped off the first chopper onto the carrier deck.

'You did okay,' Mac told him. 'Just—never again.'

Marais nominated a point west of the Rockhall basin as a graveyard deep enough for the deadly vessel. He ordered a submarine from the carrier group to an advanced position and it slammed two torpedoes into the cargo ship, slicing it in half as it entered the Maury Channel. Joe Forde watched drone footage of the action in the aircraft carrier's command post. He shivered as containers toppled and the stricken beast slowly sank beneath the Atlantic's turbulent waves.

42

When shots hit his car, Aidan Hanrahan had braked hard and on the emergency stop, the BMW's driver airbag exploded into life. The impact to his face stunned him and Kate hugged him tightly as he roused. 'Sit still, help's on the way,' she said. 'I've got to check Jack and Kenny.'

She squatted in front of Ken James as he sat upright on the gravel.

'You're alright! Oh thank God,' she said.

He unzipped his rain jacket and displayed the impacts on his bulletproof vest.

'Never leave home without one,' he winced.

'You saved my life, Kenny,' Kate said.

'Check on Quinlan,' he replied. 'I'm alright.'

SIU's first aid responders wrapped a thermal blanket around his shoulders and protected his damaged ribs. Kate ran to where she saw Sexton working on a blood-drenched Jack Quinlan and cried out when she saw his motionless body.

'Oh no, Ron. How bad?'

'Bad. We've staunched the bleeding from the bullet wound but he needs an ambulance fast.'

'Let me take a look,' Aidan Hanrahan pushed through.

'Are you sure you're okay to do this?' Kate asked. 'Your nose looks broken.'

'My head has cleared. I'm fine,' he replied and carried out a rapid assessment on Quinlan.

'Hang in there, Jack,' Kate said. 'The ambulance is coming, I can see the lights. We'll have you at the hospital in no time.'

Almost on cue, a blue light strobed the graveled entrance and drew up close to where Quinlan's unconscious body lay.

The paramedics worked on Quinlan, connected a drip to his arm, and transferred him to a gurney. When safely on board with Quinlan on one side and Ken James on the other, Hanrahan thumped the cab to get moving.

'Call me,' Kate shouted.

She was struggling to prioritize the tasks needed to keep control of the unfolding scene. She had stationed one of her crew close to the entrance to preserve the crime scene for evidence collection. The independent oversight body, GSOC, would have investigators on-site in a few hours and they would demand full access for their inquiry. She did not want to give them any cause for complaint. She was perplexed when a second ambulance drew up at the gate minutes later. Its crew descended and rushed a gurney from the rear.

'We need to get inside urgently,' they told the puzzled detective who guided the driver as he swung it around and reversed to the nursing home entrance. Kate was tripping on adrenaline, collaborating with Ron Sexton to piece together what had just happened. She paused when she saw Angie rush toward the front door.

'I've got this,' he insisted. 'You go!'

Kate faltered as she reached the ramp and grabbed its handrail to keep from stumbling. Sexton raced forward to support her. The doors swished open and a paramedic steered a gurney down the ramp in her direction.

'Oh God no!' Kate cried.

Angie leaped over the ramp's handrail to reach her, her face betraying horror at the realization of who was being rushed from the nursing home.

'No, no, no!' Kate howled, as Angie wrapped her in her arms.

Margaret Bowen lay on the stretcher, a hospital blanket covering her limp body. Underneath the oxygen mask, Kate could see her mouth open, contorted as if in a frozen scream.

Her memory of the ambulance trip was of paramedics talking continually to her mum, convincing her to keep fighting until they reached the hospital. In the emergency department, the intern treating Aidan Hanrahan's damaged nose stepped aside when his patient lurched forward and pushed past him towards the commotion of Margaret Bowen's arrival in the emergency department.

He introduced himself as her chief physician and the ED team ceded authority to him and carried out his instructions without query. He worked tirelessly but the scale of the second stroke was overwhelming. Two hours after Aidan Hanrahan believed he had stabilized her, Margaret Bowen's breathing became labored. Unable to open her eyes, she reacted to her two daughters by squeezing their hands as they talked incessantly about the wonderful person she was. Innate fear gripped Kate when her mother's breathing grew intermittent. She summoned a nurse for help.

'Keep talking to your mum, it won't be long now.'

'Do *something* for God's sake,' she begged.

Aidan Hanrahan came through the curtain and wrapped Kate in his arms.

'The time for fighting is over. Just talk to your mum.'

Margaret Bowen slipped away as her oldest friend, Doc D'Arcy, made it to her bedside and squeezed hello, goodbye into her weakening hands.

The next day Aidan Hanrahan used a consultation room at the hospital to sit down with the trio.

'Are you okay?' Doc D'Arcy asked.

He looked exhausted and had a large plaster-strip across his broken nose.

'I'm tired but I'm alright. I wanted to chat with you all about Margaret's passing.'

'You assured me everything was looking good at Brackenhill,' Kate said.

'That I did. I always emphasize the positives to keep the patient's spirits up.'

'You lied!'

'We know about Margaret's struggles with blood pressure,' Hanrahan said.

'Kate, we've known she's suffered from high blood pressure,' Norrie added. 'For as long as we can remember'

'Indeed!' Hanrahan agreed. 'And we worked on it in Beaumont. It went in the right direction, however, yesterday morning her chart showed it had spiked again.'

'Oh God, I pressganged her into talking to Jack Quinlan on the phone yesterday. To boost her confidence in her speech.'

'There was no harm in that, Kate. Your mother told me she suffered from anxiety all her life. It takes a toll.'

Doc D'Arcy looked at Kate as she processed the information.

'How is Jack doing?' she asked.

Hanrahan answered. 'He's hanging in, as well as can

be expected. He was airlifted to Beaumont last night. I'll inquire later and keep you posted.'

'So you feel Margaret's final stroke had nothing to do with what happened outside the nursing home last night,' the Doc said.

'I can't say that with absolute certainty, Doctor D'Arcy, but with an ischemic stroke, as you know, high blood pressure is a prime factor. Margaret's anxiety levels made controlling it challenging.'

'So, was it only a question of time?' Norrie asked.

'When you think of it, that's how it is for all of us,' Hanrahan replied.

'Girls, let's get on, there's lots needs doing,' Doc D'Arcy said.

***

The celebration of Margaret Bowen's life began with a wake at the home where she had proudly raised her girls. The funeral undertaker laid her out in peaceful repose in a plain casket. A neighbor helped shunt the dining table out of the front room, and the undertaker placed the casket on trestles in the center.

Kate hugged Betty Fitzpatrick tightly when she arrived from Dublin and brought her through to the kitchen. She was inconsolable when she saw Margaret laid out in the coffin. Months earlier, this lively woman had been the life and soul of her wedding celebrations.

Through the evening, neighbors filed in and occupied the chairs arranged around the best room in the house. Kate made conversation with people she barely knew or hardly remembered. Many reminded her of how proud Margaret was of Kate's transition from a worrisome, rebellious teenager to an admirable, independent woman. As darkness fell, she was on autopilot, her fingers swollen from hours of sympathetic handshaking.

Norrie's husband organized an army catering crew to work the kitchen and offered tea and snacks to everybody who came. Angie never left Kate's side and other SIU team members ducked in and out throughout the evening. When the local priest called at nine o'clock, Kate and Norrie mumbled their way through meandering minutes of long-forgotten prayers for the dead. He ran through arrangements for the following day's service and Kate locked the front door when he departed. Aidan called before midnight to let her know that Jack Quinlan's surgery was complete and he was in an induced coma to aid his recovery.

After a fret-filled night, she awoke with resolute determination to stay strong. Norrie, ever the big sister, knocked on her door, with tea and warm toast. The gesture triggered a deluge of tears that left Kate dazed, as she zipped Norrie's black dress later in the morning.

'Oh Jesus Christ,' she cried, as the zip snagged. 'I can't do anything right.'

'Kate, stop and take a breath,' Norrie said in a calm voice. 'You'll be fine.'

The morning's sounds and images etched forever into Kate's memory. The coffin screws, scraping as they found a thread and sealed in their mother. The never-ending sea of faces outside the church offering condolences. Cody O'Neill showed up among the mourners, dressed in a dark suit with Mac at his elbow. Angie overheard him inquire about the guy with the broken nose who stuck close to Kate and linked her arm occasionally.

The church overflowed with women. Some Margaret Bowen's former workmates, others, women she had helped through Rape Crisis. Many were distressed that their rock in a time of need had been ripped from this world. An all-female guard of honor formed as the coffin passed from the church to the hearse. The women walked alongside the entire journey to the graveyard.

Kate was as unprepared for the swell of sobbing when her mother's body was lowered into the ground as she was for the harsh finality of the first shovel of soil that fell on it. She leaned her head on Aidan's shoulder and absorbed memories that would live with her for the rest of her life.

EPILOGUE

U.S. Ambassador's Residence, Dublin, 4th of July

Kate stepped away from the throng celebrating Independence Day in the ballroom at the American ambassador's residence in Dublin's Phoenix Park. She made her way outside and sat on a stone bench alongside a graveled garden path. Her first official function since her mother's passing, Commissioner Fox requested she represent him at the event as Mac was recuperating from prostate surgery. With Zach Chapman and Cody O'Neill due to attend, Kate would have come along anyway. O'Neill was pulled at the last minute by his Paris ambassador leaving Chapman the only law enforcement representative.

Just three months on from her mother's death, a pervasive dullness still enveloped Kate. She smiled politely when introduced to Ambassador Greene at the receiving line in the Georgian mansion's foyer. She nodded her gratitude when he congratulated her on the recent joint operation with American forces. As she mingled with the festive crowd in the ballroom, searching for a friendly face, the noisy revelry unsettled her. Finally, she gave up and stepped out to take a moment.

'I needed air,' she said when a worried Aidan Hanrahan followed her.

He sat beside her while Kate closed her eyes, the sunshine warming her face.

'What's the fragrance, I'm getting?' he asked.

'Wild garlic,' Kate replied, her eyes still closed. 'It grows near the entrance.'

'So beautiful,' he said, squeezing her hand. 'We can go back inside when you're ready.'

'Mmm,' Kate murmured. 'So beautiful.'

'Hey there!' a familiar voice broke the spell.

With his tall, angular frame and shock of blond hair, Chapman always stuck out in a crowd. He stepped onto the patio accompanied by Pat McCarthy, the Dublin embassy's regional security officer who had picked him up from his delayed Paris flight.

Kate's composure held firm until he drew close.

'Oh Kate, I'm so sorry about your Mom,' he said extending a hand.

The sound of his voice, warm and sincere, triggered tears that Kate had long given up on trying to hold back. He wrapped her in a comforting embrace.

'It's tough, I know,' he said, gently. 'It will get better.'

Kate wiped her eyes and turned. 'By the way, this is Aidan.'

Hanrahan came alongside and shook hands.

'This is Zach, he's one of the good guys.'

'Why don't you stay out here a while and catch up,' Hanrahan suggested. 'The air will do you good.'

'I'll make sure Aidan gets a beer,' Pat McCarthy smiled. 'We'll chat later.'

'Okay,' Kate replied.

She turned and headed down a path with Chapman. The view looked onto the Phoenix Park where a herd of deer grazed languorously in the summer heat.

'Wow!' Chapman said. 'That's pretty amazing to see so close to the city.'

'It's cool. Our base is that-a-way, just beyond the Park,' Kate pointed.

'Not too shabby!' he laughed.

They strolled to the end of the path and turned right.

It's been quite a ride,' he said. 'Are you done with the paperwork yet?'

'Well Digger did get a license for Sumbal's dog,' Kate smiled.

'Did they really call it Lazarus? Chapman asked.

'They sure did. His kids adore the mutt, a born survivor.'

'What about Sumbal?'

'Facing forty years in prison. He will be tried later this year.'

She explained that final reports had just been published. The independent oversight body, GSOC, commended her handling of the case; a compliment as rare as hens' teeth that rang hollow. Digger's phone trawls verified Gary McEvoy's contacts with Junior. In the aftermath of the shootout, detectives ripped the local drug pusher's property apart and uncovered his burner phone. Fingerprints linked him to it and while he admitted to passing information to Junior he claimed he only did so under duress. Jack Quinlan was due to testify that McEvoy had alerted him to the threat against Kate.

'Junior died losing everything,' Kate mused. 'He threw his life away and ruined so many others. For what? Revenge? Jack Quinlan is paralyzed for the rest of his life. Junior's mother killed herself.'

'Oh God, that's dark.'

'Want to hear something amusing?'

Chapman stopped and looked directly at Kate. 'There's a funny side here?'

'Kinda!'

'Do tell.'

'The container that sucked us into the *Viking Prince* case was believed to have furniture with cocaine hidden in it. I passed it to a Drug Squad detective who loves the media attention that goes with a big bust.'

'One of those!'

'This time it didn't work out. He took everything on the container apart, chairs, tables, even light fittings and found nothing. So, he dumped the case and missed the obvious. The drugs gang had manufactured a false cavity at the front of the container and filled it floor to ceiling with dope.'

Chapman whistled. 'They got away with it?'

'Nope! My guy Sexton, saw the gang's enforcer, a crim called Wallace, driving a truck with the container the day it was released from seizure. Let's just say Ron and he have a special relationship.'

'I'm liking this guy, already.'

'So Ron pulls him over and they butt heads at the roadside, Wallace alleging harassment and Ron getting in his face.'

'How did he locate the drugs?'

'Angie was with him and twigged something was amiss with the container. She took a tape measure to the inside and discovered that it was three feet shy of its outside length. When they took angle grinders to the steel sheeting inside, they uncovered the drugs haul.'

'Oh man, that's a real burn for the Narcs.'

The drinks reception ended promptly at five o'clock

and Kate arranged with Chapman to eat together with everyone from SIU involved in cracking the cases. Usually, such nights turn into raucous celebrations that continue into the wee hours. However, Aidan Hanrahan collected Kate from the restaurant as most headed for a late-night bar.

'Want to spend the night at my place?' he asked.

'Love to,' Kate replied, leaning her head on his shoulder.

In Kate's dream, she watched her Grandad climb over a cattle gate. It led to their usual field for wild mushroom picking. They were on the lookout for fairies as well as mushrooms that morning.

'They're clever,' Grandad told her, 'they disguise themselves as primroses and melt into the ditches.'

'But the primroses are all gone,' she replied.

Without warning, Kate was alone; left behind as Grandad faded into the distance. He smiled at her from the field gate as he rested his elbows on its top-most bar.

'Wait, Grandad,' she cried, 'I need you to help me over.'

'You're a big girl now, you'll be okay. You'll be okay.'

Her mother appeared beside him. They smiled at each other, then at Kate, before turning and fading from view.

Kate bolted upright in the bed and screamed. Her head darted from side to side as she desperately sought her bearings in the unfamiliar room.

'You're safe, darling,' Aidan said, wrapping his arms around her.

He held her tenderly and they lay together in the early morning luminescence until her breathing calmed.

'A flashback?'

'Just goodbyes,' she whispered, as tears rolled down her cheeks.

He wiped them and kissed her. 'You'll be okay,' he said.

And somewhere deep inside, as she lay in her lover's arms, Kate Bowen knew she would.

The End

NOTES

Chapter 15

1. *Slán go fóill – Bye for now*

Chapter 26

1. *Briseann an dúchas trí shúile an chait* - Heredity breaks through the eyes of the cat.

Chapter 29

1. *Maith an cailín – Good girl!*

NOTE FROM THE AUTHOR

ENJOY THIS BOOK? YOU CAN MAKE A BIG DIFFERENCE.

I hope you enjoyed reading *Strike Back*.

Reviews, short as you like, are powerful tools. They assist self-published authors, like me, to attract new readers. Also, more reviews enable us to advertise our work on major advertising platforms so we can reach a larger audience.

You can leave your rating or better still, a few lines of review, by clicking this link.

ACKNOWLEDGMENTS

As a self-published author, I am mindful that writing is a collaborative process. I truly appreciate the assistance I received in writing Strike Back.

As my editor and literary consultant, Lizzie Harwood guided me through the project; a steady hand on the tiller. Since the series beginning, Lizzie has been visionary, enabling me to see where plot elements were holed below the waterline or when characters were surplus to requirements. I cannot thank her enough for the knowledge she has shared on writing and publishing.

To my wife, Eva, always my first reader, my eternal thanks. This time around, Eva also narrated each chapter for an enhanced perspective during editing. Huge thanks, also to my daughter, Emma, for reading drafts and sifting out errors.

Huge thanks to writers, Niamh Boyce and Andrea Carter, who took time out of busy schedules to read proofs.

A big thank you to Martin and Robyn Delaney in Perth, Western Australia for filling in background information on Oz and growing up there.

I am very grateful to all of my beta readers and especially to Philip Reilly, Michelle Dalton, and Tim Hedrick for your interest in getting the book in the best possible shape before release.

Thank you to Andrew Brown of Design for Writers for a great cover and webmaster, Andrew, who keeps my website in great shape.

ABOUT THE AUTHOR

T. R. Croke is the author of the Detective Kate Bowen mystery thriller series. He also wrote the British crime fiction novella, *One Night at the Perseverance Hotel*.

He is married to Eva and lives in County Laois in the Irish midlands. Read more at https://www.trcroke.com.

info@trcroke.com

ALSO BY T. R. CROKE

THE TRINITY ENIGMA

Set in Trinity College, Dublin, The Trinity Enigma continually charts high in the top 10 of Amazon's 90-minute Mystery, Thriller & Suspense short read category. This prelude novella is a great introduction to Detective Superintendent Kate Bowen as she uses her surveillance skills to cut short a right-wing fantasist's killing spree.

It's FREE to download on digital platforms.

THE DEVIL'S LUCK

Set in Ireland and France, The Devil's Luck finds Detective Kate Bowen, the youthful, red-blooded surveillance boss, learning fast that everything is not always as it seems. Puzzled when intelligence points to rogue terror groups conspiring, Kate trails her target to France as events contrive to threaten everything she holds dear.

A nail-biting, high stakes chase to stop a killer.

Check it out.

THE PRIZE PRINCE

Sun-drenched Cyprus. But Detective Kate Bowen is not working on her tan. She's languishing in a backwater UN posting. A chance sighting in Limassol of Dublin gang boss, Don Bailey greeting Middle Eastern contacts rejuvenates her appetite for shadowing bad guys.

She trains her sights on Bailey when fates conspire to return her as Garda surveillance boss in Dublin. She has no idea of the scale of the score Bailey is planning or that unscrambling his lofty ambitions will change her life forever.

Hard-hitting and tense from beginning to end.

Check out https://trcroke.com/ for links.

Lightning Source UK Ltd.
Milton Keynes UK
UKHW041607241120
373928UK00001B/20

9 780995 597662